Obsidian

Book Two of the Advocate Trilogy

Lindsey Scholl

ISBN-13: 978-1481112925

To John, my great support. You are better than I deserve.

ACKNOWLEDGMENTS

Many of the same people who were such a help in the writing of *The Sons of Hull* have continued to be a great support through the writing of *Obsidian*. First of all, I want to thank my husband, John. When I began writing *The Sons of Hull*, I had not met him yet. But he has been with me through the entirety of *Obsidian* and has weathered many questions, offered several helpful suggestions, and endured too many complaints about not having enough time to write. I am so grateful for his patience and his support. My parents, Patrick and Laura O'Donnell, have encouraged and assisted me in multiple ways. Dad has used his artistic skills to provide me with a map of Rhyvelad and sketches of several characters. Mom has read through drafts, offered advice, and encouraged me to write even when I was over-busy ("Laura Ingalls Wilder wrote at three a.m. with a bit of coal" or something to that effect). There are many other readers of drafts I'd like to thank: Lloyd Williams, whose advice changed the introduction; Doreen Moore, whose thoughts on Kynell were invaluable; Sharon and Keith Ridgeway, whose advice changed the introduction yet again; and Dougal Cameron, who approved the final draft and whose favorite character is Verial. To Clover and Rachel Carroll, thanks for your enthusiasm. And to Shane O'Donnell and This Dog Jumps, thanks for providing such foreboding cover art.

If there is any lasting good in this work, *gloria soli Deo.*

PRONUNCIATION GUIDE

Amarian	Uh-*mair*-ee-un	Munkke-trophe	*Muhn*-kee-troaf
Anisllyr	*Ahn*-is-leer	N'vonne	Nih-*von*
An-Sung	*Ahn*-sung	Obsidian	Uhb-*sih*-dee-uhn
Chasm	*Ka*-zihm	Patroniite	Pa-*troan*-ee-ite
Chiyo	*Chee*-yo	Prysm	*Prih*-zihm
Cylini	Sih-*lee*-nee	Relgaré	*Rel*-guh-ray
Destrariae	Des-*trair*-ee-eye	Rhyvelad	*Rih*-vuh-lad
Donech	*Dah*-nek	Tertio	Ter-*shi*-oh
Ealatrophe	*Ee*-luh-troaf	Ulan	Oo-*lahn*
Jasimor	*Jahz*-ih-more	Vancien	*Van*-cee-in
Keroul	Kuh-*rool*	Verial	*Vehr*-ee-uhl
Kynell	Kih-*nel*	Voyoté	Voy-*oh*-tay
Lascombe	Las-*cohm*	Zyreio	Zuh-*ray*-oh
Lucio	Loo-*chi*-oh		

Map of Rhyvelad

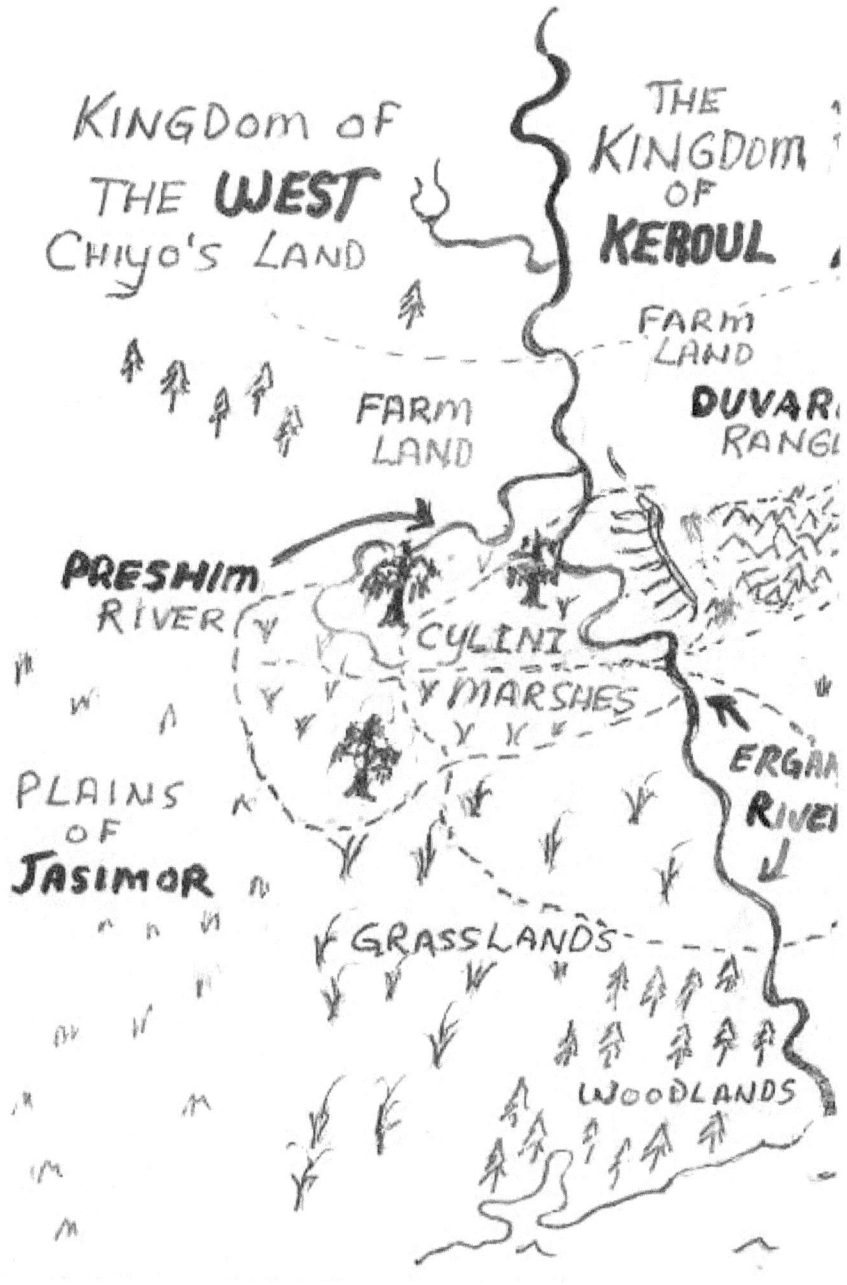

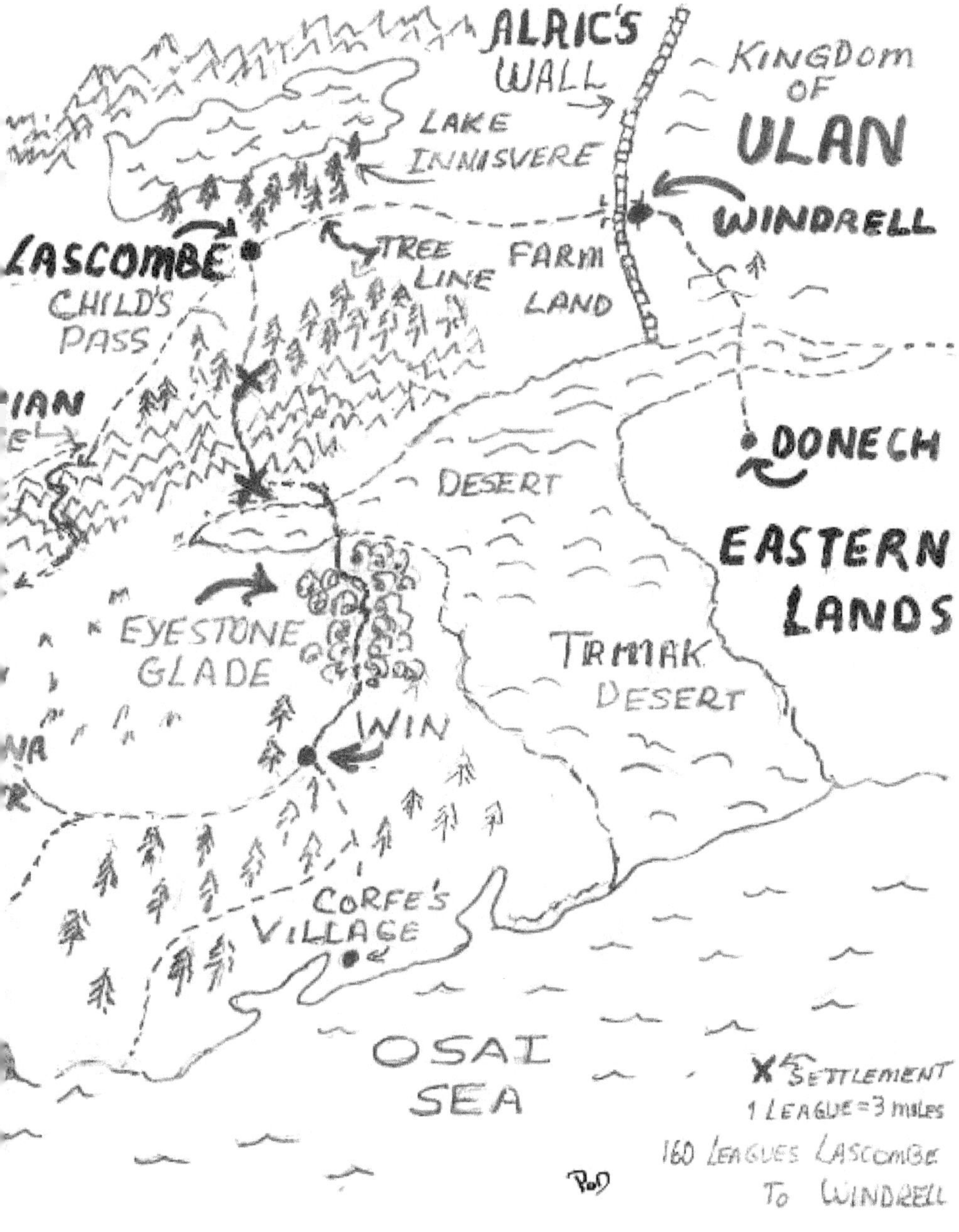

ALRIC'S
WALL
KINGDOM
OF
ULAN
LAKE
INNISVERE
WINDRELL
LASCOMBE
TREE
LINE
FARM
LAND
CHILD'S
PASS
IAN
DONECH
DESERT
EASTERN
LANDS
EYESTONE
GLADE
TIRMAK
DESERT
WIN
NA
CORFE'S
VILLAGE
OSAI
SEA
X SETTLEMENT
1 LEAGUE = 3 miles
160 LEAGUES LASCOMBE
TO WINDRELL

SYNOPSIS OF *THE SONS OF HULL,*
BOOK ONE OF *THE ADVOCATE TRILOGY*

Every world must engage in its own battle between good and evil. A world that fails to do this is either a perfect world, or wholly depraved. Rhyvelad is neither. It has recognized the good and labeled it the Prysm, which at its weakest is just a hope for better things, but at its best is an unstoppable force. The Prysm is nothing less than the spirit of truth, a fiery commitment to purity and mercy imparted from the god of the Prysm, Kynell. The Prysm has priests whose purpose is to preserve truths about Kynell, about humanity, and about Rhyvelad.

In opposition to Kynell and his Prysm stands the towering figure of Zyreio, the father of all things evil. The history of Zyreio is murky, even for learned Rhyveladians. Is he created by Kynell? Is he co-equal with him? The answers to those questions vary, and often depends greatly on the answerer's proximity to the Prysm. Scholars mostly agree that there is something derivative about Zyreio, in the same way that mold, while its own substance, has to grow out of something. Naturally, no man who is serious about Zyreio, or who clings to his banner of Obsidian, can agree with those scholars. For that man, Zyreio is a raging, primal deity in his own right; he derives nothing from Kynell. But as with so many worlds, those who best serve the cause of evil are not serious about it. They care little about scholars or gods or service. They care mostly for their own ends, an attitude that serves Obsidian quite well. For this reason and others, there are no priests of Obsidian. Zyreio is not interested in guarding anything. He is interested only in destruction. In that cause, unfortunately, many have become his allies.

Despite divine involvement, or possibly because of it, the actions of human individuals continue to carry great significance. Rhyvelad is no exception, therefore *The Sons of Hull* begins with an individual: twelve-cycle-old Amarian, who has come home from school to find a stranger alone in his house. The time of the Advocates has come, the man announces, and Amarian must make a decision. Will he choose to serve Kynell, to whom his heart is drawn? If he does, he would be consigning his younger brother to the service of Obsidian. Such is the cruel system of the Advocates, in which a pair of brothers must embody the war between the Prysm and Obsidian. It is a conflict that takes place every five hundred and forty cycles. This time, it has descended on Amarian and Vancien.

The choice lies before the elder, who feels wholly unprepared. Will he choose to become the Advocate for darkness himself, or will he allow that fate to fall on Vancien? To Amarian, there is no choice: in order to spare his brother, he mournfully accepts Zyreio's personal invitation and departs to serve the Obsidian god.

Almost fifteen cycles later, Amarian has disappeared from civilized society and Vancien has turned into a likeable young man. No one in the secure kingdom of Keroul expects anything more dramatic than the king's regular wars against border tribes. The priestly order, whose function it is to keep track of the prophetic coming of the Advocates, has become complacent. Only one priest believes that the Advocate confrontation is coming soon. Telenar pa Saauli has devoted his life to finding the young Prysm Advocate in order to train him for the coming day of battle. He has no success until, through a painful journey that involves the loss of loved ones, the Prysm Advocate finds him.

As Vancien learns to assume his role as Prysm Advocate, Amarian, now consumed by Obsidian's malevolence, plots against him. Through the help of his mute assistant, Corfe, he launches an ambitious program: with an army of humans and dark creatures behind him, he offers to help the king of Keroul subdue the border tribes. In so doing, he gains possession of not only his own army but the Keroulian regiments, as well. When the time comes for battle, Vancien will have no forces to fight alongside him.

Meanwhile, Vancien thrives under the tutelage of Telenar, who teaches him what he can about Kynell and the Ages, Kynell's holy book. Vancien is also instructed by Telenar's friend, General Chiyo of the West, who trains Vancien in the art of soldicry. As Vancien absorbs his duties and abilities as the Advocate, he learns that Kynell has given all his Advocates a Grace—the ability to restore life to one fallen comrade. Vancien does not hesitate. He wants to bring back N'vonne, the instructor of his youth, who had been a mother to him and had been killed on his journey to find Telenar. Telenar objects but Vancien will not be denied, so N'vonne's body is recovered and her life restored. It is a miracle. Yet what may be even remarkable is that Telenar, a lifelong bachelor, finds the newly recovered woman lovelier than he could ever have imagined.

According to the Ages, the fight between Advocates cannot begin until there is a consecrated time of Dedication. As the sacred moment draws near, Vancien, Telenar, Chiyo, and N'vonne set out from the capitol city of Lascombe to find the site of Dedication, as well as to avoid coming under the thumb of Keroul's militant king Relgaré, who has foolishly joined forces with Amarian.

Amarian does his best to keep track of Vancien, sending first his reptilian soldiers (the Sentries) and then trying a different tack by sending the beautiful Lady Verial to distract Vancien from his purpose. Verial is certainly a powerful weapon. Zyreio has bound her through time to be the mistress of each Obsidian Advocate, and many Prysm Advocates have wasted their resources trying to rescue her. Amarian hopes Vancien will do the same, and Vancien does almost fall for her, but Telenar and N'vonne's opposition, as well as Kynell's higher calling, prevents him from following his own conflicted desires.

But something has happened while Amarian is away. Kynell heals Corfe from his muteness, which had been inflicted by Amarian himself. Dazed and elated, Corfe comes to the surprising and misguided conclusion that he, the onetime servant of Obsidian, is the true Prysm Advocate. With the zeal of a convert, he assumes control of both Amarian's army and the Keroulian forces. When Amarian returns triumphant, carrying Vancien's body, he finds his own soldiers turned against him. Despite his recent victory, he must flee into the marshes, where he convinces himself that Zyreio has abandoned him. Now isolated from both gods, Amarian despairs, but his despair leads him to a radical act. Calling on the Prysm for the first time in over fifteen cycles, he asks Kynell to restore Vancien to him. Kynell graciously responds, allowing Vancien to return from the land of the dead.

Rhyvelad now faces an unprecedented situation: both Advocates are alive, both serve Kynell, and both face the threat of a heretical believer in control of the world's largest armies. Yet the brothers themselves are in a unique position. Amarian's newfound loyalty to Kynell is untested while Vancien, the true Prysm Advocate, must decide to fight yet another battle, this time against a well-intentioned imposter.

Despite these difficulties, *The Sons of Hull* ends on a celebratory note: the wedding of the priest Telenar to N'vonne. Vancien attends, as does the subdued Amarian. Rhyvelad has reached a temporary peace while standing on the threshold of a turbulent post-prophetic age. In *Obsidian*, that peace will be shattered in a way that shakes Rhyvelad to its very core, tearing from the heroes that which they treasure most.

PROLOGUE

The Realm of the Eastern Lands was desolate. Cold rain pelted down upon uncultivated fields and shut-up houses, trickling through un-mended roofs and splashing into waiting pools. Any housekeeper worth her salt would have been horrified at the state of disrepair. To add to the melancholy scene, a chill wind raced across the landscape, although there was no one for it to abuse. All living things had abandoned the area, even the plants. Yet it was a short cycle ago that the inhabitants of the region had been alive, industrious, and very, very excited: Amarian pa Hull, Obsidian's Advocate and Darkness personified, had ridden out to claim victory over the lands of Rhyvelad. It was only a matter of time before he became master of the world. The Easterners could already taste his triumph, as well as the rewards they would enjoy for loyal service. So they waited, patching their homes, feeding their livestock, and sharpening their blades as they counted the days until their master's return.

Amarian had told the few warriors he left behind that he would send for them when the time for battle had come. But the summons never came. Fortnight after fortnight passed, leaving the strong men with nothing to do but argue among themselves. Several of the thoughtless brutes claimed that Amarian would never return and declared themselves kings of the East. Those who were more thoughtful remained loyal. They resisted the usurpation, but were soon murdered for their constancy. After that first blood, arguments easily turned into armed brawls and brawls into battles. Old men, women, and children fled to safer lands but the mighty warriors remained, destroying each other and the land itself in their callous search for power. The fields that had once supplied an army now supplied food only for

1

the crows. The trees that had once provided shelter were razed in an effort to expose enemy clans. And the fortress of Donech, once the seat of Amarian's power, housed nothing but cobwebs and dead bodies.

Yet on this day, there was movement. It was in the great hall, under the dusty remains of a massive, cracked table, where at one time tribes of Sentries, fennels, and humans had sat under a vaulted roof. A tiny crack in the stone floor was showing activity by beginning to widen of its own accord. From within its meager depths, so small that a mouse could not have taken refuge in them, issued an eerie sound: the tiny screech of voices in pain. As the crack widened, moment by moment, so did the little cacophony. Soon its cries echoed off the walls. Voices of rage, agony, despair, and frustration all rushed through the abandoned corridors as if eager to share their story with any living thing they encountered. In doing so, they brushed past the decayed bodies of the warriors. Cold, grey fingers twitched. Eyes blinked. Skin grew warm and soft. A moment more and the flesh took on sound. The halls of Donech soon began to resonate with voices of condemned souls returning to their bodies and the boom of long-dead warriors clamoring to their feet. The Chasm was open.

CHAPTER ONE

"No, you can't go. That's final." The pale child of twelve cycles planted his fists on his hips and dug his heels into the dirt. "It's only for boys."

"Lucio, don't be such a *narfat*. I'm quicker and older than you are. Besides, you're taking Trint and he's only four cycles."

The boy named Lucio narrowed his eyes. His hair would have been a remarkable shade of blond were it not for the layer of dirt that caked it. His clothes were what one might expect of a street urchin: a mismatch of materials, torn at the elbows and knees, too tight in some areas and too baggy in others. Since hiverra had descended in full upon the land of Keroul, he had been wrapped in a bulky, oversized cloak to ward off the cold. The end result was a little comical. Still, he tried to lend his wardrobe as much authority as he could manage.

"Sorry, Teehma, but no. You *are* quicker, but you're too pretty. You will attract too much attention."

Teehma gave a snort and folded her arms, which were dark even through the cold months. "Funny coming from you. Who told you I was pretty? Gorvy?"

Lucio blushed but held his ground. "Maybe. Doesn't matter. Gorvy said it is only him, me, and Trint. You and Ester have to stay here and watch the fort."

The "fort" was just a deep alcove in the thick walls of Lascombe, Keroul's radiant capital city. She was Kynell's city, and a great deal of care had been tastefully poured into her over the cycles. Several of her streets were wide thoroughfares and all of her walls were high and whitewashed, giving

3

them a glow in the lunos light. Poetic travelers used to say that they when they saw Lascombe from afar at night, it was as if the triple lunos had bedded down on Rhyvelad for the evening. And when they saw her again at daybreak, she had transformed herself into a burning orb.

But in recent cycles, Lascombe had inspired more grief than poetry. Thanks to King Relgaré's neglect and death, the city had experienced a dramatic rise in crime and poverty. Pickpockets and other thieves roamed along the wide thoroughfares while children without parents found their home in the streets, often shepherded by black-hearted "patrons."

Gorvy was just such a man.

As Lucio and little Trint disappeared into the street, Teehma gave a sigh. "Don't you hate being a girl, Ester?"

Ester did not answer. Almost completely blind because of a childhood illness, she often kept to herself. Since a blind pickpocket was not of much use, Gorvy had only taken her in because she had insisted that she would beg and otherwise take care of domestic duties, both of which she did with quiet resignation.

So resigned was she that Teehma often found her annoying. When she received a shrug in answer to her comment, she had to clench her fist to keep from hitting the girl. But her parents, dead these many cycles, would disapprove of punching a blind person.

She looked again past the thick curtain into the night. As much as she hated to admit it, Lucio was right. She was in her fifteenth cycle and Ester was entering into her eleventh. With all the mean *narfats* out there, it was too likely that they'd be stolen away for the slave market. She sighed again. Before they had died, her parents had told her that Lascombe used to be a wonderful place where children were safe and nobody had to steal to eat. She did not believe them anymore, of course. Gorvy had taught her that the world had *always* been cruel. And when she heard Ester crying at night, she believed him.

It was almost dawn when the boys returned. Gorvy was with them, black eyes darting about the place as if the children were hiding some great treasure under their straw beds. His hair was slicked back with foul-smelling grease and each one of his multiple layers of clothing seemed to have its own, sticky smell. He had to crouch almost double to enter the fort, but Teehma figured he was used to crouching. The man had probably never stood upright in his life. He came in quietly, sitting down on one of the pallets and digging into a sack filled with clanking metal.

"The boys did well tonight," he said. "Trint is developing a knack for

4

slipping into small places. Just like you used to do, Teehma."

Teehma nodded at the compliment.

"Here you go, my little rats," Gorvy continued, tossing out a dented silver goblet. "See what you can get for this and feed yourselves. The rest I'll pawn and give you five percent."

Teehma and Lucio exchanged looks but said nothing. They did not know what five percent meant, but Gorvy had been promising it to them for almost a cycle now.

He was up on his feet again, stamping his frosted boots. "Right. You rats keep this place clean—that's your job too, Teehma. That and getting food. Careful that you do it right or I'll come calling next time the slavers are in town."

"Yes, sir."

"Be sure you watch out for them soldiers, too. They will throw you in the stocks just for being seen." He started to leave then stopped. "Oh, and one more thing." He kicked at Trint, who shied away, wide-eyed. "Keep an eye on this one. I saw him up by the palace yesterday, eyeing the rich folk. He's becoming a little too ambitious for his age." With that final encouraging word, he left, and the four of them breathed a little easier.

Trint crawled into Ester's lap, cold and exhausted by the night's activities. Teehma had long ago noticed that the two had a special connection, although she had no idea where it came from. Since the day Lucio had brought him in from the gutter, Trint had taken to Ester like a fish to water. Teehma liked Trint well enough, but Ester was more the motherly type, which was all right with her. Just the thought of being a mother was suffocating.

She hated to think how Gorvy would react if he knew what Trint was doing up by the palace. She had seen him at it a few times, putting himself in the way of the rich people, hoping that one of them would take him in. She could not blame him for trying. They had all done it at one point or another. But Gorvy would never forgive the boy if he got himself adopted.

She turned to Lucio, who was warming his hands by their small fire and coughing through the smoke it produced. "You didn't happen to see him, did you?"

He shook his head. "Things are not the same since King Relgaré died. He used to walk around town all the time. But this Relgaren don't ever come out. Don't know why you would want to see him anyway. He's just another stuffed shirt with a head too small for his crown. And then there's Corfe, that

5

friend of his." He rubbed his arms, almost choking on the name. "He gives me the shivers. That one don't seem right in the head."

Teehma kicked him lightly. "Ain't none of us are right in the head, you *narfat*. Guess you had better sleep. Gorvy might come calling again tonight."

Lucio groaned and collapsed in his pallet. "By the Prysm, I hope not. We must have broke into four different houses. There's nothing left to steal. Maybe soon we can go out when it's daylight and do some honest pick-pocketing."

The dragon dove with terrifying speed. Corfe barely had time to duck out of the way as its flames engulfed the soldiers trying to protect him. The beast heaved its body back into the air for another dive, but not before Corfe caught a glimpse of her rider. It was Amarian. He looked furious, lunging with his sword as the dragon dove again. If anyone escaped her blast, they would be caught by his blade. Then, to Corfe's terror, Amarian jumped down from his mount and walked toward him. His eyes glowed.

"Traitor!" he called.

"It's not my fault!" Corfe shouted back, ducking away. "The Prysm god healed me! It's not my fault!"

The bedchamber servants gathered nervously as their master tossed and turned on the bed. Despite the roar of battle in Corfe's mind, the lunos-lit room was quiet. Corfe groaned, muttering to himself as his shaved head glistened with sweat. He battled the dream until the head attendant ventured to tap him on the shoulder.

He jerked awake at the touch, causing the onlookers to take a cautious step back. He looked at them for a moment before exhaling in relief. Then he noticed his twisted bedclothes.

"I've been at it again, haven't I?"

"These dreams, master," said the head attendant, gesturing for the others to leave. "They're no good. Kynell knows you defeated the Dark Advocate at the dragon battle, so why do you still dream about him?"

Corfe chose not to answer the question directly. Instead, he swung his legs out of bed and began dressing for the day. "He'll be back, Kiel. You don't know him like I do. He'll come back for his revenge."

"But, sir, you killed that great nasty beast. Plus he's got no men, while you have an entire army. What's an Advocate without an army?"

Corfe stared out the window as Kiel stooped to lace up his boots. "He's still Zyreio's man. Obsidian's Advocate will never rest until someone separates his head from his body, and maybe not even then."

Kiel stood and stretched his back. He was getting too old to be bending over people's boots. "Aye, but you have Kynell on your side now. Shall I fetch you some breakfast?"

Corfe nodded and ran a hand over his bald head. He had asked the Patroniite order to shave it as an indicator of his devotion to the god of the Prysm. It was a small token, but he was proud of it. And occasionally, when no one was looking, he would talk to himself, just to remind himself of that great day when Kynell restored his speech. His own voice was evidence that he was no longer bound to the service of Zyreio. So great was his deliverance that sometimes he felt sorry for Amarian. Of course, that was a lost cause: redemption was not an option for some people.

Kiel returned with warm potato cakes, sausage, and tea. It happened to be the same breakfast that the king ate, which Kiel well knew. After setting the tray down on a delicate side table, he tried not to disapprove as the non-royal person sat down to eat. Corfe paid him no attention.

He had just finished the sausage when he heard a knock at the door. At his command, Kiel opened it to reveal a tall, reptilian soldier with sharp eyes and a shock of bright hair, closely cut. Corfe swallowed and tried to receive his guest with grace, but the sight of a Sentry—even a friendly one—was difficult to stomach in the morning. Tarl's broad ears fanned impatiently as Corfe fumbled for words to let him in.

"Lord Corfe. You wanted to see me?"

Finally, Corfe waved him in. "Any word on Amarian?"

The Sentry gurgled low in his throat. "Sir, you would be the first to know."

"He's bound to show up soon." Corfe rapped his fingers on the table. "After all, the Dedication has already taken place. He should be up to his eyeballs in Zyreio's presence by now. What's keeping him?"

"With all due respect, sir, he has lost his army. We have sought out and killed those Sentries who followed him into the marsh. Unless Obsidian raises the armies of the dead warriors as your Great Book says, it is without allies."

Corfe shook his head. "But something feels wrong. Besides, what do armies matter if you have Zyreio on your side?"

Tarl shrugged. He was not a theologian. "Is there anything else I can do for you?"

"No, that's it. Send Gair in if you happen to see him."

Tarl did happen to see Gair, who was already on his way to his friend's chambers for their morning outing. He did not stop to speak with him, however. He was a captain, after all, not Corfe's runner-boy. Gair could find his own way to the Advocate's rooms.

Even without Tarl's assistance, Gair arrived at Corfe's chamber in time for a stroll. A few more minutes and both young men had stolen out of the palace and arrived at the wide stone thoroughfares that crowned Lascombe's massive walls. The city was beautiful as always, even in hiverra, but it had suffered extensive neglect. The streets were pitted, their cobblestones stolen away for other purposes, and trash collected against the walls of dirty shops. Once their keepers had taken great pride in their storefronts. But many citizens had lost sons, nephews, and brothers in the border wars; the city's morale was sapped, not to mention its commercial spirit. The only businesses that seemed to be thriving were the taverns.

As always, Gair commented on the sight. "How long has the city been like this, I wonder?"

And as always, Corfe shrugged. "I was off somewhere fetching Amarian's slippers."

Gair watched with concern as a group of teenage boys huddled in a corner, smirking at the few passersby. A detached part of him wondered what why the adolescents were up so early.

Corfe noted the frown on his friend's face, then cringed as Gair limped up the stairs to the wall's parapet. As Amarian's former prisoner, Gair had suffered for following the Prysm god. There was a time when Corfe had thought he would never walk again, but the doctors of Lascombe were known world-wide for their skill. Not two days after they had returned from the battle with Amarian, they had fitted Gair with a prosthetic limb for the leg he had lost and a brace for the other. His friend now walked, albeit with a pronounced limp. But what made Corfe's gut turn was the tiny scar on Gair's lip. It was a small thing, given everything else the man had suffered, but Corfe winced every time he remembered the blow he had inflicted. A hundred times he had asked for forgiveness and a hundred times Gair had granted it. Still, the silent testimony to his past life troubled him.

They were on the East Wall, facing south, looking out past scores of small farms to the great Duvarian Range. Gair took a deep breath.

"One of these days, I'll have a home outside of the city. A small house with some land and maybe a pond."

"And a wife?"

Gair blushed and looked down, causing his long hair, much of it gray from stress, to flop forward. "The woman I want is unreachable."

Corfe agreed. Verial was indeed an unattainable prize. He had treasured foolish ambitions himself once—nothing so profound as Gair's attachment—but Verial was an immortal, preserved through time to be the mistress of Zyreio's Advocates. She *was* beautiful, but the woman had depths of loneliness and anger that no ordinary man could fathom.

"She'll be all right, Gair," he mumbled, "I'm sure Kynell's taking good care of her."

"I hope so. Last I saw her, Amarian had abandoned her in the woods so that she could seduce that young Vancien. Maybe she's still with him."

"Vancien's dead, remember? I saw his body before Amarian dragged it off into the marshes." Corfe shook his head. "Poor guy. Bad luck to be the brother of Obsidian's Advocate, eh? And not be the Advocate for the Prysm, that is."

Gair was happy to change the subject from Verial. "Wherever he is, he's out of the way. Besides, you heard what Patronius Supras said about the Advocates being brothers: it's all figurative."

Corfe was just about to respond when a messenger arrived with the announcement that he was wanted by the king. How he enjoyed that phrase. Who would have thought that the frightened teenager, who a cycle ago was hiding in *The Shattered Lantern* tavern, was now wanted by the king of Keroul? His conversion to Kynell had granted him a worldly status he would not have thought possible. An added perk, he thought, stepping back toward the palace.

CHAPTER TWO

The boys had departed for another night's expedition, leaving Teehma to do her chores. She knew why they had all of the adventures, but her spirit still rebelled against it. She was just about to voice these frustrations to Ester for the tenth time when she heard the scuff of a boot outside the curtain. This would normally have been no cause for concern, except it sounded as if the boot had stopped right outside the fort instead of walking by. Swallowing her angry words, she whispered for Ester to keep still.

The scuffing of the boot was soon followed by the scrape of a body sliding along the wall, then the rasp of labored breathing. To Teehma's active imagination, it sounded like a wounded man who had stumbled over the fort in an attempt to escape the king's guards. But what was he running from? Perhaps he was a thief? Unlikely. A murderer? Impossible. He had the sound of an honest man. It was more likely that the guards were after him because he had attempted a daring rescue of his true love from the palace and had only just gotten her to a safe place before he himself was seen. Encouraged by this epiphany, she summoned up the boldness to poke her head outside of the curtain, on the far side from the noises, and see how badly the hero was wounded.

There was the figure, just to the right of their small opening, sitting with his back against the wall. She could see puffs of his breath, but when she looked for a pool of blood or further evidence of injury, she could not find any. The man was simply breathing as if from a long run. After a few seconds, he took a drink from a bottle and wiped his forehead. She could not make out much, except that he seemed sort of young, kind of short, and obviously exhausted.

Eager to know more (and happy for any excuse to leave the fort), she slipped out and crept down the alley away from him. Then, about twenty paces off, she turned and walked back in the same direction, whistling casually as she went. She pretended not to notice him until she tripped on his outstretched legs.

"Oh, I'm sorry! Hey, what are you doing here? Don't you know this isn't a safe part of town?"

The man looked up, his face dimly lit by the lunos-light. He seemed amused. "You're right. It's not a safe part of town. So what is a child doing walking around here? And on such a cold night?

Teehma drew herself up to her full height. "I'm not a child! I'm fifteen cycles. Anyway, this is *my* neighborhood. If you are going to be wounded or injured or anything, you'll have to go somewhere else."

"I'm not wounded. Just a little tired. I needed a rest from a long walk."

"Isn't there anybody chasing you?"

"Not that I know of. I'm not that important. At least not around here."

Her mystery hero was turning out to be a disappointment. Teehma began to wish he would go away. After all, she could not get back into the fort with him sitting there. "Well then, if you've had your rest, maybe you should be going."

The man showed no inclination to move. Instead, he continued to look at her, taking in her shabby clothes, thin frame, and tangled hair. His gaze lingered on her face long enough to make her feel uncomfortable. "What is a girl like you doing out at this hour? And why are you talking to strange men like me?"

Teehma fished around for a quick lie. "I was just out fetching water. There's a well down that way. And I'm only talking to you because I tripped over you."

He obligingly drew his legs in. "If you're out to get water, where is your bucket?"

She blushed. "Uh, I must have forgot it."

He did not say anything as he stood, though he kept gazing at her. She could tell he was concerned for her. He was also handsome, with kind eyes and light hair like Lucio's, except that it was clean. In truth, he did not seem much older than she was.

When he spoke again, it was in a whisper. "Tell me the truth, girl. Are you in danger?"

Teehma glanced around to make sure that Gorvy was nowhere near. "I'm fine. Just a little lost. But I think I remember my way now." She started to turn away, but he put a hand on her shoulder.

"Listen to me. I don't know what your trouble is, but I want to help. You're too young to be out in the streets like this. My name is Vancien and I will be here again at this time and place in four days. If you need help, you can meet me then."

Thoroughly alarmed by now, Teehma could only nod and make her escape. She waited almost an hour behind a dump pile before she could be certain the man called Vancien had left, and that she could return to the fort. When she finally did come home, even Ester could tell that she was shaken.

———

The cold season of hiverra had descended upon other parts of Rhyvelad, as well as Lascombe, though not with the biting intensity it reserved for regions north of the Duvarian Range. In the southwest, over the gentle plains separating the Cylini marshes from the fields of Jasimor, the winter storms melted into regular bouts of driving rain. One particularly intense rainstorm was hammering a cluster of buildings just outside of the marsh's soggy tree line. The huts were rough but sturdy, organized into an efficient little compound, and inhabited by a mix of Keroulian soldiers, some Keroulian civilians, a handful of Cylini warriors, and even a few Cylini women and children. It was often a lively place, but this afternoon all its inhabitants were tucked away indoors as the rain lashed against the inter-laced broad leaves that formed the roofs of their shelters. The few unfortunate figures who did have to cross from one rude hut to another arrived at their destination soaked, as no one had yet built covered walkways. One such figure was Telenar pa Saauli, Patronius en medio.

"Blast this rain!" he muttered, hurrying into his hut and shutting the thin door behind him. He raised a damp hand to his beard. "I swear I'm starting to grow mold."

The inside of the small building housed little more than a large pallet and some traveling packs, but at least it was dry. A woman of about thirty-five cycles was tending the fire, allowing the smoke to drift upward and out through a hooded vent. This arrangement worked very well. Today, however, the horizontal winds drove the smoke back inside, creating an unpleasant burnt fog effect. Still, the woman smiled as Telenar came in. At the sight of her, he stopped his complaining, though the smoke stung his eyes.

"Perhaps today is not the best day for a fire," he said.

She frowned and starting rubbing her arms. "But I'm so cold!"

Her pout was charming. He would have responded to it, but the smoke made him cough. He hastily removed his spectacles and rubbed his face.

"Oh, I'm sorry!" she exclaimed. "Just let me—"

"No, don't!"

But it was too late. In a fit of nurturing, she had smothered the fire with a blanket, a rash action that produced even more smoke. Now they were both coughing. He struggled to her side.

"It's good to see you, darling."

She was staring ruefully at the remains of the fire. "That didn't go as I had planned."

He waved a bit of smoke away from her face. "It's all right. I like a smoky atmosphere."

"How did the meeting go?"

His answer was a sigh. "I don't know, N'vonne. It's hard to tell. The good news is that the Cylini have offered us some more of their warriors. Since the border wars have stopped, they have little to fear from Keroul at the moment. And besides, they tend to view us more as followers of Kynell than Keroulians."

"So I guess that makes us Kynellians? That's not so bad, is it?"

"Not at all. But the bad news is that Amarian is still insisting on finding the fennels. The fact that he wants anything to do with those duplicitous felines worries me. I know Vancien has faith in the man, but the thought of sending him out on his own to recruit his former allies concerns me a little. Is that so bad?"

She said nothing.

"And then there's Verial." He continued. "She's always sulking around. She has no interest in us, no interest in Kynell, and not even any interest in Vancien! The woman's a catastrophe waiting to happen."

N'vonne had been running her fingers through his brown hair, speckled with gray. She stopped, as he finished his speech. "Verial exasperates me as much as anyone, dear, but we should try to remember what she's been through. Don't you think a little confusion and irritation is natural?"

He did not answer, so she continued. "Besides, Vancien feels strongly about her. Protecting her, I mean. He would be furious if we turned her loose. Maybe we should trust his judgment. He *is* the Advocate, after all."

If she had wanted to cause her husband more unease, she could not have chosen better words. He became despondent. "That's the thing,

N'vonne. What does the Advocacy mean any more? When Amarian brought Vancien back to life, he changed history and stepped outside the pattern set by the Ages. Anything could happen now. The rules Rhyvelad has lived by are entirely meaningless."

She did not have anything to say to this. Everything he said was true, but still she did not share his fears. After all, there was always Kynell. In an effort to allay his anxiety, she shook out the blanket, wrapped it around them both, and changed the subject.

"How is Chiyo doing? Do you think he'll be back soon? I still wish Vance hadn't gone with him."

It worked. Telenar began to relax. "I think he's actually enjoying himself. As a general, he never had a chance to try his hand at spying. When he and Vancien left for Lascombe, he looked as excited as I'd ever seen him."

Now it was N'vonne's turn to become moody. "I still don't see why Vance had to go." As his former instructor, she had known Vancien from an early age and considered herself something of a mother to him. The thought of him heading into danger was very upsetting.

Telenar slid closer to her. He could appreciate her concern: he did not relish Vancien's absence either, but the Prysm Advocate was no longer a child. Plus, he sympathized with his wanderlust; they had been cooped up in this camp ever since Vancien and Amarian had returned in late autore. Nine fortnights in makeshift huts was enough to drive anyone crazy.

"Besides, N'vonne, you're forgetting that they took Thelámos." He allowed himself a short laugh. "The sight of Chiyo bundled up against that Destrariae blood is one I won't soon forget. I still can't believe that beast let him on."

N'vonne's smile returned as she remembered their departure. Thelámos was an Ealatrophe, part gryphon and part Destrariae, which were cold, ethereal, nearly invisible creatures whose blood was called *klathonus*. They lived in the Eyestone Glade and their cold was so intense that few could stand it for longer than a few moments. An Ealatrophe was perhaps the most beautiful, proudest beast in all Rhyvelad. It was an honor to ride one, though the experience was painful.

Having run out of conversation, they were both content to sit in silence until someone knocked at their rickety door. It was young Bren, Chiyo's aid.

"You wanted me to tell you when Amarian left, sir. He's just gone."

"Good. Did he take a voyoté with him?"

"No, sir. He went on foot."

Telenar nodded. That was smart. If Amarian was going to hunt fennels, taking another type of *galthis* would be a bad diplomatic move. All three types of *galthis* had been created by Kynell to be humankind's helpers. The canine voyoté, as well as the munkke-trophe (for the most part), had stayed committed to that task. But the fennels had developed an independent streak that caused them to look on the other two *galthis* as self-righteous and insufferable.

Later that night, after everyone had enjoyed a communal dinner in the mess hall, Telenar and N'vonne were sitting at the fire again, enjoying some lazy conversation before drifting off to sleep. Again, someone knocked at the door. Telenar, less than charitably, called for them to come in. It was Bren again, more agitated than before.

"What is it this time?"

"It's Verial, sir. She's run away."

CHAPTER THREE

Amarian's mission was a short one and not nearly as glamorous as Vancien and Chiyo's expedition to Lascombe. Not that he would have traded places with his brother for any price; Lascombe was the last place he wanted to be. Though no longer Obsidian's Advocate, he still shook with rage when he thought of Corfe's betrayal. Seeing the face of that traitor would most likely cause him to do something dangerous, possibly murderous. By all accounts, it was a temptation best avoided.

Yet life at the little camp was suffocating, although that was not the camp's fault. He was a man without pleasures now. The things that used to please him now repulsed him, and the things that should please him— wholesome things, like an orbset or children's laughter—only bored him. His soul felt like an empty shell, vacated of great evil, but not yet inhabited by the good.

What was wrong with him? When he had first accepted Kynell's pardon for his crimes, he had felt great release. For a few days, it had not mattered that everyone except Vancien still looked at him in suspicion and fear, nor had he been concerned by the uncertain future. He was perpetually back in that room, where as a child he had been given a choice to serve the Prysm or Obsidian, only this time the choice was not his; Kynell had made it for him and the Prysm god had chosen him *and* Vancien. He no longer had to protect his little brother from evil by becoming evil himself. The thought, as always, brought a relieved smile to his face. But that smile quickly vanished as he remembered how quiet, how aimless the world seemed now. Back when he was Darkness personified, he had had a goal: rule the world in the name of

Zyreio. Now he was no one, just another of Kynell's followers, with no rank and no purpose.

What little pleasure he did have came from his frequent conversations with Vancien. The two often sat and talked about their old village of Win, South of the Glade, their father or even Vancien's youth after Amarian had left. They never spoke of Amarian's own history. For Amarian, their conversations were a means of erasing the past, if only for a few moments. They reminded him of life before Zyreio, as well as life without the need for luxury and power. They made becoming human again seem almost desirable.

But then Vancien had left for Lascombe, leaving Amarian to his own thoughts and the suspicious gazes of others. No one, not even the priest Telenar, liked him. At the very least, they tolerated him, watching in grave silence as if waiting for him to crack under the strain of imposed virtue. No one believed that he was no longer Obsidian, nor could he blame them. At times, he wondered about it himself.

He had to get out, if only to do something to redeem himself in the eyes of his new allies. And so he suggested his little mission to the council. He had reason to believe that fennels were in the woodlands to the south. Though they had served him in the barren, wind-swept Eastern Lands, the big cats were much more at home in temperate climates, with trees to climb and enough warmth to keep their joints nimble. When Corfe had dismissed them from service to Obsidian, they would have taken the opportunity to return to their native dwelling. It was Amarian's hope that he could make some sort of peace with them; after all, if there ever came a time of conflict between his little group and Corfe's army, they would need all the allies they could get.

He left as soon as the council approved his mission, walking so quickly that it took him just two days to get deep into the woodlands. He was heading southeast, away from the marshes but also away from the Plains of Jasimor, which lay almost parallel across the grasslands from their encampment. He doubted that the fennels would go anywhere near that place. More importantly, he knew himself to be too vulnerable to go near it. It was the one place in Rhyvelad where Zyreio's influence was physically tangible. To return there would be tantamount to suicide, or a return to Obsidian's service, which would be worse.

The hiverran rains showed no mercy as he journeyed. Yet it did not take long for the trees to grow thick enough that they broke up the downpour. It was warmer here than near the marshlands. Amarian had soon stripped off his cloak, then his over-shirt. He was down to a soaked tunic and rolled-up trousers when the first fennel spotted him. The large, dark cat recognized Darkness immediately and, to his embarrassment, his tail bushed out in fear and anger before he could stop it. But rather than attack the intruder as he was inclined to do, he slipped unnoticed into the underbrush and disappeared.

Amarian continued forward, unaware of his observer and wondering how he would find the fennels at all—they were only seen when they wanted to be. Theoretically, he could be wandering around in the trees for days, hoping to bump into one or for one to "bump" into him. He did not know if he had the patience for that sort of activity; the warm rain was more suffocating than refreshing and his wet clothes were already beginning to chafe.

His will would not be put to the test. As he rounded yet another blind corner in the path, he saw one of the proud animals waiting for him. It was sitting at a distance, its mottled gray fur damp from the rain. It did not move when Amarian appeared, except for an annoyed flick of the tail. Fennels despised the rain. Amarian stopped.

"Darkness."

Amarian shook his head. "I'm just Amarian now, Koeb."

Koeb growled low in his throat. "So it is true? I had heard, but could not believe."

"It is true. My brother and I have made peace. I am no longer Zyreio's Advocate."

"Then you have not come to take revenge on us?"

Amarian noted that several other fennels had crept out of the undergrowth and were watching him intently. "No. I do not seek revenge."

"Then what do you seek?"

"I seek peace. There may come a time when we will have to battle against that pretender, Corfe. We do not want you to fight against us."

Koeb shook his head, creating a brief halo of water. "The human Corfe freed us to return here, Darkness. That is something you did not do."

Amarian had expected this objection, nor was he certain his response was adequate. "You are right, Koeb. I kept you and your kind in servitude. But I have changed. I no longer serve Zyreio. I am a follower of the Prysm now, and Kynell does not keep slaves."

The rain stopped, so Koeb took a moment to shake, stretch, and settle himself into a comfortable crouching position. He had clearly retained authority over his pack and was in no mood to return to his earlier subservience.

"I thought the human Corfe was also a follower of the Prysm. If you have both become creatures of Kynell, why would you fight?"

"I hope we will not fight. But Corfe thinks I am still Zyreio's servant. He will not believe that I have changed."

Koeb yawned. "And have you changed?"

Amarian bristled. "Enough questions, Koeb. If I had not changed, would I suffer this interview? Would I seek your help with pleas while Zyreio burned in my chest?"

Koeb blinked, unperturbed. "Does not the Prysm god burn in your chest? Is he so weak that he needs the help of the fennels?"

It was almost more than he could bear. In earlier days, those would have been the last words Koeb spoke. But Amarian was not the same man he was. And besides, he did not have a sword. So he gritted his teeth. "I am done here. Do you have an answer? Yes or no?"

Koeb stood, his eyes almost level with Amarian's. "We are not interested in gods. Nor have we been released from bondage only to return to it again. When Corfe calls, we will not answer. When you call, we will not answer. Let Kynell himself call us. We will not answer."

Amarian raised his eyebrows. Koeb surprised him. He knew that fennels were arrogant creatures, but he had never guessed the depths of their conceit—or at least, of Koeb's conceit. "So be it. When you call on Kynell, perhaps he will not answer either."

But Koeb was already walking away, followed by the others, their proud feline heads held high.

Amarian swore under his breath. All Rhyvelad could be turned upside down and the fennels could care less. But that fact did not sting him so much as the blow to his pride. He had failed in this, the tiniest of missions. So much for redeeming himself in the eyes of those Prysmites. He found himself hoping that someday Koeb would call on Kynell, only to have the Prysm god throw his arrogance back in his face. He shook his head to dispel the thought, knowing that Vancien would disapprove. Besides, had not he himself been arrogant once? Wasn't he arrogant still? If Kynell had found room for Obsidian's Advocate, surely he had patience for Koeb.

These and other thoughts were wandering through his mind when he heard a soft hiss by his left foot. He looked down and saw a small fennel, pressed so low to the ground that its brown and tan fur almost blended with the soil beneath it. It was young, just past being a kit. Its green eyes watched him intently.

"Hssst! Hssst! Darkness!"

Amarian quickly crouched into the wet foliage.

"Please do not call me that."

"Sorry, Darkness. Sorry, sir. So sorry, Darkness."

What could this runt want? "Stop apologizing," he told it. "I've already spoken with your pridehead. You shouldn't even be talking to me."

The creature nodded its enthusiastic agreement but still it continued to look at him. Since it obviously was not going anywhere and he would look a little suspicious talking to the underbrush, he told it to walk alongside him.

"It's a privilege to talk to you, Darkness. Sorry, sir," it continued from under the low broadleaves as they started walking. "Yes, a great privilege. Lord Amarian has never come to the woodlands, no never seen us at our home, no never."

"I've never had cause to."

"But Bedge is so glad he did, yes, so glad. So glad he came to see our home."

"And who is this Bedge? You?"

"Oh, yes, I am she. I'm Bedge and I'm—uff!" Her chatter stopped abruptly as the undergrowth shuddered.

"So, Bedge, what is it you want?"

The voice once again issued from the ground, sounding a little winded. "Bedge walks many places, back and forth. Bedge loves her home, yes, but Bedge gets restless. So Bedge walks and walks. One time she walked a long, long way, past the sandy dry land and into the windy land."

Amarian stopped to look in her direction. "You went back to the Eastern Lands? Back to Donech?"

"Oh, no! Big tower too far. The windy place is very different. Very, very different. Bedge was too scared to stay in windy place for long."

Amarian could not imagine the Eastern Lands being much more terrifying than during his own reign, but since this was the only news he had received of his realm, he pressed for more information. Yet Bedge grew reticent and her whispery voice started to warble.

"Yes, very different. Bedge too scared to stay."

"But what happened? What made it different?"

"Bedge left when very young; Bedge does not remember much of windy place. Bedge too scared to say."

Though he could not see her, he could tell that the young fennel was shaken. In the old days, he would have forced the information out of her. Now he felt a tug of compassion. Whatever it was that she had seen, she was still haunted by it.

"Bedge," he said, with as much tenderness as he could muster. "It's very important for me to find out what's going on in the windy place. I am grateful that you went there and I'm sorry that you were scared. What was it that scared you?"

There was silence in the underbrush for a moment, then a sigh. "Humans. Many, many humans. And big lizards. And fennels." Here Bedge almost lost her composure. "Many, many fennels, all moving, moving, and moving. Fennels talked very loud, very *bad*. The humans did not eat. Did not sleep. But all were loud. All were angry. Bedge never liked big lizards but big lizards in windy place even worse. They were not so loud as fennels and humans, but still scary. Bedge did not like it so loud, so Bedge did not stay."

If he could have, Amarian would have rested his hand on her head to reassure her. Instead, he started walking again. "You did well, Bedge, to leave." Inside, his thoughts were racing. What on Rhyvelad were so many sentries and fennels doing in the Eastern Lands? He had sent almost all of them ahead to Keroul when he was posing as Commander Hull. The only forces left should have been humans and he knew that they would not mobilize unless commanded to. Had some Sentries escaped Corfe to start another resistance? They had never showed that much initiative. Besides, the humans and fennels Bedge was describing sounded very strange indeed.

"Did you see anything else while you were in the windy place?"

"No, Darkness. I mean, sir. Bedge saw nothing but Bedge felt so scared. The bad fennels made her feel empty. So empty." Her voice drifted off, as if she was remembering the feeling.

"Have you told Koeb about this? Does he know you're telling me?"

"Bedge told pridehead everything. Pridehead laughed at Bedge, told Bedge to stop being a silly kit. Said Bedge must stay at home. But Lord Amarian," her voice brightened, "Lord Amarian has come to see us at home. Bedge must tell Lord Amarian; he came to Bedge's home."

Amarian did not follow the logic. "You did a good thing, Bedge. But now it is time for you to go home again. And stay home until the bad fennels are gone."

At this command, Bedge crept out of the bushes to walk by Amarian's side. Her head barely came up to his knee. He could see that brown and tan fur covered her in swirling patterns that culminated in thick shocks of fur around her whiskers. Her feet and ears were unnaturally large and her tail just a little bit crooked. In short, she lacked anything resembling the dignity of a fennel. No wonder Koeb did not take her seriously. Once again, she focused her big green eyes on him.

"Bedge can't go home. Bedge is lost."

Amarian frowned and pointed back down the path he had been following. "Just follow the path back to the pride. I'm sure your mother will find you."

Still the green eyes. "Bedge has no mother. Bedge can't go home. Bedge is lost."

"Look, you can't possibly be lost. All you have to do is follow the path back." A sudden, horrible idea occurred to him. "You cannot come with *me*."

The little fennel flicked her tail, preparing to argue the point. "Bedge will serve Darkness, sir. Bedge would rather serve Sir than stay with other fennels. They are do-nothings. Bedge wants to do something."

He stared at her and scratched his head. What would he do with a fennel kit? "Did you say you didn't have a mother?"

Bedge shook her head aggressively. "Bedge's mother was killed by Darkness." She gave him a pointed look, not bothering to apologize for the title this time.

He had to ask, though he was not sure he wanted the answer. "How?"

"Bedge's mother was hungry. She went hunting in the trees that were only for the hunting of Darkness' dragon-beast. Dragon-beast found her and killed her. Darkness approved, said death of Bedge's mother a good example to other fennels."

Amarian did not remember the episode, but he did not doubt it had happened. His dragon Ovna had been rapacious and he had easily valued her more than the fennels.

"If Ovna killed your mother, why are you helping me now?"

Bedge looked up at the blue sky through the trees; the clouds had finally dispersed. "Bedge has heard new things about Sir. She heard he is different in many ways. He is good now, like Bedge's mother."

"I will never be good like your mother, or like any other creature of Rhyvelad. But it's true that I have changed. I am a follower of Kynell now, of the Prysm."

The fennel nodded, appearing much wiser than her cycles. "Bedge knows. She wants to see the change herself. And Bedge has known about the darkness for a long time. She is ready to learn about the light-god."

It was a reasoning that struck home for Amarian. Still, he found his own response surprising. "You can stay with me. I may not be able to tell you much about the god of the Prysm, but I bet my brother can."

At his words, the soulful, ancient eyes disappeared, replaced by the buoyancy of a kit. "Truly? Truly, truly? Bedge is very happy to go with Sir! Bedge will take good care of Sir!" She stopped to shake herself. "Can Bedge walk in the path now? Bedge's fur is wet from the green plants."

Amarian glanced over his shoulder to see if anyone was watching them. "All right then. But we'll have to move quickly and quietly. Amarian doesn't want you to get caught."

CHAPTER FOUR

The changes that had taken place in Lascombe were more sinister than those perched on top of the thick city walls could ever have suspected. Vancien, bound as he was to the streets, could scarcely believe it. He had known it was no paradise when he had stayed there a cycle before, but now it appeared that its wounds were growing even deeper. It had been little less than ten fortnights since King Relgaré had died, reportedly at the hands of the Cylini during the border wars, although Vancien was certain that Amarian had somehow orchestrated the death. When news of the king's demise had reached the capital city, the streets had erupted with rioters. Relgaré's border wars with the Cylini had never been popular and the people hoped that his death would signify an end to the conflict. They endeavored to convey that desire by mobbing in the streets, shouting slogans such as "Let the Cylini be!" "Bring our boys home!" "The House of Anisllyr is Anis-where?" or, more ominously, "The king can have his marsh; we'll have the city!" Their cries echoed over the rooftops, through the lofty windows of the palace, and past the ears of the young king.

Relgaren had heard their cries, as well as listened to the representatives of the Square. In a rare display of solidarity, all five hundred and one of them had called for a withdrawal from the marshes after Relgaré's death. It was an easy thing to concede. With the dubious help of Commander Hull, the Cylini had been driven far into their swamplands, where they would be licking their wounds for some time to come. Relgaren had then called the Keroulian forces back home, though at the request of his new advisor, he did not disband the army. Instead, he insisted that they be quartered in Lascombe.

The city's barracks could in no way accommodate such a mass of soldiers. The citizens were consequently ordered to open up their homes and provide the troops food and shelter. It was an unpopular measure by any standard. Even the Square representatives were horrified, especially since their comfortable lodgings were first pick for the officer corps. The situation was made even more repugnant by the fact that not all of Relgaren's army was human. Sentries were now wearing Keroulian blue, thanks to the earlier infusion of forces from the Eastern Lands, which meant that many unlucky families were forced to house what they considered a walking nightmare. The result was a level of hostility and suspicion unknown to the city for the last five hundred cycles. Soldiers roamed the streets, ready for a brawl, while the citizens had to work grueling hours in order to feed their new house-guests.

Vancien had no doubt that the girl he had met in the alleyway had suffered greatly from the decisions of both Relgaré and his son, although he did not know how. The thought of her out in the cold weighed heavy on his heart, and he wished he had not told her that it would be four days before he could help her.

"Your compassionate heart is going to get you into trouble one of these days, Vance." Chiyo said after listening to his report the following night. His long, lean limbs were stretched out beside the booth they occupied and he picked at his nails as if he had nothing better to do. His gently slanted eyes, covered by a deep hood, were the only thing that conveyed his usual intensity. "I suggest you let the girl alone; maybe she did forget her water bucket, as she said."

"I'm going to help her if I can," Vancien replied, ignoring his response. He, too, was trying to look casual, though with less success than Chiyo. "There are so many people we can't help."

He leaned back, picking at his food and gazing at his dingy surroundings. *Wallow's Wake and Emporium* was not an upscale establishment. The roof leaked, the tables wobbled, and the food was mediocre. The inn was so named for a man called Wallow who had left all of his belongings, including a rickety building and some brewing equipment, toward the establishment of an inn and drinking house. The *Emporium* part was a sad collection of all Wallow's earthly belongings, replenished over the cycles with junk donated by generous patrons who did not want to throw their own garbage away. Thus, empty bottles crowded the shelves, boots without partners littered the corners, and an assembly of leather goods, all of them worn and torn, filled too many empty kegs to count. The whole place was a testament to laziness and filth. Still, it possessed the charm of being a long way away from the palace. Nor was it a drinking house frequented by Relgaren's soldiers. It was therefore the perfect place for Vancien and Chiyo to conduct their operation.

Chiyo decided to change the subject. Despite the fact that few soldiers came into the place, he still kept his hood on and his voice low: only a cycle ago he had been one of the most famous figures in the city. It would not do for him to be recognized now.

"Let's forget about the girl. Tell me what you've seen these past few days."

Vancien shrugged. "A lot of soldiers. I came across a pack of them yesterday and was almost recognized. I ran like a scared rabbit."

"Which is what you should have done. Did they follow you?"

"Only one of them saw me. I had seen him briefly during my time here before. We made eye contact but by the time he looked twice, I was gone."

Chiyo took a long pull of Lascombe Pure. "We'll have to keep our heads lower than ever. Kynell forbid that Corfe and the king start thinking of us as Obsidian spies!"

"Apparently the king doesn't show his face very often. And most people are grumbling about Corfe. You know he has become the king's main advisor. It was he who insisted that the army be quartered in Lascombe. But he does not come out much either, except early in the morning, accompanied by that fellow named Gair." He paused and sipped his own Pure, not bothering to hide a grimace at the taste. "What about you?"

Chiyo adjusted his hood and looked around again to make sure no one was listening. "My contacts in the army tell me that the dissent continues and not just between the Sentries and the Keroulians. Amarian's few battalions of humans from the Eastern Lands cause a lot of trouble all by themselves. They seem particularly put out if a Sentry and citizen manage to make peace, which has actually happened. If these troops don't have something to do before too long, they're going to make Lascombe into a war zone."

"What do you think we should do about it?" Vancien was eager to do something, anything.

"Don't think there's much we can do. We're not about to put our friend forward just to solve Corfe's problems."

"Our friend" was of course Amarian, but they had both agreed that to reveal knowledge of Amarian's whereabouts would be fatal. Corfe would surely hunt him out and their small band had no chance of defeating Keroul's army. Nor would they want to, Vancien mused. Most of the soldiers were straight-forward, Prysm-fearing men. It was unthinkable to waste their lives over a dispute between himself, Amarian, and Corfe. Despite his impatience, it was better to let things rest and hope that Corfe would forget about the Obsidian Advocate, if such a thing were possible.

"So tomorrow we go to—"

A sharp look from Chiyo cut him off. Three soldiers had come in, all of them wearing Keroulian blue, although they abused the barman in a way that most Keroulian soldiers would never have done.

Chiyo and Vancien looked meaningfully at each other. These were some of Amarian's old men. What were they doing on the far end of town? Then Vancien noticed that there was a child among them: a boy, with manacles on his wrists and a bruise under his left eye. He must have been about twelve cycles, though he did not look as terrified as a normal twelve-cycle old might in his situation. Vancien nudged Chiyo, who expressed no interest. Neither one of them said anything as they watched the soldiers propel the boy toward a stool far away from the door.

"Stay there, you little runt!" one of them commanded. "And don't be thinking about trying to escape!" He then returned to his comrades, who were already joking about thieves and slave markets.

To Vancien's surprise, Chiyo drained the last of his drink and stood up.

"What are you doing?" he whispered.

"Come on, my friend." Chiyo responded in an even voice. "It's late and we have to make an early start tomorrow."

But Vancien did not move. "Are you joking?" he whispered fiercely. "We can't leave this child in the hands of those men."

Chiyo sat down again, looking as determined as Vancien had ever seen him. "Didn't you hear the soldiers? The boy's a thief."

"But they're taking him to the slave market!"

Chiyo clinched his fists and lowered his voice. "I know. But I have a plan. We just have to get out of here quietly."

He was interrupted by a drunken voice, so near that he could smell it as well as hear it. "Hey, you two! What're you whispering about?"

Chiyo looked up to see one of the soldiers standing next to their table. He was clutching a mug and glaring at them. His lips were already wet with dark ale, which dripped down his chin into his gnarled beard. He was a big man, with a gut so substantial that it was barely contained by his belt. Chiyo did his best to appear intimidated.

"Sorry, sir! We didn't mean to trouble you."

"Well, you have. Now I suggest you get your hides out of here before I give *you* trouble."

Chiyo nodded and made to leave. Vancien followed, trusting in whatever his friend had planned, but not without glancing again at the boy on the stool. His curiosity did not escape the soldier's notice.

"What're you looking at?" the big man growled as he grabbed Vancien by the collar. His breath smelled of ale and fish.

"Nothing, sir. I just couldn't help but notice how young your prisoner was." From the corner of his vision, he could see Chiyo roll his eyes.

"Oh yeah? Well, a thief's a thief and we caught this runt climbing out of somebody's window. He's not the youngest brat to become a slave, you know."

Vancien adopted a whine. "Oh, I know, I know. He deserves it, I'm sure." He glanced again at the boy, who was looking at him with open disdain. "Yes, uh, we're grateful to soldiers like you who keep order in our city."

Pleased with the answer, the soldier let him go. "Aye, you should be. It's our job to keep parasites like this off the street." He raised a gloved hand to lay a blow on his prisoner, but found himself unable to complete the movement. Chiyo had caught his wrist.

"Pray, sir," Chiyo said, still looking submissive. "Do not strike the boy any more. It will lower his price at the market."

"Yeah? Powder covers up bruises well enough. What's it got to do with you anyway?"

Chiyo jingled his money purse. "I've come into town for the purpose of purchasing a slave. This boy here looks exactly like the type my wife wants to help around the farm. If I buy him off of you now, you'll get the money instead of some slaver."

The soldier looked at his companions, who only shrugged. Why argue with such an offer?

"Yeah, okay. What's it worth to you?"

"Twenty athas."

The soldier smirked as his companions rumbled. "Twenty athas?! A wee babe's worth more than twenty athas!"

"But if you turn him in to your captain, you won't get any money at all, will you? Just a slap on the back, which won't buy anything to drink."

Again, the logic was difficult to oppose. The soldier looked again at his taciturn comrades before accepting the offer. The money was exchanged and the boy was un-manacled, hauled off the stool, and pushed over to Vancien, who took hold of his arm. Without another word the three escaped into the street.

Chiyo maintained his silence and Vancien followed suit as they hurried away from the tavern. The boy, meanwhile, watched his new captors with a mixture of relief and fear. When they were several blocks away, Vancien let go of him.

"All right, you're free. Be sure to stay away from those soldiers. If you're a thief like they say, I suggest you consider finding another line of work."

Chiyo nodded his curt agreement, but the boy only rubbed his arm and looked at them. "You're not taking me with you?" His head was uncovered in the cold night air and Vancien noticed how ragged his hair was. It looked as if it had been hacked unevenly by a dull knife. But the child had round, expressive eyes that were looking at him reproachfully.

Vancien was taken aback by the question. "Of course not. What do we need with a slave? We just thought we'd get you out of the hands of those brutes."

But the boy glared at them. "Then you should've left me with them," he declared. "'Least if I went to the slave market, I might be bought up by someone."

"You *want* that?"

Before the boy could respond, Chiyo interrupted. "We've heard a lot about this slave market, boy. Last time I was in Lascombe, it was against the law to own slaves."

The boy shrugged and pushed his hacked and dirty hair out of his face. "They just started doing it this breach. Some country folk come in, said they had goods to sell. Turns out it was their own families! Guess they were so poor they didn't have a choice."

"But what about the law?"

The boy ignored the fact that Vancien had asked the question and kept on addressing Chiyo. "After they ran out of poor families, some *narfats* took to selling prisoners of war. Them Cylini folk. Now they have a market 'bout once every fortnight. The king doesn't seem to care. Some say it's good for the conom—econ—connem—"

"Economy." Chiyo finished for him, wrapping his cloak tighter around himself. "But these slaves can't have good ends. Why would you want to become one?"

The boy held up his tattered sleeve. "I'm already a slave. Leastwise I feel like one. I only steal for food, mister. And Gorvy takes most of that, anyways."

Both Chiyo and Vancien had more questions. Their concern about the slave market was obvious. Yet there was no sense conducting the interview out in the cold street. Since Chiyo had given most of his money to the soldier, Vancien bought the boy a warm drink at another small tavern. When they were all seated, they renewed their questioning.

Vancien began. "Who's Gorvy? Your father?"

The boy snorted into his drink. "That'll be the day the Chasm opens! My dad's dead, and my mother too. Gorvy isn't family." He suddenly turned nervous, glancing around the room as if this Gorvy might appear. It was the sort of look Vancien had seen very recently. When he spoke again, his voice was in a whisper. "Gorvy's the *narfat* who makes us steal for him. Then he takes what we get and gives us crumbs to live on."

"Us? Who's us?"

"Lots of kids like me. Our group's only got four, but I know he's got others somewhere." He took a purposeful drink, as if it had been his life's mission to discover where these other groups were.

After catching Chiyo's eye, Vancien excused himself for a moment and stepped away from the table. Chiyo mumbled something to the boy then joined him.

"Chiyo, what if that girl is in the same situation? Perhaps the boy knows her."

"I doubt it, Vance. This is a big city. This Gorvy could have hundreds of children under his thumb."

Vancien looked again at the boy, who was staring into his drink. "Still, it's worth checking out."

"And even if he did know her, what does it matter? We can't drag children around with us."

"We could find homes for them."

Chiyo's eyes narrowed in reproof. As he did so, he seemed to draw on all the quiet dignity the people of the West were known for. "We're set to leave in three days, Vance. And in that time, we're supposed to keep our heads *low*. Even if we found families, it could be dangerous for them to have contact with us. I don't know anybody in this town I'm willing to compromise, do you?"

"We've got to do something. We can't just send this kid back to Gorvy, whoever he is." As he considered their options, an unlikely image came to mind. But the more he thought about it, the more likely it became. The prospect made him smile.

"What? What are you grinning about?"

"I think I have a good candidate. I only hope he's still in town."

CHAPTER FIVE

Three days later, it was time for Vancien and Chiyo to leave Lascombe. They had found out what useful information they could and soon Telenar would begin to worry about them. But before they could sneak through the city gates and find Vancien's Ealatrophe, they had one more task to accomplish.

Upon their many assurances of good intentions, the boy, Lucio, agreed to lead them to his "group." He waited until the middle of the day, explaining that this was the least likely time for Gorvy to come by, and then led them into one of the poorer parts of the city. As the crowded buildings began to block out the orb-light, Vancien knew that his hunch was right. They were soon stopped in the same alley where he had taken rest a few days before.

"Here it is." Lucio whispered, "Wait here while I make sure everything's clear."

He went on a few paces then disappeared into the stone wall on his right. Chiyo and Vancien waited for several breaths before seeing his head poke out, then his hand, waving them on. They proceeded slowly, with hands on their swords. During their time outside, it had occurred to Vancien that there was nothing to guarantee this child's trustworthiness. What would stop him from betraying them to better his own prospects?

They arrived at the spot and discovered a thick, tattered curtain covering a cut-out in the wall. At Lucio's bidding, they ducked down and went through.

"This is it." The boy said, kicking at a pile of hay on the floor. "See why slavery don't look so bad?"

Aside from the piles of mud-spattered hay, there were three other children in the room. Lucio must have prepared them for the newcomers, since they neither ran away nor cried for help. Instead, they looked rooted to the gravelly floor. Vancien, bent low to avoid hitting the ceiling, recognized the girl from the alley. She was watching him, but did not say anything. The two others were very timid: one was a girl who appeared to be blind, the other was a small boy of about four cycles who clung to the blind girl.

For a moment all parties stood in awkward silence. Then Lucio began introductions. "These are my mates. That one there," he pointed to the girl Vancien had already met, "is Teehma. She's fifteen and can't go out stealing any more, since she might get herself stolen."

Teehma glared at him. He had obviously touched upon a sore subject.

"That one there," Lucio continued, undisturbed, "is Ester; she couldn't ever go stealing because of her eyes. See?" He waved a hand in front of her unresponsive eyes as she treated them to a curtsy. "And the little one there is Trint. He's my right hand man."

Trint surfaced from Ester's thin skirts long enough to acknowledge Lucio's compliment. It looked as if his hair had never been cut at all and though his eyes were not so round as Lucio's, they expressed great fear. One poorly healed scar decorated his left cheek and his hands were covered with small cuts. Vancien guessed these marks had been obtained by his unfortunate profession.

"So that's it." Lucio finished. "Gorvy comes back every couple of nights or so to take me and Trint out. I expect he'll come tonight, since he hasn't been in a while."

There was more awkward silence. Then Ester went over to a small trunk in the corner and began to fumble around inside. Her long skirts caught on the hay as she moved. "Can I get you a drink?" she offered, her voice small and uncertain. "We don't have much, but Trint can fetch you some water."

Vancien was touched by the offer but before he could respond, Teehma jerked the rough cups out of the girl's hands. "No need to be hospitable, Es," she snapped. "We don't even know these men. Who's to say they won't sell us into slavery?"

Trint, who had been shyly eying Chiyo's sword, gasped at the word. He looked up at the half-crouched general. "Slav'ry? We don't wanna be slaves!"

Chiyo dropped to his knee beside the boy to reassure him. "No, Trint. We will not make you slaves. We want to help you, to give you a home." As he said this, he cast a dubious look at his partner.

Vancien glanced at the curtain. They were wasting time. "My friend is right. Lucio, you know we have no interest in selling you as slaves. We are here only to help, but we're running out of time. I have a friend here in the city. He has agreed to give you a place to stay until he can find you good homes. He can feed you and give you a warm place to sleep. But you have to trust us." He looked imploringly at Teehma. "I told you I would come back to help you. And I did."

She met his look but did not say anything. Instead, she brushed her lank brown hair out of her eyes, rubbed her chapped hands, and began to pack their meager belongings. Soon she began to speak to the room in general. "Well, we've got to be sold into slavery at some point, don't we? Might as well get it over with. No good staying here for Gorvy one more night."

Trint heard the word again and burst into tears. "Slav'ry? But I want a home!"

Wishing there were a way he could shut that girl up, Vancien gently took the sobbing Trint to the corner of the room. As Chiyo rounded up the others, he slipped a cord of leather from around his neck; on it was a small metal ring with a bright chip of glass soldered onto it.

"Look at this ring, Trint," he whispered, determined to get through to the terrified child. "Do you see it? Do you like it?"

Trint stopped sobbing long enough to nod.

"My brother found it in a dried up stream a long time ago. He gave it to me when I was your age, not long before I lost him. He told me that as long as I wore it, I should remember that Kynell was watching out for me. Do you believe in Kynell?"

By now the sobs had turned into exaggerated sniffles. He nodded again.

"Good." Vancien took the leather with the ring on it and slipped it around Trint's neck. "He's watching over you now. Will you keep this for me?"

Trint rubbed a dirty finger over the glass and nodded a third time. Then he returned to Ester and whispered something into her ear. A moment later, Chiyo had them herded outside, directing them from the shadow of the city walls and towards a nicer area of town, not too far from the magnificent palace itself.

The orbs were setting as they stood outside of a slender, ornate door. Unaccustomed as they were to luxury of any sort, Teehma and Trint gawked at its delicate brass handles, intricate woodwork, and glimmering polished surface. It was carved with the most extraordinary animals: along the door's broad border prowled menacing fennels, crouching among shadowed foliage and trees, on the top of which were perched grand birds with round beaks the length of Trint's arm. Lizards—not Sentries, but funny, four-legged lizards—darted under the leaves out of the birds' sight. In the main panel itself, which was barely any wider than the border, stood an erect, frowning creature with big hands, bushy eyebrows, and delicately carved fur. It glared at them, daring them to touch the polished bronze knocker, which was carved to represent a money pouch hanging from its sash.

Notwithstanding the door's intimidating gaze, Vancien banged the knocker. "Now, remember what I told you," he said to the children as he waited for a response. "You must be very respectful toward my friend. He's not exactly like us. He's more like a. . ."

The door swung open and a short, beady-eyed primate appeared, looking very offended.

"A monkey!" Trint shrieked.

"A what?" it shrieked back.

"Sirin!" Vancien interceded, before the little primate shut the door on them. "Sirin, these are the children I told you about."

Sirin blinked his red eyes and jabbed his cane at Trint. When he was not shrieking, his voice was very deep. "You told me they were well behaved! That little beast called me a monkey! I am a munkke-trophe, sir." He stared hard at the boy, who ducked behind Ester. "*Not* a monkey."

Chiyo brushed past the munkke-trophe into the house. "Our apologies, Sirin. They've been on the street for some time, so their manners may be a little rough." He gestured for the children to follow them, which they did, staring in amazement at their new surroundings. Even Lucio, who took pride in his air of skepticism, was overwhelmed.

Munkke-trophes were known for their facility with business, and Sirin was no exception. His fluidity in many languages had allowed him to trade successfully throughout and even beyond Keroul. And like most munkke-trophes, he had a taste for the finer things in life, which included striated marble floors, Oragione cushions from Chiyo's own land in the West, and glossy wicker furniture tailored to munkke-trophe specifications (about half what a human's specifications would be). Despite the short chairs, the parlor they found themselves in had a grand feel: massive tapestries covered the walls, end-tables supported countless bits of fine ceramic, and in the corner, elaborate metal stairs spiraled up to rooms above.

Sirin bustled in behind them. "Come in, come in, if you must. I can

36

see you felt no need to wash the bratlings before bringing them here." He touched Teehma's arm with a furry finger; the girl barely noticed, so taken aback was she by her surroundings. "Dirty as a creerat. Did you roll them in manure before they came?"

"That's enough, Sirin." Vancien responded. "I didn't ask you to take them in so you could abuse them. They've had enough of that already."

The munkke-trophe shrugged and pulled a velvet cord by the door. "No matter. My servants will give them a proper bath." Sure enough, two human servants came in response to the bell; a boy and a girl, neither one much older than Teehma and both of Chiyo's descent. To Vancien's relief, they seemed healthy and content.

"Where did you get servants?"

Sirin watched as the two shuffled the nervous children up the stairs. "Where does anybody get servants? Those two bratlings are from a noble family in Ktai. Brother and sister, they are, and very well mannered. My compliments to your kind, general."

Chiyo nodded. But Vancien was confused. "Your house servants are nobility?"

Hobbling over to a large cushion, Sirin eased himself down. "It's an honored tradition, brat—I mean, Vancien. In more secure days, many of the nobility would send their children to be apprenticed in a trade. They learn humility through service, you see. Wouldn't do to have the better classes thinking themselves better, as it were. Those two," he waved a cane at the ceiling, "are learning how to barter in four different languages. And they're learning how to draw a hot bath. So when they return to their families, they will have more than their ancestry to rely on." He paused to favor Vancien with a glare from his red eyes. "But you have riled things up, bratling. Although I must say, when Corfe announced that you were dead, my little munkke-trophe heart gave a twang. Now that you're alive, I realize that I should have left you in the desert where I found you! With Telenar gone, Relgaré dead, and the new king enthralled with that misfit, the nobility of other realms are nervous. They are not as eager to send their young ones to us. Indeed, I must return these two to Ktai this warm season." He wistfully flexed his paw, an action that was becoming more painful with age. "I shall have to make sure these new bratlings learn how to mix my joint poultice."

Vancien was beginning to wonder if they really had delivered the children into slavery, but Chiyo seemed content with the situation. "They will earn their keep, Sirin, don't worry about that. Just see if you can find them permanent homes, as well. You can always get other servants."

Sirin waved off his objections. "Fear not, General. I want nothing but to dispense with my new charges as soon as possible. Now it's time for you two to depart. I have a tradesman from your old neighborhood, Vancien, coming to talk to me about smelling salts and fennel traps. The foolish man is quite taken with this Corfe upstart; it wouldn't do to have you two seen by him. Give Telenar my regards, take care on the road, watch out for strangers, and don't step in front of the big carriages."

The interview was over. Half a moment later, they were outside, the highly polished door shut behind them. Vancien stood in the fading light, a little stunned.

"We didn't even get to say good-bye to them."

Chiyo said nothing. He was staring thoughtfully at the building's second-story windows.

"Do you think we did the right thing?" Vancien persisted.

Chiyo shrugged then turned away. "They will be fed, clothed, and kept warm. Sirin has a softer heart than he lets on. They will do well. Right now, I'm more concerned about us. Sirin was right: it's time we should be leaving."

CHAPTER SIX

Verial ran as if Sentries were chasing her. Her legs burned, her chest felt like it might explode, and her vision started to swim, but still she ran. As the night turned into morning, the prairie grass rushed by, occasionally tripping her. But she picked herself up and ran harder, though she herself hardly knew why her flight was so urgent.

Part of her just wanted to run, to stretch her legs, to feel the rain soaking her skin and the wind tossing her hair. Long ago, before Obsidian's Advocates found her, she used to run for the sheer joy of it. She could outrun every boy in town, which was partly why she had felt so superior. Now, even those innocent memories hunted her down. It was her youthful arrogance, after all, that had encouraged her to view Grens as a challenge rather than a threat. All that was behind her now, of course. There were none of Zyreio's advocates left to torment her. But their ghosts, as well as her own crimes committed under their influence, were as tangible as the sharp morning air.

She ran in the direction of the capital city, stopping only to rest and take food and shelter when needed. Two long weeks would pass before she made it to Lascombe. The woman who entered through the city gates was barely recognizable from the one who fled Telenar's camp. Her clothes were torn, her feet were bruised and bleeding, her face was gaunt from cold and lack of food. But most unrecognizable was her countenance. Her old expression of resignation had been replaced by a look of ferocious independence. Feral abandon had taken the place of her usual restraint. No one would ever be her master again, *ever*. The woman who entered the city gates was determined not only to erase her past but to control her future.

Her first act of independence was to steal a knife. Some careless blacksmith had left it out on a window-sill, sharpened and ready for action. Her second, to steal food and warm clothes from an unsuspecting shop mistress who earned Verial's disapproval for humming cheerfully. Her third, to track down the one man whose existence was meaningful to her, so that she could see with her own feverish eyes that he had survived.

———————

Gair did not like staying indoors, especially in a great city like Lascombe. He would much rather wander the streets and take in all the sights that were so different than the Eastern Lands. Scarred though Lascombe had been by Relgaré's wars, it was still better than living in the shadow of Donech. The citizenry, however, was becoming almost as unfriendly as the Easterners. Relgaren's order to board the soldiers was putting the city under regrettable strain. He could see it in the resentful stares of the inhabitants and hear it in their whispered comments. Since Corfe had become Relgaren's most prominent advisor and Gair himself was Corfe's frequent companion, he received a hearty dose of hostility. After several hostile glances and one shameless attempt by a schoolboy to pin a dead moth to his prosthetic limb, he decided that he would get his fresh air from a palace turret instead of the city streets.

He was halfway up the spiral stairs on the east tower when a messenger hailed him from behind.

"My lord Gair! Here you are!"

"What is it?"

"I come from the king, sir, as well as the Advocate and the king's brother, Patronius Lors. They request your presence in the Council Room. We've been looking for you for some time."

Gair grunted. Was that council meeting tonight? Didn't they just have one a few nights ago? "All right. Tell the king that I'll be there as soon as I can." He started limping down the stairs as the messenger rushed off with his good news.

It was several minutes before he arrived at one of the most august chambers in the palace. The Council Room had been built by Ruponi the Great, grandson of Erst, the Prysm Advocate whose victory had ushered in the current (now ending) era of ten thousand score of mornings and evenings. Ruponi had been a skilled musician as well as king. During the restoration of the council chamber in his third year as king, he had ordered the room to be mapped out to precise mathematical proportions, in accordance with the musical theory of his day. The theory behind this arrangement is too complex for description. It involved a great deal of geometry, as well as visual techniques such as vanishing points and foreshortening, all of which were explained on a long, often ignored plaque in one of the room's eight corners.

The room itself, as its eight corners suggest, was octagonal with a peaked ceiling, each of its eight walls bearing a panel that depicted a symbol from ancient Keroulian pictography: a circle to symbolize the order and unity of peace, a narrow wedge breaking a crooked line to represent the sometimes necessary destruction of war, and so on. Underneath each pictograph was a detailed portrait of an individual—not a prince or priest, but a tradesman, market woman, or soldier. Although each of these portraits were based on actual individuals, they served to remind all the members of the council that behind their abstract theories were individuals who would suffer or gain from their decisions. Finally, in the center of the octagonal table was a large prism: a warning to all of the council members that Kynell himself presided at their meetings.

The men inside watched patiently as Gair entered. Relgaren did not, of course, rise to greet him, nor did his brother Lors. But Corfe jumped to his feet and pulled out a chair for his friend.

"Glad you could make it. We were wondering if you'd forgotten about us."

Gair bowed to the king and made a slight obeisance to the prism before taking his seat. "I'm sorry for my tardiness. I did not realize we had called another meeting for this evening." He directed his penitent gaze toward Relgaren, who was the most likely to be offended. The young king had taken over his duties with considerable ability. As a new promotee, however, he was zealous for the honor of his office. Even Corfe was careful to show him deference. It was Relgaren, after all, who commanded the Keroulian troops that Corfe needed so much.

Relgaren accepted the apology. With his thick red hair and broad forehead, he bore a striking resemblance to his father. Yet Relgaren was more thoughtful than his predecessor. He often diluted his desire for action with a healthy amount of caution, which was partially the reason Corfe had been given such prominence at court: Relgaren liked to keep wildcards close, and Corfe was the wildest card of the age. His younger brother was not always so prudent. At a mere fifteen cycles, Lors was a passionate young man. He had embraced Corfe whole-heartedly, promising and obtaining the support of the Patroniite Order. Now he insisted on being present at any meeting as a spiritual representative, however insignificant the meeting might be. Gair could appreciate the boy's enthusiasm, although he did not share it. At just twenty-five cycles, he felt old, a feeling encouraged by the awareness that he was the oldest person in the room.

Corfe seemed to read his thoughts. "We are young, Gair. But maybe Kynell has appointed youth to govern the country for a reason. The older generation, though well intentioned, was not without its faults."

Gair nodded. For having his voice so recently restored, Corfe was putting it to good use. "Is anybody else coming?"

Relgaren responded. His voice was low for such a young man, maintaining the perfect level of gravity for a king. "The other advisors have not been included today because of the sensitivity of the issue we need to discuss. As you know, we have sent Farlone to the Kingdom of Ulan to call upon their aid. You may remember that our sister Dorylen is married to Huran, heir-apparent to the Ulanese throne?"

Gair nodded again. The Ulanese were good allies. He knew them well, since their small kingdom was sandwiched between the regions of Keroul north of the Duvarian Range and the Eastern Lands. Only a narrow strip of the Trmak Desert separated the Ulanese from Amarian's realm. The Dark One had frequently encouraged his people to raid the Ulanese, but their neighbors had always put up a stalwart defense. Whatever trinkets the Easterners had been able to take away from the ventures were not worth the resources lost. Farlone, the king's brother and first general, would approve of his sister's militant new home.

"Has there been any response, my liege?"

"Not yet. In truth, his return has taken longer than anticipated. We," he gestured to the men in the room and perhaps to Keroul in general, "are beginning to get concerned. There have been strange reports coming out of the Eastern Lands."

The ominous statement did not surprise Gair much; the Eastern Lands and the great castle of Donech belonged to Obsidian's Advocate. Only the Plains of Jasimor, where Zyreio had buried his deceitful tongue, could produce more evil than the realm of the Dark One. "What do the reports say?"

It was Lors's turn to answer. "That an army is gathering there."

"Of course there's an army. Amarian left behind some reserves when he came as Commander Hull."

But Lors was shaking his head. "These aren't reserves. We've heard reports of Sentries, fennels, and humans too numerous to count. They're very agitated. Our scouts say that they're preparing for war."

"But where would such a host come from?"

Finally, Corfe spoke, staring at the prism as he did so. "From the Chasm. They're Zyreio's own dead come to fight for Amarian."

Gair tried not to laugh out loud. It was all very well to believe that Corfe was destined to fight Amarian, but armies of the undead? He knew that the Ages spoke of such a thing but had never given the possibility much thought.

If the king and the others noticed his amusement, they did not show it. They waited for him to respond and when it became obvious that he had nothing to say, the king leaned forward intently.

"We must find out what happened to my brother. He was due back many days ago. We believe that the Ulanese may be in trouble and that Farlone stayed to help them."

"If that were the case, we should have received messengers telling us so."

Relgaren leaned back into his chair. "That's precisely our problem. We've heard nothing."

Throughout the conversation, Corfe had been shifting in his seat. Now the look he gave Gair was troubled. "We need somebody to find out what has happened, preferably a soldier who is familiar with the Eastern lands."

Now it was Gair's turn to stare at the prism. He had already been called upon to sacrifice so much for Kynell. Surely the Prysm god would not send him back to the place of his torment? His skin began to prickle at the thought. "We have many of Amarian's former men here. I'm sure any of them would be willing to return."

"Which is why none of them can be trusted." Corfe's response was not without compassion. He was well aware of the horrible thing he was asking of his friend. "You know you are the best man for this task."

Gair resisted the temptation to shake his head in protest. He was a soldier, after all, and soldiers were trained to follow orders. Still, it took several seconds before he could respond. "Who will be riding with me?"

Relgaren took over. "It will have to be a small group—small enough to infiltrate the Ulanese capitol if it's under siege or, Kynell forbid, completely run over. We have five of the fastest voyoté available ready for you."

"When do I leave?"

"Tomorrow at dawn, if you can gather your men quickly enough."

Tight-lipped, pale, and anxious, Gair forced himself to stand.

"Permission to make preparations, your majesty?"

Relgaren stood, as well. Although he knew it had to be done, he did not relish sending Gair back to face the Easterners, or whatever they had become. "Our prayers go with you, Gair. Find my brother. And take care of yourself."

"I will, sire."

He had barely left the room when Corfe caught up with him. The two walked in silence together until they reached the same turret Gair had been heading for earlier that evening. When they reached the open parapet, Corfe spoke first.

"It was my idea."

The statement startled Gair but he tried not to let it show. "Perhaps you could have mentioned it to me before the meeting?"

Corfe shrugged as the lunos-light glinted off of his bald head. "I would have liked to. But the scout reports about the Easterners came in only this morning and by the time I realized what had to be done, I couldn't find you." He waited for a response and when he received none, he added. "I wish I could go with you."

The comment was well intended but insincere, as Gair knew. "It would serve no purpose for you to go. You cannot face the Easterners or Amarian until our army is complete." He paused as another thought occurred to him. "What about our own forces? If Zyerio's followers have indeed risen up to fight for him, what about Kynell's own faithful?"

He could tell by Corfe's dark expression that he had considered this, too. "I wish I had a good answer for that. Kynell is apparently only allowing me to gather worldly forces, for now, at least. Perhaps soon I will be able to summon our dead brethren."

Gair nodded. There was no need to press the issue further. "All in good time, I suppose." He looked sourly at the rising lunos, rubbing his hands against the cold. "I have to get some men together."

"Can I make a suggestion?"

"Of course."

"Take a munkke-trophe with you. They fight like the Chasm's own and can speak more languages than you or I even know of. I'm guessing you don't speak Ulanese."

"But is it possible to get one on a voyoté?"

Corfe smiled for the first time that day. "Take one from the king's guard. Then it won't have a choice."

44

Verial went straight to the palace grounds. The reports they had received in Telenar's camp had indicated that Gair was much in the pretender's company and therefore frequently at the palace. Fortunately, today was a market day and the throngs made it easier to slip past the guards at the gate and get close without being seen. She picked a spot next to a fish vendor that was dark and out of the way. To her surprise, she saw him almost as soon as she sat down. He had aged a great deal since she had last been with him. All the youthful bravado was gone. Instead, he walked with a pronounced limp. His dark brown hair had grown long and was marked by shocks of gray. Worse, disfiguring scars covered his face and hands. How much he had suffered for his religious devotion! Before she could study him further, he disappeared into the palace where she dared not follow him.

The day passed slowly as she endured the stench of the vendor's stall, watching the good people of Lascombe pick out their penacle, thrup, and gavins. The capital city was much too far from the sea to enjoy saltwater luxuries, but the citizens did well for themselves from nearby lakes and streams. Since Verial herself had never cared for fish, she spent most of the day berating herself for selecting such an offensive place to hide.

Finally, when her back was stiff from waiting and her stomach growling for satisfaction, the vendor packed up his goods for the evening and left her to breathe freely. The orbs were setting, making the hiverran air even more biting, yet she dared not move from her position. It was possible that Gair would exit on the same path he had entered. And so it proved. Not long after all the stalls had been put away for the evening, she saw him hurry out of the palace, crossing the market grounds with great, awkward strides. If possible, he looked even more grieved than before. He was soon in front of a building at the far end of the grounds, which Verial discovered to be the royal barracks. She watched him go inside, waiting just a few moments before she slipped over to one of the windows, creeping as close as possible to peer in.

He was talking to a munkke-trophe, of all things, and it did not look like the conversation was going well. The creature was gesticulating wildly, pointing first to the soldiers gathered round, then to Gair, and then toward the ceiling. Gair just stood there, resolute, repeating what looked like the same words over and over again, though Verial could not hear them. When it appeared that the munkke-trophe had accepted defeat, he turned to three other men and spoke briefly. They all nodded and soon Gair was back outside, this time heading stiffly toward the stables.

Now was her chance. The courtyard was calm and quiet; she should not have to work hard to draw his attention. Keeping as close as she could to the shadows, she called out his name in a hoarse whisper. He stopped, looked around, but continued onward. She called his name again, a little louder. This time he peered in the direction of her hiding place.

"Whoever you are," he called, "I suggest you show yourself. Creeping around the palace will only get you put in a prison cell."

Verial bit her lip to keep from shivering. Too late, she began to wonder how he might receive her.

He was getting impatient. "In the name of the king, show yourself!"

The courtyard was well lit that night; no clouds dimmed the glow of triple lunos as she stepped into the light. "It's Verial, Gair. Do you remember me?"

At first he showed no reaction, except to widen his eyes and loosen his grip on his dagger. Then he drew in a sharp breath and stumbled to one knee. "Lady Verial!"

Encouraged by the emotion in his voice, she hastened to his side, dropping to her knees as well. "You remember me? Truly?"

He stared at her, trying to convince himself of what he saw. Verial. The last time he had seen her, she had been on her way to lay a snare for that Vancien fellow. But now Vancien was dead and Amarian in hiding. What was she doing here? Now?

"How could I forget you? But what are you doing here? Are you alone? Did you make it to Vancien's camp?"

She saw that it pained him to ask that last question. To herself, she had to acknowledge that his fears were well founded. Amarian had originally sent her to seduce the Prysm Advocate; who was to say she had not succeeded?

"I did. But I'm all right and yes, I am alone. I escaped Amarian." She hesitated, trying to find the right words. "And Vancien is no longer important. I came to find you."

She had never seen anyone so overwhelmed. It was embarrassing.

"Perhaps we should get up off the ground."

He nodded, still speechless, but he had difficulty getting back to his feet. Only when he lurched upwards did she notice that one of his legs below the knee was nothing more than a wooden shell. Now it was her turn to gasp. "What did that monster do to you?"

He was holding her hand, which he now grasped even tighter. "It doesn't matter. It's over now."

The pain shooting up her fingers told her otherwise.

"Besides," he continued, brightening. His soft voice was a balm to her. "We have a strong champion now, you and I. You must have heard that Corfe has turned to Kynell. He's the Prysm Advocate. Soon Amarian and Vancien will be just a bitter memory."

She smiled weakly, not sure what to say. Should she tell him of Amarian's conversion? She owed the Dark One nothing. Nor did she have an obligation to Vancien. And although she despised Corfe, she could not bear to see Gair's spirit crushed by her revelation. She decided to hold her peace.

Gair noticed her hesitation, but he interpreted it incorrectly. Against all appearances, did she still harbor feelings for Amarian? He could not believe it to be true, but why else would she flinch at his downfall? He looked at her. She was still as beautiful as ever—more beautiful, perhaps, since she seemed more human. Her fair hair was tangled from much traveling, her blue eyes were reddened from lack of sleep, and even her clothes were ill-fitted and dirty. Although she still carried herself like royalty, there was a fierce look about her that he had never seen before.

But she was starting to shiver, so he led her to a quiet corner in the stables.

"Verial." He ran a hand across his forehead. "You have no idea how happy I am to see you. I was so terrified for you. But I've been assigned an errand for the king and I have to leave tomorrow."

"Then I'll come with you."

He was already shaking his head. "No, I can't take you back there with me. He's sending me to the Eastern Lands."

The name was a douse of ice water. Surely she had misheard him. "But why go back there? You've only just escaped."

"I don't have a choice. The king has ordered me to go."

"Then disobey the king. Run away with me." She flushed even as she said it. Now that the offer was made, however, she had no wish to take it back.

"I can't. I have to do Kynell's will. I have to return to that place—even if I hate it."

She could not believe her ears. She had just found him and now he was leaving her? It was hard to tell if she was more hurt or insulted. "What does Kynell have to do with it? It was following Kynell that got you into this mess in the first place." She pointed accusingly at his leg. "Don't be a slave to the gods."

He clenched his jaw in response then let go of her hand. "I am not a slave to the gods. Only to Kynell. And if he desires me to descend into the Chasm itself, I will."

Now she stepped back, shaking with anger. He was no better than the others, all of them pandering to gods who used them like playthings. If he thought Kynell commanded it, he would probably use her, as well. "You may be willing to run back to the Chasm, but I am not. I have been a tool of those brutes long enough."

"Verial, wait." He tried to take her hand again, but she had lost interest.

"I have to go," she declared. Before he could stop her, she slipped back outside.

CHAPTER SEVEN

Amarian returned just as the rains were lifting. Some of Chiyo's men were on duty to guard the camp that day. They eyed him with suspicion at the best of times. Now, as he approached with a small fennel bounding at his side, they had no idea what to make of him. Not knowing what else to do, they gripped their spears harder, in case the kit turned out to be a spawn of Zyerio.

Bedge thought they were funny. "Look, sir! Look at the strange men over there! Bedge thinks they don't like you."

He stopped while they were still several paces off. "Do you remember what I said? When we get close to camp, no jumping around. And don't speak to anybody unless I tell you to."

"Yes, sir. Bedge says not a word. Not a sound from her. Not a—"

"Enough. Here we are."

The guards let them pass without challenge, but they had not taken two steps past the low timber fortifications before N'vonne noticed them. She looked almost happy to see him.

"Amarian! You've returned safely. Telenar will be so interested to hear what you've learned. But who are you, little one?"

"My name is Bedge. Bedge came along with Sir after he argued with Bedge's pridehead."

Seeing the sharp jerk of Amarian's hand, she flattened her ears and looked apologetically at the ground. "Bedge is quiet now," she whispered.

Amarian did not give her a chance to start up again. "I need to speak with Vancien. Where is he?"

N'vonne shook her head, shifting the basket of herbs she'd been gathering. "He's not back yet. Will you speak with Telenar?"

Amarian looked thoughtfully down at Bedge, who returned his gaze. He and Telenar had spoken very few words since his return in late autore; he knew the priest struggled with trusting him. He would much rather have spoken with Vancien first. But if his brother had not returned then there was no choice. His news could not wait.

"Of course. Where can I find him?"

"He's just come back from hunting. The Cylini were teaching him how to shoot a bow. He should be in the mess hall by now. I'll walk over with you." She looked ruefully at the herbs. "Hopefully the cook will be able to get some use out of these."

He doubted it. N'vonne had gathered hartroot, which was used to cure digestive problems. Its similar appearance to rosemary had fooled many a person before, but its disguise lasted only until it was boiled. Then the acrid smell could choke a voyoté. But the cooks would figure that out soon enough.

The three walked in silence until she spoke again.

"Have you seen Verial?"

"She's missing?"

"Since the night you left. We thought that she might have followed you."

Anger flared up in him. Would these people ever accept that he had changed? "Well, it wouldn't have been to make up with me."

N'vonne grew even more flustered. Telenar's decision to not send a search party for Verial still irritated her. "We didn't figure she was much of a threat; she did not take any weapons and you are a trained fighter."

"But a woman's vengeance is a fearful thing. So you thought we two villains would battle it out ourselves? Not a big loss either way, was it?"

She flushed in embarrassment and he knew he was being unfair. He also knew the decision to not search for Verial was Telenar's, not N'vonne's. And N'vonne was not the type to undermine her husband in front of others. "No, I saw no sign of her. Perhaps she went to find her beloved Gair."

"That was our other thought."

They found Telenar finishing up a bowl of yemain stew and discussing hunting tactics with one of his tutors. His Cylini had improved greatly since the start of their adventures. When he saw Amarian he immediately excused himself.

"Amarian, you've made it back. How was your journey? Are you hungry?" When Amarian nodded, he asked the Cylini warrior to fetch another bowl of stew. Only then did he notice Bedge, who was standing excitedly by Amarian's leg, trying not to chase down every scent that wafted from the tables.

"What is this? A fennel kit?"

Amarian sighed and gestured for her to hop up on the bench. "Her name is Bedge. It's a long story."

While N'vonne tried to rustle up some food appropriate for a fennel, Telenar returned to his seat. "So?"

Amarian watched the priest for any sign of suspicion or of softening. He saw neither. Apparently bringing Vancien back from the dead and returning from his first solo undertaking was not enough to garner credit with the man. No matter. Telenar could spend his whole life not trusting him for all he cared.

"It was unsuccessful. Koeb will not help us. But neither will he help Corfe."

Telenar nodded then gestured toward Bedge, who had been silent for an amazingly long time. "Then why her?"

"She insisted on returning with me. Her parents are dead and it turns out that she's a bit of an explorer."

"Does she speak?"

It was too much. "Oh yes, Bedge speaks! Bedge loves to speak Keroulian." She lengthened out the "oo" sound until it became almost a purr. "Bedge is happy to meet a holy one of the light-god."

Telenar nodded graciously and even smiled. "I am far from holy, but I am happy to meet you too, little one. How did you know I was a priest?"

She sniffed. "Holy ones smell the same. Like books."

Impressed, Telenar opened his mouth to respond, when she added, "And Sir told Bedge."

"I see. Amarian says you like to explore?"

"Yes, yes. Bedge likes to wander many places, back and forth."

Amarian accepted a bowl of stew as N'vonne returned with a meaty bone for Bedge. "Tell the holy one what you saw in the windy place."

It took longer than the original telling but eventually, in-between bites, Bedge related what she had seen in the Eastern Lands. When she had finished, Telenar and N'vonne sat in stunned silence.

"Bedge needs to run. Can she go?"

Amarian nodded, not taking his eyes off of the others. "You may go.

Just stay away from the hunters."

She left and Amarian returned his gaze to the other two. "Well?"

N'vonne spoke first. "I don't understand it. How can there be a howling army of Zyerio's dead servants without an Advocate to lead them?"

Telenar nodded agreement. The same question had occurred to him.

Amarian, on the other hand, allowed himself a moment of grim satisfaction. His new friends had no concept of Obsidian's determination. "He doesn't need an Advocate. He never has. I suspect that he feels victory has been snatched out of his teeth and he wants it back." Even as he said the words, he had to fight down a shiver.

"Do the Ages say anything about this?" N'vonne asked Telenar.

"No. When Amarian defeated Vancien and then brought him back from the dead, the pattern Kynell had set was broken. We've moved beyond the prophecies." He looked at Amarian. "So what do we do now?"

"Take cover. It's all we can do."

His words were lost to a loud screech, followed by the shouts of men. All three of them jumped to their feet and ran outside with the other diners. Vancien and Chiyo had returned.

The orbs were beginning to set, casting a dramatic light for the arrival of the great Ealatrophe, who was as intimidating as ever. His fierce gaze cut through the throng of men as his dark wings, spread wide for landing, cast a chilly shadow. Satisfied that all was as it should be, he landed and allowed his charges to dismount. Poor Chiyo was shivering in starts and fits; the padded saddle and multiple layers of clothing were about as effective as medical gauze in the face of the Ealatrophe's cold. Only Vancien could stand the Destrariae *klathonus*. Everybody else who approached had to suffer heart-stopping chills.

Bren, the Ealatrophe's self-appointed handler, hurried forward and checked it for signs of fatigue or injury. He had made himself a "cold suit," which allowed him to come closer than most, although he looked and moved like an overstuffed scarecrow. Crooning softly, he led the Ealatrophe away from the crowd.

Vancien watched them go. "Thelámos likes him."

But Telenar had grabbed him by the arm. "Yes, Bren is a good boy. Now come with me. We need to talk."

They followed him, N'vonne, and Amarian into Telenar's hut without comment. Telenar was not known for his social skills, but they could tell that he was agitated beyond his usual brusqueness. Even so, they made him wait for a few seconds while Chiyo demanded a bowl of warm soup and Vancien insisted that he stretch his legs. A three-day journey on an Ealatrophe was no casual matter. Finally, both men settled in enough to ask what was bothering the priest so much.

After looking hesitantly at Amarian for a go-ahead, Telenar began. "As you might guess, Amarian has been to visit the fennels in the southern woodlands in order to feel them out as allies."

Chiyo nodded. "We knew that was in the works before we left."

"Well, I didn't meet with any success," Amarian took over. "But one of the fennels—a kit—sought me out privately. She told me that she likes to go out exploring, often far afield from her new home." He fixed his dark eyes on his brother, and though they held no trace of cheer, the shadows around them were disappearing. Despite his complaints, life at camp had been good for his constitution. "Vancien, the armies of Zyreio's dead have risen. They're preparing for battle."

Vancien almost laughed out loud at such an absurdity, then he looked again at his brother, then Telenar and N'vonne. The looks on their faces told him that they were serious enough. But what they were telling him was impossible. Kynell had won the battle, albeit by unorthodox means. Zyreio was to be stilled for the next ten thousand scores of mornings and evenings. The only "enemy" they had now was that duped Corfe.

While he was still processing the news, Chiyo spoke. "How did you say you found out about this? A fennel kit?"

Amarian nodded. "As unlikely as it seems, yes."

"Why would you trust a fennel informant, even a young one?"

"Hang on." Amarian jumped to his feet and went to the door. Opening it a crack, he looked outside. Soldiers were wandering here and there, going about their chores. Some wives who had chosen to join their husbands at camp were doing laundry in the distance, outside of the ring of rude buildings. The voyoté were stabled in a large pen to his right. One of them was fixing an intent gaze on an adjacent woodpile, giving him the clue he was looking for.

"You can come out, Bedge. Come over here."

Two eyes peered out from the shadow of the logs. Then a streak of brown and tan raced toward his feet.

"Bedge did not run for long. Bedge saw great big wings and was scared. Bedge followed Sir."

"It's all right. I want you to come in. There are some people who would like to meet you."

He opened the door wider and allowed her inside. Bedge instinctively went to sit by N'vonne, who began to pet her.

Chiyo looked displeased. "What in Rhyvelad persuaded you to bring back a kit?"

Amarian shrugged. In his mind, the only person whose opinion mattered was Vancien's. "She insisted on coming. Her parents are dead."

Chiyo grunted but said nothing.

Vancien was fascinated, never having spoken with a fennel before. "Do you speak Keroulian?"

Bedge had started purring under N'vonne's ministrations. "Bedge knows Keroulian." Again, the long "oo."

Vancien nodded. She must have been born in the Eastern Lands, where Keroulian had been spoken ever since Varrin, himself a Keroulian, had taken up residence there. He realized with a start that he did not know the nationalities of the other Advocates. Were they all from Keroul? Surely not. He had a dim memory of Tryun and Grens being from the West.

The fennel kit stretched, bringing his attention back to the present.

"What's your name?"

"Her name is Bedge." Amarian interceded before the fennel could answer. Well-meaning as she was, her introduction of herself went on too long. "She followed me because she heard I served Kynell, or 'the light-god,' as she calls him." He turned to her. "Tell them again what you saw in the windy place."

Although originally terrified of recounting her expedition into the Eastern Lands, Bedge had begun to warm to the tale. Amarian noticed that the fennels had turned more eerie, the humans had become extremely violent and vicious, and the eyes of the Sentries were now red. Still, the meat of the account was the same.

Vancien had started pacing as she spoke. When she finished, he did not bother restraining his frustration. "How is this possible? Kynell won! He *won*. Zyreio can't do anything."

He was cut off by his brother. "Zyreio can, Vancien. And if he can, he will. Think of it from his point of view. He was betrayed and now he wants vengeance. In his mind, the next ten thousand scores are his."

N'vonne resumed stroking Bedge in the hopes that the fur would hide her shaking hand. "Forgetting that it shouldn't happen, if we assume that it did happen, what do we do now?"

Amarian's response was much the same and this time he had Chiyo to agree with him. "After all," the general observed, "we don't even know how to fight this type of enemy."

"But we can't just sit here and do nothing." Vancien objected.

"So what do you suggest we do? Fight Zyreio with a handful of Cylini?" Amarian certainly believed his own protest, but he would have been lying if he said he had no ulterior motive: the thought of going back to the Eastern Lands made him almost sick.

Vancien turned moody, so Telenar took over. "To respond to Chiyo's point, there is no recorded means whereby living soldiers can defeat Zyerio's, er. . ." He stopped, wondering how to describe them. ". . .shall we say 'reanimated' army. This type of conflict has only happened once before. The battle between the first Advocates, Tryun and Grens, is the only struggle that lasted long enough for both forces to form and be deployed. Varrin and Heptar, Nejona and Erst. One brother was dead before either could raise his own followers."

Bedge yawned. N'vonne shushed her but Telenar took the hint. "There must be something we can do," he concluded lamely. "There are still Kynell's own faithful to consider."

All heads turned to Vancien, who looked as helpless as they felt. "I haven't tried because I didn't see a need. Surely Kynell will hear me now, though."

Telenar nodded, happy to seize the hope. "Kynell responds in his own time. The point is, we no longer have any reason to stay here. We must head toward the Eastern Lands. Perhaps we can confront this army before it does any damage. "

Later that evening, Vancien caught up with his brother as he was walking outside the camp. Bedge was hunting a little distance from them.

"Do the fennels know she's gone?"

Amarian nodded then cursed as a gust of wind blew chaff into his eyes. He dug at his face with the corner of his coarse sleeve. "The Chasm take these plains!" Then he looked at his stained and dirty clothes; the exquisite wardrobe he had brought from the east so long ago was stored away. "We live little better than beggars here."

Though itching in his own clothes, Vancien had to disagree. "Not better than the beggars I saw in Lascombe. It's wretched to be poor in the city, surrounded by people who don't know how to help or else don't want to. 'Ian," He put a hand on Amarian's shoulder. "Did you know that they've started a slave market there?"

"A slave market?" Amarian had, of course, possessed slaves of his own in the Eastern Lands—mostly unwanted children or people kidnapped from the Ulanese. He still cringed when he thought of their misery. How did Kynell ever manage to forgive him for the things he had done? "I thought those abominations were outlawed in Keroul."

Vancien shook his head, grieved by what his country was becoming. "It started this past breach. Apparently things are bad enough that people are selling their families. Now they've started selling Cylini captives."

"I wonder how our friend Corfe justifies these new developments."

Vancien had been wondering the same thing, too. A Prysm Advocate had never sanctioned slavery before; it was understood as a sign of man's distance from Kynell. "I think he means well, in that he thinks he wants what Kynell wants. But so many things can get distorted when you think you're an Advocate."

Amarian grunted. Nobody knew that truth as well as he did. "When do we leave for Donech?"

"Do you think they're still there?"

"It'll be even worse for Rhyvelad if they're not. Better that they stay close to home."

At that moment, Bedge came bounding up, to the considerable relief of both men. It was hard to dwell on the negative with someone like her around. After dropping the gift of a dead bird at Amarian's feet, she sat down.

"Nice hunting, Bedge." Vancien commented, watching his brother's reaction with amusement. Amarian was torn between retaining his gloomy dignity and acknowledging the gift with the warmth it deserved.

"Thank you, Bedge," he prevaricated. "But you know that this is not enough to feed a man."

The little fennel purred loudly. "Bedge knows. But Bedge's other kill is too big to bring to Sir."

Amarian and Vancien exchanged looks. Other kill? What exactly were fennel kits capable of? Curious, they followed her a little further into the meadow and were astonished to find a dead bohide—a large, slow bison-type that had killer instincts when cornered. Bedge gripped its tail in her teeth. "Bedge cannot carry slow-cow on her own."

The entire camp ate well that night, with enough meat left over to salt and carry with them on the journey. The cooking team both grumbled and rejoiced at the provision, while Bedge instantly became the soldiers' mascot. They took turns talking with her, petting her, and offering her choice tidbits.

56

Amarian thought that such displays were unnecessary but the kit glowed under the attention. As he watched her preen, he had to remind himself that she had lost her mother at a very young age. A little extra attention surely would not hurt her. Even so, he was gratified that she still came when beckoned. He was jealous, though he would never admit it.

It took a few days, and some convincing, to get the small force ready to leave. The question that plagued them was whether it was better to inform the troops of their unsavory mission, thereby risking mass defection, or to keep their undertaking secret. Telenar, at Vancien and N'vonne's urging, decided that it would only be right to tell the Cylini what they were in for. Chiyo could do with his own men what he chose, although once the word was out it would be impossible to contain.

The reaction among the Cylini was dispiriting. Telenar told them the news in their own language. As he did so, they began to murmur, then fidget, looking anxiously back over their shoulders to the trees. Many of the warriors had wives and children in those marshes and were unwilling to travel far from home to combat a mythical undead army. In the end, a handful remained: predictably, they the ones with no dependent loved ones. Chiyo's men had a little more time to decide. Their route would take them through the marshes then south of the Duvarian Range, before crossing the Trmak desert and drawing near to the Eastern Lands. In a little over a week, they would be directly south of Lascombe. Those soldiers who wished to return to the city could do so at that point.

CHAPTER EIGHT

The mood was sober as Vancien and his companions broke camp one wet morning, packed away what was transportable, and made their start. By afternoon of that day, they were back in the marshes, moving swiftly in Cylini boats. The air was still as the boats glided through the murky waters. A few creatures in the trees made their calls, but the large number of vessels forestalled any more ominous interruptions. Rather than reassure them, however, the placid environment only added to the tension. It was as if the marshes were taking satisfaction in leaving the humans to their morbid imaginings.

Chiyo had his share of dark thoughts, though his concerned the past, not the future. He clenched his jaw as he remembered the last time he had entered this territory. His best lieutenant, Hunoi, had been killed during a Cylini ambush, felled by the first arrow of the assault. He had not even had a chance to bury him properly. Now they were gliding over the same waters that covered his friend's body, aided by the same people who had taken his life. What a funny, horrible place the world was.

Telenar watched Chiyo with concern. The general's commitment to Kynell was absolute, but sometimes Telenar wondered what he thought of their unusual circumstances. Chiyo had, after all, come from the West to serve Relgaré and the House of Anisllyr. Now the king was dead and Chiyo had broken ties with the throne—what was worse, he was leading a small force that could potentially become hostile to the House of Anisllyr, should Relgaren make as many unwise choices as his father had. Telenar was not a soldier, but he understood the importance of loyalty, and in some ways Chiyo was showing more loyalty to the throne by opposing it. He could always have returned home to the West and let the Keroulians deal with their own problems (however short-lived an illusion that would be, since Zyreio was everybody's problem). Yet here he was, in a Cylini boat, ready to lead a tiny group of men and women against a massive and unpredictable enemy. Telenar shook his head. The general may not be a scholar of the Ages, but he was committed to the right things.

The observation brought Telenar some comfort, but not much. There still remained the problem of how they could possibly confront Zyreio's army. He had spent the past few days studying not only the Ages, but the few books of history he had brought with him. As always, the Ages had proven more useful: those histories written under Relgaré's reign were worthless for his purposes. According to them, the Advocates existed only as figurative representatives of moral epochs, whatever that meant. But the Ages were refreshing in their bluntness. The struggle between Tryun and Grens had been bloody and drawn-out: Grens' reanimated Obsidian forces collided with those of Tryun in the Battle of the Knuckle, which turned out to be a complete disaster for the Prysm. The theater of war at that time was the Trmak Desert, which had once been lush rolling hills and the most sought-after land in Rhyvelad. Grens had held the high ground, a ridge running north to south called the Knuckle, so named because of its uneven, undulating surface. Although Tryun's army was large, it struggled to capture the ridge. At first, the Prysm Advocate had forbidden his living soldiers to participate in the fight because of the danger from Grens' reanimated forces. Only when his own reanimated soldiers had been cut down by Obsidian did he command his living men to flank the Knuckle on the north and the south. They did, and although they caught the reanimated troops by surprise, they discovered that living men could not prevail against dead ones. Tryun ordered a withdrawal, but during the course of the retreat, a flaming arrow pierced him in the eye. He was killed instantly and with him, the Prysm's chances of overcoming Obsidian. It was said (not by the Ages), that the despair of good men and women was so great that it turned the rolling hills of Trmak into barren desert. Telenar thought it was a fitting legend, but subscribed to the belief that a dramatic climate change occurring about a hundred cycles after the battle accounted for the Trmak's fate. He had the history books to thank for that.

So there it was. He looked around at the others, admiring their resolution. Yet without Kynell's armies, their case was hopeless. Vancien had told him that he had tried to summon the faithful every day since they had first received the news, but with no success. On the other hand, Corfe had thousands of men at his disposal. Men, Telenar considered grimly, who would soon be slaughtered if Corfe persisted in his delusion. How desperately Corfe needed to be convinced of his mistake, but mere words would never persuade Corfe he wasn't the Advocate. Still, if he could be reminded of Tryun's failure, maybe he could set up defenses around Lascombe to fend off Zyreio's forces, at least long enough to realize his mistake. Perhaps by then, Kynell would have answered Vancien's prayers.

Yet even if they joined Corfe at Lascombe, he would never trust Amarian. For the moment, Amarian only complicated things. If he could lie low for a time then perhaps he, Telenar, could attempt to dissuade Corfe of his delusion while Chiyo oversaw the city's defenses. As for Vancien, it wouldn't hurt to have him lie low, as well.

A splash interrupted his reflections. One of the younger voyoté had grown anxious in the confined space of the boat and had jumped into the water. Now its handlers were having a great deal of trouble getting him back into the boat. No harm was done, though there was a great deal of angry shouting. He sighed. Cetla, Lansing, and Nagab—their own faithful voyoté who had carried them so far last cycle—had long ago been sent back to Lascombe. The royal head groom had been nervous about letting them go in the first place; the least Telenar could do was to return them, unharmed, when he had thought their journey was at an end. Truth be told, he missed their strength and agility. The Cylini kept a healthy stable on the border of their territory, but the plains voyoté tended to be scrawnier and less reliable than their royal counterparts. If he had to go into battle against Zyreio, he would at least prefer to have Lansing under him.

His anxious thoughts then returned to Vancien and Amarian. It seemed more necessary than ever to have them out of the way, if only for a time. He looked nervously at N'vonne, wondering what she would think of his strategy and promising himself that he would tell her and the others before they reached the road to Lascombe. Until then there was no point in disturbing them.

———————

Ester and Trint had the easiest time adapting to Sirin's strange habits. So grateful were they to have three square meals a day, with snacks in-between, that they submitted to the routine of the house with no complaint. Teehma and Lucio struggled the worst. Living with a munkke-trophe did not suit their independent natures. While Ester, with her gentle spirit, quietly learned to mix his joint poultice and Trint fetched his brocade slippers whenever Sirin asked, the other two spent their time recalling the "freedom" they had enjoyed under Gorvy. The city and life in general, it seemed, was passing them by as they batted carpets, cooked their own meals, and polished those beautiful front doors.

More than two weeks had passed when Lucio, as usual, was thrashing one of Sirin's rugs, the one with the macaw bird and the gigantic purple snail.

"By the Chasm, that old monkey sheds more than three voyoté combined!"

Teehma, who was holding the great rug for him, looked nervously at the door. The "dupes," as they called the two other servants, were away with Sirin on an errand, but she still feared their ingratitude would be reported. "He's a munkke-trophe, Lucio, not a monkey. And aren't you happy to have a hot meal and a soft bed?"

"You mean a lumpy bed and the same meal every other day? We work like slaves." He gave the rug another thwack and watched the dust particles fly off the snail and into the cold air. "We *are* slaves."

They switched positions. Now it was Teehma's turn to beat the snail. "No, we're not. Sirin didn't buy us. He's looking for a home for us."

Lucio snorted. "If this is what a home is like, I think I'd rather be on my own."

Teehma agreed. She had been only seven cycles when her parents, weak from hard living, had both succumbed to illness a few months apart. All she remembered of the life up to that time was her mother's exhaustion and her father's dangerous flashes of anger. Sirin's house was a great improvement on that life, and on the wretchedness of working for Gorvy, but she was still a drudge: fetching for others, cleaning up after others, and cooking for others, with little benefit to herself. Who was to say that this new "home" she was supposed to find would be any different?

"Besides," Lucio continued, "who would want us? Someone might take Trint. And they would have to take Ester, too, if they took him. But we're too old. We're not cute like Trint," he rolled up the rug and threw it in the corner, "and we're sure not as nice as Ester."

Again, Teehma had to agree. But she wasn't about to let Lucio have the joy of being right. "We're old enough to be apprenticed. We could learn a trade, like the dupes are doing."

"And go on doing more drudgery." He leaned over the balcony and squinted at the distant peaks of the Duvarian Range. "What would it be like to get out on our own? To get up when we wanted? Eat when we wanted? Sleep when we wanted?"

Teehma followed his gaze. "If you're thinking of escaping to the Range, you're a silly *narfat*. The mountains would kill you and if they didn't, some wild fennel would."

"Shows how much you know. Fennels don't live in the Range. They like the woodlands."

"Oh yeah? How do you know?"

He shrugged and scratched his head. His now-clean blond hair had been neatly trimmed for the first time in his life and he was still getting used to it. "One of the old monkey's lessons. He says if I ever learn to read, I can find those things out for myself. I guess 'till then I have to listen to him go on about them."

Teehma gave an unlady-like grunt and followed him into the house. Sirin was teaching them both how to read, but only Lucio was getting the geography lessons. The munkke-trophe, who believed that all girls should know how to keep house properly, had put her under the charge of the female dupe, Lidia. Every morning, she was forced to learn the domestic arts, while Lucio learned about more exciting things like military history and where fennels lived. Lidia was a gentle and effective teacher, but her efforts were wasted on a girl like Teehma, who equated being female with being cooped up inside or being sold as the worst sort of slave. Though she would never admit it to him, she was jealous of the privileges Lucio enjoyed just for being a boy.

Crossing by the top of the spiraling staircase, the two were surprised to hear Sirin's voice below. He was not due back for several hours yet, but nevertheless they heard his sonorous tones in conversation with another, lighter voice.

"You've come for the boy, no doubt," they heard the munkke-trophe say. Lucio and Teehma looked at each other in alarm.

"If the boy needs a home," said the other voice, "my wife and I would be happy to give it to him. Ever since we lost our own Nes."

Sirin interrupted. "You know the child is very dependent on the blind girl. He'll barely talk with anybody clse."

Teehma stifled a guffaw. What four-cycle old wouldn't be scared stiff around Sirin? Trint talked to her and Lucio plenty.

The other voice continued, sounding very earnest. "We understand that he's very attached to the girl. If you don't think the boy will be happy without her, we would be willing to take her in, as well. You say that she's very useful around the house."

"I'd say she's more helpful than the others combined. The two older ones mope as if they've been whipped."

"If we could return to the boy."

"The boy is yours, but you had better take the girl, too. I'll come around tomorrow to your house to make sure everything is in order. Then if all is as I see fit, you'll have yourself two new bratlings."

Teehma and Lucio did not bother with the rest of the conversation. They had to talk to Trint and Ester before Sirin did. Trying to ignore the feeling like they'd been punched in the stomach, they hurried to the kitchen. Ester was there, washing some vegetables, while Trint was sitting at the butcher-block table, kicking his feet and fingering the necklace the man Vancien had given him. When they came in, he jumped to his feet.

"Ester says I have to eat all those veg'tables tonight!" he announced. "She says Sirin won't be happy if I don't eat them all. But I don't *ever* see Sirin eat veg'tables."

"Hush," Lucio ordered, steering Ester away from the washbasin and toward the table. "You both just sit down and be quiet. We have some news." Then he looked at Teehma, uncertain how to begin.

"Sirin's found you a home." Teehma blurted out. Better to have it done and over with.

Trint gave a loud whoop and started running around the table. But Ester did not move. "For whom has he found a home?" she said, so quietly that Teehma barely heard her.

Teehma was not given to discernment or compassion, but one would have to be a stone not to sympathize with the girl. She was relieved that her answer was a good one. "He found the same home for both of you. You and Trint will live together."

The sigh that Ester released sounded as if she'd been holding in it for cycles. She reached for Teehma's hand, and when she found it, Teehma could feel her shaking. "That is good news. I don't know what I would have done without him. But what about you? And Lucio? Will you come, too?"

Teehma fought back tears while Lucio forced Trint back into a seat. The boy's excitement and Ester's profound relief only exacerbated their own disappointment. "Sirin only talked about you and Trint. I think that we'll stay here."

"Like the great green Chasm we will," Lucio interrupted. "The day you and Trint leave, Teehm and I are going too."

Trint's jubilation ceased as soon as he figured out that Teehma and Lucio would not be accompanying them. "Are you gonna follow us?"

Teehma glared at Lucio. "Lucio and I are not going anywhere. And I'm sure that, if you want, your new family will let you come visit us."

Trint's eyes grew even wider as he wailed, "I don't wanna visit you! I want you to come with us!"

"We can't, Trint," Teehma replied even as Lucio proclaimed, "We're not staying!" The two girls ignored him in their efforts to comfort Trint; they barely noticed him stalk out of the room.

Two days passed awkwardly. Ester and Trint were torn between excitement about their new prospects and reluctance to leave the other two. Teehma, on the other hand, had her hands full trying to keep Lucio from flying off the handle at the slightest provocation. Sirin did not help matters. After officially announcing the news, he proceeded to order the older two to wait on the younger two. Lucio was supposed to polish Trint up and teach him to mind his manners, while Teehma was pushed into all the chores Ester would be leaving behind. The result was more awkwardness and resentment. Consequently, when the day came for Ester and Trint to leave, Teehma and Lucio suffered from violently mixed emotions.

Sirin woke them all up early that morning and told them to come down to the parlor. After some quick washing, they staggered downstairs and laid eyes for the first time on Trint and Ester's new masters.

The man was tall, so tall that Trint barely came up to his knees. He looked like a giant standing among the miniature furniture of the parlor, there being no comfortable place for him to sit. He had a kind face and a ready smile. There was a lady standing next to him, whose plump figure complemented his height. She wore a plain dress, a plain apron over it, and a colored scarf which hid all of her hair. Her face, too, was cheerful, although a little sad. When she saw Trint, she gave a little gasp and then retreated to the corner.

Sirin took up the introductions. Pushing Trint and Ester forward, he said, "These are the two brat—er, children. Trint and Ester. You can see that they've had hard lives." He pointed to the scar on Trint's cheek and to Ester's unseeing eyes. "I trust you won't make life any harder for them."

The woman stayed in the corner, but the man crouched down in front of Trint, who watched him nervously. "Hello, Trint. My name is Tertio. I own a

65

store not too far from here, where I sell all sorts of food and clothes. This is my wife." He pointed to the lady, who was watching the proceedings at a distance. "Her name is Alisha."

Trint looked at him, then at her, then at Ester. Then he gave a jerky gesture in the direction of the last. "This is Ester."

Ester, ever timid and polite, gave a small curtsy. "Hello, sir. I am pleased to meet you."

The man looked back again at his wife before responding. "Ester, my wife and I are very glad to welcome you to our home. We lost a boy about Trint's age two cycles ago, but we've never had a daughter. We understand that you and Trint are very close; we will not try to separate you."

Ester managed another small curtsy and a quiet "thank you." Then the man brought his wife forward and began talking some more with the two children. Teehma was beginning to wonder why she and Lucio had been brought down at all when, to her surprise, the man fixed his gaze on them.

"You must be Teehma and Lucio. Sirin told us about you."

Teehma had been so focused on the scene before her that she had not noticed that the munkke-trophe had fallen asleep on a cushion. At the mention of his name, however, Sirin jerked and rubbed bleary eyes. "What? Are you still here?"

The man ignored him and continued talking. "I understand that you are the ones who have protected Trint and Ester for much of their lives. I can't tell you how grateful we are for what you've done." Behind him, his wife nodded her shy agreement. He continued. "Unfortunately, Kynell has not given us the means to support four children; we can only take care of two. But we know that it must be hard for you to be separated and we want you to know that you can visit Trint and Ester anytime you want."

Lucio nodded stiffly and Teehma felt tears come to her eyes. Why couldn't they just take Trint and Ester and leave? Why did they have to make it so emotional?

As if reading her mind, the man stood. Trint, sensing what was about to happen, ran to Lucio and hugged him fiercely. Lucio, trying to appear as grown-up as possible, patted him on the back. But Teehma could see that he was biting his lip so hard it was bleeding. Somehow the good-byes were made, then the two young ones were gone and only Sirin remained with them in the front parlor.

"Well then," he said briskly. "That's two down and two to go. Not bad for a fortnight's work, eh?"

Later that night, Lucio vented his full wrath.

"To the Chasm with Sirin! To the Chasm with those two strangers! To the Chasm with everybody!"

He would not be calmed, nor would he be diverted from cramming everything he owned (rather, that Sirin had given him) into a canvas bag. Teehma had tried every means she could think of even being nice to slow him down. She had even tried being nice. But he would not listen.

"Lucio, just calm down. You heard Sirin. We can go visit them tomorrow if we want."

He stopped packing just long enough to glare at her. In his fury, his speech degenerated into its roughest form. "Why? So we can sip tea and talk about how we aren't good enough to be adopted? Maybe we can tell Trint and Ester about our chores while they tell us about how that woman tucks them in at night and sings them lullabies!"

"So what's your great plan then? Are you going to kidnap them? Is there room for them in that great big sack of yours?"

"Don't be a *narfat*, Teehma." He slumped onto his small cot. "Those two need a home; they aren't strong like you and me. Besides, they've already forgotten about us."

Teehma slugged him hard across the arm. "They've only been gone a day! You think they've got the memory of a swamprat?"

"No." He rubbed his arm, deflated. "But they're happy now. They've got to be."

"So why are you packing? If they're happy, maybe Sirin will find a home for us, too. Maybe we're not too old."

He shook his head, slipping into his characteristic fatalism that was so infuriating. "There's nothing left for us here. Sirin won't find us homes and even if he did, we wouldn't like them. Our only hope is to leave before he separates us."

Teehma crossed her arms. "Well, I'm not going out there to starve again. We may not like it here, but at least we won't freeze to death."

Lucio stood up and moved to the window, where he pressed his hand against the glass. "We won't freeze. Hiverra is almost over; autore is pretty much here."

"So?"

The look he gave her was as resolute as all his twelve cycles could manage. "I'm leaving, Teehma."

"Not tonight, you're not."

"No, maybe not tonight. But in the next few days, soon as I come up with a plan. Then I'm getting out of Lascombe, even if it kills me."

Teehma kicked at the empty air to vent her frustration. In truth, she felt just as trapped as he did. "Let's be sensible. Where would we go?"

"Probably east. Away from the city, that's for sure. I could work on a farm somewhere."

"And what would I do?"

He shrugged. "Cook. Clean. How should I know what women are supposed to do?"

She almost slugged him again, but given his depressed state of mind, she restrained herself, settling on a haughty tone. "This *woman* can do farm work just as well as you can, Lucio."

His response was to take his clothes back out of his pack. Then, he pulled out a slate that Sirin had given him.

"So what do we do first?" he asked.

"First, you should learn how to read and write. Then you'd be able to get more jobs. But since we don't have time for that, we'll have to start by smuggling food out of the kitchen."

CHAPTER NINE

They were out of the marshes. After fording the Ergana, which formed the eastern border of the wetlands, Telenar and his company turned north toward the Duvarian foothills. In a few days, they would be at a good location for the Keroulian soldiers to return to Lascombe, if they so desired.

On the morning of the third day out, Amarian was returning from a walk with Bedge when he noticed that Telenar had drawn Vancien aside and was speaking with him quietly. As he drew closer, he saw the distress in his brother's manner; it looked as if Telenar was conveying some unpleasant news. Not bothering about their privacy, he introduced himself to the conversation.

"A beautiful morning, isn't it, priest? Vance, Bedge missed you on our walk today."

As if on cue, the fennel kit said, "Bedge wanted Sir's brother today! Bedge almost brought down small running beast, but Sir said no."

Vancien looked distractedly at her, then at Amarian. "Good job, Bedge. 'Ian, will you excuse Telenar and I? We're in the middle of something."

Amarian felt a flare of irritation. "I'll be happy to dismiss Bedge, but I'd rather stay, if you don't mind."

Much to his annoyance, Vancien looked to Telenar for approval. The priest nodded. "It's all right, Vance. This concerns him, too."

"Now," Amarian continued after having sent Bedge off, "what's this all about?"

When Telenar made no effort to explain, Vancien responded. "Telenar thinks that we should return to Lascombe and help Corfe."

"Help Corfe? Why?"

"Because he's a young man in great need of help," Telenar cut in. "Soon he'll be sending innocent soldiers out to confront Zyreio's forces and he has no idea how to fight them."

"He can't fight them."

"Yes, *we* know that, but he may not. If he sends innocent Keroulians out to meet Obsidian, they'll be massacred. So I'm hoping that maybe he'll listen to us and proceed with caution."

"What about going to the Eastern Lands?" Not that he was in any great hurry to go back there again, Amarian reminded himself.

"I can't pretend to predict the movements of Zyreio's forces. But Lascombe is as defensible a city as any in Rhyvelad. If we're going to make a stand against Obsidian, that's a good place to do it. And Corfe's troops, though not able to defeat with Zyreio's whatever-they-are, may at least hold them off."

"So what about Vancien and me? I don't think Corfe is ready to see us, nor we him."

Telenar cleared his throat, adjusted his spectacles, then cleared his throat again. "The presence of the two Advocates might cloud the issue. If Corfe believes that I am allied with you, Amarian, Kynell only knows what might happen."

"I can't leave him behind," Vancien interrupted.

"I know that, Vance," Telenar responded. "Corfe thinks you're dead, anyway. From what Amarian told us, he may have seen your body before Amarian fled to the marshes. So I think you and your brother should lie low."

Amarian snorted, stung by the reminder of his defeat. "And where should we do that?"

"Listen, unless you have Kynell's faithful behind you, you are both vulnerable, to Corfe as well as to Zyreio. Vance, if indeed you are the only one who can call the faithful, then you *must* stay alive, no matter what happens to us. And Amarian," Telenar turned an unkind eye toward the convert. "I presume Kynell spared you for a purpose. It's best to keep you alive until we find out what it is."

"So where should we go?" Vancien asked shortly. He did not approve of Telenar's tone.

"That I don't know. Somewhere close enough to be helpful but out of Corfe's range."

Amarian couldn't believe what he was hearing. Where did the priest get off ordering the Advocates around? *They* were the gods' chosen, not him. "So you expect us to go hide in a hole until you call for us?"

Telenar clenched his fists. He had meant what he said: he presumed Amarian was still alive for a reason, but how simple life would have been if Vancien had slain his brother, instead of the other way around! "All I know is that Corfe needs better guidance than what he's getting. And that your presence in particular, Amarian, would not help the situation."

"Have you told your pretty wife about this? How will she bear to let her pet out of her sight?"

"Enough, 'Ian!" Vancien interrupted. "Telenar, is N'vonne all right with this?"

"I told her last night. She knows you'll be close, so she's fine. The plan is that we will all go through the Pass together, but once we get close to Lascombe, we will find a place for you and Amarian to stay. Still," he hesitated, looking back towards his tent, "a word from you would encourage her."

Vancien took the hint and left to speak with her as Amarian eyed the priest with open disdain.

"Think you can fight our battles for us, do you?"

"I mean to do the best I can, for as long as I can. One hopes that, given the grace Kynell has shown you, you would do the same."

"Don't worry. I'll take good care of my baby brother."

"Vancien can take care of himself. Just see that you don't start relying on your own strength instead of Kynell's."

The same could be said of you, old man, Amarian thought but did not say. Instead, he went to find Bedge.

Gair left at dawn, just as he had been ordered. During the first fortnight of his journey, the weather was as forgiving as it could be. Hiverra melted away, allowing for the first inroads of autore. The terrain was also pleasant. The road heading east out of Lascombe ambled through Keroul's richest agricultural region. Gair's company could see the farmers out testing the condition of the soil and preparing the fields for planting.

Despite the tranquil scenery, the company was tense. The three Gair had chosen were good men and good soldiers. This last quality was no doubt the cause of their apprehensive mood. Gair had told them about their mission when they departed, and not one man among them relished joining a losing battle, or worse, discovering a massacre. Who knew what they would find

71

when they made it to the Kingdom of Ulan? The last days of a siege? A pile of dead Ulanese? A kingdom in ruins? One thing they did know for certain: they would be facing a supernatural enemy whom they had no idea how to fight. These considerations subdued even Ragger the munkke-trophe, who had managed only three solid days of bitter complaints before retreating into a silence.

After sixteen days of hard riding, the Wall came into sight. They had just come out of a wooded copse and rounded a bend when there it was, running from north to south like a second horizon. Gair sucked in his breath at the sight of it. Alric's Wall, so named after the Ulanese king who built it, was a testament to the dark periods of Rhyvelad's past. A hundred cycles after the beginning of the second Obsidian era, Keroul and the Kingdom of Ulan were immersed in a bitter war. Yet even in those dark times, some countries were less given over to evil than others. Keroul, in particular, was known for its sporadic resistance to the Obsidian despots. The remnants of Prysm followers would often try to flee there, including those among the Ulanese; King Alric therefore built the Wall not just to keep the Keroulians out, but to keep his own people in. It was a grim project promising a future of misery and captivity for those whom it affected. Despite frantic attempts to stop it, the Wall continued to rise to its present, awe-inspiring height. Such blatant containment worked for many cycles, until the Ulanese trapped in their own kingdom eventually caused so much internal dissension that Alric's son, Osgard, had to resort to the most horrific means of subduing them. It was a massacre of catastrophic proportions. Many Keroulians had even feared that the Ulanese had died out behind the great stone edifice. When Erst defeated the Obsidian Advocate, Nejona, ushering in an age of freedom, one of his first tasks was to send a Keroulian force to break down the gates of the Wall and liberate Windrell, Ulan's great capital city. For the past five hundred cycles, the gates to Ulan and Windrell remained open, allowing trade between the two former enemies to flourish.

As imposing a sight as Alric's Wall could be, it was not what drew the eyes of Gair's men. It was the smoke rising from behind it that caught their attention. And the noise. They had heard the distant clang of battle as they drew closer, but the trees had broken some of the sound. Now, as they stepped out of the thick wood, the horrible cacophony hit them in full force: inhuman screeches, howls, and shrieks piled on top of each other as if each were competing to be the first over the mighty wall. A wave of sound washed across the field, buffeting whomever it encountered. So chaotic was it that it seemed impossible to distinguish the victims' voices from those of the victors, if the victims' voices could be heard at all.

It took a moment for Gair to notice something else, something more immediate: the mighty gate that served as Ulan's portal to the outside world looked different. Digging out his range glass, he tried for a closer look. Where there was once a gate, there was now a crude pile of boulders that completely covered whatever opening there may have been. King Relgaren's concern had been well-founded. The Ulanese had been out of contact because they were trapped in their own city! Gair wondered how Farlone had made it inside; the gate must have been walled in after his arrival.

All around the base of the Wall were posted guards. That is, Gair assumed they were guards. In reality, they were the most agitated things he had ever seen. At first glance, it was hard to tell if some of them were human, so troubled were their movements. Most were batting at their own clothes, as if trying to beat off a swarm of biting insects. Those who were not writhing were showing signs of extreme anger and distress, either bawling out the figures closest to them or methodically pulling at their hair. Only the Sentry element of the guard stood still, but even its members flexed their muscles and limbs again and again, as if uncomfortable with their own bodies.

Gair had seen enough to chill his blood. "Back into the trees!" he hissed. Men and munkke-trophe immediately obeyed. The Wall was still more than a league away, but there was no sense in exposing themselves to the fiends. Once in the relative safety of the copse, they tried to take stock of the situation.

"What in the Chasm is going on?" the first man whispered through gritted teeth.

"I'd keep a close guard on that word, Sedgar," Gair replied. "You don't know how accurate it is."

Sedgar paled. "So that's them? I was expecting them to act more, well, dead."

Merto, who was a scout by training, volunteered to go in for a closer look. "There must be another entrance. I've heard that there are smugglers' tunnels dating back to Alric's reign. Those Chasmites can't have clogged all the ways in."

Gair shook his head. "We're few enough as it is. Besides, if any of the smugglers' tunnels were left open, wouldn't the Ulanese have found them?"

The wiry little man shrugged. "I see what others have pass over."

But the other two agreed with Gair. Reyn, the oldest and most experienced of them all, spoke with gravity. "The captain is right: we are already too few. I imagine those Easterners," he refused the more colorful name Merto had given them, "would crush any one of us with pleasure. To split up until we have more information would be too dangerous."

Merto was not convinced. "And how will we have more information if we don't split up? It'll be much easier for them to track five of us than one."

Sedgar looked at his companion with skepticism. "And how are you going to get closer to the Wall? It's open terrain between here and there; you'll be lucky to find a rabbit warren to hide in."

Merto was just about to respond when Ragger the munkke-trophe held up a paw to silence them. He was sniffing the air. "I can smell the smoke," he declared.

"So?"

The primate's beady red eyes were wide. "It is not just the smell of burning buildings; it is much more foul."

As he processed what Ragger was saying, Gair's heart sank. "Then the battle's already over."

The munkke-trophe nodded. "You don't burn bodies while you're fighting."

The group fell silent, each one considering the enormity of the catastrophe. Windrell was Ulan's greatest city, as well as the city closest to the Wall. It was her smoke that they were seeing. They all knew that if Windrell had fallen then the Easterners must have pushed their way through the width of the Ulanese kingdom, no doubt destroying everything in their path. Gair looked unhappily in the direction of the gate. The Easterners had not only run through the kingdom, but had sent forces through the Trmak desert to skirt the southern end of Alric's Wall and come up the outside, thus enclosing the Ulanese in a massive net.

"What do we do now, Captain?" Reyn's question was barely audible.

Sedgar took it upon himself to answer. "What can we do? We go back and tell the king that Ulan is destroyed."

Gair silenced him with a look. Sedgar was just a few months younger than himself. Gair had chosen him because of his loyalty to Corfe and his skill with a bow but had heard nothing remarkable about his bravery. "You surprise me, Sedgar. We've only just gotten to the battlefield and you already want to leave it?"

Sedgar turned crimson. "No, sir. I only meant to say that the battle is already over."

With a grunt, Gair stood up and checked the straps on his voyoté's saddle. "We won't know that until we get a better look. Merto, how close do you think we can get without getting detected?"

Merto also stood and peered through the trees. "The grass is tall, but other than that, there's little cover until we reach that rocky field there." He pointed to an area of ground about three-quarters to the Wall that was protected by a small scattering of boulders. The turf around it was torn up. "That must have been where they got the rocks to block the gate. There's no sense making a move until nightfall, though. Let's just hope those Chasmites can't see in the dark."

"And after that?"

"I vote we move south, away from the gate; that's the spot where they'll be looking for action. But we must be careful. You said that you saw Sentry Chasmites as well as human: one from any tribe would be trouble, but remember that the Urabi are night watchers."

Gair agreed and told the men to rest as well as they could. Then he sent the munkke-trophe up into the trees to keep watch. Corfe had been right: despite his complaints, Ragger was a useful scoundrel who had a sharp eye and needed less sleep than his comrades.   Night finally fell and the small troupe made its move. The horrible smoke had turned to an orange glow, bathing the Wall in a malevolent light but not extending its light to the field. They crept to the boulders without trouble, from which vantage point they could make out the individual shapes of the Easterners who guarded the Wall. To their surprise, the creatures were moving, starting to draw in toward where the gate had been. They had lit several torches so that their shadows crept high up the stones behind them. Their agitated movements were now cast in the eeriest of silhouettes. Several large Sentries appeared—Mholi, from the look of them—and started to lash ropes to the rocks piled up against the gate. Then, when the bottom boulders were secured, several of the Mholi took up the lines and started pulling. As the lower boulders shifted, the higher and smaller ones began to roll down. Any other soldiers would have jumped out of the way, but the Easterners, both Sentry and human, simply let the torso-sized rocks knock them to the ground. A second later they were up on their feet as the Mholi continued to pull.

Gair could feel Sedgar shaking, or possibly it was himself. Was this the type of enemy they would be fighting? How could they possibly overcome things against which the rocks of Rhyvelad were useless?

A crash resounded through the night, audible even over the cacophony of voices. The Mholi had not taken long to bring down the barricade. The boulders that remained in the path were hastily pulled away and the road was cleared. The spies watched, riveted, as the door opened and a dark screeching mass began to pour through it. The Easterners were on the move.

They tried not to panic, although Merto couldn't keep his voice from trembling. "Skies above, do you see what they're doing? There's only one city on that road."

Gair shared his alarm, but he tried not to succumb to it in front of the others. "At least they'll move slowly. Such a large force—even one like this— can only go so far in a day."

Ragger had started wringing his hands. "Yes, but no doubt they can travel by night, as well. They'll be in Lascombe in less time than it took for us to get here."

Sedgar jumped to his feet, eying the spot in the trees where they had left their voyoté. "Then there's no time to waste; we have to beat them back."

Reyn pulled him back. "Get down, you fool! Do you think you're invisible?"

Gair stared gloomily at the orange sky over Windrell. Was there anybody alive in there? "Here's what we do. Sedgar, Reyn, and Merto, move as quick as you can back to Lascombe. Warn the king."

"And you, Captain?" Reyn asked.

"I cannot move as quickly as you." He knocked his wooden leg. "If anything were to happen to my voyoté, I'd be a hindrance. Ragger and I will stay here to search Windrell. Perhaps there are some Ulanese still alive." He did not mention that he might find Farlone among them. Such a hope seemed too far-fetched.

"As you wish."

"Now go. Rest only when you need to. Reyn, you're probably right about the Easterners: they may move slowly, but it doesn't look like they will stop. You *cannot* let Lascombe be taken unawares."

The men saluted and hurried off, leaving Gair and Ragger, to settle down and wait. It would be a long while before that gate had vomited forth its last Obsidian regiment.

CHAPTER TEN

The triple lunos were high in the night sky when the final group of Easterners had disappeared beyond the horizon. The gate stood empty. The victors had felt no need even to shut the doors behind them. Gair suspected that they had not bothered to leave behind a garrison either, but he took no chances. As stealthily as they could, he and Ragger moved from shadow to shadow until they made it to the base of the Wall. Then they crept to the edge of the dark opening.

If a garrison was stationed there, it was hidden under the debris. Gair had never seen the city of Windrell. He had heard stories that it was a lively town, not quite up to the artistic level of Lascombe, but still a hub of trade and learning in its own right. For the Ulanese kingdom, Windrell was a gateway to the west, to the rich plains and majestic peaks of Keroul. Now, the famous gateway had become a tomb. The silence was deafening, and Gair tried not to get sick as he looked at the remains. With no one alive to bury them, bodies were left where they had fallen. It looked like many were clustered around the gate in a last ditch effort to escape or perhaps to keep the fiends from moving toward Lascombe. Most of the bodies were men, but it did not take much searching to find the women and children who had tried to hide. They, too, had been brutally murdered. Gair shuddered at what their last visions might have been. He was sure that many of them had put themselves into Kynell's hands before falling under Zyreio's wrath, but eternal peace for their souls did not save their bodies from being ravaged.

Shaken yet emboldened by the stillness around them, Gair and Ragger picked through random piles of debris, listening for any sounds of life. Once, as they were investigating an area at the base of a building, the wall above them came loose and they almost shared in the fate of the Ulanese. Only Ragger's quick reflexes saved them. After two more close calls and a few more hours of searching, Gair was ready to leave.

"There can't be anybody left alive," he whispered. Talking aloud seemed sacrilegious in this place. "And if there are, they're further back in the city and can fend for themselves."

Ragger, as submissive as Gair had ever seen him, agreed. The two were about to return to the gate when the munkke-trophe held up a paw. "Wait, Captain. I smell something."

Gair raised his eyebrows. "How can you smell anything but burnt flesh?"

Ragger didn't answer. Instead, he scampered down the street, away from the gate, and disappeared into a doorway. Gair followed, although he traveled much slower on his artificial limb. When he arrived, Ragger was climbing, monkey-like, down from a ruined balcony, the staircase to which was nowhere to be seen. He was cradling something in one arm.

"It is a human child, Captain."

"I can see that, Lieutenant. Is it alive?"

"Yes, sir. It looks healthy, just a little hungry and messy." He looked down at the child's tattered diaper.

"And the mother?"

"She is with Kynell now, sir."

Gair nodded as he stared down at the infant. It was young; he had no idea how old it was, but not old enough to walk or possibly even crawl. It was crying, although it was so weak that the cry was really more of a whimper. He looked around the remains of the building. What could they possibly give it to eat?

Ragger was stroking the child's head, which had the most meager amount of thin, dark hair. Gair had no idea he could be so gentle. "We must get her out of here," the munkke-trophe announced. "She needs food."

"Her?"

"Yes, sir."

"All right then." He stopped and looked around again. His artificial limb was beginning to chafe; he longed to get out of this place of death. "Are there any more?"

Ragger shrugged. "I cannot smell any more. It's amazing that this one survived."

"Then let's get her some food and, uh, some fresh clothes."

On their return to the gate, they dug up some clean rags that would serve as diapers, some more clothes to keep the chill off the little girl, and even a small store of food supplies. They found a bottle of milk that, while not fresh, was not yet rancid, and even some produce that they could mash down for baby food.

It was well past dawn by the time they made it back to the copse. Ragger, whose hidden talents were revealing themselves through this new development, changed the child's clothes and gave her some food. But Gair was anxious to press on. He watched impatiently as Ragger rocked her to sleep.

"Get up, Lieutenant," he ordered. "We have to keep moving. We will deposit the child at the first village we come across."

Ragger said nothing. Moving to his voyoté and mounting carefully, he continued to croon into its ear. Then he started. "Captain, I smell something."

Gair's nerves, already frayed, caused him to jump at the sudden announcement. "What is it this time?"

"Another human, sir. About ten yards through the trees."

"Ulanese?" His voice dropped to a whisper.

"Her smell is difficult to place."

"Another her?"

"Yes, sir."

Gair drew his sword and approached the trees carefully. Ragger dismounted again, placing the child between the protective front paws of the voyoté before he drew his own weapon. Together, they pushed through the leaves until they saw a woman standing in a small clearing. It was Verial.

She looked thin, torn, and even wilder than when Gair had seen her last. Her clothes, which were only rags, were supplemented by bits of small animal pelts, rudely dissected. She clutched a knife and there was blood under her fingernails.

"My lady, what are you doing here? How did you get here?" Gair couldn't decide if he was relieved or angry to see her. When he hastened to cover her rags with his cloak, she only flinched away from him. She had come close to cursing Kynell the last time he had seen her. Had she decided to return to Obsidian?

"It's my own business. I stole a voyoté. It ran off. I wanted to make sure you were safe."

He looked at her small knife and thin arms, and tried not to smile at the thought of her protecting him. Ragger, meanwhile, retreated to tend to the child.

"Kynell kept me safe."

She flinched again, but did not respond.

He waved a hand in the direction of the gate. "You didn't follow me in there, did you?"

She shook her head, causing matted blonde strands to fall around her face. "No, I couldn't. I saw those horrible creatures and hid." She dropped her gaze.

Now that he knew why she was there, he wanted to comfort her, to put his arms around her and tell her that Kynell could defeat all of Zyreio's efforts with a word. But of course he could not. Instead, he offered her his cloak again, which she took. "You did well to hide. *We* hid. I fear the Easterners are brutal."

She nodded. "I've seen them before, a long time ago, at a distance."

Gair grimaced. He had allowed himself to forget her age. Of course she would have been seen the battles of Advocates past.

"Is there anything we need to know about them?"

"They don't eat and they don't sleep. They're constantly tormented by their own anger. They only do Zyreio's bidding, which usually means they destroy whatever is in their path."

"So we don't stand a chance."

"No."

Her resignation, so evident and habitual, galvanized him. They may not have a chance, but they had to try. Besides, Kynell was more powerful than Zyreio. He voiced this observation, but Verial only shrugged and followed him back to camp.

Her meekness disappeared, however, when she saw the child.

"What is that thing?"

"A child. What else could it be?"

"Where did you get it?"

"Ragger found her among the Ulanese dead. The Easterners must have missed her, or else not considered her worth their time."

She eyed the sleeping infant as if it would bite her. "Yes, but why did you bring it with you?"

He looked at her, not comprehending the question.

"I assume that you want return to Lascombe to warn them about those fiends. A child will only slow you down."

He mounted his voyoté, not liking where this conversation was going. "And what do you suggest we do with her?" The child in question had woken up and started to cry. Ragger offered her some mashed fruit.

She would not relent. Rather, her voice took on a tone that Gair never thought he would hear from her. She began to whine. "Better to let it perish as the Easterners intended. At least then it would be spared suffering. And you would be free to do what you think you ought."

He could not believe what he was hearing. In his wildest, most carefree moments, he had thought about taking this woman as his wife. Praise Kynell that he had not done so!

"My lady, need I remind you that the child is a 'she,' not an 'it'? And my duty to Kynell is to help those in need. Can you conceive of any creature more in need than this abandoned child?"

She retreated into a resentful silence and he had no desire to argue further. "If you care to join us, my voyoté can carry two. But we must hurry. The Easterners already have half a day on us."

The Easterners thrashed rather than marched, but they thrashed consistently in same the direction. They passed many villages on the road, much to the terror of the inhabitants. Fortunately, the villagers, unless they happened to catch the eye of a tortured soldier or ravenous fennel, were in no imminent danger. Somehow the writhing mass kept close ranks and therefore made good time. The army appeared to have only one destination in mind: Lascombe, Kynell's city.

It was only by changing voyoté at every town and sleeping while mounted that Sedgar, Reyn, and Merto were able to keep ahead of it. As they shifted in their saddles, they wondered if their warning would do any good. The creatures had appeared unstoppable. Walls and gates were little hindrance to them, as Windrell had shown. They tried to warn people as they passed, but it was news that no one was ready to receive. Nor did they have time to explain it. It was if a tidal wave were roaring through the Trmak desert; how do you tell creatures who have never seen more than a stream of water that a wall of it was coming?

In the end, Reyn decided to tell them that the Cylini were attacking. It was a ridiculous lie, but years of Relgaré's wars against the Cylini tribes had fired the Keroulians' imagination into paranoia about the marsh dwellers. It was not hard to convince his hearers to flee while they still could.

It was the three men's good fortune that even they did not know the truth of who marched in the middle of that army. He was the only one of the thousands around him who looked untroubled. He surveyed his forces from the back of a common voyoté. He knew many things, though not everything. Of course he knew that three soldiers were racing ahead of him like hunted prey. And of course he knew that Verial had followed Gair in a pathetic chase. What he did not know was what his opponent's next move would be. Kynell's plans were hidden from him. And that traitor Amarian was so covered by the Prysm's protection that he looked like a wall of light. Zyreio could no more decipher the movements of his own Advocate than he could those of that Prysm slave. Indeed, when it came to any Prysmite, his vision consisted of illuminated splotches. At best he could tell where on Rhyvelad they were moving about. At worst, their brilliance seared his vision altogether.

He sighed, and the air around him shivered. If only that useless, fickle woman had stayed where she belonged. At least he could have gleaned some information from her. But that was no matter. He had trumped the Prysm before and he would defeat it again. Except this time, he was tired of Kynell's game. When he became victorious, he would be victorious for eternity. The days of the ten thousand scores were over. Zyreio was tired of cycles.

CHAPTER ELEVEN

A few days after the Easterners left the gates of Windrell, Telenar reached Lascombe with his small force. They had parted with Vancien and Amarian at the outskirts of town, leaving them in the care of a loyal old friend of Chiyo's. The brothers were not happy about the arrangement, but neither were they prepared to meet with Corfe. Vancien, in particular, was content to wait. He preferred to encounter the usurper with the risen Prysm army at his back.

Telenar wanted to present himself to Corfe as soon as possible and get the unsavory meeting over with. He did not even allow N'vonne time to brush the dust from the road before he was pounding on the palace gate—or rather, glaring at a palace guard who did not share his sense of urgency.

"Sorry, priest. The Advocate is occupied today."

Telenar felt N'vonne give his hand a reassuring squeeze. He looked towards her, hoping to draw from her patience. What he saw were the Sentries behind her, guarding the streets of Lascombe as if they were native Keroulians. How Rhyvelad was changing. He was glad now that he had left all the Cylini troops outside the city walls and let the other men return to their families. There was no sense in provoking an unnecessary fight. He turned his attention back to the guard.

"Listen, I must speak with him. Tell him my name is Telenar pa Saauli. He will recognize that."

But the human guard was unmoved. "Sir, I don't have direct access to the Advocate. And I can't leave my post to relay your message."

"Can't you call a courier or something?" N'vonne asked. "It's a matter of the city's security."

"Sorry, ma'am. That's not my concern."

Telenar was just about to ask how it was possible that the security of Lacombe was not the soldier's concern when he felt Chiyo move to stand next to him. Not being sure of his reception, the general had kept a low profile up to that point. Now he stepped forward with affronted authority. "I am General Chiyo. What's your rank and name, soldier?"

The guard was still unmoved. He must have been one of Amarian's men. "Ensign Henny. I've never heard of any Chiyo, but since you say you're a general, I'll call over my sergeant."

He gave a short whistle. Then they waited for a few minutes until a corpulent fellow with short bristly hair burst through the thick door Henny was blocking. "Henny, if you whistle at me one more time, I'll have you sleeping with the Sentries! Doesn't that thick block head of yours know how to use a courier?"

Henny was unrepentant. "Sorry, sir, but I didn't see one about. This man here," he waved a lazy hand toward Chiyo, "says he's a general. Chiyo, was it?"

The sergeant was clearly more aware of recent events than his subordinate. When he saw Chiyo's face and heard his rank, his hand snapped up in a salute. "General Chiyo! We thought the marshes got you!"

"No, the marshes did not 'get me,' as you say," Chiyo retorted, brushing past the sergeant into the hallway beyond. Telenar and N'vonne followed, slamming the door shut on the offensive ensign. "And I should say that my men's subsequent concern for my welfare was lacking to the extreme. Since when do we leave whole battalions unaccounted for out in the field?"

The sergeant, who of course had nothing to do with Chiyo's predicament at the time, still rose to the bait.

"I'm sorry, sir! I truly am! We none of us could stir a finger under ol' King Relgaré, not with that Hull fellow tramping about. The king was sore besotted with that man, if you ask me."

Chiyo cut him short. "I did not ask you, sergeant."

The officer was cowed. "Y-yes, sir. What was it that you wanted, sir?"

"To speak with Corfe."

The sergeant nodded, running a nervous hand over his bristles. He was stuck between a rock and a hard place. "I believe the Advocate is in meetings with the king today, sir. He's not seeing anyone. Perhaps I could find you some lodgings and check with him tomorrow?"

It was an unsatisfactory response that gave Chiyo the opportunity to swell with indignation. "What was your name, Sergeant?"

"Burtee, sir."

"Sergeant Burtee, Patronius Telenar, his new wife, and I have traveled many leagues and for many days in order to have this interview with Corfe. Now that we are here, you tell us that he is occupied?"

The man looked from Chiyo to Telenar with equal surprise. "Telenar? The wandering prie—I mean, the famous Telenar? We have heard much about you."

Telenar, too, was more than willing to assert his authority. "And you'll hear much more if you don't show us to Corfe. Lady N'vonne has already been standing for too long."

N'vonne took the cue and tried to look faint while the sergeant, now under the mistaken assumption that she was pregnant, showed them to a small chamber. Then, he offered Chiyo another hasty salute.

"This is just to get the lady off her feet, you understand. We'll let the Advocate know of your arrival and, er, tell him you'd like to speak with him immediately. I'll send a man along to take you to some nicer quarters."

Chiyo, ever willing to encourage repentance, returned the salute. "That'll be fine, Burtee." He looked around the small, closed room. "Just don't forget about us in here."

The man looked horrified. "Oh no, sir! That'd be the day! I'll just go and see what can be arranged." Continuing his protests and provisos, he backed out and disappeared into the hall. Chiyo shut the door behind him as N'vonne tried not to giggle.

"That was almost enjoyable."

Chiyo shook his head. "Are these the sort of men guarding Lascombe? Our cause is lost."

Telenar leaned back in his chair and began to polish his spectacles. "Come now, Chiyo. We wanted to make a quiet entrance and, well, those are the types of men who guard quiet entrances. But I think you have the sergeant on our side."

"At least until Corfe scares him worse than I did." Chiyo allowed himself a smile as he looked at the boxes along the walls. "Is this a storage room?"

N'vonne picked up a label from a large canvas sack. "Rice meal. I guess if he locks us in here, we won't starve."

Their concern was unnecessary. Once Corfe heard of their presence, he showed himself just as eager to meet with them as they were to speak with him. They were not in the room twenty minutes before a respectful knock sounded at the door, followed by the presence of a very well dressed, very polite servant.

"I'm so sorry for the intrusion," he began, staring at the floor. "Please allow me to show you to some more appropriate chambers, where the Lord High Advocate will see you."

Telenar flinched at the exalted appellation, but the three of them followed the servant, who never once dared to raise his eyes, down a maze of hallways. After what seemed like an endless walk, they found themselves in familiar territory: the king's antechambers.

Telenar gave a low whistle. "I guess what we heard was true. Corfe is in it up to his ears."

"In what, may I ask?"

They turned to see the young man himself. He had been sitting in a chair just inside the entrance. Now he strolled over to them, obviously comfortable in his royal surroundings.

Telenar could not hide his distaste. "You shaved your head. Do you think that makes you more spiritual?"

Corfe spread his hands expansively. "So good to see old friends, or old enemies, whichever the case may be. What brings you under my roof?"

"Your roof? I think you mean the roof of the house of Anisllyr."

Corfe acknowledged the rebuke with grace. "Well said, Patronius. I serve Keroul and all Kynell's people now."

Telenar bit his tongue. He had not planned to open with hostilities, but as usual, the words just came flying out of his mouth. Corfe, meanwhile, invited them to sit and ordered an attendant to bring in some refreshments. "You look as if you've come straight from the marshes."

N'vonne smiled, hoping to inject some sort of geniality into the conversation. "Almost. It's been a long journey. We're thankful that you're willing to see us."

Surprised and grateful for her tone, Corfe directed his full attention toward her. Despite his polished appearance, it was easy enough to tell that he had lost several hours of sleep recently. "And how have you been, Lady N'vonne? The last I saw you and your company was in the foothills of the Range. I believe that you proceeded from there into Cylini territory?"

N'vonne hesitated before she answered. They had agreed beforehand not to pretend to acknowledge Corfe's advocacy, yet they were walking a fine diplomatic line. How much could they say about Vancien and Amarian before they lost Corfe's ear? She opted for a subtle digression.

"We did have the privilege of meeting the Cylini. They are a good people; King Relgaré, may he rest well, might not have given them their due."

Corfe laughed out loud. "I agree with you. I have learned many things since Kynell touched me and one of those is that he created all living beings with strengths and weaknesses. Even the Sentries," he waved a hand toward the windows and the courtyard beyond, "have their place."

Chiyo had been quiet up to this point. Now his curiosity got the better of him. During his time in Lascombe with Vancien, he had noticed that some Sentries had indeed changed for the better. "We had heard that the Sentries were employed in your service. How is that working out?"

Corfe relaxed even further. The conversion of the Sentries was one of his favorite topics. "Kynell's service, General, not my own. For the most part it has been a success. The key has been to know the limits of the men. They have a lot of understandable prejudice against the Sentries. Kynell knows that I spent enough time with them while under Amarian. But as long as we content ourselves with gradual integration, things go along just fine."

He leaned back in his plush chair and watched them. He was very curious as to why they had come; surely the priest Telenar would blurt out the reason soon enough. The man seemed to be sitting on pins and needles.

He did not have to wait long. With an irritable wave of his hand, Telenar cut off Chiyo's next question. "We are all curious about how you've been managing your affairs, Corfe, but we don't have time for digressions. Do you know why we are here?"

"You came to acknowledge my advocacy?"

N'vonne and Chiyo glanced at each other but Telenar gave a short bark of laughter. "Hardly. We are grateful to Kynell for your healing, but you surely know that we do not consider you the Prysm Advocate."

Corfe nodded. He had expected as much. "Then what brings you here?"

"Your scouts have informed you of the Eastern army?"

"Yes. They are from the Chasm. Amarian must have called them out."

Telenar shook his head. Corfe would never believe that Amarian was not the enemy until he saw it with his own eyes. Better to focus on what he *would* believe. "Amarian did not raise them. Zyreio must have done it."

Corfe paled, though he tried to appear unmoved. "Zyreio? What makes you say that?"

"Because of Amarian." Telenar fiddled with his sleeve, uncertain how to proceed. "Amarian thought that Vancien was the Advocate. We saw him several months after your battle. He was still in the marshes. Your scouts must have told you that the army is already in the east and potentially moving west. Why wouldn't Amarian have called the army to himself and struck at you from west of the city?" He paused, waiting for an objection but hearing none. "Having slain Vancien, Amarian considers his job done. But for some reason, Zyreio is not satisfied. We believe that his forces will strike at Lascombe, since it has always represented Kynell's presence on Rhyvelad." He stopped. That was close enough to the truth.

Corfe was silent. Telenar's report confused him. Had Amarian been so convinced of Vancien's advocacy? And if so, believing that he was victorious, why was he not setting up his rule? Was the priest telling lies? He couldn't fathom any reason for Telenar to come into what he might consider enemy territory to spin such a story, unless Telenar had somehow allied with Amarian. But even if that were the case (which he doubted, even of the priest), the presence of the Eastern Army was indisputable. What would Amarian, through Telenar, gain by helping Corfe defeat Keroul's most serious threat? Surely preparing for a Chasmite army without a head would equip him to fight Amarian, whenever that situation might arise. In the end, he had to shrug. No matter what Obsidian force was coming his way, he wanted to be ready.

"I owe you gratitude for this new piece of information. It seems Amarian may not be the immediate threat that I thought him to be." Then he nodded graciously toward N'vonne. "And my belated condolences. Vancien was a fine young man. I'm sure you're still grieving for your loss."

Telenar responded before Corfe could notice N'vonne's startled expression. "There's more. We've come to help you fend off the Easterners, but you should know that, without Kynell's risen forces, you'll only be able to stave off the inevitable for so long."

Corfe winced. He hated to expose his weakness, especially to Telenar. "Kynell will grant me success in due time, I'm sure. Even you must admit," he continued with a grim smile, "that, with Vancien gone, I'm your best chance for an Advocate."

Ignoring the theological absurdity of the comment, Telenar looked at Chiyo, who shrugged. Then he glanced at N'vonne, who raised her eyebrows as if to say, "Let's get this over with." With the small encouragement those two reactions provided, he cleared his throat.

"Vancien is alive."

"Excuse me?"

"Vancien is alive. He's camped close to here, where we can communicate with him."

Corfe shook his head. "That is impossible. I saw his body. And I know what dead bodies look like."

"You did see his body. He was dead. But now he's alive and willing to meet with you, if you desire."

"How can he be both dead and alive? You're not making any sense, Patronius."

The look Telenar gave him was not unkind. After all, it had not been that long ago when the same young man had sat in his office. He had tried to pass himself off as an Advocate then, as well. "I fear that your education in the Ages has been scattered and rushed. You know just enough to get you past the current situation, but have never taken the time to delve deeper into their mysteries. If you had, you would know that every Advocate is granted a Grace—the power to bring someone back from the dead. That is what happened to Vancien. He *was* dead. But he's been restored to life."

Corfe could not believe what he was hearing. "And who brought him back?"

"I think you know the answer to that question. Who's the only one who could?"

"No. No, no, no. I don't believe it." He rose, mystified and offended. "Even if such a thing could be done, Amarian would never do it."

"He did do it. And we have proof. Amarian killed his brother then raised him up from the dead."

Corfe was pacing now, still shaking his head. "You don't understand. Amarian would never do something like that. Never. He hated Vancien, hated him so much that he talked about him all the time. The man was obsessed."

N'vonne whispered something in her husband's ear. When he nodded and whispered back, both she and Chiyo quietly excused themselves and stepped outside. This was an issue better handled one-on-one. Her intuition was confirmed when Corfe did not notice them leave.

When they were alone, Telenar leaned forward, trying to catch Corfe's eye. What would it be like to have a cruel master follow you into redemption? How could you believe that the same god who forgave you would forgive him also?

"Corfe, you must listen to me. The fate of Rhyvelad depends on it. Kynell did a great thing when he healed you. A miraculous thing. And I have no doubt that he is still working through you. But there was a reason Amarian was obsessed with Vancien. *They* were the brothers destined to fight. They did fight. Vancien lost. And that's just the first marvelous thing you're going to have to accept."

Corfe sat down. "How can I, when it's so clear that Kynell chose me to lead these armies?"

"Unless you do accept it, those armies of yours will be devastated. And you will have to answer to Kynell for the life of every man, woman, Sentry, and fennel among them."

But Telenar's warnings were falling on rocky ground. Corfe returned to his moral pedestal. "What you don't understand, Patronius, is Amarian's true nature. Even if, for argument's sake, he brought Vancien back from the dead, so what? Have you considered that he may have done so with an ulterior motive? Perhaps something that served Amarian and not Vancien?"

The idea had not occurred to Telenar; he shook his head to clear the troublesome thought. "Corfe, he is a follower of the Prysm now, just like you."

"Ha! Now *that's* impossible." Corfe rose again and moved toward the door, as if relieved of a great burden. "Amarian a follower of Kynell? Now I know that you're more confused than I could ever be. I would like to stay and talk hypotheticals with you a little longer, Patronius, but I need to be going."

Telenar rose, as well. "Believe what you want about Amarian. You'll see the truth soon enough. But at least agree to meet with Vancien."

Corfe had slipped into his earlier, imperious attitude. "You and your party are welcome to join me at dinner tonight. And if you can somehow conjure up Vancien, as well, so be it."

CHAPTER TWELVE

Vancien was twenty cycles old. He had been an orphan. He had lived in a palace. He had kept extended company with a munkke-trophe, traveled *over* the Duvarian Range, lived among the Cylini, battled with a man older than himself, died, and been brought back to life. And still he felt like an amateur.

"Look, Vance, you're doing it wrong. Didn't Papa ever teach you to skin a yemain?"

Vancien gripped the knife tighter. "No. He died, remember?"

Amarian ignored the bait. "When you were twelve. Plenty of time to teach you before that. I knew by the time I was twelve."

"Yeah, well, Papa never was quite the same after you left, 'Ian."

It was a low but true blow and Amarian could say nothing in response to it. Vancien, meanwhile, wiped the sweat from his eyes and the blood from his hands. He had not meant for it to come out quite like that.

"Sorry. I guess part of me envies your time with him."

"Well it's a pity he didn't teach you how to skin an animal. Here, give me the knife." He took the bloody implement out of Vancien's hands and proceeded to divest the woodland creature of its skin. They had been hunting in a thin line of trees not too far from their hideout, which was nothing more than a one-room house outside the city walls. Their hostess, Ming, was an elderly widow who barely had enough food for herself, let alone two healthy men. So in gratitude for her taking them in, the brothers had decided to supplement her diet with some good red meat. Normally, Amarian would have put Bedge on the task but the fennel had disappeared several days before they had arrived in Lascombe, presumably to hunt for herself or perhaps out of wanderlust. Amarian had known her to do this sort of thing, although not for so long. He was beginning to get worried.

As they finished dressing the carcass of the dead yemain, Amarian tried to ignore the unnatural cold over his left shoulder. The Ealatrophe was watching them with idle curiosity. Thinking that Thelámos would attract too much negative attention, Vancien had directed his mount to stay among the trees; the beast had joined them not long after they had brought down the yemain. Though Amarian figured he wanted a piece of the kill, Vancien insisted that he was merely bored. Either way, Amarian didn't like it. The sacred nature of the creature always made him feel as unworthy as he knew he was.

"Where could that brainless fennel be? The army will be here by the time she gets back."

Vancien said nothing. Fear often spoke with the voice of anger and for Amarian, this was particularly true. Just as he was about to suggest that they start back to the house, Thelámos gave a loud shriek of welcome. They both looked up to see Bedge burst out of the trees. Her swirled brown fur was missing large patches, she was favoring one paw, and her eyes were half-crazed.

Amarian dropped his pack. "Bedge, where in the Chasm have you been?"

By way of an answer, she limped over to him, ran her thin body across his legs, and collapsed. Now much alarmed, he dropped down next to her. "Bedge! Idiot fennel! What's gotten into you?"

Vancien knelt next to him. After listening to her breathing, he passed a hand over her to check for wounds. The limp was caused by a large thorn, recently acquired. She appeared simply exhausted.

Amarian muttered as he, too, ran his hand across her limp head and down her neck. She stirred under his touch, but did not open her eyes.

"What do you think happened to her?" he asked.

"Looks like she's come a long way and in a great hurry. There's no way we can know until she wakes up."

The day was beginning to fade, so Amarian draped the unconscious kit over his shoulder as they gathered up their kill. The movement woke her up. With a howl, she tried to scramble to the top of his head. Amarian howled himself as she did so.

"Bedge! Shh! Hold still, it's me! By the Chasm, you've got claws!"

Pinned to his shoulder like a huge housecat, it took a while for her to calm down. "Sir? Sir, we must go," she rasped into his ear.

"What are you talking about? We are going. Go where?"

She shook her furry head and jumped down. "Bedge went very far. First for good hunting. Then Bedge followed the orbs coming up in the big, pretty fields. She ran and played. Played, played, played. . ." she ran a paw distractedly across the dirt. "Bedge likes to play, but Bedge stopped when she heard them."

"Them?"

"Him. And them. They were in the fields." She shuddered. "Bedge heard bad noises before she saw them."

The brothers stared at each other as she began to avidly lick herself. Vancien spoke first. "She saw the army. And if she went east towards the rising orbs, she was in the fields or the wood between here and Windrell."

"And him?" Amarian was pale.

Vancien looked at the fennel, then at the sky, then at Thelámos, who was preening himself, oblivious to Bedge's news. "I think there are only two 'hims' who could be riding with the Eastern Army. And you're here."

Amarian's stomach turned. He wiped a shaking hand across his forehead, which was beginning to glisten. "Surely not. I mean, we knew he raised them but he couldn't ride with them, could he? He's never done that before."

Vancien was disturbed by the idea, as well, but he didn't want to admit it. "None of this has been done before, 'Ian. Starting when you chose Zyreio against your will."

"We can't fight him, Vance. We can't. Who knows what he'll do?"

Bedge had begun pacing. "Sir not fight? Sir must fight. Evil army will reach big city in days. Bedge, Sir, and—" she glanced at Vancien, for whom she had not yet found a satisfactory label, "—Sir's brother must fight loud bad fennels."

Amarian had knelt on the ground, struggling to breathe. "I can't," he rasped. "I can't face him."

Vancien laid a hand on his shoulder. "It's all right, Amarian. Kynell is with us. Zyreio is no match for him. I'm sure of it."

Amarian continued to sway, senseless to everything but his fear. The nightmare that had been his advocacy came rushing back, paralyzing him and casting his current reality into darkness. He could feel Bedge purring up against him, trying to calm him, but he could not move to touch her. He heard her voice soothing, "Sir is too scared, Sir will be fine, Sir has Bedge and the light-god," but he could not catch his breath well enough to respond.

Amarian shook his head and began swearing under his breath. Then he felt a great claw shove him to the ground, digging its talons into his chest. For a moment, he thought Zyreio himself had struck him, but then he felt a debilitating cold seize his body.

"Thelámos, stop!" Vancien cried, horrified. He shoved his shoulder into the Ealatrophe, who ignored him. Bedge had thrown herself onto Thelámos' back, going instinctively for his great neck. He only plucked her off and tossed her to the side.

Amarian lay pinioned on the ground as Thelámos glared at him. He heard Vancien's shout and saw Bedge attack. But those images began to mingle with other images, and other voices.

"Tell me again," he heard his own voice insisting. *"From the beginning."* Then his reality disappeared altogether. All he could see were the walls of his childhood, and his father looking down on him.

Hull bent down low, scooping him into his lap. "It's a long story, son. And it's about time you go to bed."

Amarian squirmed at that last word. "Not yet, Papa. I'm not tired."

Hull looked at Chera, who only shrugged. It was Hull's job to put Amarian to bed, and she would let him make the decision.

"Okay. Just once. But tomorrow night you go to bed early."

Amarian nodded. It was worth the sacrifice.

"Do you remember who never, ever changes?"

"Yes. Kynell. He is always the same."

"And who is ever-changing and inconstant, except for his lies?"

"Zyreio. He never means what he says, except when he wants to."

"And who is in-between?"

Amarian thumped a small hand on his chest. "Us. We change but not always. And we only sometimes lie. But we shouldn't," he added quickly.

Hull settled back in his chair, his voice low and strong. "Long ago, in the days after the great city of Lascombe was first founded, Zyreio came to Kynell and said to him, 'I am tired of exile. I want all of Rhyvelad to be mine.'

"'You cannot have it.' Kynell told him.

"'Then I want a champion,' Zyreio had said. 'And I want you to have a champion, too. They will fight as enemies and one will die. Whoever's champion triumphs will rule Rhyvelad for a time. Then we'll do it all over again.'"

Here Amarian straightened and looked his father in the face. "But why would Kynell do that? Why did he listen to Zyreio?"

"I don't know, son. Not completely. Do you want me to finish the story?"

Amarian nodded and put his head back on his father's shoulder.

"At first Kynell did not respond. Zyreio's heart fell, or whatever he has in place of a heart. Kynell would not accept his plan. But then Kynell, with a voice that made Zyreio jump back, said 'They will be called Advocates. And they will be brothers.'"

"No!" Amarian popped up again. "That's too mean! Brothers shouldn't fight."

"Shh. It's okay. We have to trust Kynell. If he wanted the Advocates to be brothers, he must have had a reason."

"But that's not how the story ends, is it?"

"They talk some more. About the cycles, and how long each would have control of Rhyvelad. What could be done, and what couldn't be done. That sort of thing."

"Why did Zyreio get his way?"

Here his mother interceded. "Zyreio only got his way for a short time. Kynell always triumphs in the end, and that means love does, too, including the love between brothers."

"Why can't the gods fight themselves, instead of the Advocates?"

His father took up the conversation again. "Kynell can defeat Zyreio with a word. But if Kynell allows Zyreio to resist, the whole world could be destroyed by their fighting."

Kynell can defeat Zyreio with a word. The words rang again and again in Amarian's head as he pictured Zyreio in that army. The whole world could be destroyed, but Kynell can defeat with a word. The cold continued to course through him, pounding at his fear, bringing him relentlessly back to the fear of Kynell, whose voice even Zyreio feared.

He had stopped moving. Vancien was frantic, plowing repeatedly into Thelámos' shoulder. Finally, Thelámos released his hold and sat back to admire his handiwork.

Amarian lay still a moment longer then coughed and curled into a fetal position. Vancien covered him with his cloak but it seemed to have no effect. He still clutched at his chest, which bled only a little, and stared into the trees. Finally, in a thin voice, he spoke.

"It's okay. I'll go."

Vancien nodded, but glared at Thelámos. It had been a brutal way of getting Amarian's attention. Amarian saw the look and managed a smile.

"Don't. He is holier than we are." Then his speech was stopped as Bedge, anxious to help, curled up next to his chest and rested her head on his face.

Night had fallen when Amarian recovered; when he did stagger to his feet, he said not a word. They walked the short distance in silence. Ming, who was waiting for them, had only to look at his shivering form before she put another pot of hot water on the fire in addition to the one with boiling vegetables. Like most of Chiyo's people, she operated with impressive efficiency. After she hurried Amarian to the chair next to the fireplace and wrapped him in a blanket, she started asking questions in her thick Western accent.

"What has happened to this man? What did you do to him? And where did that lady go?"

Vancien and Bedge kept their distance, happy to let her do the preparations for dinner. "He has taken a severe chill," Vancien responded. He pointed to the big, bloody sack they had brought in. "We were hunting yemain. That bag is for you. What lady?"

"This lady," N'vonne answered as she stepped inside. "I just stepped out to see if I could find you. What took you so long? And what happened to him?"

Vancien shook his head. "Long story. But we have more news."

"Save it for now. We've got to get you to the palace. Corfe wants to meet with you tonight for dinner." She looked out the door. "Right about now."

When he didn't move, she threw him a bundle of clothes she had been carrying. "Hurry! Put these on. They're loans from the palace so we can at least look respectable."

He did as he was told, instructed Bedge to keep a close eye on Amarian, and followed her out into the night. The early autore air still had a bite in it; he could see his breath as he jogged to catch up with her.

"Corfe knows I'm alive then, does he?"

"I don't think he'll believe it until he sees you. We're all interested in what his reaction will be."

"He still won't believe I'm the Advocate."

She nodded, her auburn waves bouncing a little in the lunos-light. He noticed that she had also dressed up for the occasion.

"We need to talk to Telenar, as well," he continued, dropping his voice as they entered the city gates. No need to cause a panic quite yet. "Bedge went exploring, and she saw the army between here and Windrell."

That caught her attention. "Here and Windrell? It's already gone through the Ulanese?"

"Apparently so."

"So Telenar was right. It's headed straight for Lascombe."

"Which means we have a lot of work to do in the next few days."

Corfe entertained them in high style. It had been a long time since they had enjoyed good, warm Keroulian food. Vancien's appreciation of it was dimmed, however, by the knowledge that Amarian was still shivering in Ming's poor cottage. Wine flowed, followed by delicious greens, marinated poultry, and finally, sweet glazed honey cakes. Corfe did not say much to him beyond a formal greeting when he first arrived. It was a private party, consisting of Corfe, Telenar, N'vonne, Chiyo, and Vancien, yet their host kept to surface conversation during the course of their meal. Vancien, who alone knew how imminent the threat was, could not sit still.

Finally, when the last of the honey had been whisked away and replaced by hot tea, Corfe acknowledged his presence by more than a shallow formality.

"I have to say, Vancien, you look very much alive and healthy. Much more so than when I last saw you."

"Much has changed since then. You yourself look more alive now that I can see Kynell in you."

Corfe flushed at the unexpected compliment, but before he could respond, Vancien continued. "We can't dwell on the past, however. I have just found out that the Eastern army has moved beyond Windrell and is marching through the fields towards Lascombe as we speak. We may have just a few days before it's here. And Zyreio rides with it."

Telenar choked on his tea. "Did you say rides with it?"

"Bedge said that she saw a 'him' with 'them.' And she was terrified."

Corfe jumped in, glancing at Telenar. "Perhaps the 'him' in question was Amarian?"

There was an awkward pause as several of them considered how to proceed. Vancien, not knowing how much Corfe had been told, held his tongue. Telenar sighed. "Remember when I told you that we saw Amarian in the marshes? That was not entirely accurate. Since that time, Amarian has been traveling with us *as*," he laid great stress on the word, "a follower of Kynell. Consequently," he continued, looking again to Vancien, "there's just one other person that Zyreio would trust with his army: himself."

"Look," Corfe cut in, beginning to rise from the table. "I don't know what game your little band of brothers is playing. First Vancien's dead, now he's alive. Then Amarian is Obsidian's Advocate, now he's not. I have half a mind to throw you all out on your heels."

At the far end of the table, Chiyo had been scratching plans into its wooden surface. He had not spoken at all during dinner, except for muttering to himself. Now, when Corfe's voice escalated, he slammed down his knife.

"You will do no such thing, Corfe. Sit down." Surprised, the young man obeyed as Chiyo continued. "Do you know what I've been doing while you've been discussing Kynell knows what?" He pointed a calloused finger towards the scratches. "Planning evacuation routes. Preparing to defend the city. Figuring out how to keep people alive. Do you or do you not believe that a large force will soon be laying siege to this city?"

They all nodded.

"Then I suggest we start acting more like soldiers and less like theologians. Send for your commanding general. We need to evacuate the women and children immediately. Have him bring me layouts of the palace, the city, and the surrounding areas. After that, send for the king. He needs to know what's going on. Vancien, find the palace carpenter. We'll need his help. N'vonne, find the kitchen master. We must know how long we can hole up in this place. Telenar, find what helpful priests you can and get all the useless ones out, away from the soldiers."

Vancien was already on his feet. "And Amarian?"

Chiyo paused. "It might be best to keep him out of sight. If any under his former command see him, who knows how they will react?"

Everyone, even Corfe, was galvanized into action by Chiyo's words. By min-lunos, the king and his chief officers had been informed of the approaching danger, and Chiyo was already conferring with the carpenter on how to build barriers against the enemy. Shouts started reverberating in the streets as word spread of the evacuation.

It was still several hours before dawn when the soldiers banged on Ming's door. Amarian withdrew into a corner as the older lady limped to the door, wiping sleep out of her eyes as she went.

"Yes?"

A flushed young officer bowed. "Sorry to disturb you, ma'am. The city is being evacuated. We must ask you to remove yourself and any dependents inside the walls to report for immediate departure. Please do not flee yourself but report to the city for appropriate evacuation orders. Please do not take anything with you but warm clothes and food. Shelter will be provided."
Having finished with his speech, he hurried away to the next house. Ming shut the door, lit a candle, and looked at Amarian. "Do you count as a dependent, my son?"

"No, but I'll help you get your food ready for the road."

98

CHAPTER THIRTEEN

The night before Chiyo ordered the evacuation, Lucio and Teehma made their escape. After several tense days of planning, Lucio had wanted to leave the city as quickly as possible, but Teehma insisted that they say farewell to Trint and Ester first. She had asked Sirin where they were living during supper. Unsuspecting, he had described Tertio's shop to them and even how to get there. So later that same night they crept down the street, avoiding eye contact with anybody and hoping they could see their two comrades one more time before they left the city forever.

Sirin's directions were accurate. In about twenty minutes, they found themselves outside of a small house, with two windows facing the street and, around the corner in an alley, two more windows. It did not take long for Lucio, using Gorvy's training, to find the window that looked in on both Ester and Trint sleeping in bunked beds. But his small whoop of triumph was cut short when the door to their room opened and Tertio looked in. Holding their breath outside the window, Teehma and Lucio could only see the outline of his head. It looked like a contented outline. Teehma felt a pang; it had been a long time since an adult had bothered to look in and see how she was sleeping.

After a few minutes, Tertio left and Lucio sprang the window's lock. They climbed inside, using a worn-out old dresser as a ladder down to the planked floor. Tertio certainly did not live like Sirin, but the place was clean and warm. Trint was sleeping like a baby, but Ester jumped when Teehma scuffed her foot on the floor.

"Hello? Who's there?"

"It's us, Ester," Lucio responded in a hoarse whisper. "We're here to say goodbye."

"Lucio? Is Teehma here too? Where are you going?" As she swung out of the lower bed in the pale light, Teehma noted her soft nightgown with envy. She had left hers behind at Sirin's, not seeing the need to sleep in anything but her clothes during the journey. She sighed. No more luxuries for her.

"Me and Lucio are leaving Lascombe, Ester," she began. "There's nothing for us anymore at Sirin's, now that you and Trint are safe."

Ester felt about wildly for her hand, which Teehma provided. "You can't leave," she whispered. "You haven't even visited us once yet! I told Trint that you would come see us soon. He's been so upset. He's been saying you've forgotten us. You haven't forgotten us, have you?"

It was the most they had heard her speak in cycles. Even Lucio began to feel some remorse. "Of course not, Ester. You're family. We're not gonna forget you. But we have to go. How can we stay at Sirin's, knowing nobody wants us? Not even the old munkke-trophe? You and Trint have a home now." He looked around the room, admiring its size. "A good home."

"What will I tell Trint?"

"I'll tell him." Before Ester could stop him, Lucio had clambered up to the top bunk and was shaking the boy awake. "Hey Trint, wake up! It's Lucio."

Trint obviously did not appreciate the importance of the occasion. "Go'way, Lucio," he muttered, shoving his head even deeper under the pillow.

Lucio was undeterred. "Don't be a *narfat*, Trint. Wake up. Teehma and I are coming to say goodbye."

Trint poked his head out from the bedding. "Goodbye? What for?"

"Teehma and I are leaving Lascombe. We don't know when we'll come back, but we'll come visit when we do."

Trint did not seem as upset by this news as Teehma thought he might be. "When? In a few days?"

Lucio looked at Teehma for help, but she was staring stonily out the window. Maybe coming here had not been such a good idea after all.

"Uh, maybe a couple months."

"Months?" Trint's grogginess disappeared. To a child of four cycles, months lasted an eternity. "But Ester said maybe tomorrow."

It was more of a protest than Lucio's short reserve of tenderness could handle. With a quick pat on the boy's head, he jumped down to the floor.

"Sorry, Trint. We gotta go."

Teehma offered some gentle goodbyes but Trint was already in tears. They left, trying to ignore the sounds of his sobbing and Ester's attempts at encouragement. The window shut on the sound of Tertio coming in to find out what was wrong with his two new charges.

It was a few blocks before they spoke again.

"Nice one, Teehma. Such a good idea to stop in and give our respects." He kicked at a stone. "So much for slipping away, unnoticed by anybody."

"Yeah, well, if you weren't such a brute, he wouldn't be so upset."

Lucio said nothing in response but kicked at the stones harder. They carried on in this fashion until they reached the eastern gate. The guard there happened to be somebody they had known from their days under Gorvy. He had always taken pity on them, even to the point of bringing them tidbits from his small garden outside the city walls. After a few questions and pleasantries, he unbarred a small door adjacent to the gate and let them out.

Outside of Lascombe's south-eastern corner was a whole other city: a poorer, more impermanent version of the capital itself. This was where much of Keroul's peasantry lived, in clusters of dwellings far enough out to tend the fields, yet close enough to seek the mighty city's protection in times of danger. Lucio and Teehma had been this way a few times before—enough to know that there was little worth robbing—and could creep through the dirt-packed streets with relative ease. By mid-lunos they were almost to the last of the sloping houses and by dawn they had traveled far enough to rest by a shallow creek.

"How far are we going, anyway?" Teehma asked as she fluffed her pack up into a pillow.

"Don't know. I'd like to get out of view of the city." He waved his arms toward some fields on the horizon. "I bet those farms don't have people like Gorvy or Sirin."

Teehma yawned, trying to disentangle her long hair with her fingers. "Sirin wasn't so bad."

"Yeah, but he wasn't for us."

She didn't bother asking what *was* for them. Yet when they resumed their journey later that afternoon, their predicament continued to trouble her. What chance would they have if they failed to find a farm to work on? With no family, no money, and very little skills, their prospects could not be good. At least with Sirin, they would have had the opportunity of learning a trade, even if they were never placed in a home. She tried this argument with Lucio as they walked, but he would hear nothing of it. His anger at Sirin for taking Trint and Ester away from them had built up to an irrational level. In his mind, anything, including starving under the open stars, was better than living under the roof of "that monkey." Since she wasn't about to leave him to his own devices, she dropped the subject and concentrated on replenishing their small food supply.

Several nights later, they had had little success among the farmers. Lucio had spent one day helping a man plow his field, thus earning dinner and a night in the barn for the both of them, but no one was interested in taking on two youths long term. Mostly they just received sympathetic wishes and a few bits of coin.

They had made camp a little bit off the road, dined on some meat sticks provided by a charitable blacksmith, and drank the last of the tea stolen from Sirin's cupboards. Exhaustion claimed them not long after and they fell into a deep sleep, punctuated only by Lucio's light snores and the sound of a chipperwick chattering above them. Lucio had tried to bring it down with his sling earlier that evening, but it had evaded his clumsy attempts. Now it was determined to remind him of his failure by keeping up a constant monologue.

Far into the night, they were awakened by sounds far worse than an annoying chipperwick. A combination of stamping feet, clashing metal, and angry shrieks filled the night air. It sounded as if it were right next to their heads. Awaking with an oath he had learned from Gorvy, Lucio jumped to his feet, then covered Teehma's mouth before she could cry out. The horrible din was coming from the road. In the dim light cast from the triple lunos, they could see thousands of shapes marching past, some of them human, many of them contorted, all of them convulsing as if their veins were on fire.

The two remained as motionless as statues, partly from an instinct for survival, partly because the sight passing before their eyes produced the type of terror that numbs the brain and the body. Teehma's breath came in short spurts, but she made no sound, even when Lucio removed his hand. Lucio had given up swearing. Instead, he was digging deep for the few Prysm prayers he knew.

It took hours for the horde to pass. None of the gruesome soldiers thought to look into the copse of trees for sport. Each one seemed preoccupied with his own torments. By the time the last twitching shadow disappeared, the morning orbs were beginning to peak over the horizon. Teehma hissed as she moved her aching muscles.

"What was that?"

Lucio looked just as horrified as she felt. "I don't know. But it made me feel sick." His voice sounded dull. "Like when my mom would come home late from the tavern. And father would hit her for being so drunk. And then she'd hit me." He shook his head violently, trying to dispel the feeling. "I feel all empty inside."

Teehma nodded, feeling thirsty, hungry, sore, and desolate all at once. "Maybe we should keep going and get as far away from those men as possible. The orbs will come up soon and we'll feel better."

Lucio nodded as he began to pack up their few things.

There was no way Gair would be able to catch up with Obsidian's army. With one voyoté loaded down with two passengers, he'd be lucky to get to Lascombe by the end of the siege. It didn't help that the road they traveled on was strewn with debris from the passing mob: bits of torn cloth that tangled the voyoté's legs, some broken weapons, and, occasionally, the remains of some poor soul who had gotten in the Easterners' way.

Despite the delay, Gair turned a deaf ear to Verial's repeated requests to abandon the child. Providing a home for her had proven more difficult than he had thought. The few villages they encountered were the same ones who had seen the Easterners pass. They were the ones who had not heeded Reyn's warning that the Cylini were coming, and so they had witnessed invaders far worse than any Cylini. Not surprisingly, they had also turned superstitious overnight and refused to take in a stray. It took several days of searching, a great deal of groveling, and a sizable monetary gift, before they found a family willing to take her in.   Only Ragger was sad to see her go. Verial had been openly offended by the child's existence and Gair was anxious to get back to Lascombe as soon as possible. He did hope that he had done the right thing. Parents who needed flattery and monetary persuasion to take a baby in need would be unlikely to give it a supportive home. He shook his head. Such considerations were secondary now. What was done was done.

The grueling days passed and Gair knew the army must be drawing close to the city. One foggy morning, that knowledge was pressing upon him. The munkke-trophe, too, seemed depressed while Verial stared moodily ahead. About mid-day, they were all surprised to hear a rustle behind a hedge line that followed the road. Gair help up his hand for them to stop, gesturing for Verial to hide on the other side of the road. Then, with the voyoté growling behind them, he dismounted, drew his sword, and motioned for Ragger to approach the hedge with him.

What they beheld was nothing more frightful than a girl of about fifteen cycles and a boy of about twelve. They looked rough, as if they had spent their entire lives behind the hedge. The girl spoke first.

"Sir, don't hurt us. We haven't been involved in anything. We don't want any trouble."

The boy appeared both terrified and grumpy. He looked annoyed with the girl for having spoken, although he did not offer up any words himself.

Gair hastened to sheathe his sword. "Get up, if you can. Have you seen an army pass this way?"

The girl looked around at the rubble. "Yes, sir, we saw it. A few days ago. We've been running like scared coneys ever since. Several of the towns are deserted, and those people who were left wouldn't take us in. I don't know if they thought we'd escaped from it, or what. You're the first person to talk to us and offer us food."

Gair raised his eyebrows at this conclusion. The children did look hungry. He waved Verial over and ordered Ragger to get some rations out of the packs. As the two made short work of the fare, he asked them where they had come from.

"I'm Teehma," the girl volunteered. "We are traveling to, ah, search for some sort of work. Lucio here," she waved at the boy, who continued to glower, "said we could find work in the farm fields. But it looks like nobody's interested in farming these days. What *was* that, anyway?"

Gair did not relish telling them the news, but he had no choice. They would find out soon enough, if Obsidian had its way. "The army you saw was not made of regular men. It consists of, er, individuals released from the Chasm. Rhyvelad is going through a prophetic time and there's about to be a nasty battle, probably around Lascombe."

"Lascombe?" the two cried in unison.

"Do you really think," the boy said, "that it will attack Lascombe?"

Gair nodded. "I'm sure of it. We're hurrying back there now to help." He stood and pulled on his riding gloves. "I suggest that you two keep traveling east. Find somebody from a village off the road who will take you in. And don't bother traveling to Ulan. The army's already been there."

The boy and girl looked at each in silent communication for a moment, then the boy crossed his arms. "We're going with you."

Verial, who had watched the exchange with disdain, could not hold back a bark of laughter. "Ha! Why would we want two scavengers to come with us? You'd just slow us down."

Gair flinched at her condescension, but he had to agree. "I'm sorry, but you can't come with us. We shouldn't even be stopping as it is. Keep all the food I gave you and be on your way. But please, follow my advice and save yourselves for as long as you can."

Without another word, the party mounted and rode off, leaving Lucio and Teehma alone again.

"That settles it." Lucio said. "We have to go back."

"Don't you think Tertio will protect them?"

"Did he look like a fighter to you? Ester has more of a backbone than he has."

Teehma did not argue. She, too, knew her place was between Trint and Ester and that horrible army. But she did not relish the walk back. The soldiers' rations would last them a while, but it would be a long, hurried journey. Already her feet were sore and bleeding.

"All right. But before we go, let's gather up some of these scraps. My feet are going to fall off if they don't get some help."

He helped her get together a small bag of material. Then he picked up a pole-ax, the pole of which was broken about midway down, making it almost his size. Teehma dug up the shattered lower half of a sword. Its splintered end looked sharp enough to run anybody through at least once.

"Do you have any idea how to use one of these?" she asked.

"Not one of those," Lucio responded, hefting his own weapon. "But I imagine you use one of these just like you're cutting down a tree. This time, though, the tree might cut back."

She did not smile at his joke. "We'll just have to do the best we can."

"What do you know about the Chasm?" Lucio asked as they started back the way they had come.

"Not much. Before we saw those things, I would have said it didn't exist. My mom believed in it and in Kynell and Zyreio and all that stuff. Father said she was being a silly woman. I always thought he was right."

"What did your mom say about it?"

Teehma fingered the hilt of her broken sword. It was made of dark metal, with some sort of coarse black cloth wrapped around it. She wondered what sort of hand had held it last. "She said that's where people went who had turned their backs on Kynell. People who thought they didn't need him or didn't believe he existed. People like me and my father." She paused. Had her father been a part of that mob?

"You don't believe in Kynell?"

"Why should I?"

"That great big nasty army might be one reason."

"That just proves the Chasm exists, not that Kynell does. Do *you* believe he exists?"

Lucio nodded. "When my father was thrashing my mom and she was thrashing me, I never knew why they were doing it. But I knew it wasn't right. And sometimes I'd feel protected, somehow, even though she was beating the life right out of me. Or at least I knew something was there with me, making the blows sting a little less. I always figured that was Kynell."

Teehma looked at him with interest. He had never talked so much about his parents as he had in the past few days. She thought that she'd been through a lot, but when she heard Lucio's stories, she had to be grateful that her parents had kept their abuse to mere words. Not that verbal poundings were much fun, she reminded herself.

"Well," Lucio continued, brightening a little. "Looks like you might have to start believing in Kynell soon enough. If those soldiers were from the Chasm, it's gonna take something from the Prysm to stop them."

Sedgar, Reyn, and Merto were in sight of Lascombe. They had ridden hard, but if it hadn't been for the Easterners stopping to build siege engines, the army would only have been a few hours behind them. As it was, Merto figured they were about a day and half ahead.

To their relief, they rode toward a city already preparing for battle. The residences outside the walls were evacuated, and a high, slick barrier was being erected less than a quarter of a league out from the permanent fortifications. Behind this new defense a deep trench was being dug, filled with sharpened timbers. The ground in between the temporary wall, which terminated at the tree line on either side, was filled with hunting traps of all shapes and sizes, some just large enough to trap a coney, others made from whole logs, strong enough to trap a dragon. All around the traps, the men knew from experience, were buried large, thin, empty clay jars, positioned on their sides. The turf had been dug up then carefully replaced over the jars. Any man—or better, the wheel of any siege engine—putting his weight on those areas would crash through the thin layer of soil and clay and become immobilized for a time. Finally, large groups of sweaty, tired men were pouring tar in copious amounts over the city's once brilliant white walls. Casing tar was made from a type of tree found throughout Keroul. It dried very smooth, so smooth that it would not afford man, beast, or even grappling hook a sure hold. All in all, it looked to the newcomers as if these were measures meant to immobilize an army, rather than eliminate it.

The preparations were far from complete, and it appeared that only men were working on them. As they rode up to the gate, shouted their names and were let in, they could see why. The women, children, and elderly stood in long lines throughout the streets. Where the lines were going, the evacuees themselves did not know. Even Merto, with his sharp eyes, couldn't tell. But the lines moved forward nevertheless, sometimes crossing each other, sometimes going opposite directions, but always moving. Intriguing though it was, the men did not have time to stop and figure it out.

Marching up to the palace's main entrance, Reyn announced that they were scouts sent from Captain Gair. The guard on duty hastily allowed them in, led them to a sergeant, who turned them over to a lieutenant, who directed them to a captain, who placed them in front of General Chiyo.

Chiyo was encouraged to see them. "Welcome back. Have a seat. You must be exhausted. Captain," he gestured at the man who had brought them in. "Send a man to kitchens. Tell them to have some hot lunch ready for these three." The man saluted smartly and hurried down the hall.

"Now tell me your news."

Reyn, as senior officer, began. "Sir, Obsidian's army has destroyed Windrell. Captain Gair and another officer stayed behind to search out survivors; the Captain sent us in advance to try and stay ahead of the force. As of yesterday, the army was camped about two days out. They had just started constructing siege engines. I would expect them by tomorrow afternoon at the earliest, provided that they, Chasmites though they are, take the proper time to prepare their equipment."

"And the nature of this force?" Reyn and his associates were the first people Chiyo had talked to who had actually seen the enemy. Telenar had tried to prepare them all as best he could, but even his knowledge was limited.

Reyn shifted in his chair, trying to find the right words. "They're not like anything I've ever seen. They don't sleep, don't eat, don't do any other natural things. They behave in a very agitated manner, as if their skin is constantly irritated. They fight among themselves, but the blows they give to one another do no damage. Actually," he paused to consider, "this inability to hurt each other seems to aggravate them even more. Most of them carry weapons, of course. Though they look like standard fare, we were not able to get close enough to inspect them."

"And their leader? Who commands the armies?"

"There doesn't seem to be a commander, sir. At least, not that we saw. Some of them were riding voyoté, some of them were walking, but none of them stuck out as someone in charge. You'd think a wild army like that would disperse, but *someone's* telling them where they should be going. Just can't see who."

"Numbers? What size of force are we dealing with?"

Reyn glanced at Merto, who had a good eye for counting. Merto responded, "It's impossible to tell, sir. It was big. It could outnumber the population of Lascombe twice over, at minimum. Plus, they were hard to pin down, being so agitated; no one moved in ranks or regiments. They look more like one big mob rather than an army."

"No sign of Farlone?" Chiyo had been apprised of the initial reason for their mission, but he asked the question out of protocol. After a report like that, there could be no real hope.

Merto shook his head sadly. He had always had a great deal of respect for Keroul's fighting prince. "No sir. If anybody survived that attack on Windrell, it would be a miracle."

Chiyo bowed his head for a moment then rose, obliging them to do the same. "Thank you, men, for your service. Follow my aide down the hall where they will take down your report. Then get some rest. I don't want to see you out and about until tomorrow morning. Understood?"

All three expressed polite agreement and shuffled down the hall, eager for a warm meal and a soft bed. Chiyo, meanwhile, fell back into his seat with a groan. Tomorrow afternoon? He had to find Telenar and Vancien; he had no confidence that his man-made defenses would hold off the fiends for longer than a few hours. By tomorrow night, Lascombe would be overrun.

CHAPTER FOURTEEN

Trint and Ester were just beginning to settle down with their new family when the call for evacuation went out. Two mornings after Teehma and Lucio's night-time visit, they were awakened with a start. Tertio had been called upon to help with the city's defenses, leaving them with a scared but resolute Alisha. This was certainly not the arrangement they would have chosen. In the days since their arrival, Tertio had been the one to play games with them, read to them, and tuck them into bed. All Alisha had done was speak to them occasionally and fix their meals. Ester figured that her cold behavior was because she still missed her other child, the one who had died, though the woman never said anything about it. Indeed, she rarely spoke about that other child at all, even to her husband.

"Hurry up, children, and make a pack of clothes for yourself. Ester, make sure Trint gets at least three outfits into a bag, including one for cool weather. Then both of you come help me in the kitchen."

Too bewildered to ask questions, they obeyed. When they returned to the kitchen, they found her packing dried and canned goods into a small cart. Without further words of explanation, she ordered Ester to fetch some water and Trint to pack some bedding. By the time Ester returned, the little cart was almost full. After putting the water into canteens, jars, or whatever else she was able to find, Alisha pronounced them ready to go. Together, the three of them trundled out into the chaotic streets as the orbs began to rise.

Trint huddled close to Ester, who had to clutch Alisha's skirts so she didn't get lost. Alisha, meanwhile, gripped the handles of the cart with fierce intensity. After she stopped and asked a guard where to find the nearest evacuation point, Ester finally found the courage to ask what was going on. Alisha's response was not very comforting.

"They didn't tell us much, child. Just that the city's being evacuated and all the men are being summoned to help with defense. I guess all these soldiers hanging around the streets will finally do some good."

Ester's heart sank. They had just found a home and now they were going to lose it? It didn't seem fair, especially now that Lucio and Teehma were gone. Even Tertio, whom they were just beginning to like, had disappeared. Everybody was abandoning them.

Alisha saw the look of distress on her face and instantly regretted her tone. Why was she being so cruel? These were children, not replacements. With a soft exclamation, she wheeled the cart over to the side of the street and pulled them to her. They resisted at first. Her attitude was beginning to strike them as slightly mad.

She tried again, opting for a light grip on their hands rather than the bear hug her impulsive nature was inclined to give.

"I want you to know something," she began, once she was sure she had their attention. "I don't know what's going on and I don't like it any more than you do. Lascombe's never been attacked in my lifetime, nor my mother's, nor her mother's. I don't know why we're being attacked now, or by whom. My mind's a whirl. But when Tertio and I agreed to take you into our home, we wanted to give you not just food and shelter, but a family. We wanted you to consider us as the two grown-ups in the world whom you could always trust. I know I haven't been as open as Tertio, but I intend to take care of you kids. Even though we may not have a building to live in at the moment, you still have a home, okay?" She took a moment to brush away a strand of hair that had fallen into Ester's face. The unexpected movement made the girl jump, but she did not object.

Both children nodded. Then she pulled them into an embrace, hugging them so close that Trint wriggled to get free. This was funny enough to lighten the mood, which gave Ester the courage to ask another question.

"When will we see Tertio again?"

Though Ester could not see her face, she could tell that Alisha struggled to find a good answer. "I don't know, Ester. I hope soon. We'll just have to trust that Kynell will take good care of him."

The time for conference was over. A Sentry approached and asked them brusquely to hurry along to their evacuation point. They obeyed by joining the general throng. They were destined to spend their whole day in the crowd,

110

shifting their aching feet, avoiding sharp elbows, and wondering where and when the line would end. When they were hungry, Alisha would feed them something from her cart and when they were bored, she would tell them a story from her childhood. As the afternoon passed, both children began to enjoy having a mother again.

The line jerked forward for the thousandth time. Ester secured a firm hold on Alisha's and had just grabbed Trint's hand when she heard a familiar voice behind her.

"There you are, you little rat! Thought you could escape, did you?"

Then she heard Trint cry out and felt his hand pulled out of her grasp. Hearing their exclamations, Alisha turned around just in time to see the boy, slung over a man's shoulders, disappear into the crowd.

When Relgaré died in the battle against the Cylini, he left behind not only four children, but a handsome, healthy wife. Quinia still bore herself like a queen. She had not approved of her husband's extensive campaign against the people of the marshes, still less of his ill-fated alliance with Commander Hull. Nor was her grief over Relgaré's death eased by the "converted" Corfe fellow who had taken over the palace, running Sentries here and there, and stealing the ears of two of her sons. On top of this offense, she had not heard from her daughter, who had married an Ulanese prince, for many months, and her other son had disappeared behind Alric's Wall. She was beginning to despise the Ulanese, however friendly their past may have been.

To add to her frustration, the entire city was now being evacuated and she had no clue why. Like the populace at large, she knew that Corfe was intending to fight the man named Amarian, who was claiming to be the Obsidian Advocate. Like the populace at large, she figured the fight was imminent, since soldiers were roaming the streets. And like the populace at large, she was fearful, though she wasn't quite sure what she was fearful of. How she despised being on such equal footing with the populace at large! Relgaren had told his mother nothing the past few days, which had forced her to make her own observations. Observation number one: the garrisons on all the walls had been doubled. Observation number two: the representatives of the Keroulian Square had all been sent home to their constituencies. Observation number three: Relgaren had reverted to chewing his nails, even while sitting in court.

Her attempts to sound him out had been rebuffed. And Lors was no better. Now he was so full of his own self-importance that he had no time for her. So be it. She sighed, running a brush through her long black hair in the light of the morning orbs. Only a few cycles ago, unwelcome gray hairs had started to peek in, but she had managed to pluck them out. Yet the recent stress of her husband's death and her children's absence had caused them to come in greater numbers than could be managed. Oh well. Forty-six cycles was not a bad time to start going gray.

The silence of her two sons troubled her more than she cared to admit. She had always tried to maintain an open relationship with her children: she had refused to farm them out to nannies when they were young, and when they were older, she had insisted on personally educating them in all the social graces, drawing from the considerable insights she had gained as queen. Most remarkably, she was one of those worthy mothers who enjoyed her children's company. They therefore grew to respect and to like her. Then Corfe had come. Before the arrival of that imposter, Relgaren had spoken freely with her about his new duties. Now, he was as silent as a tomb. Perhaps he felt that she would speak against Corfe, in whom he put so much stock? She had so far said nothing on the subject, although her lack of enthusiasm was palpable. On the rare occasions when Corfe was presented to her, she had been courteous and had even gone so far to address him as "Lord Corfe." Of course the man merited no such title, but she couldn't bring herself to label him "Advocate." The whole notion of advocacy was superstitious nonsense, and she refused to take part in it. Kynell and Zyreio did things as they would. They did not need human puppets to do their dirty work for them.

A discreet knock echoed through the room. With a slight wave, she sent her waiting ladies into another chamber and answered the door herself. It was her man, An-Sung, a distant relative of General Chiyo. He had come from the West around the same time as his cousin and had served the House of Anisllyr just as loyally, if not as famously. As captain of the Queen's Guard, he had long assisted Quinia in public transactions. Now their shared dislike of Corfe had given their association a conspiratorial air.

"My queen," he said with a bow. His voice was low and rough, as if he had eaten pebbles for breakfast.

"Yes, come in, An-Sung." With a glance down the hallway, she closed the door and conducted him to a chair, only to have him insist that she sit first. When she had complied, he perched himself on the edge of a low settee.

"Now tell me what in the world is going on," she insisted. "Why are we evacuating?"

An-Sung was a handsome man, as graceful as his fellow countrymen but

112

taller and with softer features. Quinia had long ago admitted to herself that this was the reason she was happy to have him as her captain. That he had used this trait to good effect with women in the past, she also knew, though it did not bother her. She had always been faithful to Relgaré, so jealousy was not an issue, and he had also kept his indiscretions quiet, so as not to embarrass her. An-Sung was not the type to fall in love or allow a romance to interfere with his duties. If anything, his affairs had made him more cynical. Now, as he sat upright before her, she thought they made a fine pair: an attractive skeptic and an aging, worried widow.

"There is an army coming toward us from the east, my lady. The king is attempting to ensure the safety of the women, children, and elderly. I am to escort you away from danger."

"I'm not going anywhere, An-Sung. You know that."

He bowed his head but said nothing.

"And whose army is this? Where does it come from?"

He opened his mouth then shut it, as if reconsidering. "To be honest, my lady, I am not the best person to describe it to you. Perhaps if you will see Patronius Telenar and General Chiyo?"

The name of an old friend, so suddenly dropped, brought a flush to Quinia's cheeks. Chiyo had been a steady support for her house and his absence had caused her great pain. In his last letter to her, Relgaré had said that he had been dissatisfied with his general and so had sent him with a small regiment into the marshes. She had been appalled at his decision but not surprised. General Hull, now known to be Amarian, held almost complete sway over her husband in his final days. She had always assumed that Chiyo perished in the swamps along with his men. Now he was back, with that Patroniite in tow. The priest she could dispense with, but the general might very well restore some common sense to this place.

"I am glad to hear that General Chiyo is still alive. Tell him that I would like to see him at once. He may bring the priest if he must."

"Yes, my lady." He stood to go.

"An-Sung."

"Yes, my lady?"

"No more talk about evacuation. A queen's place is with her people and her children."

"But my lady."

She held up her hand and he said no more.

The balance of power was shifting in Lascombe. The king, with Corfe's support, had given Chiyo backstage control of the evacuation as well as of the defenses. Corfe, of course, would continue to be the liaison to the public, since it was in him that they were all placing their hopes. Fortunately Corfe had no pretensions about conducting a successful defense; when not making morale-boosting appearances to the troops, he spent most of his time closed up in his room, praying for his Prysm army to appear.

As soon as the three scouts from Ulan had left the room, Chiyo had summoned Telenar. When Telenar arrived, the general was pacing up and down, nervously fingering a copy of the Ages.

"You know, all of us throughout the West, as well as here in Keroul, are encouraged to read this. But you, Telenar, seem to have an uncanny knowledge of how to interpret it."

"I try not to do too much interpreting. What's wrong?"

"Everything is wrong. I've just heard from three scouts whom Corfe sent out a few weeks ago. They have returned in advance of the army, which will be here by tomorrow afternoon at the latest."

Telenar felt like he'd been punched. "Tomorrow?"

"If they take the time to build proper siege engines, which we might assume, but should not plan on."

"Tomorrow?" Telenar repeated lamely. It seemed an odd time for the end of the world.

"I'm assuming Vancien has had no success with his efforts?"

"You would be the first to know, I think."

"And has Amarian tried?"

"Sorry?"

Chiyo rubbed his chin as he tried to voice to his unformulated thoughts. "Kynell knows that I'm a soldier, not a theologian. But Amarian has changed so many things already. Why not this, as well?"

Telenar was flustered. He could scarcely admit it to himself, but Amarian's story was not pleasing to him. The man was still so arrogant. It seemed to Telenar that there would be a certain degree of humility in being the Advocate for the wrong side, and Amarian continued to bear himself like a prince. Now it would be Amarian, not Vancien, who might be the key to defeating Zyreio? It was hard to stomach.

As was his habit, he took off his glasses and began to clean them. "I had just assumed."

"We've all assumed, maybe too much. Perhaps we should call both of them in here as soon as possible."

Still processing this new direction, Telenar nodded and was about to embark on his mission when they heard a knock at the door. It was An-Sung.

Chiyo had too much on his mind to offer a polite welcome. "An-Sung? What are you doing here?"

The other man, several inches taller than his cousin, saluted. "I come at the request of the queen-mother. She is pleased to hear of your return and requests your presence as soon as you are able to join her."

"I am sorry, but as you can see, I'm a little occupied. I hope the queen is preparing for her departure?"

"She has chosen to stay in the city. And she requests your presence as soon as possible," he repeated.

Chiyo had dealt with his cousin before and knew it would be quicker to oblige him than ignore him. "Very well. Telenar, get Vancien and his friend and bring them back here."

An-Sung nodded to the priest. "Patronius Telenar. The queen-mother requests your presence, as well."

"Sorry, but I have a task to complete."

Again, An-Sung insisted. "It will only take a moment of your time."

Telenar growled under his breath. What could Quinia possibly want that was so urgent? In some ways, she was too much like her departed husband. And he had to obey her.

They found her waiting patiently, resting on a low settee, dressed in a black mourning gown with her long dark hair pulled up and held tight by a silver wire net. Though no longer the acting queen, she still maintained an aura of dignity and beauty that would put many younger women to shame. And she was obviously happy to see Chiyo. With a broad smile, she rushed up to him and took his dark, scarred hands.

"General! We feared you were dead."

Chiyo bowed low. "My queen. It is an honor to come back to you alive. Allow me to express my condolences for the loss of our great king, your husband." She tipped her head graciously as he continued. "Allow me also to present Patronius en medio Telenar, whom you may remember. His lovely wife N'vonne, whom you have not met, is currently working on our evacuation efforts."

Her nod to Telenar was brusque. "A pleasure to see you again, Patronius. Now, about this evacuation. Isn't it a little extreme? Relgaren has told me nothing."

"My queen, the threat is very dire. I suggest you depart now, while there is time."

She laughed, a high tinny sound that Telenar would not have expected to come from such a dignified lady. "Now, General, you and I both know that I can't go anywhere. Where would I go?"

"My queen, if you knew the nature of this threat."

She cut him off. "That's just it, general. I *don't* know the nature of this threat. What in the Chasm is going on?"

Telenar winced at her wording, a motion she caught out of the corner of her eye. "Why do you react like that, Patronius? Has your order become so sensitive to extreme expressions that a lady cannot vent her frustration in your presence?"

"Oh no, my queen." He bowed low for effect. "It's just that your wording is quite appropriate in this instance."

"Oh? Tell me more."

He glanced over his spectacles at Chiyo before proceeding. "I know that the subject of the gods is not a favorite topic with you, my lady. But in a short time, their actions will become very relevant. Zyreio has formed an army of his own followers that, even now, is less than two days away from Lascombe. You may remember in the Ages that such an army has arisen in times past."

The lady lost some color at his remarks but retained her distant attitude. "Corfe talks of nothing but that nonsense. But surely you know, Patronius, that these so-called followers of Zyreio—really the henchmen of that Amarian fellow—were all killed in the Battle of the Dragon, or whatever it is they're calling it. Either killed or 'converted' somehow."

Telenar swallowed. The queen-mother would certainly not accept what he was about to say. He wished N'vonne were there. She had the gift of diplomacy that he was lacking. "The Ages speak of another type of army, my lady. An army formed from the souls condemned to the Chasm. It is *that* army of which we speak."

"Ha! Superstitious nonsense! General, do you honestly believe this?"

Chiyo was fingering the edge of his tunic; he was about to tread on very painful ground for her. "Pardon me, my queen, for asking a personal question. I only do so because of the urgency of the situation we are in. How long ago did Prince Farlone journey to the Kingdom of Ulan?"

She stopped laughing. "Farlone was due back weeks ago. His Majesty says that he may be performing a tour of the Ulanese hinterlands, which would explain the delay."

Telenar could not hide his incredulity. Had Relgaren really kept this poor lady so much in the dark? And for what purpose? He could not see any, nor did he feel any need to perpetuate a farce. "My lady, three weeks ago, Captain Gair was sent to investigate rumors of a mysterious force attacking the western region of Ulan. The fact that the king has heard nothing from his brother, nor from anybody else in that realm for some time, indicates that the Ulanese are undergoing a great danger. Indeed, our scouts say that they have already succumbed to it."

The words hung in the air for a moment as Quinia absorbed the news. She clasped her hands to stop their shaking, but she could not hide the tremor from her voice. "And Farlone?"

Chiyo interposed. "Farlone is a fighter, ma'am. We both know that. If there is any resistance left in Ulan, he will be involved in it."

Her smile was grim. "He would fight anything to the death. And Dorylen…" Here her composure began to fade. For a few minutes there was silence as she took several short, sharp breaths.

Chiyo looked at the ground. There was nothing he or Telenar could say. It was An-Sung who broke the silence. "My queen, I have told the general and Patronius Telenar that they would be allowed to return to their duties. May I dismiss them?"

As abrupt an interruption as it seemed, his words offered a merciful break to the tense silence. She regained her composure enough to thank them and dismiss them. Chiyo knelt next to her before leaving.

"My queen," he whispered so that only she could hear. "Please leave this city. Extend your life so that you may help others. And although I know you will not listen to a priest, listen to a soldier and an old friend. Put your trust in Kynell. He is the only one who can help us now."

She nodded through her tears. Having made his plea, he kissed her hand and departed. When he looked back through the door, he saw that An-Sung had drawn close and was murmuring something in her ear. Whatever he said, it broke the queen's composure. Chiyo shut the door before her cries could be heard in the hallway.

CHAPTER FIFTEEN

The rain started early that evening. Great sheets of it crashed onto the rooftops of the city, soaking all those attempting to maneuver through the crowded streets. Outside the city walls, some of the poorly maintained houses started leaking. This circumstance would have annoyed their inhabitants, except they had already gone off to help in the defense or else join the long evacuation lines. Only one house was inhabited. It was occupied by a man and a fennel sitting around a candle, eating the cold remains of cooked yemain.

"Bedge sorry to see rain come. No like to fight in the rain. No like rain at all."

Amarian stared at the roof, listening to the barrage. "You never know, it might be helpful. Maybe those Chasmites'll have a hard time keeping their footing."

"Kasim-ites don't scare Bedge. Wet fur does." She shook her coat for emphasis.

Amarian smiled a little before returning to his thoughts. He felt helpless, cooped up in this little shack, waiting for somebody to come get him. At least, that was what he assumed would happen. Ever since Ming had left to evacuate with everybody else, he had sat here, waiting for Vancien or N'vonne or even Telenar to come seek him out. For what purpose, he did not know. He could offer his services in battle, but his presence might cause more harm than good. Maybe his friends had decided that it would be better for him to wait it out here, outside the city walls, the first and most worthy victim of Zyreio's wrath. He had a hard time believing that Vancien would consent to such a plan, but he wouldn't put it past Telenar.

The rain began to fall even harder and a leak developed not too far from their candle. He got up, went to the corner, and pulled out a heavy pack. Inside were the clothes he had worn on the day he defeated Vancien, as well as the smoky gray armor he had had made for the occasion. He glanced at Bedge, who was watching him with interest.

"Sir has new clothes."

"These are not new, Bedge. I committed a great crime in this outfit," he said as he began to strip off his old clothes and don the dark garments. "Now I'll do some good in it. Either way, I don't want to go to battle in rags and this is the only suit of armor I've got. Come over here and pull these buckles for me."

She obliged and after several labored minutes, he was ready.

"Sir going to sleep in metal shirt?"

"Sir's not going to get much sleep tonight. And neither are you. Who knows when these fiends are coming?"

Bedge sniffed the air. "Somebody's coming."

Amarian had just drawn his sword when Telenar appeared at the door.

"So you've heard?" were the first words out of the priest's mouth.

"Heard what?"

Telenar shook the rain off his cloak carefully, so as not to put out the candle. "Scouts came in this afternoon. The army will be here tomorrow at the latest. The only reason they're not here now is that they've stopped to build siege engines."

Amarian nodded. Even the most immortal of enemies would have to get past Lascombe's walls somehow. "Is the evacuation almost complete?"

Telenar tried to wipe his glasses off on his shirt, which was already damp. Bedge kindly offered her fur, which was no help at all. "I'd say about sixty-five percent. It will continue through the night. There are only twelve evacuation points scattered throughout the city, many of them through people's cellars, leading into the network of tunnels below. The women and children will be able to hide out there if the city is sacked. From what I heard about Ulan, if the enemy is victorious, they won't stay for long. There are cities in the West they'll want to subdue." He had stepped away from the candlelight, so that only his silhouette was visible.

"So what now?"

Telenar was quiet for a moment, which annoyed Amarian. All of this work to be done, and the priest was standing in the dark, thinking. He didn't know that Telenar was choosing his words carefully, as well as forcing his mind to make a transition it did not want to make. Finally, he stepped back into the light.

"Chiyo sent me to fetch you. Both he and Vancien want to speak with you. And I need to ask your forgiveness."

"My forgiveness? For what?"

"You know for what. I have had no love for you, not when you were my enemy and even less when you were my ally. I haven't had any patience for you either. Your easy manner with Vancien tells me that you have forgotten all about murdering him."

Amarian set his teeth. The priest was lousy at apologies.

"Sorry. That was too far. And that's between you and Kynell. The point is, I have not welcomed you as a brother or a son, which I should have done. I am a priest, after all, and all followers of the Prysm should be brothers or sons to me. And as Vancien's brother, I should have welcomed you all the more. Not to mention the fact that Kynell gave you such a great salvation—"

"Got it. You should have been more friendly."

"I should have loved you as Kynell loves you. Or at least as Vancien does. And I didn't. So I'm asking for your forgiveness."

Amarian did not say anything at first. Telenar's words were a comfort to him, a much-needed encouragement from an unexpected source. To show his gratitude and lighten the mood, he buckled on his sword belt and gave Bedge a pat on the head. "I've never granted forgiveness before. You shall be the first." He nodded slightly in Telenar's direction. "There. It's done. Now we should go."

"First, put on your cloak. And for goodness' sake, don't show your face, especially in that dreadful outfit. Whoever recognizes you will think that Obsidian's already here."

They plunged into the rain and were soon battling the crowds in the city streets. The evacuation lines had thinned a little. By morning, they would be almost gone. Amarian was careful to keep his hood well over his eyes, a natural enough task in the deluge, but he was not the one to attract attention. He could hear whispered exclamations as Bedge passed. A fennel kit was a rare sight in Lascombe and the bystanders pointed to her as one bright spot of interest in an otherwise anxious and depressing day.

They were soon inside the palace, where Bedge shook off the rain. Amarian, however, kept his hood lowered until they were in Chiyo's chambers and the soldiers with whom the general was conferring had been dismissed. Only then did he look up from the ground to see Vancien, Telenar, and Chiyo watching him.

"What? Should I not have worn the outfit? It was all I had."

Vancien responded with a big smile and slap on the shoulder. "I've seen you looking more cheerful, I'll give you that. Nice armor."

Amarian allowed himself a smile, as well. "You should know. It deflected your blade well enough."

"Hopefully my blade's improved since then."

"All right," Telenar cut in. "We need to discuss something."

"Many things, no doubt," Amarian responded. "Chiyo, I see you've been working on some counter siege efforts. Your ballistae are misplaced, though, and will be less effective than the trebuchets and catapults, anyway. Large rocks might pin them down, at least. A big ballista bolt will only make them angry."

Chiyo was nodding. "You've got a point, Dark One. But with your help, we might be able to do more than pin them down."

Amarian, whose spirits had been buoyed by Telenar's earlier comments, bent over the city plans Chiyo had spread out on a large table. "Hmm, perhaps. What did you have in mind?"

"We were thinking you could summon our allies for us."

The statement took him off guard. "And which allies are those? Any support we have from the West is already here and I don't think the Cylini are sending any more."

"I meant those Kynell has provided for us. It's time you and Vancien sought his help together."

Amarian gave a nervous laugh. "I think the stress is getting to you, General. Vancien is the one Kynell will listen to."

Telenar had been watching Vancien while Chiyo and Amarian spoke. Vancien had at first started, then flushed, then tried unsuccessfully to hide his resentment. Telenar could sympathize. He, too, resented Chiyo's idea.

Now all three of them were looking at the Prysm Advocate. "Did you come up with this?" Amarian asked first.

Vancien shook his head. "I probably should have, but no, I didn't. This is the first I've heard of it."

"And? What do you think?"

Vancien thought for a moment, looking first at the curtains, then at the map, and then squarely at Amarian. "I don't like it. It's an insult. I've given my life to him and now he won't hear my prayers? Why? Why would he listen to you and not me?"

Amarian lowered his head. His own unworthiness washed over him. "I don't know. I wouldn't deserve it if he did."

Vancien, too, dropped his gaze. "That's just it. Neither one of us deserve it, not really. But maybe with the both of us asking in his name, he'll grant our request."

There was nothing else to say. Telenar and Chiyo departed, leaving the brothers to their thoughts and their prayers.

———————

Torches lit up the wet streets as crowds of terrified people shuffled past doorways that were closed and locked. N'vonne was standing near the entrance of a blacksmith's shop, directing people inside and down into the cellar, where another woman pointed them down a wide tunnel lined with small, burning bundles of tar-soaked hay. The evacuees, having been told nothing, asked questions of every person they could, but the only response they received were kind reminders to keep following directions. N'vonne hated to see the fear of the unknown in their faces, but it was for the best. If all the helpers (who themselves were not informed of the whole situation) stopped to answer questions, no one would make it to safety before the attack came.

Not long before twilight, she was accosted by a distraught woman and girl dragging a cart behind them. The woman was repeating the same thing over and over again, pointing frantically back into the street. The girl said nothing; she appeared stunned. It took some moments before N'vonne could make any sense of what was wrong.

"Please! He took my boy! It was Gorvy, she says! I didn't see him, but she heard him. We know it must be Gorvy!"

Determined not to make the crowd more edgy than it already was, N'vonne pulled the woman aside. "Shh. You must calm down. Who took your boy? Who's Gorvy?"

The woman took several deep breaths. "I didn't ever see him, but Ester here says she heard a familiar voice. Gorvy's voice. He's the man who used to keep the children. Then she heard Trint cry out and I looked just in time to see him over a man's shoulders. Then he was gone. We tried to follow, but the streets are so crowded. We've been searching for hours. Can't you send the guards?"

N'vonne doubted if any guards could be spared, but she assured the woman that she would see what she could do. "Where did you see him last?

How old is your boy? What does he look like? Can the girl describe what the man looked like?"

Ester quickly found her tongue, a little pleased that the lady did not notice her handicap. "My friends told me that he's tall, with dark, greasy hair. He wears a smelly leather vest with leather moccasins. No boots, though. I think he also has a mustache."

"Do you have any idea where he lives?"

The girl shook her head. "Gorvy lives all over the place. He steals for a living, you see, and he used to make us steal for him. We never knew where he lived."

N'vonne looked again at the woman. "And this boy? He's your son?"

The woman nodded her head firmly. "He is now. And I've got to find him."

N'vonne could understand that sentiment. Pulling aside the woman who had been helping her, she told her that she would be back as soon as she could. Then she followed them into the street. On the way, she snagged a Sentry to help them search. It was just a Mholi, his eyes glazing over as he kept watch over the lines in the street, but he would strike the fear of Kynell into that villain Gorvy, if they could find him.

The Sentry listened as Ester described the man they were pursuing, then he jogged ahead, his ears fanned wide to listen for a cry of distress over the other noises. Ester tried to describe to them where the old 'fort' was located, but her clues were difficult to put together: a well twenty paces left of the door, a noisy tavern forty-five paces straight ahead, a continuous wall running along to the right. This last was the best clue, since it told them that it was dug into the city wall. So they started searching that perimeter, in the hopes that Gorvy would take Trint back to his original place of captivity. Soon they were outside the old fort, now inhabited by other unfortunate children (the enterprising man had been quick to fill the shoes of his lost four). These, upon questioning, had not seen Gorvy recently. Both N'vonne and Alisha were horrified. Despite the children's natural fear of Sentries, the women sent them packing with the Mholi with the orders that he attach them to a willing family for the time being. Then they continued their search, shouting out Trint's name until their throats were hoarse and praying that they could somehow find him in the wet and sprawling city.

Trint had never been so scared in his life. He screamed and cried and kicked until Gorvy tossed him to the ground, clamped his hand over his mouth, and threatened a good lashing if he did not stop. His face was so close that Trint got a whiff of his breath, which smelled like rotten fish. Then Gorvy jerked him to his feet and led him through the crowds.

"Can't go back there," he was muttering to himself. "She'll remember how to get there. She's blind, but she's not stupid. Gotta go to Point Four."

Point Four, as Trint soon found out, was the attic of a fabric shop, accessible from the street by thin, rickety stairs. Gorvy marched them up these. When he reached the top, he produced a jumble of keys. Holding Trint with one hand and juggling the keys with the other, he located the one he wanted. The door unlocked with an ominous clank, swinging open to reveal the barest of rooms, lit by one small window high up in the ceiling and furnished with a solitary chain attached to the wall.

"I know you're good at getting in and out of tight places," Gorvy said as he attached Trint's thin wrist to one end of the chain, "But I figure this'll keep you. The lady downstairs is deaf. She can't hear anybody screaming. So there's no sense wearing yourself out over that. Just sit tight for now. I'll be back in a bit to deal with your mutiny."

Trint did not know what mutiny meant, but the chain spoke loud enough for him to understand. He sat mutely as Gorvy cuffed his ear before going outside, locking the door as he left. After the footsteps of his kidnapper faded, he began to cry.

The evening turned into night, which turned into eternity as Trint watched the door with dread. When would he come back? Would he bring something to eat? To drink? Terrified as he was of Gorvy's presence, the boy realized that he was his only link to food. He was therefore both scared and relieved when Gorvy arrived long after nightfall. After lighting a candle and setting it on the floor, he tossed him a dried meatstick and a canteen of water.

"Here. Take this. Not that you deserve it, you little traitor."

Trint ate, but his appetite left him when he noticed Gorvy unwinding a thick knotted rope that was looped around his shoulder.

"W-what's that for?" he stuttered.

"It's to show you what the punishment is for traitors 'round here. And I plan on making it a lesson you won't soon forget."

Trint dropped his food and started to sob, drawing himself back against the wall as much as he could. Gorvy took a step forward then stopped, his attention drawn towards something to the boy's right.

"How did you get here?" he snarled.

Trint looked up to see a bow-legged, sturdy man, completely out of place, looking placidly around him. Though he would swear he had never seen the man before, he knew exactly who he was.

"Daddy!"

When the man's gaze fell on the boy, his expression lit up. "Trint? Is that you? My, how you've grown!" He crouched to take him in his arms, then noticed the chain.

"What's this?"

He looked up at Gorvy, who, in his astonishment, still had his arm raised. "Who are you? And what are you doing with that rope?"

Gorvy attempted to stand his ground. "I don't know who you think you are," he stuttered, "but you've interrupted something. If you don't mind stepping outside, I've got to teach this boy a lesson."

The man stood, placing himself in front of Trint. "I do mind. Now tell me what you were doing with my son."

Gorvy raised his eyebrows, trying not to appear intimidated but already planning his escape. "Son? So you really are his old man? Trint, you never told me," he wheedled, edging his way toward the door. The man noticed the movement and grabbed him by the collar.

"Not before you unlock him," he growled.

Faced with the threat of direct force, Gorvy obeyed and soon found himself locked up with the same chain. Then the man, with a protective arm around Trint, shut the door on him, although not before kindly promising to send a guard up his way.

CHAPTER SIXTEEN

The three women were exhausted. Poor Ester was almost incoherent with grief and worry. She kept whimpering to herself, "It's because I can't see. If only I could have seen where he went." N'vonne and Alisha had tried to comfort her several times on that score, but she would not listen and soon, they were too tired to try.

Nightfall had not deterred their efforts, but as the hours dragged by, their despair of finding Trint became acute.

They had stopped to rest in an alley. Ester had become very still in her grief, while Alisha was doubled over, rocking back and forth.

"How could I let him go?" She muttered. "I have lost two sons. I cannot be trusted with sons. I have lost them both."

She was repeating this refrain over and over, when Ester suddenly raised her hand.

"Shh! Alisha, do you hear that?"

She jumped to her feet and ran down the alleyway, turning left, then right, not caring whether the two women were keeping up with her. When they caught her, she had stopped on another quiet street (so many of the side streets were deserted now), and was listening intently.

"It's coming closer." she whispered, her voice quivering with excitement.

The words had just escaped her mouth when a man rounded the corner with a small boy perched on his shoulders. They were both singing.

"Trint!" Alisha cried, startling both the boy and the man.

Trint waved as they rushed up to him. The man, meanwhile, recoiled as Alisha started pummeling him with her fists.

"Let him go, you monster! Drop him this instant or you'll have me to deal with!"

But Ester tilted her head to where she thought Trint would be. "Trint, are you okay? Who are you with? He doesn't sound like Gorvy."

At the sound of her question, Alisha stopped her attack, stepped back, and studied her young charge. It certainly did not look as if he was being kidnapped.

Trint was beaming from ear to ear. "He's my daddy."

Ester frowned. "Trint, your father has been dead for almost four cycles."

Trint shrugged, clamored down off of his father's shoulders, and allowed Alisha to swallow him in a hug. "Still," he responded, his voice muffled by Alisha's dress, "he's my daddy."

N'vonne had watched the scene first with relief, then delight, then with amazement. She alone of all of them could suspect what had actually happened. She approached the man cautiously, as if approaching a cornered animal.

"Sir, are you this boy's father?"

The man, a picture of health and energy, nodded enthusiastically. "It's been a while since I've seen him but, oh, I'd know that boy anywhere. My name's Wake."

"Okay, Wake. How did you find Trint?"

The man scratched his head before stooping to pick up his son again. "Hard to say. I was with Kynell and some others, then suddenly I was in this room. Dingy place. Nothing Kynell would have done. There was a man." His face darkened at the memory. "He was about to hurt my boy. I stopped him, of course, chained him up. Then Trint and I decided to go for a walk, didn't we, little guy?"

Alisha and Ester had started listening to their conversation as N'vonne continued. "And do you know why you're here? I mean, pulled out of Kynell's presence?"

"Don't know if I'd say 'pulled,' ma'am. I was happy to go, especially when I figured out where I was. Beyond saving my boy from that scoundrel, I imagine I'm here to help fight Obsidian. It's about that time, isn't it?"

N'vonne could not hold back tears, nor could she refrain herself from embracing this cheerful stranger. "It finally worked!" she exclaimed. "Vancien did it!"

She blubbered for a few seconds along similar lines as Wake politely returned her embrace, then asked the way to the palace. He was not familiar with this neighborhood, he explained.

N'vonne pulled herself together and told him to follow her. Trint, meanwhile, had latched onto his father's hand. Ester had grabbed Trint's other hand and Alisha followed them all like a mother hen.

They arrived on a main street completely changed. Anxious silence had been replaced by joyful shouts and tearful greetings. Everywhere they looked, loved ones were hailed, children scooped up, and women swept off their feet in long, intense embraces. It was as if, on the eve of invasion, the people of Lascombe had decided to host a family reunion. For Trint, the change served as a confirmation of the joy he was already feeling. Alisha and Ester, however, were mystified. Mystified, that is, until Alisha saw her parents talking with a dear, departed friend. And with them stood a young man whose appearance stopped her in her tracks. At first she said nothing, but it was obvious that she was torn between running to her loved ones and staying with Trint. She wavered until Wake assured her that he would watch his son as well as Ester. After making hasty arrangements to meet up later, she ran to join them. Then Wake wandered off with the children, leaving N'vonne alone, trying not to watch the crowd for the one man she wanted most to see: the man she had not seen since that fatal accident had deprived Vancien of his father.

She found him standing in front of a seed shop, looking in the window and pointing out items to the woman next to him. She was short, with a round face and expressive eyes. The way she cocked her head was so familiar that N'vonne could not restrain her cry, the sound of which made them both turn around. When they saw her, both their faces lit up in recognition and before she knew it, she was in Hull's arms, sobbing, as Vancien and Amarian's mother stroked her hair.

"It's all right," the woman soothed. "See? It all turns out all right."

Feeling a little awkward about hugging Hull with his wife watching on, N'vonne stepped back with a sniffle.

"I can't believe you're here. I mean, you—you're both here," she stuttered. Hull's kind blue eyes were the same as they'd always been, only more intense.

"N'vonne," he began, although he had to stop as she regained her composure. "N'vonne, I want you to meet Chera, Vancien's mother."

Chera's smile was warm, without the slightest hint of jealousy. "So you are N'vonne! I've heard so many things about you. You were the one who took care of Hull after I left and then, when he joined me, you took care of Vancien. How can I ever thank you? Vancien needed a mother so badly."

With that comment, she wrapped N'vonne in an enthusiastic hug, broken only when Hull politely interceded and asked to be shown to their children. "I've never been in such a big city," he added. "Will we be able to see Amarian and Vancien soon?"

N'vonne nodded eagerly and hurried them through the streets, glancing back at them again and again, trying to assure herself that they would not disappear as suddenly as they had come.

Vancien and Amarian, meanwhile, continued to pray in Chiyo's room. The candles had burnt out and the chamber's thick walls prevented almost all outside noise from entering. Sometimes they would take turns, each asking Kynell for mercy, for protection of their loved ones, and always for the return of his faithful. Sometimes they would pray in silence, each opening his heart to the Prysm god. Sometimes they would be on their knees, sometimes pacing around the room, occasionally with their eyes open and often with their eyes shut. Amarian, who had so recently felt what it was to fear Kynell through the Ealatrophe's talons, prayed as humbly as he could manage, submitting everything to his will. If the god wanted Rhyvelad destroyed, well, who was a converted Advocate of Obsidian to stop it? Vancien approached the god boldly, relying not on his past service but on his assurance that the Prysm god was an accessible deity, one who forgave wrongs and listened to human petitions.

Amarian was just considering lighting another candle when they heard a voice coming down the hallway. It was indistinct, though they could tell it stopped right outside their door. It continued muttering to itself as the door opened, allowing light from the corridor to spill in and cast its form in silhouette.

"Now, he told me I could find them here," the voice grumbled, "but blast it, it's so dark! Is the treasury so depleted that they can't afford candles?"

The voice, now recognizable, brought back a flood of memories for both of them. Memories of opening packages sent from far away, of breach harvest and the festivals that went along with it, and of a generous-hearted uncle whom as children they loved to see.

"Uncle Naffinar?" Amarian asked hesitantly.

"Ah, so somebody is in here! Amarian, be a good boy and light a candle."

Amarian did as he was told. Soon the room was lit again and the brothers were reunited with their beloved uncle—one who, not two cycles before, had been slain before Vancien's very eyes by Amarian's orders.

Vancien could not contain his excitement over Naffinar's sudden presence, as well as what that presence meant for Rhyvelad. He would slap Naffinar on the shoulder once or twice, then race to the hallway to see who else was there, then return to pound Naffinar's shoulder once more. Amarian held back and fiddled with a candle.

"Amarian, lad!" Naffinar exclaimed as soon as he could get a word in between Vancien's exclamations. "Come here and give your uncle a proper greeting. It's been a while since I've seen you. You've grown into quite a man!"

Amarian pulled himself up to his full height, emphasizing the already considerable difference between his stature and his short uncles'.

"Uncle," Amarian began, "I cannot forget how it was that you left us so abruptly. Were it not for my actions, you would still be with us. I owe you an apology, although I understand if you don't accept it."

Naffinar was so silent that Vancien feared that Amarian would not be offered the grace he had requested. He should have known better. Naffinar's time in Kynell's presence had improved him, not impoverished him. He gestured for Amarian to come stand before him, placing his hand on Amarian's armored chest.

"Amarian, how could I, who have been forgiven so much, not forgive you for something you did before you even knew Kynell? Perish the thought. But remember it!" He could restrain his smile no longer. "By Ruponi, it's good to see you!"

The name sent Vancien's head spinning. "Ruponi! I bet he's here in the palace!" He ran to the open door. "The Ages say that *all* the dead of the past ten thousand score will. . ." his voice trailed off as he stared down the corridor.

"What is it, Vance?" Amarian called, following him to the door. He, too, stopped as if he'd seen a ghost. Naffinar, muttering again, poked his head out behind them.

"Ah, Hull and Chera! And N'vonne! Come on in! The boys'll be happy to see you."

The boys were happy to see them—so happy that they stood mute. Vancien, who had never seen his mother, stared at her as if she were a portrait. Amarian felt tears well up in his eyes. The last time he had seen his father was the day he had left to serve Obsidian.

No one but Naffinar spoke until Hull, Chera, and N'vonne were in the room. An unknowing onlooker might have thought the two brothers were facing an enemy, so hastily did they back away from the visitors. For Amarian, this was not far from the truth. He had departed from everything his father had taught him, used the name of Hull for the purpose of evil, and had killed Hull's child with his own hand. His father had every right to judge him, and his mother too.

To forestall the inevitable, he seized on the one good thing he had tried to do. "I wanted to take care of Vance after I left," he mumbled, not sure how to begin, "but Zyreio would not let me. And I couldn't fight him. He was too strong."

But Hull did not speak at all. Instead, he pulled him so close that Amarian became a frightened boy again, crying because he had seen something scary next to the fireplace.

"I'm proud of you, 'Ian," he whispered. "You tried to protect your brother the only way you knew how. You must have been terrified. I'm so incredibly proud of you." He repeated that last phrase over and over, until he knew without a doubt that his son heard it and believed it.

Happy reunions were taking place throughout the city as lost loved ones from all over Rhyvelad were called to muster at Lascombe. The city swelled with the increased numbers, but no one noticed or cared. Few were the individuals who did not encounter a spouse, parent, child, cousin, grandparent, or friend who had chosen to follow Kynell, if not always in life, at least in death. The old city saw more tears of joy that night than it ever had of sorrow. But Lascombe could not forget the cause of its current happiness; the orbs would soon rise and with them would come Obsidian's army.

Telenar and Chiyo had enjoyed their share of delightful reunions. Chiyo had been delighted to see his old friend, Hunoi, whom he had promptly assigned to the south-east gate. Yet Telenar was happiest when N'vonne made it back to his side. When he met Hull along with the others, he tried to be as amiable as possible. N'vonne had been open about her feelings for Hull and at the time, Telenar had not felt much jealousy over a man who was dead. Now he was intimidated at the tall, muscular figure who glowed with life. Nor did he feel more at ease when Hull pulled him aside for a quiet conference.

"Telenar," he whispered, "may I have a quick word with you? I know we have much to do."

"That's an understatement," Telenar huffed. "The great hall is filled with faithful monarchs and generals of the past; all of them anxious to have a role in tomorrow's battle. Did you know how many faithful members of the Square there were in the past ten thousand score? And how many of them

132

have diplomatic leadership skills but do not know how to hold a sword? Still, the good news is that Kynell seems to have taken care of the language barrier for the ones risen among the Cylini."

He was prattling, he knew, and he kicked himself for it. But Hull was undeterred. "Yes, my friend, we will have to face many challenges very soon. But first," he lowered his voice even further. "I want to tell you how much I admire your courage."

"Courage?"

"You had the boldness, Telenar pa Saauli, to tell the Patroniite leadership the truth at great risk to yourself. Then you had the patience to wait for Vancien, instead of trying to make it work with a pretender or giving up all together. And if that were not enough, you had the audacity to court one of the most beautiful women in Rhyvelad."

Telenar allowed his eyes to drift to N'vonne, who was chatting with Vancien and Chera. She caught his eye and smiled.

"Kynell knows *I* did not have the guts to seek her hand," Hull continued, "even after Chera had passed on and I felt free to marry again. You are a bold soul, you are," he concluded, slapping him on the back. "It will be a pleasure to fight next to you."

Telenar's response was forestalled by Chiyo, who was rapping on a table for attention. Not a man to be distracted from duty for sentimental reasons, he had taken it upon himself to call the defenders to order. Everyone in the small chamber gave him their respectful attention.

"I am as happy to see our loved ones as anyone," he began. "We must thank Kynell for his timely provision." They murmured assent as he continued. "But the time for action is just beginning. It appears to me that the first order of business is to divide our resources. Risen Ones," he bowed to Hull, Chera, and Naffinar, "allow me to suggest that your women facilitate our evacuation efforts. If, Kynell forbid, we should not triumph above ground, your women will be some protection for our precious ones in the evacuation tunnels. Meanwhile, all of the remaining Risen Ones should gather in either the Stoa or the Royal Courtyard under the main tower of the eastern wall, there to await orders. Hull and Naffinar, I would appreciate it if you would take these orders to the men and women waiting in the Great Hall. I am sure they understand that, since I've been appointed to my post by the king and, I hope, the Advocates," he tilted his head to Vancien and Amarian, "I intend to retain my command over the situation for the time being."

With these orders distributed, the men and women said their goodbyes.

For Hull and Chera, it was the farewell of a moment. Whatever happened, they would be reunited in Kynell before too long. But for N'vonne and Telenar, as well as for Chera and her sons, it was a painful parting.

"My precious boys," Chera sighed, holding both of them close. "I'm so proud of both of you. Vancien, I missed so much. And Amarian," She put a hand on his cheek. "What a strong man you've become. I know you'll fight well. Kynell is so kind." At this point, she could go no further without crying. They, too, were fighting back tears and only drew back when Hull gently pulled her away.

N'vonne and Telenar had withdrawn to a quiet corner where he kissed her on the forehead, the cheek, the mouth, and then the forehead again. "You have to stay safe," he whispered, "I trust Kynell, but if I lost you—"

She nodded, her heart too full to speak. Though she could not have expected it, her recent reunion with Hull only made her love her scholarly, impetuous husband even more. Running her fingers through his graying hair, she murmured how much she loved him and promised him that she would stay as safe as she could.

Then it was time to go. Hull and Naffinar departed to the Great Hall, while N'vonne and Chera set off for the difficult task of rounding up the celebrating evacuees. Chiyo and Telenar went to explain things to the king and find Corfe. Vancien and Amarian left with their father, following him like two shadows.

When the four men arrived at the Hall, it was like entering a historical costume ball. If Vancien, who had a great love of history, had had the time, he would have sat and interviewed each person he saw. He would have taken careful note of their differing accents, their costumes, their political philosophies, even their physiognomy. But although time moved no faster on this night than on any other, every moment of it could mean a life saved or lost, a battle won or surrendered.

Hull hurried to the dais where he jumped onto a chair to command attention. "Lords and ladies!" he called over the din, repeating the summons until the room was almost quiet. "Lords and ladies," he said again, "my name is Hull. I am the father of the two Advocates who have summoned you here. And I come now under the orders of General Chiyo, the commanding officer of this operation. Please listen to my orders and obey. Ladies, your help is needed at the several evacuation points throughout the city. The evacuation effort is under the command of Lady N'vonne. When I have finished, please make your way down to the southern end of the hall, where she will meet you and take you to those points. Should those of us guarding the city fail in our efforts, you will be called upon to defend the women, children, and elderly of Lascombe. Generals and monarchs, as well as anyone else who believes they can contribute significantly to overseeing the city's defense, please stay here in the Hall. General Chiyo will be in to confer with you. For the rest, please report to either the Stoa at the Square or the Royal Courtyard under the main eastern tower. Those of you unfamiliar with the city of Lascombe will find several natives ready to assist you, I'm sure. As you go, if you see any of more of us Risen Ones, pass along these instructions. Thank you."

The hall was silent as he spoke, breaking into polite murmurings only when he stepped down from the chair. It was a surprise to Vancien and Amarian, though not to Hull, that no one questioned the orders. Instead, all dispersed as they had been told, with just a few questions for clarification. When the brothers expressed their amazement to their father, he smiled with satisfaction.

"What you are seeing, boys, is the work of Kynell. These people have been cleansed from the insatiable pride that Zyreio brought into this world. They no longer have a desire to aggrandize themselves. They only want to help where they are needed."

A few minutes later, Chiyo had arrived. When he entered, Hull, his sons, and Naffinar allowed him to claim a place of prominence on the dais, though as he did so, he was approached by a stout little man with a full beard and flushed cheeks. He offered Chiyo a short bow then approached without waiting for an invitation. When he spoke, it was quiet enough that only Chiyo and those immediately around him could hear.

"Am I right in believing that you are General Chiyo?"

"You are right," Chiyo responded, wondering who this little man was. "But I don't yet have the pleasure of knowing your name."

The man bowed low. "Ruponi pa Kellehern, at your service. I have some familiarity with this city and its defenses."

The sudden appearance of Ruponi the Great, the most celebrated Keroulian ruler of the past ten thousand score, gave Chiyo pause. He bowed, too, as deeply and humbly as he could.

"Your Majesty, it is my privilege to serve *you*. If you wish, the city is yours to command."

The man shook his head, as if the offer were the furthest thing from his mind. "No, no. Please, you are clearly the man Kynell has placed here. Far be it from me to challenge you. My desire is to know what has happened to the king? Why is he not here speaking with us? Fighting with us?"

"It grieves me to say it, but King Relgaren has taken a great interest in the false Advocate, Corfe. His attention to Corfe has made him less aware of immediate happenings. I believe that currently he is enjoying a reunion with his father, Relgaré."

Ruponi's face grew red. "He is meeting with his father while we are here?"

"Yes, but it has been a strange night."

"General Chiyo, I must excuse myself. I will be back."

"Of course, but remember he's very young."

Another look at Ruponi's face indicated that youth was no justification. Before Chiyo could object further, he was off.

CHAPTER SEVENTEEN

Not long before the appearances, Corfe had been having a late, private dinner with the king and Lors when they were joined by the queen mother. She burst into the room most unexpectedly, catching all three men off guard and causing Relgaren's quick temper to flare.

"Mother, why are you still in the city? Why haven't you evacuated?"

Quinia swished into the room, her full black gown rustling against every piece of furniture it encountered. "I'll ask the questions around here, young man," she shot back. Her tone, so familiar a reminder of his childhood, made him resume his seat and his silence. Lors followed his brother's lead. Corfe watched the scene with interest until she rounded on him.

"You, Corfe. This is going to be a private family meeting. Please leave."

Corfe looked at Relgaren, but did not move.

"Lord Corfe stays," the king interceded. "We've received word that the armies of Obsidian will be here tomorrow. There is much to discuss with him."

"Discuss?" Quinia retorted. "Discuss? Since when have you been interested in discussing anything? Do you know what I heard today from near strangers? That both Farlone and Dorylen may be dead, or have been dead, possibly for weeks! Did I hear that from my son? Oh no. The king was too busy *discussing* things with his pet here to let his mother know about this loss of her—" At this point, her fury began to melt into grief; she could not prevent the tears from stopping her tirade.

Relgaren sprang to his feet, put an arm around her shoulders, and led her to a chair. Corfe, who had no relationship with his own parents, had once persuaded him that his accession to the throne placed him at a distance from his mother. But her outburst gave him a pang of guilt.

"I am sorry, mother. We thought it would be best not to tell you until we knew for sure."

"And when would that have been?" she asked, trying to control her shaking. "When their bodies are recovered months from now? The whole city appears to have known of this before me."

Lors narrowed his eyes. The expression was meant to convey suspicion. Instead, it highlighted his freckles, making him look even younger than his few cycles. "Who told you about this, anyway?"

She stood firm. "It is none of your business, young man. You should have. But you did not."

Relgaren held up his hand in gentle reproof. "It was my doing, mother. I chose not to tell you, and Lors followed my wish. Besides, we don't know anything for certain yet. We may be grieving prematurely."

"All the same," Lors said, "I bet it was Chiyo and Telenar. They've had it in for Corfe since their arrival. Now they've managed to stir up more trouble."

Relgaren shot his brother an angry look while Corfe tried to hide his amusement at the boy's immature loyalty.

"Chiyo and Telenar are the reason we're this far along in our defense," Relgaren replied. "If not for them, we might have been taken even more off guard."

Lors shrugged. Corfe was about to suggest that they convene with the general and the Patroniite about tomorrow's battle when all eyes in the room abruptly turned to him, or rather, to the curtains just behind him. He paused, looked behind him, and felt his stomach lurch.

There stood Relgaré, one-time patriarch of the House of Anisllyr. He was humming a child's tune and looking not at all surprised by his sudden appearance. For a king, his clothes were simple. He wore no crown, no blue sash, only a simple linen tunic and breeches. He had a sort of traveling pouch slung around his shoulder and his feet were bare.

Relgaren spoke first. "Father?"

Relgaré gazed at his eldest. Then recognition dawned; he gave a great smile and opened his arms wide. "Children! Quinia! It's good to see you! And Corfe, well, you've certainly changed since we last spoke. Or rather, *I* last spoke." He chortled, amused at his own joke.

The family was too shocked to respond in kind to his warm greeting.

Quinia approached him very slowly, touching her hand against his clothes as if to make sure they would not fade between her fingertips.

"Relgaré?" she whispered, almost to herself. "But you're dead."

He nodded. "Well, sort of."

She was shaking her head. "This is impossible. I must be dreaming. Relgaren, tell me I am dreaming."

But Relgaren was just as astounded as she was. He had collapsed in a chair and was regarding his father as one would regard a stuffed animal come to life.

Corfe, who alone had been expecting Kynell's hand to move so dramatically, dropped to his knees. "Your Majesty," he said to the ground. "Welcome back to Rhyvelad."

Relgaré pulled him to his feet. "Now, now, none of that, young Corfe. I'm no more a 'Your Majesty' than you are an Advocate."

His words, though meant as a reassurance, struck Corfe like a blow. "What did you say?"

Embarrassed, Relgaré looked around for help but found none. "Well, things have changed, you know. Up with Kynell. I'm no more a king there than you would be an Advocate down here. The very thought!"

Corfe took a step back and was about to protest when he considered the source. Relgaré, who had been quite dead just a few moments ago, had been raised through Kynell's power. Relgaré had been *with* Kynell. Even if he had died before Corfe's conversion, he would certainly know who was the god's chosen and who was not. Suddenly, his ears started burning and he felt that sickening knot in his stomach start to turn. Not trusting himself to speak, he turned on his heel and left the room.

Relgaré watched him go. "Poor fellow. He looks upset."

Lors, too, had turned pale. When Corfe left, he wavered between following him out and remaining with his father. But old loyalties overcame new ones; he stayed with Relgaren and Quinia.

Quinia remained very near her husband, studying him. Corfe's sudden exit did not trouble her. She could care less about the Advocacy. "Why are you here?" she repeated, still sounding as if she were talking to herself.

"To help fight Obsidian's army, of course. But Kynell was generous enough to let me see my family first."

"You believe all that?"

He looked at her as if she had lost her mind. "Of course! I believe that the ground and sky exist, don't I?" He paused to give her a probing look.

"Quinia, I know you've been skeptical in the past, but surely you can't doubt now. Look around you! Our children are preparing for a great battle and we must help them. Speaking of which, where are Dorylen and Farlone?"

Relgaren started from his position in the chair. "They're not with you?"

The old king laughed. "I think I'd know it if they were! So where are they?"

"I—we thought that they had perished in Ulan."

This seemed like news to Relgaré, who considered it for a moment. "I think I would have known if something had happened to them. Surely they didn't turn to Obsidian." He shook his head to dispel the hateful thought. "No, they must be alive. Somewhere."

It was one shock too many for poor Quinia. The idea of Farlone and Dorylen, believed to be dead, and now possibly alive, put her into a swoon. Relgaré caught her and deposited her gently on a couch. While they were trying to revive her, Relgaren ventured a comment.

"I'm not going to ask about Corfe not being an Advocate, but I want to know what you meant about not being king."

Relgaré laid a gentle hand on his son's shoulder. "It was a valuable lesson for me, Relgaren, one that you and Lors would do well to learn now."

"There are no kings in Kynell's country?"

"No, there are not—although that's not so much what happened. Surely you remember what I was like in my final cycles."

Relgaren and Lors nodded in unison, not offering further comment.

"I was very proud of my station. Proud when loyal subjects bowed before me. Proud when I was able to subdue my enemies. *My* enemies, not necessarily Kynell's. That pride caused me to persecute a people who had long since ceased to be a threat. It was a criminal obsession that took many lives. That hateful alliance with Obsidian was the culmination of my blindness."

During his speech, Lors had started looking out the window. He seemed to be struggling with something.

"Go ahead, son. Say what's on your mind."

Lors continued to fidget for a moment before blurting out his thoughts. "If you were so wrong then why aren't you, you know, with them?" He pointed in the general direction of the advancing army.

The question was honest and appropriate. Still, it provoked a strained silence. Relgaré hung his head as the memories swept over him. His answer was so quiet that they had to bend low to hear. "I should be. The night of my greatest folly, when we slaughtered the Cylini, I was attacked by Amarian's Sentries. My just reward, I'm sure. They took their time about it, and I suffered a great deal. But if they had finished me off quickly, who knows where I would be? Instead, their meticulous care allowed me to realize that all of my pride, my obsessions, and my crimes had brought me to this: being torn apart by Obsidian itself. With my dying breaths I called out to Kynell for mercy, not from the Sentries but from his justifiable wrath. I knew that a thousand eternities could not pay for all the wrongs I had done, the wrongs I had believed."

He stopped as Quinia started to wake up. He watched her tenderly for a moment.

"Now, in the Prysm," he continued, "I am no king. Why should I be? What had I done with my kingship in Rhyvelad? Instead, I'm happy to be the lowest of the low. I, who should not have been allowed into the Prysm in the first place!"

Another silence followed, broken by the soft sighs of the queen as she came to herself. Neither Relgaren nor Lors knew what to say. They had been so accustomed to seeing their father exercise total authority that they were still unable to comprehend his humble gratitude. But he did not mind their confusion. With a final kiss on Quinia's forehead, he rose to his feet. She, meanwhile, seemed content just to watch him.

"Boys, I must be about what I'm here for. Take good care of your mother and tell her what I told you."

He was about to open the door when the door opened for him. It was Ruponi, flush with righteous indignation.

"Ah, Relgaré," he said. "Glad to see you. I think you're wanted at the Stoa."

Relgaré nodded meekly and stepped out to obey the summons, but not before looking again at his family. "Please remember what I told you. You may not have the time to reflect that I had."

With those ominous words, he was gone. Ruponi did not watch him go; he was focused on Relgaren.

"Now then, young king. It appears you are having a family reunion while your city's about to go up in smoke."

Relgaren gave a great shudder, as if waking from a dream. "Yes, I'm sorry. And you are?"

Ruponi's introduction was enough to stir him into action. Without another word to his family, he followed him down to the Great Hall, the duty of what lay before him weighing heavily on his shoulders.

Telenar was lingering alone outside the corridor running past the king's chambers. Chiyo had come with him to inform the king of the resurrections, but upon overhearing Relgaré's voice inside the chamber, the general had decided to proceed to the Great Hall. Telenar had been left wondering whether he should disturb the interview. He was still unresolved when Corfe stumbled out with an expression so distraught that Telenar decided it would do more good to follow him.

Corfe did not see him at first, nor was he paying attention to anything else but his own thoughts. He made his way to one of the palace's many towers, avoiding eye contact with anyone he encountered. Consequently, he was twelve steps up the narrow spiral staircase of the northeast tower before he realized someone was following him. The close quarters prevented him from seeing his follower, so he was forced to bark out an irritated "Who's there?"

Telenar made haste to answer. His response elicited a grunt and more climbing. In a few moments, they had both emerged under the wet sky. Corfe acknowledged Telenar's response with a slight movement of his hand, then proceeded to the far edge. It was still raining, a warm, steady drizzle.

"Corfe, what's wrong?" Telenar called out through the rain, fearing that if he approached too quickly the young man might do something drastic.

Corfe did not answer, so Telenar took a few steps forward. "I know I'm probably the last person you want to see right now, if you've just learned what I think you've learned."

"The last person I want to see is Vancien, priest. But you're close."

"Vancien is down in the Hall. He has no idea we're up here."

Again, Corfe did not answer, but resumed looking out over the city. Telenar did not press the issue. He would talk in his own time. His limited patience was taxed, though, as Corfe continued to stare out into the rain for several minutes. Finally, he spoke.

"You had better go inside. You're needed much more in there than out here."

"I'm not confident of that."

"You think I'm going to throw myself over the edge? I'm not planning on it. But if I did, what is it to you?"

"A waste is what it would be. Kynell did not save you from Zyreio to have you hurl yourself from the top of a tower."

"He'd rather I made a fool of myself instead?"

"That was your doing, not his."

Corfe drew a deep breath. The city below seemed to mock him, as if it had known of his mistake this whole time. He was racking his brain for signs of where he had gone wrong—*how* he had gone wrong, especially when he felt that he had been doing so much right. To buy time, he digressed.

"If you had known what I would become that day I was in your office, what would you have done to me?"

"Done to you? What should I have done? Locked you up? The hold Amarian had over you was spectacular, Corfe. It was not my place to punish you for it."

"You would have saved us all a lot of trouble if you had."

Telenar wished that Corfe would at least turn around. It was awkward talking to the back of his head. But at least he was talking.

"Kynell saved you. And no matter what has happened since, that's what you have to remember."

"And I should just block out these past months?"

"Yes. And do it quickly, or we will catch our death of cold before Zyerio's troops ever lay a hand on us."

Corfe turned toward the entrance of the stairwell. "One of these days, priest, you'll have to point out to me where I went so horribly wrong."

"If we survive that long," Telenar responded, following him into the shelter, "I'd be happy to." He paused on the top step. "If you don't mind my asking, how did you find out the truth?"

Corfe's voice echoed up to him as they made their way down the stone staircase. "Relgaré made me the butt of a joke. I don't think he realized what had happened."

"Ah, Relgaré," Telenar sighed to himself, "still the same, even with the Prysm."

"There's another problem," Corfe said after they had reached the bottom of the stairs. Though his voice was calm, he was clenching and unclenching his right fist with manic intensity. "Most everybody here believes that *I* am the Advocate. If I just go out and say 'No, sorry, I was wrong,' what will that do to them?"

"Would you rather they die believing a lie?"

"I'd rather they fight before they die than just give up altogether. Half of them don't even know Vancien exists."

Though he did not like it, Telenar could see the validity of Corfe's point.

Still, he could not sanction heresy, even for tactical purposes. "I do not have an answer to that," he replied frankly. "But maybe somebody else does. We must hurry to the meet the others. It will be daylight in a few hours."

CHAPTER EIGHTEEN

Though several Risen Ones had already dispersed, the massive room remained filled with past notables, both from Keroul and other countries. Their murmurings rose to the vaulted ceiling, bouncing off the timber rafters and creating a productive din. The figures themselves were all gathered around a large table, looking at something. Several cycles ago, Chiyo had ordered a small-scale model of the city to be constructed in as exact a manner as possible, insisting that it was essential to the city's defense. Relgaré, who at that time feared the Cylini might encroach so far as the capital, had supported the project. The mock-up had sat unused for cycles, except for when Chiyo would come and stroll around the great table on which it sat, reviewing the city's weak points, ordering adjustments both to the real and miniature fortifications as he saw fit. The miniature city was so large, however, that Chiyo soon had to rig up a system of mirrors that would allow him and others to study its interior, which was impossible to examine from the perimeters.

He was now employing those mirrors to great effect, using a pointer to indicate the locations of the barracks, storehouses, etc. Occasionally he referred to a map of the city that hung on the wall nearby, but he seemed to take the greatest satisfaction in showing off his model to an appreciative audience.

"Those of you new to Lascombe should know the general layout of the city. You see that we've constructed a makeshift wall three hundred yards out." He pointed to a thin miniature wall built of wood scraps. "The model does not show it, but we've made it as traction-less as possible. It's finished on the eastern front. I have a team working on the western front as we speak.—if they have not been completely distracted by your arrival, that is," he added with a smile. The resurrection of the faithful had given him new life. Although he never enjoyed battle, at least now he could find satisfaction in the challenge confronting them, knowing that all hope was not lost.

A tall, elegant lady leaned over the miniature. She was dressed in leather armor, her thick hair pulled up in a business-like manner. Her name was Jana. All the Risen Ones treated her with grave respect. Originally, she was from further south than even Vancien's territory, past the Osai Sea. Her people, like Corfe's, were sea-faring. Although Corfe had taken pains throughout his life to forget his connection to the sea, Jana obviously enjoyed her heritage, lingering over her accent like it was a prize in itself. Chiyo had never heard of her before, but he already liked her: her questions had shown that she had a keen awareness of strategy and urgency, and her accent was sweet to his ears.

"They will dig under the wall if they do not tear it down," she was saying.

He nodded. "Yes, most probably. And we won't be able to see where they're digging. We could not prevent that in the time we had. But at least we can slow them down that much more."

Jana appeared satisfied with his answer. She leaned back, folded her arms, and listened as he resumed his speech.

"The tar teams should have everything slicked down right before orb-rise. Casing tar takes a few hours to lose all of its tackiness, so hopefully the scouts are right and we won't be in for a dawn arrival."

Telenar and Corfe slipped in as he spoke. No one noticed them, except for Relgaren and Lors, who were standing among the other dignitaries. The brothers of Anisllyr glanced at their old ally, then back at the table. They had realized no less than Corfe the gravity of their mistake. Corfe did not blame them for ignoring him.

"I don't see Vancien or Amarian." Telenar whispered.

Corfe started. "So you were telling the truth? Amarian really is here? How can you trust him?"

"The same way I can trust you, or think I can."

Corfe had a retort but decided to keep it to himself. Telenar was his only friend at the moment.

"Come on," Telenar hissed again as Jana asked another question. "We're not needed here. Chiyo, Ruponi, and whoever that lady is will get along without us. We've got to find Vance."

"Where would they be, if not here?"

"My guess is at the Stoa or the Courtyard. Hull's not here either. Chiyo must have sent them all on."

"So what do we do?"

"We need to find Amarian."

"Not Vancien?"

"If we find one, we'll find the other. But it strikes me that if Amarian is allowed to fight at all, he'll need your public endorsement, or else your armies will turn on him."

As Corfe pondered that, Telenar slipped over to Chiyo's side and said a few words to him. Chiyo paused long to respond with a brief comment. When Telenar returned, his tone was urgent.

"He's at the Stoa. Hull is going to direct the forces there and Vancien and Amarian are with them. We should hurry."

The Stoa was a large portico with columns dating back from Erst's reign as Advocate. They were the oldest Prysmite architecture in Keroul, since followers of the Prysm were not allowed to construct long-standing buildings in the first two Obsidian eras. Although a few earlier scraps of rough stone structures survived throughout the countryside (rude pyramids with K's inside indicated their orientation) the columns had symbolized the Prysm from the time they were erected. They were older and more respected than even the Square that surrounded them.

The portico itself was long and narrow, with one broad side facing an open square and the other pressed against a high retaining wall. Although just seven paces wide, it was a hundred and fifty paces long and set above the surrounding pavement by four deep, almost impracticable steps. When the Stoa was first built, the columns would have been painted in rich colors, with their leafy capitals overlaid in gold. Over the many cycles, however, the vibrant colors had faded and worn off, the leaves turning from gold to bald stone once more.

Despite, or perhaps because of, its age, the Stoa continued to serve as the city's most respected assembly point. It was the hub of the Square's political activity. Here, stump speeches were made, taxes announced, and scandals publicly regretted. That night, like the rest of Lascombe's residents, the representatives of the Square were either involved in the defense or commanded to evacuate. Now the courtyard facing the Stoa was beginning to flood over with Risen Ones. Living soldiers intermingled with the crowd.

The constant metallic clink of armor and blades also filled the square. Lascombe's armory had been depleted by the influx of troops under Corfe, although reportedly reinforcements were coming in from the West with extra arms. Yet the added support would not arrive soon enough, and many of the living soldiers feared that they would have to surrender their arms to the Risen Ones. But the Risen Ones were already equipped. Mundane blades, Hull had told his sons on their way to the Stoa, were of no use against the Chasmites. Only weapons forged in Kynell's furnaces would be able to slay the enemy. Every man and woman of the Prysm's army was equipped with the means of sending Zyerio's followers back to the Chasm from which they came. What those means were, he added, might not be revealed until the battle itself.

When they arrived at the Stoa, the rain had still not let up. Hull could barely see the crowd, though he knew it must stretch for hundreds of yards into the surrounding streets. "Fellow soldiers!" he called, projecting his voice as well as he could. There was no response. He tried the call again. In the end, it took four bellows to get the Square to quiet down.

"I am here to give you directions, not a speech. I trust that those Risen Ones who can hear me will relay my words to those who cannot. I was sent here by General Chiyo. But I am also the proud father of the two Advocates. They have been granted the authority to give orders. Vancien is young," he brought forward his youngest, who was lingering behind a column. "But he will have charge of—"

His words were drowned out by shouts of protest. The Risen Ones looked on in amazement as Lascombe's soldiers started a cry of "Imposter!"

One of the men close to Hull rattled his sword. "That boy's not the Advocate!" he bellowed. "Lord Corfe is!"

Despite the calm, reasonable murmurs of the Risen Ones to the contrary, his cry was taken up by others around him. Hull was beginning to think he was going to have to take coercive action when Corfe himself, accompanied by Telenar, appeared at his side. They had obviously been running.

As soon as the soldiers saw him, they gave a hearty roar. But Corfe, once he had caught his breath, put up a hand to stop them.

"Good men and Sentries of Lascombe," he shouted hoarsely, "do not shout my name. My name is nothing. I am nothing. I have made a horrible mistake."

The roar stopped, first in the front, then towards the back as his words were passed on.

"Though I love the Prysm," Corfe continued, "I was in error. I am not

148

the Advocate. I never was the Advocate. But this man," he put a hand on Vancien's shoulder, "*is* Kynell's chosen. He is the one equipped to lead you into battle. He is the reason that we have the Risen Ones among us."

Before the troops could protest again, he gestured to the Risen Ones. "If you do not believe me, believe them. They have come from Kynell himself! Do they not acknowledge Vancien as the Advocate?" he asked urgently.

The Risen Ones did not disappoint. As one, they saluted Vancien and cried "Vancien pa Hull, Advocate of the Prysm!"

They did not stop their chant there, however. Changing the angle of their salute, they shouted again, "Amarian pa Hull, Advocate of the Prysm!"

Amarian had also been hiding behind a column, watching the scene. When he heard his name, he stepped out. The crowd, excepting the Risen Ones, cried out in anger when it saw him. Some of them threatened to rush the Stoa, so enraged were they by the sight of him. The Sentries were as confused as they had ever been.

Amarian flinched but did not retreat. He watched with no small amount of distress as the Risen Ones restrained the troops. But they could not stop the shouting. Cries of "Murderer!" "Traitor!" and even "Dragonmaster!" all piled on top of each other in a chorus of accusation.

Both Corfe and Hull were shouting at the top of their voices to stay the crowd. Bedge, who had been following Amarian, moved protectively between her master and the soldiers. With front paws planted and hackles raised, she growled, a deep, throaty sound Amarian had never heard from her before. Some of the men laughed at this show of defiance. Those who were better acquainted with fennels gave her wide birth.

It was the piercing shriek of an Ealatrophe that stilled all protests. Thelámos's cry cut through the shouts and the rain as he swept low over the assembly, landing in a hastily cleared area at the base of the steps.

There was a rider on his back. Unlike everyone gathered in the Stoa, he did not carry a sword or a shield. He dismounted, patted Thelámos on the neck, and led him up the steps, out of the rain. The crowd watched in surprise. Most of the Lascombian soldiers had never seen an Ealatrophe before, and the Risen Ones were just as taken aback by its presence as their comrades.

Once under the protection of the Stoa, he shook his head and clothes free of excess water, then pushed his hair back from his forehead. Then he began to study the crowd, as if he had come for no other purpose.

Vancien, a little offended that someone would dare ride Thelámos, decided to speak first. He did not know who this newcomer was, but clearly some questions were in order. "Who are you? Have you been sent from Chiyo? How is it that you can ride an Ealatrophe?"

The stranger began to roll up his sleeves, giving his answer to the stones at his feet. "I have not been sent from Chiyo. And Thelámos is an old friend of mine."

Vancien started forward. "Then who are you? Why don't you look us in the eye?" He glanced back at his father, who was also staring at the man. "You are not a Risen One."

The man still gazed at the stones. "No, I am not a Risen One. Neither are you. Not yet."

Vancien, keenly aware of the Obsidian army's proximity, did not want to waste any more time in conversation. "Is that a threat? Look, I don't know how you got on Thelámos, but if you can state your business, we can get on with ours."

The man lifted his gaze even as Vancien heard Hull shout a warning. Then he felt his heart constrict as it had not done since his first experience with the Destrariae. He heard his name, but saw only Amarian as a young boy, stolidly taking a lashing for something he, Vancien, had done. He tried to look away, but other realities crowded in. Some of them he recognized from his past, some from his imagination, and some from his dreams. He felt himself try to embrace Verial, a woman forbidden to him, and felt again the rush of anger at Telenar for stopping him. He became aware that deep down, he was faithless, but that knowledge was no comfort. It was just a trivial admission from a small soul, whose punishment should be the greater for its pettiness.

The man was still looking at him, but it was just a look, the same as any man would give. At first Vancien wanted to blame him for such horrible visions, but the man had only revealed the truth. Vancien could not accuse him of anything; his own shallow failings were too obvious. He felt impure, because he knew himself to be in the presence of purity itself.

He looked around and saw all the Risen Ones kneeling in the rain.

"My God," he whispered, sliding to his knees.

Amarian and the others watched Vancien go down, then saw the Risen Ones kneeling in worship. They felt their hearts pricked by something both terrible and delightful as the thought began to occur to them, "Could it be?"

Then they, too, were on their knees before Kynell, god of the Prysm, the Light of Rhyvelad and the Deliverer of Every Age.

CHAPTER NINETEEN

When Kynell spoke, his voice had the clarity and force of rushing water. He addressed his comments to everyone, and even those at the back of the crowd could hear him. Not everyone could tell at first who he was, and when they did hear the truth, every reaction was different. Several knelt, some tried to push to the front, many stood in shock, and a large handful shook their heads and slipped back into the dark streets, muttering about too many apparitions for one night.

"People of Lascombe, some of you know me, and it is good to see you!" He emphasized the word "good," and those nearest him could see that he really meant it. His face was bright with cheer, as if he had just come from a tremendous feast and desired nothing more than to share it with others. Even the weather gave him cause to smile; he held out his hand to the rain in a gesture of invitation and several raindrops obligingly dropped into it. Then he reached out and rested one hand on Amarian's shoulder and another on Vancien's.

"These men have served me well. I am pleased with them."

A couple Risen Ones nodded, as if they had expected Kynell might come for the sole purpose of commending the Advocates. But he was not finished. "The Ages have told you about the time of the Advocates. As you know, it has come many times in the past. It is here now. But now I am going to do something—"

"He's not really the Advocate is he?" A slender man in the front interrupted, his finger pointing at Vancien. He was quickly hushed by the men around him, though Kynell had already stopped his speech to glance down.

"You think that I was lying? Let him go," he added, as the man began to disappear beneath a pile of scandalized Risen Ones.

The man returned to his feet. He had a bookish appearance, as if he had just left the library to fight a war. "I just don't understand it. I have scarcely even heard of, of—what's your name, young man?"

"Vancien pa Hull," Vancien supplied.

"Vancien. Now I know that Lord Corfe has been with us for a while and of course, he's a good man. He follows you, after all, although I wonder who you really are. I have read the passages that talk about the Advocates, and it seems clear that a man with his dramatic story could serve in the role. Like I said, I have never heard of that one." He pointed again at Vancien.

The crowd watched the god of the Prysm, wondering if the rude fellow would be struck by lightning or vanish in a mist.

"What's your name?" Kynell finally asked.

The man grinned. "You know that as well as I do."

"I do. Your name is Clive."

"Earnest. Clive Earnest. With an emphasis on that last syllable, as you also know. It's because of my Ulanese heritage."

Vancien could not help rolling his eyes. The man was not only rude, but a bore.

But Kynell had fixed his gaze on him. "Clive Earnest, you are acting like a fool. And you have left your son at home. Why hasn't he been evacuated with the other children?"

Clive fidgeted. "He's very weak, as you know. A serious cough. The dampness of the tunnels. I fear it would do him in. But I've placed him in a safe location." His voice wavered, as if he would like to be more certain of the boy's safety. "I didn't have a choice."

Kynell dismounted the steps to stand in front of him. "Go to your son," he said, speaking so Clive and those around him could hear. "He is well. Take him into the tunnels and stay there with him. And go without shame."

Clive's eyes lit up. He stared at Kynell for a moment, as if not comprehending what he had heard, then he turned and began pushing his way through the crowd, which tried its best to let him through. Those who could see him as he broke free later said that they had never seen a man move so quickly as did Clive Earnest.

Kynell hurried up the stairs to face the crowd. He clapped his hands again on Vancien and Amarian. "These two have served me well," he repeated, and his voice clapped like thunder. "But they are no longer my

Advocates. I will be your Advocate now."

The dawn brought a reprieve from the rain. But it also brought a dim shadow on the horizon. Obsidian's army had arrived. The watchers on the walls tried not to sound panicked as they shared what they saw, but panic was inevitable. Telenar made no attempt to hide it.

"They're here! What in the Chasm are they doing here? They're not supposed to be here until the afternoon!" He was standing with Chiyo on the eastern wall, gripping a range glass in his hand. Chiyo was staring in shock. Both men had woken up from a very short night's sleep just minutes before. For a moment, they had both forgotten what Telenar had seen personally and what Chiyo had learned from witnesses: Kynell himself was in the city.

"So what do we do?" Telenar asked, beginning to pace. "They're already here! What can we do?"

Chiyo watched his friend slosh through the puddles that had gathered on the battlements. Telenar was a great priest, but no soldier. His temper was too volatile.

"If what you say is true, Kynell is here with us. I wish I could be with him."

Telenar ran a hand over his spectacles. What right had he to panic when the god of the Prysm was here among them? He looked down at the men who were soaking the buildings in the hopes of preventing fiery missiles from doing too much damage. He could see Kynell in the street below, his sleeves rolled up, taking a bucket in his turn and heaving its contents on exposed timbers. Telenar's mind still reeled. If asked earlier what would be the effect of the Prysm god on common men, Telenar would have said they would be so awestruck as to be immobile, useless for anything but worship. But he saw instead that Kynell invigorated everyone around him. Instead of falling on their faces, they went to their task with renewed energy. He even heard laughter drifting up into the gray sky.

"Does he know, do you think?" Chiyo asked, following his gaze.

"He must. The question is, should we wait for him to say anything or go on with the plans we've already laid out?"

"If I send a messenger to ask him, he will only join the soaking crew. I've already lost two men this morning. Let's tell the Risen Ones and the generals, though I'm guessing they already know."

After his conversation with Telenar, Chiyo went about his duties like a machine. When he had heard the news of Kynell's arrival the night before, he had sent a messenger (the only messenger who returned) to offer the Prysm god command of the city. The messenger had this statement to relay: "Keep to your post. I did not come to command." And so Chiyo, after wisely getting a few hours' rest, continued in his task, not taking time out even to see Kynell in person, as many of his men had done.

The women, children, and elderly had completed their evacuation a few hours before dawn, despite the stir caused by Kynell's arrival. It was only at his urging that they reluctantly left him to descend into the dark labyrinth beneath the city. All of the access points into the tunnels had been sealed shut, guarded on the inside by the women Risen Ones. The people who now remained in the city were those men, women, and Sentries who were determined to give their lives to protect it.

Construction crews were called back from the extramural defenses, and all soldiers were ordered to their posts. Teams were soon appointed to man the siege weapons mounted at intervals along the eastern wall. The few Risen Ones who were trained in siege warfare were paired with living soldiers to conduct that aspect of the defense. Fortunately, they still had time; the stillness of the enemy's weapons meant that the advancing army was yet out of range, something most trained eyes were already able to tell. The rest of the Risen Ones were gathered at points throughout the city, by the entrances and possible breach spots, ready to ride out in sorties or stymie the attackers if they should penetrate the walls. Final weapons checks were conducted as every soldier was equipped with a blade of some sort, even if it was a sharpened pitchfork.

A few hours after dawn, most of the soldiers, both living and Risen, stood soberly at their stations. Kynell, despite earnest requests from almost every individual in the city to be at their side, remained with the soakers, buckets at ready. His presence had given the defenders new life, but several also noticed that he had offered no promises of deliverance, nor had he chosen to manifest himself everywhere at once, as he surely could have done. He meant for the battle to proceed, leaving a few to wonder why he had bothered coming at all.

By noon the shadow was a dark, writhing mass. Massive siege weapons towered above it like bony jail-keepers. The wooden frames of trebuchets were just discernible, along with the bulky siege towers. The catapults and ballistae were not visible, but lurked behind the advance guard. As the evil vision drew closer, it was accompanied by a horrible clamor. It took a moment for the Lascombians to realize that what they were hearing was not the distant clanking of armor or even weapons; rather, it was the tortured, furious cries of the Chasmites. The sound was constant, like an agonized drone, chilling the hearts of the defenders.

As the third orb peaked in the sky, the air was marred by the sound of a whistle. The garrison on the East Wall had just enough time to duck as a small boulder went soaring over their heads and crashed into the houses below. It was immediately followed by several others. The army of Zyreio had come into range. The battle had begun.

———————

Gair rode his voyoté hard, despite Verial's added weight. A few days after the encounter with the children on the road, they came across the remains of a wooded copse. They were not too far from Lascombe now; if his own sense of direction had not told him that, the shattered remnants of the tree trunks did. The army must have stopped to construct its engines. From the look of the raw wood and torn-up ground, they had been gone from the spot a few days at most. He was just about to spur his voyoté forward again when he heard a thoughtful harrumph from Ragger.

"What is it?"

The munkke-trophe was looking in the direction of the city. "I wonder, Captain, if we are doing the wisest thing?"

Even Verial was surprised by his question. "What else could we do?"

Ragger pursed his lips. "If we somehow make it past the attackers and into the city, what then? We join Lord Corfe and fight to the death, no doubt. But if we remain outside the walls, behind the Easterners, perhaps we could be more effective?"

Gair shifted in his saddle. "In what way? We don't know how to fight against them."

"You point out a weakness, sir. Also, we are very few, and they are very many. But if we go inside the walls, we become just two more soldiers—and a lady—with no tactical advantage. Out here, we may at least have the element of surprise."

He had a point. Gair stared at the ground, mulling it over. Once they went inside, if they could make it inside, they would lose whatever small advantage they had. And it was a distinct possibility that they could somehow be of better service to Kynell and Corfe outside the city. But that meant more watching and waiting and less fighting, which annoyed him greatly.

From behind him, he could tell Verial was dealing with a similar struggle. "So we raced all this way just to stare at the backs of those fiends?"

He held up a hand. "Shh. I'm thinking."

She repositioned herself and, in the process, her slender arm tightened around his waist. The ordinary movement reminded him instantly of how attractive she was; thoughts of war dissipated with ludicrous speed as he was overcome with the urge to take her hand in his. Then he recalled what she would have done with that innocent child and his passion cooled. He wanted no relationship with such a woman.

A few minutes passed as everyone sat absorbed in their own thoughts. The voyoté whined, more than ready for a rest. Gair patted his mount absent-mindedly.

"Just a little longer, girl. Bring us within sight of the army and we'll let you rest."

It sounded like the beginning of a plan, so they moved forward.

———————

"By the Chasm, what happened here?"

Lucio whistled as he surveyed the torn tree stumps, the scattered branches, and the dirt crisscrossed with deep ruts. "Looks like something exploded. Hang on. Maybe this is what I think it is."

"What? What are you going on about?"

"Sirin made me hear about all these old battles. In a couple of them, they would build huge towers and catapults and things so they could tear up the walls of the cities they were attacking. I bet most armies don't carry that much lumber around. Looks like this is where they got it from."

Teehma was impressed. Lucio had listened to his teacher.

"That means we must be getting close."

Lucio nodded. "Maybe a couple days' walk."

Teehma shuddered. She was not anxious to encounter that horrible army again. And once they got there, what would they do? Would they be able to creep into the city? Her stomach rumbled. The food the soldier had given them seemed like a distant memory.

"I wonder how Trint and Ester are doing."

"Hopefully better than us," Lucio responded as he picked his way through the wood. "Not that that would take much." He would never admit it, but he was kicking himself for leaving Sirin's and angry at Teehma for letting him do it. But how could they have known? Nobody had been running around shouting that an army was coming to town.

"I wish we were older," Teehma said to the ground, "then we'd know what to do."

Her sentiment angered Lucio, though the idea had occurred to him as well. "You think the adults know how to fix this? How could someone like Gorvy take on an army like that?"

She had to admit that Gorvy would stand no chance. But when she remembered that young man who wanted to help them find a home, she thought that maybe the adults might know what they're doing, after all. At least, she hoped that was the case.

By the end of the day, they had moved past the torn remains of the woods. The twilight was coming fast, and although the autore season was upon them, the nights could still get very cool. Along the road, they had collected extra scraps and garments to keep them warm. They wrapped these around themselves as they staggered on.

"So do we have a plan?" Teehma asked in a whisper. It was probably unnecessary to lower her voice, but she did not want to take any chances.

"Find Trint and Ester."

"Yeah, but how are we going to get into the city?"

"I don't know."

He stopped as a movement caught his eyes. There was something just off the road ahead of them, moving in their direction. The three lunos gave them only enough light to see that it was about their height and moving in a heavy lope. They crouched down and began to crawl into the ditch on their right. But the figure noticed them and switched its direction. Before they could retreat, it was upon them.

It was Sirin.

"There you are!" he shrieked. He looked tired, his clothes were disheveled, and his eyes had a wild look. They could not tell if he was angry or triumphant, but their own surprise was so great at seeing him that they could only stare.

"Well, what have you got to say for yourselves?" He tapped his cane impatiently on the ground.

Teehma found her tongue first. "What are you doing here?"

Her words failed to satisfy him. "What am I doing here? Well, that's a fine question. I might ask the same of you. Why are you wandering around in the dark? And where have you been these past days?"

"We ran away," Lucio replied stoutly. "Since Trint and Ester found a home, we didn't figure we would be good for much more than slave work, anyway. Why did you follow us?"

Teehma hissed a warning at him under her breath; the stupid boy was

157

going to turn away their only hope of food. Sirin, however, did not seem as offended as he might be. In fact, he looked sympathetic, which everyone knows is an unusual attitude for a munkke-trophe.

"You misunderstood, child. When young Vancien places charges under my care then I mean to take care of them. I've been searching all over Lascombe for you. Only late last night did I hear from some irresponsible guard that he had let you out of the city. Do you know what I went through to get past that horrible army? Do you? Well, don't ask."

Lucio looked at the ground, abashed. "We didn't expect you to come after us," he muttered.

Sirin took his cane and knocked him lightly on the arm. "I wouldn't expect so, young man. You've never had anybody try to chase you down—unless it was for the purpose of arresting you. But you're worth much more than that to me."

This brought a surprised smile to Lucio's face. Teehma watched in amazement as his surliness vanished.

"Well then," Sirin went on, feigning not to notice the transformation. "What's our plan now?"

Teehma looked in the direction of the town. Now that they had to voice it out loud to a grown-up, their rescue attempt seemed rather silly. "We were going to try to get into Lascombe, find Trint and Ester and, well, take care of them."

"Tertio did not seem like a fighter to you, either?"

"Not really."

Sirin took off his short cloak and wrapped it around her shoulders. Then he gave Lucio his traveling pack, told him to open it, and distribute what he found. "Do not underestimate Tertio. He'll do what he needs to do to protect his family. And I suspect that Alisha has the two young ones well underground by now. The bombardment had not yet begun when I left."

"What's a bombardment?" Lucio asked around a mouthful of sweet roll. Munkke-trophes did not like to go without their comforts, and Sirin was no exception: he had brought a pack full of sweet rolls, jerky, cut vegetables, and jars of water. It weighed a ton.

As Lucio passed the food around, Sirin directed them to the side of the road in order to make camp. Then he began collecting kindling to start a fire. "A bombardment," he began in a teacherly voice, "is when a series of missiles, such as rocks, boulders, sometimes dead livestock or decapitated heads, is launched by siege engines the walls of a city for the purpose of distressing, upsetting, and injuring the inhabitants of that city."

Lucio paused, the gears in his head turning. "So that army is already attacking Lascombe?"

"By now, it certainly is."

Teehma was shocked. "But what about everybody in the city? What about all the children?"

"Your young friends are most likely safe," Sirin finished for her. "Like I said, there are underground evacuation tunnels where all the women, children, and elderly have been sent. Trint and Ester may be bored out of their minds, but they're protected."

Both children breathed easier at his explanation. Now it did not seem like such a horrible fate to be outside of the city, away from the fight.

"I admit I am at a loss as to what to do now," the munkke-trophe continued. "If it were me, I'd charge back in." He shook his cane for emphasis. "But I do not relish the thought of taking you young ones back into danger."

Lucio bridled at his words. "We've been in danger before! Worse than any ol' army. Gorvy's more dangerous than the lot of them!" He waved his hand in the general direction of Gorvy.

Sirin sighed. "Gorvy is a deluded, corrupted, foolish man. And to you he was a tyrant. But do not be foolhardy, Lucio." His beady eyes narrowed in the firelight. "The army we face is very dark; we will need to rely on the power of the Prysm, not our own strength, to defeat it."

Teehma bit her lip. She'd never heard Sirin talk that way before. Nor was she was excited to hear him talk that way now. "Yes, well, what can we do out here?"

"More than we can do inside, I think." Here he began to awkwardly trace patterns in the dirt with his cane. "I've never been much for praying to Kynell in front of people. Munkke-trophes are known for their independence. But perhaps now may be a good time to start. Maybe the Prysm will provide us with an opportunity to be of some service."

Lucio nodded. He rose, went to the edge of the firelight, and began pacing. Teehma assumed that he was taking Sirin's suggestion literally. She groaned and stretched out under Sirin's cloak. Maybe she would say a prayer to the stars as she drifted off to sleep. Just to make the old primate happy.

CHAPTER TWENTY

A few hours after Kynell had appeared at the Stoa, Alisha, after her own tearful goodbye to her son, made the children bid their farewells to Wake. She had heard rumors of Kynell's arrival, but it seemed too good to be true. Those who remained above ground had heard the story, as well, but theirs was a mixed reaction. Some dropped everything to race to the Stoa. Some stopped in the streets, as if paralyzed. The recent arrival of their loved ones and now Kynell's coming had so stirred them that mundane matters like saving their lives had fled their minds completely. Only when another Risen One came along to hasten them on their way would they move. Alisha herself was just as torn. Was it possible that Kynell was here, in Lascombe? If the god of the Prysm had come, shouldn't the whole city be on holy fire or something? Surely he would not just slip in, hiding among the Risen Ones?

She could not wrap her mind around it and she did not have time to try. Kynell knew she loved him; he knew how much she longed to see him. But he also knew that she could not rush the children all over in search of him and get back to the evacuation tunnels before dawn. There was no doubt in her mind that her immediate duty was to Ester and Trint; it was Kynell who had given them to her, after all.

Her mind was made up, but she still had to pull Trint away from his father, a parting made worse by the fact that Wake could not assure his son that he would see him again soon. If the Prysm lost, he would be with Kynell. If the Prysm won, who knew? He would probably still be with Kynell. In the end, he had to assure his boy that one day, he *would* see him again. This he could promise, even though he might have to wait until Trint was a grown man for it to happen. It was also Ester's ingenious idea that if Alisha could teach Trint how to write, he could write to his father whenever he wanted. Wake had jumped in. He was pretty sure he would not be able to write back, he said, but he felt certain that Kynell would allow him to read Trint's letters as often as he wrote them. To this plan, the distraught boy agreed.

Before they parted, Wake took him aside for one last discussion. Alisha watched them talk, holding Ester's hand in her own. She kept seeing her own boy grown, happy, and healthy. It had been wonderful to see him, but oh, how much harder it made tonight! Would he even miss her as he fought this battle? Would he die again? Would Tertio see him?

Wake was bringing Trint toward her. Trint was trying to look determined. When they were close enough, he took Ester's hand from Alisha's, as if he were the girl's protector, not the other way around.

"Dad says you'll be my mom and I need to listen to you."

Alisha could see the tears he was trying to hide. Her instinct was to scoop him up and hold him close, but she knew that would be fatal to his young dignity. Instead, she nodded, gave Wake a short wave, then pulled the two children toward the nearest evacuation point.

Wake watched as they walked away, waving again every time Trint glanced back. When they turned the corner and moved out of his vision, he listened for wails or shouts of protest, ready, despite everything, to run back to his son. He heard none, so he began jogging towards his post, weeping openly as he ran.

Alisha, meanwhile, tried not to think about the figure fading into the background, or of her son, or of her own parents, both of whom had determined to stay aboveground and fight, or of Tertio, who was only Kynell knew where. Perhaps he was with Kynell himself, if the rumors were true. Perhaps Kynell would end the battle before it even started. She hoped that would happen, and she glanced up at the sky in the hopes of seeing the coming dawn turn to brilliant white. But there were no dramatic changes to the sky, and she could hear shouts of alarmed men as they spied something from the top of the walls. The Obsidian army had been spotted, and whether Kynell was in the city or not, it was still coming.

She gripped her little cart of provisions tighter and pushed through the emptying streets. They were the last to descend into the same evacuation tunnel where she had earlier enlisted N'vonne's services. The woman who was now guarding the entrance watched her come, not bothering to hide her relief. She had been anxious to close and seal the door before orbrise. Amid all of her chatter, Alisha made out that N'vonne had placed her under strict orders not to seal the door until the first missile struck or Alisha and her children were inside, whichever came first. The woman was grateful that she did not have to wait for the first occurrence.

Inside, a wide and well-paved tunnel sloped gently downward. Alisha had no problem maneuvering her cart down the broad street, although she had to pay close attention to her guide. The entrance-keeper carried the only light in the passageway. As they walked, the flames of the bright torch illuminated a series of doors on either side of them, each one made in the same fashion: thick, rough-hewn planks bound together with solid iron, hanging on massive hinges. Their only decorative element was a soft arch at the top. When Alisha asked what all the doors were for, their guide, Bertrice, said that they were mostly dead ends, meant to deceive invaders.

"Can I open one?" Trint asked. He had been terrified of the doors, but his confidence was increasing as one by one passed without anything jumping out to get him.

Bertrice hesitated, resting the end of the torch against her thin hip. "Sure. But make it quick."

Before his courage could fail him, Trint ran over to a door and pulled on the handle. The door did not budge. He tried pushing, but even shoving his little shoulder against the wood failed to move it.

"It's locked!"

Bertrice gave a wan smile as she continued walking. "They're locked from the inside."

Ester pursed her lips as she dragged Trint away from the door. He was still trying to figure out a way to open it. "How is that possible?" she asked.

"I said they were *mostly* dead ends. In the back of each is a small tunnel—barely a crawl space. Each crawl space leads out to another tunnel that runs parallel to this one. When the tunnels were carved and the doors put in place, many, many cycles ago, a team of eight munkke-trophes were assigned the job of crawling in and locking them on the inside. It was said that the task took them three days, though I think munkke-trophes will give you a different answer, if you ask them."

Ester pursed her lips again. "If all of them are locked, wouldn't it make it easier for the invaders to find the one that's opened? The one that leads to us?"

Bertrice's smile grew warmer, which was encouraging since the torchlight made her narrow face look very harsh. "You're a smart girl. No,

163

they're not all locked. The idea was to get them to waste time smashing through the locks in some of the doors closer to the entrance. Eventually, of course, they would realize that all the doors lead to a dead end." She stopped and indicated a door on the left with her torch.

"Try that one, young man."

Trint did so, and when he did, the door swung open. "Hey, it worked!"

"But if you were to follow that tunnel—which I don't advise you to do—you would find that it leads into some pretty nasty curves and pitfalls. It could be very dangerous for you, or for anybody else who goes that way."

"Like the 'vaders?"

"Exactly. A couple of doors like this are hidden among the locked doors." She continued walking as she spoke. "It's almost impossible to tell which one is the right one." After a few minutes, she paused in front of another door that looked like all the others.

"One hundred and fifty-seven doors down, on the left."

"Pardon me," Alisha had to ask as the woman produced an odd-shaped, thin sliver of metal, which she then slid between the door and the wall. The door clicked and swung open. "How do you know all of this?"

Bertrice ushered them into another, smaller dark tunnel. "Lascombe has always had women trained for a time such as this. No one, not even the king, knows all the secrets of these tunnels. But I do. So did my mother, and her mother before her. Someday, I hope to pass my secrets along to my daughter—or perhaps my niece."

Trint's voice dropped to a whisper. "There're more secrets?"

"Oh yes. Many, many more. I would not advise wandering around these tunnels without a guide, young man."

He nodded solemnly as she closed the door and they continued, passing yet more portals. These were open and cavernous, yet nobody asked what was beyond them. Even Alisha felt as if she had learned enough about the city's subterranean world.

They began to hear voices. Alisha had been noticing for some time that the angle of their descent was steeper than at first. When they stopped at what looked like a sheer rock wall, she was surprised to hear the voices coming from above them. She looked up into the darkness, but could see nothing.

"You'll want to put your cart here," Bertrice said, pointing with her torch to a small platform with fence slats on its four sides. She removed one of the slats, helped Alisha load the cart, replaced the slat, and yanked four times (three quick, a long break, then a fourth) on the rope that connected the platform to some unseen point above.

To Alisha's surprise and Trint's delight, the rope became taut in response and the entire platform, cart and all, began to ascend until it disappeared into the darkness.

"Wow!" Trint exclaimed. "Can I ride?"

"No, you cannot." Alisha responded, rather sharper than she was intending. "I mean, it looks your ride has already left. Maybe there's another one."

But Bertrice was shaking her head. "It's the stairs for us." She waved her torch to a spot of darkness on her left. The firelight revealed a narrow opening in the wall. "If you're claustrophobic—that's scared of tight places," she added for Trint and Ester's benefit, "I'm afraid this will not be very pleasant for you. But it's the only way up." Then she disappeared into the cleft. Alisha, Ester, and Trint hastened to follow before she was too far gone, though they would have easily found their way: the cleft held nothing but a steep set of stairs with walls close on either side and no ceiling. These stairs went up in a straight line, with the exception of one sharp turn to the right.

Alisha, who did struggle with claustrophobia, concentrated on the voices, which were getting closer and closer. It also helped her to realize that there was nothing but empty space over her head. In fact, if she peered hard enough, she could just make out a distant glow of light above them. She would have commented on this, but they were all saving their strength for the climb. By the time the stairs stopped, even Bertrice was out of breath.

"This," she gasped, "is Haven."

The walls disappeared and the staircase turned into a flat surface. They found themselves standing on a giant field of stone, brightly lit, and populated by thousands of women, children, and elderly. The sudden sight of so many people was overwhelming; Trint hid behind Ester's skirts and Alisha stepped instinctively in front of both children. Ester and Bertrice alone seemed unfazed.

"It's very loud here," Ester said, raising her own voice to be heard above the din. "Is that safe?"

"It can't be helped," Bertrice responded. "By the time the invaders make it to this point, it won't matter. We'll either be gone or be raining rocks down upon their heads."

Ester smiled at the mental picture. "I wish I could see their faces if that happened."

Bertrice ruffled her hair. "One day Kynell will restore your sight, my girl. And then think of all the things you'll see!"

Ester nodded with enthusiasm and began passing a hand in front of her eyes as if the miracle had already been performed. Alisha, meanwhile, was looking around for a place to settle.

"Please, where can we put our things?"

"Just follow me," Bertrice said. She began weaving her way through streets of barrels, tents, and even a few campfires. After about ten minutes of walking, during which Alisha completely lost her bearings, she stopped in front of a low canvas tent.

"The tents are helpful for privacy and warmth," she explained, as if embarrassed by the redundancy of tents under a stone ceiling. "Just makes the place feel homier. This is your tent, number 4501. Remember that in case you get lost. Any woman with this on her sleeve," she indicated a dull orange band that Alisha had not noticed before, "will help you find your way back. The dining tent is in the center of the residentials; it's technically Number 5, but you won't be able to miss it." Indeed, as she pointed back over her left shoulder, Alisha could see the canvas peaks of a large pavilion. "There are waste houses not too far from the dining tent, and also at the end of every street. We are fortunate that Ruponi's miners discovered ample amounts of trepofam down here, which dissolves human waste with minimal fumes. It's even recyclable."

Both Ester and Trint wrinkled their noses.

"Right, so those are the main things you need to know about. Women and healthy elderly are encouraged to volunteer at the dining tent or for refilling the W.H.'s with trepofam. The trepofam's not as bad as it sounds—at least you're not stuck in the kitchen all day. Children should consider it their duty to stay well behaved, clean up after themselves, and carry their own dishes to the dining tent and back. I believe that various streets have organized prayer meetings, as well, if that's something you'd like to do. Oh, and one more thing."

She stared off into the distance for a moment, then pointed to the furthest point of light. "Do not go beyond the light. We are on a high plateau; the torches mark the edge of it. If you go beyond them, you're liable to fall to your death."

Alisha did not appreciate Bertrice's flair for the melodramatic. "I'm sure that's quite enough information for us to get started," she said. "Will they be bringing me my cart or will I have to pick it up?"

"Oh, yes, they'll bring it around. Should be here in a few minutes. And I'll tell Lady N'vonne that you've made it."

"Thank you."

Since Alisha's tone did not allow for further discussion, Bertrice took her leave. Alisha watched her go, took another brisk look at her surroundings, then ushered the children into the tent. The first thing was to get some sleep; the children had not slept for almost twenty-four hours. Three thin mattresses and three heavy blankets had already been provided. She tucked them both in as well as she could, prayed with them, and kissed each of them on the forehead. Then she set herself up outside of the door to await the cart and Lady N'vonne, if the latter should decide to come by for a visit.

CHAPTER TWENTY-ONE

Though the defenders had greater range for their engines than the attackers did, the bombardment was still severe. For several hours, boulders a little larger than a man's head rained down on the city, tearing down walls, crushing rooftops, and crushing to splinters Lascombe's own siege engines. Chiyo was furious. Forced to take cover with some of his generals at the base of the thick eastern wall, he started to pace like a cornered animal.

"How many engines do they have? Our crews are working like animals and still three boulders come in for every one we put out! And what in Rhyvelad is Kynell doing?"

General Tengar fought the temptation to swear. He had served under Relgaré in his campaign against the Cylini, had been present to witness Corfe's conversion, and had done his part to march the Sentries into Lascombe. Only last night he had been told that Corfe had abdicated his position of power. Then Kynell had shown up. Not to win the battle, apparently, or even to fight it. No, the Prysm god, the Deliverer of All Ages had posted himself with the soaking crew and refused to do anything helpful. He had not even come up to the battlements since his arrival.

Yet Tengar was also frustrated with himself. He knew he was partially to blame for the city's desperate situation: if he had understood the true nature and imminence of the threat, he would have done more to prepare against it. Instead, this blustery Western general comes in and begins acting like he owns the place. He knew Chiyo was a good man and obviously *the* man to galvanize the city into action. Still, it galled him that King Relgaren and Prince Lors had so little spine that they let themselves be commanded about first by Corfe, and then by Chiyo.

Relgaren had, admittedly, taken more responsibility for his city in the past few hours. After joining the leaders in the Great Hall, he had offered his full support to Chiyo, claimed he was willing to meet with and publicly endorse Vancien, and even sent his young brother Lors to take shelter and pray with the other Patroniites. Then the arrival of Kynell had changed everything. With one phrase, he had swept aside all Advocate authority: "They are no longer my Advocates. I will be your Advocate now."

It was hard to overestimate the effect this statement had on the city's defenders. It was as if, at the dawn of an invasion, the king had disbanded the Square, claimed all power for himself, and then holed himself up in the palace. The only thing Tengar could think that would have been worse would have been if Kynell had added, "Oh, and don't pay attention to General Chiyo either." Indeed, if it had not been for Chiyo's iron grip, the men would have had no leader at all. As it was, they were energized by Kynell's presence, but confused as to what to do about Amarian, Vancien, and Corfe. But Vancien and Amarian had made themselves so useful (and Corfe had made himself so scarce) that no one had much of an opportunity to react to them one way or another.

Old Relgaré, meanwhile, had encouraged his wife to go underground with the other evacuees. She had resisted, of course, but Tengar knew Relgaré was a man not to be refused. The last anybody saw of her was her entering a small grocer's shop a stone's throw away from the palace. Tengar had been a member of her escort from her chambers to the evacuation point. She had borne herself like a queen, but he could tell that the past few days had taken her toll. She looked lost, following the gentle guidance of Captain An-Sung with an aura of fearful innocence. Tengar's heart had gone out to her. He had heard the report that Prince Farlone and Princess Dorylen may be dead, may be alive, or may even be with the Chasmites. He knew his own teenage girl, along with his wife, were alive and safe underground. But what would it be like not to know?

Chiyo was saying something to him. Something about a sortie. "I'm sorry, general!" he shouted over the crash of the boulders. "You wish to attack?"

"How else are we going to stop this barrage?"

"Sir, it would only be a massacre, unless we send out our whole force now."

Chiyo smiled as the dust from the roof showered down on them. "I was thinking of a particular type of attack. Where is Vancien?"

Vancien was not hard to find. He and Amarian were mending a tower on the northeast corner. Bedge was with them, running in and out of the rubble, digging out valuable materials when directed and using her delicate hearing to warn them of incoming missiles. Both brothers were soaked with sweat and bleeding in various places. Vancien looked upset.

"This is ridiculous!" he spat over the crash of yet another boulder. "The city is being reduced to rubble!"

Amarian, who was more trained in the ways of war than his brother, just shrugged and helped Bedge shove a boulder off of a pile of bricks. "They'll run out of boulders soon enough, Vance. When they do, they're going to have to rely on less wieldy objects, such as tree stumps. Those will be less accurate and take them longer to load," he grunted as he and Bedge gave the large stone one last push, "which will give our guys more of a chance."

"Amarian's right," Chiyo said, announcing his presence. Both men snapped to attention. "At ease," he added, though he was surprised to get such an acknowledgement from Amarian. "On the other hand, we don't know how much ammunition they brought with them. It could be days of bombardment. We'd prefer not to wait that long."

"Big rock coming!" Bedge shouted. A second later, they, too, heard the warning whistle and ducked for cover. This one crashed into the top of the tower, sending debris raining down on them.

"Vancien!" Chiyo barked through the dust clouds. There was no more time for conversation. "Come with me! Amarian, keep up the good work! We need this tower in fighting shape!"

Amarian shouted an affirmative as Vancien's shape emerged through the haze. Soon he was trotting next to Chiyo as they headed away from the rubble.

"What is it, General?"

"Where is Thelámos?"

"He's in the stables west of the palace. Why?"

"I have an idea about how to slow down these cursed boulders. I think Thelámos will help."

When they arrived at the stables, they found the Ealatrophe in a restless condition. Bren was trying to calm him, but to no avail. He looked relieved when he saw Chiyo and Vancien.

Chiyo shivered as he entered. Outside it was a warm, early autore day, but that made little difference in the Ealatrophe's presence. In fact, the beast seemed even more frigid, if that were possible, since Kynell's arrival.

"Bren, you can go for now." Chiyo said. "We will take care of Thelámos."

When Bren had left, shedding extra layers as he went, Chiyo turned to Vancien. "You can see that this beast is ready for action."

Vancien nodded, laying a soothing hand on his neck. "He's been going crazy ever since the boulders started. What can one Ealatrophe do against an army like that?"

"A lot, I think." Chiyo pulled Vancien over to a clear spot on the floor and started forming a map with sticks and bits of hay. "This is Lascombe here." He pointed to a block of wood. "Here are the Easterners." He indicated a semicircle of hay partially encircling the block. As he positioned little upright twigs among the hay, he pondered his creation. "We need to find a way to take out those engines," he said, indicating the twigs.

Vancien was beginning to catch what he was saying. "But we can count at least ten of the trebuchets and undoubtedly more catapults. I might be able to take down one or two, but they'll target me before I can get to the third."

Chiyo nodded. "Which is why we will coordinate your attack with an ambush on this flank," he indicated the hay bits that stretched toward the southern end of the city. "How strong is Thelámos?"

The Ealatrophe seemed to understand the question and screeched an indignant answer. Vancien seconded his response. "He's strong enough to do what's required. Which is what?"

"Is he strong enough to grab the tip of one of those things and pull it over?"

"I should think so."

"Great. So here's what I'm thinking."

Even Thelámos bent low to listen as Chiyo outlined his plan. It would be their first foray into the enemy camp and Vancien's first battle since he had fallen to Amarian.

The attack had to take place at night, preferably in the darkest hours before orbrise. That meant the city would have to suffer a full day of bombardment. Even with rotation, their own siege crews were getting tired— the living soldiers, that is. The Risen Ones drew from an unlimited supply of energy.

The enemy army had stationed itself in a shallow valley between two wooded hills. The trees on the periphery of the army had already been cut down for security reasons, but thick groupings of timber were still standing about a hundred yards from the main force. Some intrepid scouts had already gone out and returned with the news that small regiments of Easterners were starting to infiltrate the woods, hoping to skirt to the north and south of the city. Fortunately for the Lascombians, the Easterners were not practiced in stealth. Even the Sentries, who in their waking lives had been able to disappear into shadows at will, fidgeted constantly. This made them noticeable to the scouts, who reported their movements.

Chiyo had already appointed Ruponi head of extramural activity. Despite the old king's beefy appearance, he was a clever, calculating soldier who could move as quietly as a yemain. The ground around the city had been cleared of tall grass and outbuildings as much as possible to prevent the enemy from approaching the city undetected. This posed a problem, however, for anyone who wanted to leave the city unobserved. Ruponi solved this by leading his men out the west gate, skirting south to the cover of the foothills, and then creeping into the tree line where it joined the hills. Another group was performing a similar maneuver to the north, although without the aid of the undulating hills. The leader of the northern sortie was a Risen Sentry, of all things, who surpassed even Ruponi in the art of stealth. Chiyo had given the two only one order: keep the Easterners from surrounding the city or else send up a warning if they could not stop them. Ruponi had every intention of stopping them.

Two munkke-trophe scouts were sent out to find these parties and advise them that a larger force would soon be joining them in the woods. There was no need to contact these newcomers, unless reinforcements were absolutely necessary. Ruponi and Brag, the Sentry captain, were to allow them passage, then return to their mission of containment.

That evening, after Chiyo had ordered him to go and get some rest, was the first time Vancien had a chance to think about what had happened the night before. Though he was bone-tired, he could not sleep yet. Instead, he kept replaying the events of Kynell's arrival over and over in his mind: his ride on Thelámos, his own reaction to him, his healing of that man's son, his words. . . that last brought a hard lump to his throat. "They are no longer my Advocates," he had said. And then, as if Vancien and Amarian meant no more to him than any common Lascombian did, he had stepped down from the Stoa into the soldiery. Vancien had heard him say something about soaking down the city, and then he had disappeared. Vancien remembered looking back at Amarian, stunned. His greatest hope, the one around which he had built his life, had stripped him of everything then left. And since every delusion of virtue had been shattered, he had no justification for calling it back.

Amarian must have read the pain in Vancien's eyes, for he had hurried to his side. Having had dealings with Zyreio, he had not expected Kynell to act much differently. "It's okay," he said.

"I'm not an Advocate? Am I anything?"

Telenar was also quick to join him. He, too, had looked dumbfounded. "I don't understand," he was muttering. "I don't understand." He had absentmindedly clapped a hand on Vancien's shoulder, then wandered off toward the palace.

If not for Amarian, Vancien had no idea what desperate thing he would have done. As it was, Amarian forced him into service, ordering him to check minor problems here and there, keeping him far away from other men, when possible. Before Vancien knew it, his mind was too tired and his body too sore to do anything but put one foot in front of the other. Then Chiyo had come, explained to him his assignment, and distracted him even more.

He had thought that he could figure it all out if he could get a moment to himself. But now that he had that moment, in the quiet next to Thelámos' stable, he only felt the pain of Kynell's rejection. What had he done wrong? Everything, as Kynell had silently reminded him. The other things Kynell had said, something about serving well, were fuzzy and unimportant. But that one phrase, "They are no longer my Advocates," hammered again and again at his brain. It made him angry. He clenched and unclenched his fist, wanting to break something. He had never been seriously angry at Kynell before, but now he wanted to let him have it. That night, up in the mountains, when he had determined to follow the Prysm no matter what, had Kynell even heard him? Or if he had, perhaps he had just checked off Vancien's name under the category of "easy victories." But his anger was mixed with guilt, which reminded him with brutal force that any real service was impossible for him—that it had always been impossible. His own inadequacies made his commitments paltry and delusional, little more than a speck in the plans of either Obsidian or the Prysm.

A quiet knock on the doorpost interrupted his thoughts. It was Amarian. He looked battered and tired, but composed.

"Telenar sent me to look for you," he said, as if apologizing. "It's been so crazy today. He wanted to make sure you were all right."

"I could ask the same question of him." Vancien's voice was harder than he had intended. He could not blame Telenar. They were both caught in the same trap. "I mean, how is he doing with Kynell?" He was not sure how to phrase the question, but Amarian knew what he meant.

"It's hard to say. He's not talking about it."

"Why didn't he come himself?"

Amarian sat down beside him. Vancien could smell the dust on him. "Chiyo has him counseling the soldiers. They all have questions. Relgaren is with him, too, trying to keep them at their posts instead of flocking to the soakers."

"Maybe we should flock, too."

Amarian gave him a look, but did not respond. After a moment, he picked up a piece of hay and started splitting it down the middle. "When I was with Zyreio, he always acted as if he didn't need me, as if he could barely stand me. I always thought he was a little ashamed of having an Advocate. Maybe that's why he despised me so much. Maybe Kynell feels the same way."

"Kynell is not Zyreio." Vancien replied.

"Of course he's not. But they're not like us. Kynell is a god, just like Zyreio seems to be." That sounded awkward, he knew, but he also knew Vancien's sensitivity on the point.

"I just don't understand," Vancien broke in. "I don't know what I am to him. If anything."

Amarian was about to answer, but he was interrupted by Chiyo standing in the door.

"I figured you might still be up," he said to Vancien. "I was not kidding when I said to get some rest." He looked at Amarian. "Vancien needs to get some sleep."

Both of them nodded, but not without feeling the shame of being ordered about like ordinary men. Amarian got to his feet. "I've got to find Bedge anyway. I think she was going to try and sneak in with the soakers." Yet when he reached the door, he stopped. "They're just not like us," he repeated, then left Vancien to his sleep.

Vancien did try to rest, and he finally succeeded, although it felt like he had just closed his eyes when he heard Chiyo's voice again.

"Vancien, get up. It's time."

As he rubbed his bleary eyes and yawned, he noticed that Chiyo was carrying a bow and a quiver full of arrows in one hand. In the other, a deep bucket.

"Take this bucket and strap it to Thelámos," Chiyo began, not waiting through another yawn. "Make sure it's within easy reach. Thelámos does not get nervous around fire?"

Finally waking up, Vancien shook his head and led the Ealatrophe out of his stall. Then he started lashing the bucket above Thelámos' right shoulder. "I don't think so. I've never tested him."

Chiyo did not say anything. Instead, he pulled out some flint and in a few quick strokes, had the hay burning at Thelámos' feet. With a shout, Vancien jumped to put it out, but Chiyo held him back. Thelámos, meanwhile, fixed a disdainful eye on Chiyo, then on the small blaze. Delicately moving his claws away from the heat, he bent down and breathed over it. The fire disappeared, leaving only a tendril of smoke from the ashes.

Chiyo nodded with satisfaction. "Telenar was right. Okay then." He clapped his hands together and turned toward Vancien. "The bucket you just put on Thelámos is lined with casing tar, which is non-flammable. At the bottom of bucket is a thick layer of gruel, which is a sticky, flammable substance that one of our fine chemists has cooked up. The ends of these arrows," he pulled one out of the quiver, "have been wrapped with rags to soak up as much gruel as possible. Before you take off, you need to light the gruel. Its burn is low but intense—the bucket is deep enough to hide its glow, I think. Then, as Thelámos starts tipping each machine, you dip an arrow into the gruel and stick it on to whatever part of the machine you can reach. When the slightest amount of wind comes in contact with lit gruel, it will burst into a full flame. That's great once it is on the machine, but be careful when you pull the arrow out at first."

"So what's the bow for?"

"In case you have time to shoot at a couple of catapults or ballistae. But focus on the trebuchets and siege towers. Make it a clean approach. Quick, quiet. I imagine you'll be able to get at least two machines on the first run before they know what's going on. Then you'll have to lie low before you strike again. Dawn is still a few hours away, so we should have plenty of time to do some damage."

Vancien nodded. His stomach was in knots.

"You will attack the northern machines first. Like I said, try to get two. They're going to be confused by the first long enough to try a second. After that, disappear back over the woods. Then fly south around the back of the army. Keep your distance: we don't want a chance arrow taking you down. There will be a force awaiting you in the trees south of the Obsidian forces.

How strong is Thelámos's sense of smell?"

"I think his sight is better."

"Okay. I was hoping he'd be able to smell it before he could see it, but it should still work. Relgaré has requested to be in charge of the sortie. He's been equipped with a tall metal tube that fits over a small campfire, so it's only visible from the air." He grimaced. "That's the plan, anyway. We're hoping you can see it and make contact with Relgaré."

"Relgaré, huh? So how will I know it's him and not a party of Chasmites camping out?"

Chiyo dug a small pouch out of his belt. He held it out to Vancien. Inside was a foul-smelling brown powder. "Chur-root. It'll make the fire burn green for a few moments. They've been instructed to burn it every five to ten minutes. So watch for it. When you see the green, land, make contact, then take to the air again. All his men will be ready to move. The plan is for them to attack the southern flank of the Easterners a split second before you take down the engines on that side. When you hear their shouts, attack."

Vancien looked dubiously at the bucket tied to Thelámos and the quiver in his hands. "And the retreat?"

"Do not try to take on the whole army by yourself. When you have taken down some more engines on the southern side, fly straight back to the wall. Just have Thelámos give a screech before you go. Relgaré knows to listen for it and retreat as soon as he hears it. We do not expect his crew to do much damage; they are there as a diversion for you."

Vancien shouldered the quiver and the bow and stepped toward the Ealatrophe. "Anything else?"

Chiyo did not respond immediately. He gave Vancien a thoughtful look before holding out his hand. "May Kynell keep you safe, Vancien. It has been a privilege to serve alongside you."

They shook hands and Vancien led Thelámos out of the stall before his fear could show. Chiyo's words reminded him again of how dangerous his mission was. But then he remembered his anger. What was it to Kynell if he died tonight? Would he even know, caught up as he was with his precious soaking crew? The thought made him shiver. He had never feared death before, especially after having gone through it, but this was different. Tonight of all nights, the god of the Prysm would not be with him. And Zyreio was in that army.

He shivered and leaned against Thelámos for warmth. Soon they had walked to a clear enough space that the great Ealatrophe could spread his wings. Without a further thought, Vancien swung himself up onto his back and gripped his neck tightly. Lascombe was counting on him—more than that, Chiyo had put his faith in him. Whatever Kynell might think, there was no backing down now.

Soon he was over the northern tree line. The air was cool and the night was cloudy. He was glad for his armor; the padding kept him from feeling the chill of the air as it rushed by him. Normally, he would have taken comfort in the steady whoosh of Thelámos's wings, but tonight he could not hear them, so great was the chaotic sound coming from the army as he drew near. Night did nothing to still their torment. He fought the urge to cover his ears with his hands; not only would that be unpractical, but he could not think of a less manly way to enter battle.

He realized with a start that he had forgotten to light the gruel. With a frustrated grunt, he pulled Thelámos back and directed him into a circular path over the trees. Then he dug out the flint pieces to strike a spark. It took him a few tries: bending over Thelámos's shoulder while reaching into a deep bucket proved awkward. Nor could he see what he was doing; the sudden heat on his hands, however, must mean that the gruel had caught. He leaned back, watching to see if flames would shoot out of the bucket's top. They did not. He could barely discern even a faint glow. As usual, Chiyo had been right.

Now it was time to move. He closed his eyes and urged Thelámos forward, toward the campfires of the Easterners.

CHAPTER TWENTY-TWO

The Ealatrophe had keen sight; even though the areas around the machines were poorly lit, he had no trouble finding the first one. As he drew near, Vancien grabbed an arrow from the quiver and thrust it into the bucket. Thelámos's talons seized the tip of the engine—a trebuchet—and started to pull. Vancien jerked the arrow out of the bucket, leaned back behind Thelámos's flapping wing, and lodged the incendiary in the machine's top joint.

He heard a creaking and a quiet whoosh of flame, but before he could survey his handiwork, Thelámos was taking him to the next machine, this one a siege tower. It was much taller than the trebuchet, so Thelámos entered a steep climb while Vancien heard the chaos below him take on a sharper pitch—presumably in response to the falling trebuchet. He tried to ignore it and prepare the next arrow. But Thelámos hit the side of the tower a little hard and low. Recovering quickly, he scrambled to the top ledge, but he had lost all of his forward momentum and had to flap backwards, pulling with his legs. This made Vancien's task that much more difficult, but he managed to get low enough over Thelámos's shoulder to plant the arrow just as gravity began to take over. Another machine down.

Arrows were whizzing around them, but the Chasmite humans had little better vision than their mortal counterparts. As the second machine crashed to the ground, Thelámos was able to fly back to the trees. So far, so good. Vancien had never been so grateful for a cloudy night; if the Chasmites had been able to see him at all, there would have been holes in Thelámos's wings. As it was, they remained intact and carried them far behind the army, then south to meet up with Relgaré's men.

The Obsidian forces filled up the breadth of the wide, shallow valley that indicated the end of the plains and the beginning of Lascombe's hinterland. Vancien had never realized how broad that valley was until he was crossing it in the echo of the Chasmites' fury, counting the beat of Thelámos's wings and looking for the tree-line that held the old king.

Finally, the air changed around them and Vancien could tell they had made it.

"All right, Thelámos," he whispered, "look for the green fire."

The great beast responded by dropping his altitude and humming low in his throat. It was a sound Vancien had never heard before this night, but one that he was beginning to associate with battle and stealth.

If he thought it had taken a long time to cross behind the army, he was unpleasantly surprised at the length of time it took to find that faint, green glimmer among the trees. Thelámos circled endlessly, adopting a sort of crisscross pattern to cover a wide area in the least amount of time. Just as Vancien thought it was impossible to find them before orbrise, Thelámos gave a tiny screech. Vancien rubbed his eyes and saw a green glimmer below and to his right. The Ealatrophe did not need any guidance; he headed straight for it. After hovering a moment far above the small flame to make sure all was well, he landed.

The atmosphere in the small camp was sober. All was dark, but he could hear the sound of swords being sharpened and voyoté shifting. He could hear quiet comments here and there, but could see scarcely anyone. Fortunately, Relgaré was right there to meet them. Vancien recognized his voice, and to his surprise, found it comforting.

"Vancien, it's good to see you," he said. "We were concerned that the night was waning too fast."

Vancien returned the greeting and jumped to the ground. He needed to stretch his legs before the next attack. "Two machines are down."

"Yes, we heard the pitch change about an hour ago."

An hour? Was that all it had been? Vancien wiped his brow and realized he was hungry. "Do you have any food?"

"I'll get you some. But first, come with me." Vancien felt a hand on his arm, leading him away from the other sounds. He heard a whispered "Here he is" and felt the hand let go. Had Relgaré been speaking to him?

Then another voice, the source of which Vancien could not see, said "Thank you." He felt another hand on his arm, pushing him gently toward the dim shadow of a log. "Please, sit."

The night was horribly dark and Vancien wanted badly to see who was talking to him. Instead, he had to settle for a desperate guess. "Kynell?" he breathed.

He felt the warm hand again, insisting that he sit. "Hello, Vance. I'm glad to see you made it safely."

Vancien stared in the direction of the voice; it was so dark that all he could see of Kynell's face was a shadowy outline. "What are you doing here?" he blurted out. "I thought you were with the soakers."

"I will return to them shortly," Kynell responded. "They need me more than you might think."

"*I* need you." The words were out of his mouth before he could stop them.

"I know. That's why I have come to talk with you. Vance, surely you know that you and 'Ian are very dear to me."

Vancien, still struggling with his anger and guilt, remained quiet.

"There is much I would say to you, but there is not much time. You have both been my Advocates. But I will be the Advocate now. What I'm about to do is something you could never do."

Vancien, assuming he was talking about defeating the Chasmites, quickly interrupted. "I know I'm not you. I am too insignificant. But I had hoped to be by your side."

There was a touch of cheer in Kynell's voice. "That's where I want you to be. But the time of the Advocates has passed. This new age will be my own."

Vancien forgot his guilt as hope leapt up inside of him. "Then why are we talking about this in the dark? We should be shouting it from the rooftops! Surely your age would be better than all the others."

"It will."

"And Zyreio will be defeated?"

Kynell's voice was low. "He will."

"You sound upset."

There was a pause, then, "Zyreio was once my creature. I will not delight in his downfall, but neither will I grieve over it. Since you ask, I will say that something else troubles me, something that is coming very soon."

"What is it, Lord? Tell me, and I will do what I can to help."

He felt Kynell lean close. "Vance, never forget that justice demands a penalty for every wrong deed. I demand this penalty. But the price is too high for my loved ones to pay it and survive."

Unbidden, the memory of Verial's hand in his came back to him. It was a hand he should never have touched. There was a need to reconcile Kynell's words and that image, but he had no time to figure it out. He could already hear footsteps behind him. It was Relgaré. He had some dried meat and water, which he pushed into Vancien's hands. "I am sorry to interrupt, Lord" he whispered to Kynell. "But if we are going to do this, we should do it now."

Vancien nodded. There would be more time to talk later. For now, he wanted to get this done and over with. Eating the meat on the way, he hurried to Thelámos and mounted. After checking to make sure the gruel was still burning, he urged him to flight. Kynell's words still buzzed in his head, but he could not make sense of them. It was not possible that every wrong deed could demand a penalty. No one could pay such a high price. And to whom would it be paid? People could not be parsed out based on their actions; that made things too complicated. Instead, they were judged by their allegiance, which affected their actions. After all, the spiritual world of Rhyvelad consisted of one very simple dynamic: followers of Zyreio went to the Chasm, followers of Kynell went to be with him. That was how justice worked, and the fact that it worked was spread out on the ground under Vancien like a writhing, twitching blanket.

The enemy camp was mobilizing. From the circles of light cast by the campfires, he could see soldiers being beaten and forced into ranks. The normal din of sound had been reduced to a low murmur, interrupted by staccato commands, usually followed by the crack of a whip. In many ways, this concentrated activity was more disturbing than the previous chaos. It meant that the mob was capable of being directed, which served to remind Vancien of who was doing the directing. He shuddered, trying not to question the wisdom of Chiyo's plan.

Thelámos had reached the closest machine. He circled above it, hopefully far out of the enemy's sight. Only then did it occur to Vancien that the fennels and Sentries should be able to spot him, even on a cloudy night. Were they all stationed away from the machines? He had no time to pursue the thought; a shout from the trees meant that Relgaré was attacking. He took advantage of the moment and urged Thelámos into a dive. The Ealatrophe responded, folding his wings and plummeting them both down to the trebuchet below. He pulled up just before they reached it, snagged it with his talons, then waited until Vancien plunged another arrow tip into the gruel. Thelámos gave a mighty yank, Vancien fixed the arrow on the nearest piece of timber he could find, and down it went with a magnificent groan. As it fell, Vancien spotted a catapult close by, its wheels and trappings illuminated by another campfire. Without thinking twice, he unslung the bow, dipped an arrow into the gruel, and let off a shot. His aim was true. The Chasmites, with their attention torn between the falling siege engine and the ground attack, barely even noticed it go up in flames.

Vancien could only indulge in a brief moment of satisfaction. No sooner was the trebuchet on its way down than he heard a chorus of twangs below him. With a shout, he urged Thelámos upward as a hail of arrows rushed their direction. They escaped unscathed, but it was only a matter of time before a chance arrow would hit its target. He decided to attempt one more machine and then head for Lascombe.

The last engine went down with little trouble. The night was so dark that the Chasmites had no idea where he was or when he was going to attack. There was another volley of arrows as the fourth machine crashed to the ground, but again, with no damage. If so much had not been at stake, Vancien might have enjoyed watching the big, lumbering devices fall. But there was no time for that. He had to return to the city.

The sounds of the battle were still going strong. He resisted the urge to go help; Chiyo would never forgive him if he lost Thelámos on such a foolish venture. They would be of limited assistance in close ground combat, anyway. Instead, knowing that it would give away his position, he urged the Ealatrophe to let out his sharpest cry. Now Relgaré would know the mission was accomplished and he could retreat. Then he turned west for the short flight between Obsidian's army and the walls of Lascombe.

But Thelámos had not gone far in that direction when he gave a small, alarmed screech.

"What is it, Thelámos?" he asked in a low voice. The Ealatrophe dipped his wings to the north in response, looking pointedly at the ground to their right. Vancien followed his gaze. Thelámos' sharp vision had picked up on what no one else, either in the city or in the woods, could see: a dark, quiet mass of troops moving across no-man's land. They had already dug their way under the barrier wall and were entering the second line of defense.

Early in the morning before Vancien's night-time flight, Gair, Ragger, and Verial were close enough to the army's southern edge to hear the Chasmites' groaning. At Gair's request, Ragger had led them to within an arrow-shot of their southern flank. Gair had hoped to do something with the engines themselves, but they were too far off. Hastening through the woods for a better view, they beheld the Obsidian army spread out before them like an ocean.

"It's horrific." Verial hissed.

Ragger had already drawn his blade and was watching the Chasmites intently. His eagerness did not pass unnoticed by Verial.

"What do you think you're doing, primate?"

Ragger gave her a dismissive glance. "I'm preparing to make a difference, what else?"

Gair, too, had already loosened his sword in his scabbard. As he opened his mouth to tell Verial to dismount and go hide in the woods, she held up a hand in exasperation.

"You two aren't honestly planning to fight the Chasmites, are you?"

Gair's pulse was already starting to race. On the ground, his legs would not support him. But on the back of a voyoté, he planned on being invincible. Why must that woman be a hindrance to everything?

"I bet we could do some sort of damage."

"Yes, but look at them. What can you do against that?"

She had a point. The Chasmites writhed with an unholy energy. In an effort to release that energy, they pounded and beat at each other. The blows, even those delivered by sharp blades, had no effect, except to make the receiver angry.

"Ragger," Gair breathed, "I think this fight is beyond us. Come on, let's see what else we can do."

But Ragger was silent. When Gair turned to look for him, the munkke-trophe and the voyoté were gone. Only he and Verial remained hidden in the trees.

"Where did he go?"

Verial was no longer watching the Chasmites. Her eyes were fixed in the opposite direction, toward a spot of darkness at the base of a tree.

Gair's own voyoté began shaking underneath him. Then it began whining so piteously that he dismounted to have a look at it. No sooner had he touched the ground than it, too, abandoned him for the safety of the trees.

"Verial, what's going on?"

"They're escaping, Gair," she said, in an uncharacteristically worried tone, "and I think you should, too."

"Escaping what? What could possibly scare them?"

His question was answered as a dark spot at the base of a tree grew into the form of a man. He did not look like much: a short fellow with a bit of a paunch and thinning hair. Yet he made Gair's stomach turn. He was reminded, only more careless.

The three stood in silence for a moment. The short man obviously enjoyed watching the other two squirm. The orbs were just beginning to rise; the cool dawn placed in stark colors the thick underbrush and sparse trees. The man was a few paces away from them, across a meager little path that before this day had seen more animal traffic than human. He leaned casually against a thin trunk, content to let them speak first.

Gair had no desire to open his mouth. It was Verial who started the conversation

"Aren't you supposed to be with *them*?" Though her words were bold, Gair could hear a quiver in her voice.

The man shrugged, rubbing a dirty finger across his nose. "Oh, I don't know. They seem to be doing all right just now." He pulled out a bit of churr-root and set about lighting it. When he was done, it dangled from his lips, burning a dull green. The rank smell of the root was so pungent that they could almost taste it.

"So what are you doing here? Surely Lascombe is about to fall." The quiver in her voice was growing stronger.

The man puffed at his makeshift cigar. "I think the more pertinent question," he responded, turning his gaze to Gair, "is what are you doing here?"

Gair stiffened. "I'm here to protect the lady." If he had been honest with himself, he thought, he would have known that that was his mission ever since he first stepped foot out of the Eastern Lands. The realization gave him strength, but he doubted it would be enough to face whoever it was that was speaking with them.

The man nodded. "Yes, I figured that's what you would say."

Verial looked from Gair to the man. "We must be on our way."

"Your 'protector' here is free to leave. Sadly, he's beyond my grasp. You and I, however, have a debt to settle."

Verial narrowed her eyes. "Haven't you already taken enough of me? What else is there to take?"

The man stepped forward, but Gair pushed himself between them. "Listen, I do not know who or what you are. As I said, I'm here to protect the lady."

The man stopped, shaking his greasy head. His voice gurgled in his throat. "Oh, I know what sort of protector you are. First, you allow her to go off and cause trouble for the Prysm. Then you allow her to be manipulated by Obsidian. And the first chance you get, you go off to live in a big city, abandoning her to her enemies. *That*," he pointed at Gair with his glowing churr-root, "is the type of protector you are. Now I will tell you again. Leave the lady and go back to the city that you enjoy so much." He laughed, a crude, liquidy sound that mutated quickly into a fit of coughing.

Gair was confused. How could he know all of that? Who *was* this character? This guy knew more about his time with Verial than even Amarian did. He looked at Verial again. He had never seen her look so afraid. This was not a Chasmite. He did not twitch, and he knew too much. But he was not a man, either. It took a moment for the awful realization to come.

"Zyreio."

The man looked at him disdainfully. "That name sounds so foul on your lips. Now leave, Gair. Or you'll deal with me directly."

"I thought you said I was beyond your grasp," Gair managed to respond.

The man wiped the phlegm off of his chin with a dirty sleeve. "I may have lied about that."

Verial had watched the exchange with a mixture of pride and terror. Zyreio's presence was suffocating. She could not conceive how Gair could stay of his own free will. As for her, her legs were immobilized just as surely as if they had turned to stone. Her mouth, however, was not.

"Gair, you should go. I'll be fine," she lied.

Though his face had gone white with fear, he gave her a sharp look. "Verial, you've been lying your whole life. Now, in the presence of *him*, you lie again?"

She did not respond. How could he know? How could he have any clue what she had been through. What she was about to go through? She almost wished he would leave so she could get on with it.

He caught the hostility in her gaze but it did not change his resolve. Zyreio, on the other hand, was growing impatient. "Gair, son of Edgar, did you know that your father walks with me? He fights in that army, against the Prysm. He is a true soldier who will be faithful to the end. You, however, prefer to choose the path of greatest comfort. You did not make your colors known until after you had left the Eastern Lands. You suffered prettily for your lady love here, but when the time came to follow a new hero, you left her. You are nothing. The Prysm does not need you. I do not want you. Even she will not follow you." He gestured toward Verial.

186

The words hit Gair's resolve like a flight of arrows, each one finding its mark. He knew Zyreio was a liar, but this time he spoke truth. It had been no sacrifice to follow Corfe back to Lascombe. It had only led him into more luxury than he had ever known. He recalled that first night Verial had sought him out. He had been living in comfort while she had traveled the greater part of Rhyvelad, killing for food, shivering in the cold, tearing at her hair in misery. And when she found him, he had offered her a way out of her agony. He had offered her the Prysm. But she had scorned that, just as she had scorned everything else. So little was his influence on her that she mocked the thing dearest to him. Further, when she followed him to Ulan, she did so only to mock him further, suggesting that the precious life of that poor baby was more of a hindrance than a blessing. Now, in the face of Obsidian himself, she was sending him away. What was the point of protecting a woman like that?

He exhaled, thinking how hungry he was. When was the last time he had eaten? It was time for this interview to end. He took several steps backward and was about to leave altogether when he caught a glimpse of Verial's face. She was watching him. And she was crying.

The sight stung his conscience and struck at his heart. Without thinking, he drew his sword and advanced toward Zyreio.

"In the mighty name of Kynell and all that the Prysm sheds light upon, I will send you back to the pit from which you came."

Zyreio held up his hands in mock surrender. "Oh my! So you do have a little spring of courage in you. How inspiring!" He grinned, displaying a row of brown and crumbly teeth.

"Leave!" Gair barked.

"Like I said," Zyreio continued, "You're beyond my grasp. But she is not." He moved forward, brushing aside Gair's sword as if it were a sewing needle.

"Verial!" Gair shouted, "come to me! Come to Kynell!"

But Verial only stood there, allowing Zyreio to reach out a grimy hand and catch her by the waist. "I can't, Gair," she said, her blue eyes still moist. "I'm not like you. And I'm so tired of fighting."

She allowed Zyreio to lead her through the trees, toward the field filled with his children. Gair stood there, helpless. And when she disappeared from sight, he sat down, dazed. He shouted after her once, but there was no response. She had gone. There could be no redemption for her now. He had failed again.

CHAPTER TWENTY-THREE

Sirin kept watch at the camp for most of the night. Knowing they had such a guardian, the children slept better than they had in weeks. It was only toward dawn that their guardian drifted off into a well-deserved sleep.

A sharp, pungent odor woke him awhile later, as the orbs were rising. A munkke-trophe's sense of smell was always reliable, even at absurd distances. In this instance, he smelled what was coming long before he saw it.

It was another munkke-trophe, riding a voyoté. The sharp smell had been a blend of fear and canine lather. As the pair drew closer, the munkke-trophe saw Sirin and started furiously waving his paws. Sirin jumped up and hurried to meet him, eager not to wake the children before it was necessary.

The other munkke-trophe was dressed like a soldier. When he saw Sirin coming his direction, he jumped off his mount and bent over double. Sirin could see that he was panting. Where could he have come from? Before he could ask, the other munkke-trophe gasped out his message.

"Sir," he spat, "I knew I was right to come this way. My captain needs your help. Please come."

"Who's your captain?"

"Captain Gair, sir, of Lascombe. He serves as a scout for Lord Corfe."

"And where is he now?"

The munkke-trophe pointed back from the direction he had come. "In the trees south of the valley, sir. Please. It's probably too late, but we must hurry."

Sirin nodded, then persuaded the soldier to come back to camp and at least get some water before making the return journey. The soldier complied and soon Lucio and Teehma had been shaken awake, told to gather their things, and make haste. They did so without complaint.

The journey back took most of the early morning. They left the road, veering south, away from the army. They spotted Gair as soon as they came close to the tree line. He must have been watching for them, for once they came within sight, he stepped out of the trees only long enough to catch their attention—a pale dot against the dark wood—then disappeared again to wait.

When they arrived, he met them with a despairing smile. "Lieutenant Ragger, I was wondering where you had gone."

"To get help, sir. It is good to see you survived. Where is the lady?"

Gair's expression turned stony. "She has gone where we cannot follow her."

Ragger bowed his head. "I am sorry, Captain."

Gair did not respond immediately. Instead, he turned toward Lucio and Teehma. "I did not think to see you two again so soon."

Teehma had the presence of mind to curtsy. "We want to thank you again for your help, Captain. Your food kept us alive."

"You came all this way to thank me?"

"No, sir. We came with Sirin."

A few more introductions were made, then Gair suggested they move deeper into the trees, closer to the mountains. "The Easterners," he said, "will not be kind to children." No one felt any need to disagree with him. He looked so haunted that even Lucio was content to give him some berth.

"What's the matter with him?" Lucio asked as he and Teehma trailed behind. "He looks as if he's seen a ghost."

Teehma rolled her eyes. "We've all seen ghosts now, if that's what you want to call them. He must've seen something much worse."

Lucio snorted. "What can be worse than a Chasmite?"

Teehma just looked at him. It was not a conversation she wanted to pursue further.

But Lucio was undeterred. "Have you noticed how he limps? Wonder what caused that? Just look at his scars!"

"You seem pretty enamored with him. Why don't you go ask him yourself?"

Lucio's response was to hit her arm. It was a playful tap, with no trace of anger. The transformation that Sirin had wrought the day before was still in effect. Much of Lucio's hardness had evaporated.

Gair did not prove to be very talkative. He was too absorbed with his own thoughts, allowing Sirin and Ragger to lead the way to a safe camp. The children, to their delight, took turns riding the voyoté. Only toward lunch time did they find a location all the adults felt comfortable with. It was a sort of dug-out, caused by the recent rains. The soil had eroded from a steep hill, leaving a sheltered, fairly dry location where they could see anybody coming for at least thirty yards. While Ragger went out hunting, the children helped Sirin gather wood for the fire. Yet Gair still seemed lost in his thoughts. One of his legs seemed to be hurting him. He flexed it compulsively. Other than that, he did not move. He just sat on the ground, staring into the trees.

Lucio and Teehma were too intimidated to disturb him, but after a few hours of Gair's grim meditation, Sirin decided enough was enough. Leaving the children to tend the fire, he loped over to where Gair sat silent and cross-legged.

"I say, young man, you're rather sober this evening."

Gair did not move.

"I said," Sirin persisted, "you look like you've been through the mill, as it were. What troubles you?"

After a few seconds, Gair turned his head to look at the munkke-trophe as if he'd never seen one before. "What do you want?"

Sirin stamped his cane down on the ground. "I want you to come out of your shell. You're scaring the children."

Gair shook his head, his long, dirty hair falling down around his face. "I'm sorry. I don't mean to be rude." He stopped, giving Sirin an evaluating look. "I have failed to take care of the one thing I was supposed to protect."

The munkke-trophe's eyes narrowed. "There are many assumptions behind that statement, young man. But we'll let it go. Was it a woman?"

"Of a sort."

"Of a sort! What sort of response is that? Well, I suppose I'd grieve for her—have a mourning party or two—then move on."

"But she's not dead. She just made a horrible mistake. So horrible that I can't even begin to describe it. And she will not let me help her. She has never let me help her."

The man's frustration was so raw that Sirin softened his tone. "It is hard to watch others make poor choices. But Kynell will help her."

"But it's Kynell whom she's rejected."

Sirin harrumphed. "Usually the first of many bad decisions."

Gair was shaking his head again. His voice cracked as he voiced the bitter truth that had been cycling around and around in his head. "And now she's gone. She would not listen to me and now there's no way of saving her. I was supposed to protect her."

"Now, now," Sirin soothed. "If she is still alive, there's still hope. Though she has rejected Kynell, the Prysm may not have given up on her. Perhaps she'll come around."

Gair gave him a hard look. "You don't understand. She is with Zyreio. Right now. In his physical presence."

Sirin considered. He was not surprised by much, although the woman's plight was unusual. Still, there was an answer for everything, and he usually knew it. "And how long do you think it will be before she realizes her mistake? When she does, who will be there to offer her a way out? Who will be there to point her to Kynell?"

He watched as his words sunk in. Gair shook his head again, then clinched his fists, rubbed his leg, stood up, sat back down again, then jumped to his feet. "You think I should go after her?"

"I think you'd be a fool not to be there when she needs you. And it sounds like that could be at any time."

Gair was pacing with renewed energy. "Yes, you're right. I can do that, at least, though Kynell knows how. But I should leave soon. Immediately. Who knows what she's been through already?" He stopped and turned to Sirin. "I hate to do this, but I need the voyoté. Can you spare it?"

Sirin agreed. By the time Ragger returned from hunting, Gair was gone, and Sirin was left wondering who the woman was who had tormented him so much. When he asked Ragger, the lieutenant replied that it was Verial.

"Verial? That old witch from the Ages?"

"Yes, sir."

"But that's impossible! She's pure evil! She's no good! Of all the lame-brained, love-struck young men," Sirin sputtered. "If I had known who she was, I would never have told him to go after her."

Ragger nodded respectfully. "But you didn't know, sir, so you did. Perhaps it was for the best."

Sirin scowled at the ground. "Hmph. All the same, it seems like such a waste to upset oneself over *her*."

"Yes, sir."

———————

Amarian was the first one to spot Vancien's return in the dim morning light. He had been standing on the battlements, scanning the horizon for any sign of his brother. Bedge was with him. When Thelámos's silhouette appeared through the haze, they both gave a loud whoop and jogged to the place where the Ealatrophe touched down.

"You did it, Vance! The assault is a fraction of what it was. Well done!"

"Whoo-hoo! Sir's brother is alive!"

Amarian's face was so flushed with joy that Vancien scarcely recognized him. For a second, he forgot the unpleasant report he had to give and simply enjoyed his praise.

"Thanks, 'Ian. Thelámos was fantastic. You should have seen him! He toppled those towers like they were toys. I saw Relgaré, and I talked with Kynell." He waved a hand toward the battle scene. Yet as he looked back in that direction, he remembered what was coming.

"We have to find Chiyo," he said, interrupting Amarian's question about Kynell. "Quickly! The Sentries and fennels have broken through the barrier walls."

Amarian swallowed his comment and nodded. "I figured it was just a matter of time. Chiyo is down at the base of that tower. It's where he's set up headquarters. Fly Thelámos down. I'll meet you there."

Vancien did as he was told. He soon found Chiyo in conference with Tengar. They were arguing over how to use one of the Risen battalions. Tengar wanted to reassign them to repair the siege engines, Chiyo insisted on keeping them near the gate to which they were already assigned.

"But they're not doing anything there!" Tengar protested. "At least we could put them to work for a while."

"General Chiyo!" Vancien called as Thelámos landed. He jumped to the ground as both men came out to greet him.

"Welcome back, Vancien!" Chiyo said, shaking him by the hand. "It's good to see you alive and whole. Well done!"

"Generals," Vancien nodded toward Tengar. "I have bad news. The Sentries and fennels have broken through the outer wall. It will not be long before they either tear it down completely or come to the base of the city wall itself."

Chiyo turned toward Tengar. "The battalion stays at the gate. Lady Jana and Captain Hunoi are commanding them; they'll know what to do. Go tell the engine teams to change their trajectory and be on the lookout. Fennels are smart climbers, but the casing tar should hold them for a while."

Tengar saluted. "Of course, General." He trotted off, not a little annoyed.

Chiyo, meanwhile, had another mission for Vancien. "I think you should go and find Telenar. Those Patroniites need to be ready for anything, especially with the fiends so close."

Just then, Amarian ran up. He must have plummeted down the stairs, so quickly did he arrive and so winded did he look. Bedge was at his feet, looking as if she were enjoying herself.

"Sir fell down the big stone steps!" she cried joyously. "Bounce, bounce, he went! Until Bedge stopped him."

Amarian looked a little sheepish. "I tripped. So, what's the plan?"

Chiyo took a moment to decide. "Vance, go find Telenar. Amarian, come with me. We need to alert everyone at the gates." But Bedge's energetic maneuvers had caught his eye. He knelt down to her level, pondering a better idea.

"You have a lot of energy, don't you, little one?"

"Oh yes! Bedge can bounce and hop all over the city!"

"Do you think you can run to each Risen battalion along the wall? Will you tell them that the Sentries and fennels are coming soon?"

Bedge did not stop bouncing. "Yes! Yes! Bedge can do that!"

"Good. Go do it. And then come find Amarian."

Eager though she was, she did not take off at once. First she looked at Amarian. Only when he told her to go, and be quick about it, did she take off like a shot.

"That's quite the partner you have there, Amarian."

Amarian gazed at her trail of dust. "She does have her uses. Vance, what are you waiting around here for?"

Vancien jolted to attention. "Oh, right. Telenar." After sending Thelámos off to the stables, he ran toward the palace.

To his surprise, he found Telenar in his old office, alone, or close to it. Corfe was sitting in a corner, staring out the window.

"Don't mind him just now," Telenar said as Vancien came in. "He's wrestling through some things."

"I thought you were out doing some counseling."

Telenar gestured for Vancien to sit, which he was happy to do. It was comforting being with his mentor. Despite all that had happened, Vancien knew he had much to learn from him.

Telenar started wiping his spectacles, as he always did when he was stressed. "I was counseling. I went all around, looking for those who were refusing to go into the tunnels, or who wouldn't let the Risen Ones go about their duty, or who kept clamoring to be on the soaking crew. But then, sometime before dawn, I just stopped. There was nothing I could say. After all, I didn't understand him any more than they did. They kept asking me questions about the Advocates, and what he meant, and why he was not with everyone at the same time." Through glasses that were almost as smudgy as they were before, he looked at Vancien. "And I just didn't have an answer for them. So I came back here to wait," he tapped the desk in front of him, "and read." He ran his hand over a much used, heavily marked copy of the Ages that lay open on the desk. "He came in about an hour ago. Hasn't said a word."

Vancien looked over at Corfe, who was still staring out the window, not moving. The sight of him in the corner and Telenar reading behind the desk was eerily calm in contrast to the heavy activity outside.

"I spoke with him again, when I was out tonight."

Telenar's head jerked sharply. "Have you? What did he say? I confess I don't understand what he's doing here. It's strange, but I feel more distant from him now than I did before he came."

Vancien nodded. "I know. I felt that way too. But then he came to me, out at Relgaré's camp, before I took Thelámos over the army. And he talked with me. Just me," he added, as if marveling at it.

They heard loud cries outside of Telenar's window and hurried over to look. Men and Risen Ones were all racing toward the eastern wall. Even the soaking crew, distinguished by their wet clothes, were heading in that direction. Both Telenar and Vancien looked instinctively for Kynell, but they did not see him. Telenar drew back and looked at Vancien.

"You have to find out what's going on. And I can't just leave him." He jerked his head toward Corfe, who had shown only the slightest reaction to sudden noise.

"What will you do?"

"Try to put him with some of the other priests. I believe several of them are on soaking duty."

Vancien did not spare a glance for Corfe as he left, but he could not help looking back at his friend. Telenar was sitting again at his desk, flipping through the Ages.

"You should go to him, Telenar. He'll talk with you."

Telenar shook his head, and Vancien could not stay to discuss the point. He took off down the hallway, pulse racing. When he emerged out into the orblight, he began to jog through the streets, squinting at the distant battlements to see what was happening. Occasionally, a boulder would whistle overhead, forcing him to take cover. Even when he made it to the Eastern wall, it was almost impossible to tell what was going on.

After a few moments, Hull found him.

"Vance! Thank Kynell you're here. The Sentries and fennels are at the base of the wall. They've found a way to scale the casing tar, though they can only do it slowly. There are thousands of them!"

"Aren't we dumping rocks on their heads?" Vancien asked.

"Yes, but it just knocks them back a bit. It won't kill them. And we're running out of rocks."

"So what's our plan then?"

"Chiyo is over there." He pointed to the general's temporary headquarters. "We'll find out soon enough."

"Is Kynell there, too?"

Hull gave a sharp jerk of his head. "No. He's with the soakers again. I don't know why."

Vancien did not either, but he was relieved to see that even the Risen Ones were confused about the Prysm god's behavior.

"Glad to see you made it back safely, son," Hull added.

"Me too. I guess it was fortunate for me that the Sentries and fennels were already on their way." He bit his tongue, but not before all the words came out. How selfish that sounded!

Hull clapped him on the shoulder as they headed in Chiyo's direction. "It was a good thing. I prayed for you to come back in one piece."

"But why? I mean, if I had died, I would have come back as a Risen One, right? And then I would only be stronger."

Hull shook his head. "The Risen Ones are here and the living ones are here. A man can die only once in this fight. It's Kynell's wisdom—otherwise, it could only end when everyone on Rhyvelad was killed. Plus," he added, "I don't want to outlive you."

They had arrived at Chiyo's base. He was again arguing with Tengar.

"A sortie is our only option," Chiyo was insisting. "We have to move before they get their claws into that tar."

"And I'm saying that we maintain the defense at the top. Tarl, what do you think?"

The Sentry captain scratched one long claw under his chin. He had recovered well from Corfe's failure. The presence of Risen Sentries made him believe anything was possible, even serving Kynell. He fanned his ears in and out, looking over the handful of men who had assembled to face of this new danger.

"It is tough to say, General," he responded to Chiyo. Tengar he viewed as little more than a nuisance. "Once they get to the top, they will come over in droves. But to send out a sortie would be a massacre."

"See? The top is our best option!"

Chiyo shot Tengar a withering look. "One moment. We must think about this carefully."

But he had only begun to ponder the problem anew when a young lieutenant came racing up on a voyoté. "General! General Chiyo!" His words were overwhelmed by the sound of trumpets rocketing through the city. It was a long, solitary note, signaling that Lascombe was being invaded.

"It's the south-east gate! We've been betrayed!"

CHAPTER TWENTY-FOUR

It had almost been too easy. Did the fools think that every soul in that city was a follower of Kynell? Zyreio knew human nature very well, yet he never ceased to be amazed by its naiveté. Did they not think that somewhere in those swells of men, women, Sentries, and cursed munkke-trophes there would be one person—just one—who would sell out his neighbors for money? Or vengeance? Or even simple curiosity?

Coercion had not been necessary. Zyreio had found his man tied up in a shop attic, foaming at the mouth, almost a full day after a shiver had gone through the very fabric of Rhyvelad. Of course the burst of power had come from Kynell; Zyreio knew the Risen Ones had appeared the moment it happened. Their arrival did not trouble him much. The presence of Kynell himself was a little surprising. But so far Kynell had done nothing but water down a few buildings. Zyreio's more immediate concern was the wronged and bitter individual chained to the wall. Those types were usually the most eager for conversation with him.

The man was exhausted and hungry, too worn out and full of self-pity to be surprised at his appearance. He had simply looked up from his position on the floor, with his arm dangling from a chain above him. His greeting, as Zyreio recalled, had been less than ceremonious. Something to the effect of a snarl and a "What do you want?"

"Oh, it's not about what I want," Zyreio had purred. He had chosen a fancy wardrobe to impress the man with his power. Humans were especially susceptible to such shallow displays. "It's about what you're willing to do to get what *you* want."

"And what do I want?"

"I assume you want revenge for being jilted by a man and his four-cycle old son."

The pathetic man had started snarling again. "What do you know of it?"

Here Zyreio had felt it appropriate to get down on his level. So he crouched down, making sure he had his complete attention. "Many days ago, you were robbed of four good workers. Then, when you tried to get back a little of your own, a man appeared out of nowhere and chained you to a wall! Now I am here to offer you revenge and you're asking questions?"

His victim glanced at the door. "How can I get revenge? I'm chained up like a galley slave."

"Now we're on the same page. Come, let us talk together like men."

And so Gorvy had agreed to pick out a handful of men and Sentries like himself, unwillingly trapped in the city. At the appointed hour, armed with blades and violent indignation, they created enough distraction at the southeast gate for Gorvy and three others to loosen the two great bolts that held the gate shut. As the massive metal pins were lifted out of their sockets, the Sentries and fennels outside gave a mighty pull. The gate opened. Of course, Zyreio would have preferred to open the gate with a simple word of command. But that was not how this game was played. And as much as he hated it, he was not in a position to make the rules. Not yet.

Gair ran the voyoté so hard that by the time the lunos had risen in full, the beast was exhausted. When they reached the spot where Zyreio had first appeared, it refused to go another step. Gair dismounted to give the animal a well-deserved rest, but to his dismay, it vanished again into the trees. Perhaps it was just as well. He could not imagine that it would survive the Chasmite army.

He went the rest of the way on foot. It did not take long until he was a stone's throw from the Chasmites. They had been beaten into order and were now standing in agitated formation. Occasionally, one would give in to a burst of anger or start pounding its head to shake out whatever evil spirit was tormenting it. When that happened, an officer, himself just as jittery, would whip the soldier until he had cowered back into the ranks or was a gibbering mess on the ground.

He spent several hours watching, waiting for his move. The orbs were beginning to rise when, as he looked on, the whole force started forward. He spared a glance toward the city. Was Corfe ready? He shook his head to clear the thought. That was not his concern just now.

The grim parade marched on before him. He tried to spot Verial, but it was impossible to see anything in that writhing mass. He had to make a move soon, though, or she would be carried off with the tide. Who knew? Maybe she was already gone. The thought seized him so violently that he almost panicked. Could it be? Maybe he was too late. Even now, maybe she was bound in the Chasm, suffering her punishment.

Visions of her distress assailed him. Clutching at his stomach, he rocked back and forth, trying to shake off what he knew was Zyreio's own doing. Obsidian would be happy to paralyze him with fear. And it was working. He started to sweat, moaning at his own impotence.

Then, as clear as the toll of a bell, he heard a voice. It was his own, echoing inside his head, cutting through the fog that gripped him. He was speaking words from the Ages: *My children are my own. I have sent them for a good purpose. The plans of the evil one will come to naught.*

They were familiar words, words that his mother used to speak to him as a child. They had given him comfort then. Now they became a lifeline.

"My children are my own," he breathed as he staggered to his feet, "I have sent them for a good purpose. A good purpose."

Slowly, he relaxed his arms and straightened his back. "My children are my own. I have sent them for a good purpose."

There was nothing else to do. The army was moving. If he failed to act now, he might not have another chance.

"The plans of the evil one will come to naught," he said to himself one more time. Then he stepped out of the trees and into the flow of Chasmites.

The evacuees were oblivious to what was going on above ground. They could no more tell if the attack had begun than if it was rainy or orblit outside. The hours slipped by as they went about their daily task of self-preservation.

Haven was not without its difficulties. Quite apart from the stress of having husbands, fathers, brothers, and friends above ground was the tension between the evacuees themselves. Being thrown into a new, primitive, living arrangement while surrounded by thousands of women and elderly in the same position brought out some of the evacuees' darker sides. By the end of her first full day there, Alisha noted that the orange-banded "hosts" had been called upon to break up at least three fights and investigate four accusations of theft.

Alisha tried to stay away from trouble as much as she could. She had volunteered for trepofam duty, which meant that she visited most of the "neighborhoods," and often was brought in as an impromptu judge over a dispute. The trepofam she did not mind so much. Having to decide whether a portly old man needed a hands-breadth more cooking space than his younger, thinner neighbor was what she loathed. Usually, she just called a host over and relayed the argument to her. The host never seemed pleased to inherit the problem, but Alisha figured that she was at least better trained to handle it.

To return to the tent from trepofam duty was her chief delight. Trint and Ester were always there waiting for her and Ester made it her duty to have food from the dining tent already prepared. That was fine with Alisha; after hours of overhearing squabbles and cleaning waste houses, socializing was the last thing she wanted to do. Instead, after their meal, she would read to the children from the Ages, or they would swap stories about their lives. There was so much to learn about each other. Often enough, Alisha would break down in tears over what the children—her children now—had been through.

Ester, in particular, delighted to hear about how she and Tertio had fallen in love. Alisha never would have guessed that the girl had a romantic streak a league wide. This tendency was not helped by Bertrice's frequent visits. Their one-time guide had become their friend, so she would often stop by when she was off duty to regale Ester with romantic stories from far-off places. Alisha doubted the truth of these accounts, but since Ester never took them too seriously (except for swooning over a handsome prince), she figured little harm was done. It was much harder to find stories to impress Trint. Tertio's life had been steady, with minimal amounts of swordplay and adventuring, which were the only things Trint wanted to hear about. And though Bertrice's stories had plenty of combat, she always lost the young boy at the kissing parts. Yet he was content enough to play with some of the toys he had brought along. And, of course, he lived for the times when N'vonne would come visit.

Although she was the chief administrator of Haven, N'vonne still found plenty of time to stop by Alisha's tent alone. On the second morning after the evacuation—the same day that Vancien returned with news of the Sentries and fennels—she stopped at their tent for over an hour, chatting with Alisha, helping Ester with some dishes, but above all, sitting on the floor playing with Trint's set of wooden blocks. Together, they built lofty towers, squat castles, and Trint's favorite, a rounded arch, complete with a wooden keystone. This was his building of choice because it was necessary that they rig up a support for the arch in order to build it and then, when the keystone was in place, they would remove the support. There the arch would stand, as if by magic. He would giggle with delight and then, with N'vonne's permission, send it crashing to the ground.

After an hour or so, N'vonne had to leave to go about her other duties. On her way out, though, Alisha pulled N'vonne aside and thanked her for spending so much time with Trint.

"I've never had the opportunity to have children of my own," N'vonne said, a little embarrassed. "So it's a privilege to be around Trint and Ester. Plus, I guess Trint reminds me of Vancien."

Alisha nodded. The night before, over tea, N'vonne had shared her distant past. She knew of N'vonne's career as an instructor, of her interest in Hull, and of her care for Vancien. Though she had never met Vancien himself, she had nothing but gratitude for the young man who rescued Trint and Ester from Gorvy. So she took N'vonne's comment as a compliment.

Alisha checked to make sure both children were distracted, and her voice cracked as she responded. "Yes, my boy was just a little younger than Trint when the sickness took him."

"Did you see him among the Risen Ones?"

Tears welled up in Alisha's eyes. "Oh, yes. He was just like he always was." She turned her face away.

N'vonne waited, and after a moment, she had collected herself. "My Nes—that was short for Nesbert. He was named after his grandfather. Tertio never cared for the name, but I always kind of liked it. Anyway, Nes was full grown. And yet so young!" Her eyes took on a distant expression. "Seeing him again was the most amazing gift Kynell could have given me."

"And yet you could not see him for long."

Alisha shrugged, trying not to relive the parting. "No. But a lifetime would not have been enough. It was good to know he was safe. And besides, I've got to take care of these little ones now. They need me more than my Nes does." She looked tenderly back into the tent.

For a moment, N'vonne had nothing to say. How much selfless love must it have taken for this woman to pull herself away from her son for the sake of two street kids she'd only just adopted?

Now Alisha was looking up at the black space above them. For a moment, she looked very peaceful.

"Wonder what's going on up there?" N'vonne asked, following her gaze.

"I don't know. I can't even tell if it's day or night. I know we have not been down here for very long, but still, the waiting is difficult. Do you think the Risen Ones would know if anything happened?"

N'vonne shook her head. "I've asked them several times. They keep telling me it's better not to know. Frankly, I don't like the sound of that."

Alisha sighed and then glanced around. "I'd better tend to the children. I think I can hear Trint getting into trouble."

"Are you on trepofam duty today?"

"Yes. But not for a few hours yet."

"If you like, I'll go with you. I could stand to do something more practical here than wandering around all day with the Risen Ones. Besides, being with them reminds me of Telenar." Now it was her turn to look away. What was her husband doing right now? Praying? Fighting Sentries? Talking with Kynell? She had briefly heard of Kynell's arrival before she had gone underground. She knew it had to be wonderful for Telenar, to be up there with him.

Alisha pretended not to notice her distraction. "I would like that very much. The kids and I will be at the dining tent for lunch, if you want to meet us there."

N'vonne nodded then took her leave. It would not do to be sniffling or dreaming over Telenar in front of a woman who had already lost so much. They parted with a quick hug before Alisha went back into her tent and N'vonne took the long road back to her lonely little dwelling. She had never before so sharply regretted not being a follower of Kynell in her youth. If she had been, maybe she would know some of the Risen Ones who now stood guard over her. Instead, she was certain that her mother and grandmother had chosen the way of Zyreio. The thought that they were now among Obsidian's army was like a dull, reverberating ache that she could never entirely ignore. Her family had never followed the Prysm; to her father, it was just another corrupt organization that siphoned money for the king. And her mother was so bitter towards life that hope had no room to grow. With two such parents, N'vonne had grown up a defensive, cynical young woman. Though she had never told Vancien this, Hull was the one who had introduced her to Kynell. No wonder she had fallen for him! He had shown her life: the fullest, most abundant sort of life. It was enough to divert her from her youthful angst. Now she lived and breathed the Prysm like it was her lifeline. And on top of that, she was married to a priest!

These thoughts carried her back to her own tent, where she decided to steal a quick nap before going about her duties. Only when she crept into her bedroll did she realize that she did not feel lonely at all. The One who had brought Hull to her, who had given her to Telenar, and who now was presenting her with a friend in Alisha was still there. He had walked with her the whole way. And even while he walked on Rhyvelad, she knew he was still standing guard over her. She felt as certain about that as she did the rock underneath her. So she slept.

The munkke-trophes were all for staying put. Even though Ragger felt some obligation toward his captain, it was easy enough to assure him that where Gair had gone, he could not follow. So, like a good soldier, he assigned himself the post of first sentry and chief hunter. Sirin fretted about what he was going to do. Lucio and Teehma were equally restless. Not a few leagues away, the battle to end all battles was taking place and they knew nothing about what was going on. It was maddening and reassuring at the same time.

"D'you suppose the city's been overrun?"

"Lucio, for the last time, I don't know!"

"But Trint and Ester are safe, right?"

"Listen, young man, if you ask me that question one more time I shall use this cane on you."

So Lucio, having annoyed both Teehma and Sirin past the point of conversation, took up with Ragger. The munkke-trophe had a soft spot for children, so he was happy enough for Lucio's company. He even took the time to show him a few combat moves, which caught Teehma's attention, as well. Soon both children were learning how to wield a long-staff and a sword.

Sirin did not approve, but neither did he object. "Good for the muscle tone," he grunted once when Teehma asked him about it. "Not that I think you'll be doing any fighting. When you come up against a Chasmite, only Kynell will be able to help you. Not some sliver of metal."

Teehma was feeling particularly independent at that moment. She had just had her first lesson from Ragger and he had complimented her on how well she moved with the long-staff. The world was at her feet.

"Yeah, well, what if I don't believe in Kynell?"

Sirin looked at her with sad eyes. "I know you do not believe in him, child. Or I figured as much."

The insightful comment stung. "Huh. Well, you're right. So what?"

The munkke-trophe narrowed his eyes. "You are not ready to have this conversation. Here, right before your very eyes," he waved a furry arm in the general direction of the battle, "is proof that Zyreio exists and plots against us. Only a fool would not believe that Kynell exists, as well. And only a very lost little girl would not want him to exist."

"But Zyreio we sort of see." Teehma protested. "We saw his army, anyhow. We haven't seen Kynell or his army."

"You've seen Captain Gair and Lieutenant Ragger. Are they not enough for you?"

"You know what I mean. The dead soldiers. We haven't seen them."

"I fail to see why you should want to see a dead soldier when you do not even acknowledge the living ones," Sirin sniffed.

Teehma suppressed a growl. "You're impossible to talk to."

"I know exactly what you're saying," Sirin continued. "But it seems to me that you are so resistant to the truth that a vision of Kynell himself would not satisfy you. What disturbs me is why you do not want him to exist."

"I want him to exist plenty," Teehma said as she watched Ragger and Lucio duel. "But wanting doesn't make it so. Trust me, I've wanted lots of things and they haven't happened."

Sirin had finished scraping the pelt from one of Ragger's kills. It was warm enough in the afternoon that he could start bleaching its underside in the orblight. Teehma hoped that it would soon contribute to their bedding; she missed the soft mattresses of the munkke-trophe's house.

"Sometimes," he said so softly that she had to lean in to hear him, "your soul desires something because it exists to be desired."

His comment brought the conversation up to an uncomfortably philosophical level. She was puzzling out a response when, to her relief, Lucio trotted up.

"Come on, Teehma," he panted. "Ragger says he'll teach you how to block and parry, if you want."

No offer was more readily accepted. She jumped to feet and bolted over to Ragger, leaving a surprised Lucio in her wake.

"What's up with her?"

Sirin shook his head. "She's struggling with some difficult questions."

Lucio sat himself down and began munching on a piece of fruit. "Oh yeah? Like what?"

"If you're so curious, why don't you ask her?"

Lucio spat out a seed. "Maybe I will. So," he continued, changing the subject, "how long are we going to stay here? Because I've been thinking of ways to build a shelter, if we need it. It still gets pretty cold at nights, and it

206

might rain again." He blushed at his own forthrightness.

"And what have you come up with?"

Lucio hefted his shattered pole-ax and began talking. Soon the two had wandered over to the trees, testing their thickness and flexibility. Sirin provided guarded guidance while Lucio hopped from one candidate to another, giving emphasis to his ideas with great swoops of his arms.

Ragger and Teehma, meanwhile, went through the prescribed motions. It did not take long for the munkke-trophe to realize his pupil had lost some of her zeal.

"It seems to me, young miss, that your focus is not what it could be."

Teehma dropped her makeshift weapon, not bothering to hide her frustration. "I'm sorry, Ragger." Suddenly, and quite to the consternation of her instructor, she burst into tears. "I just don't want to know!" This last part came out as a wail that caught even Lucio's attention, though Sirin, with great composure, steered his attention back to the trees. Ragger hastily put down his sword.

"Don't want to know what?" he soothed, laying an awkward paw on her shoulder.

"Anything! I don't want to know what's going to happen. Or that my father is in that horrible army. Or if all the Prysm stuff is really true."

"Goodness, I can see why you would not want to know about your father. But if this 'Prysm stuff,' as you call it, were true, why wouldn't you want to know?"

Teehma sat down on the grass with a thump. All she could manage was a meek shrug. "It's too scary," she threw out. Then, through her tears, she tried to rephrase. "It's too big for me. And if Kynell's really out there, what does he think of me? Why did he let my parents die? Why did he take Trint and Ester from us?"

Ragger sat down next to her. The girl's questions were impossible for him to answer, but his heart still went out to her. He picked a blade of grass and started to tie it in knots.

"I wish I could answer your questions, little one. Nobody can do that but Kynell. But I can tell you this: he loves you. More than Trint and Ester ever could, I think. And he loves your parents."

Teehma wiped a hand under her nose. "If he loved them, why would he let my father become a Chasmite?"

Ragger sighed. "I did not know your father, of course. But I suspect your father had a say in that. Those who do not choose the Prysm are given what remains. And that is Zyreio."

This was of little comfort. "But what if he made a mistake? We're all allowed mistakes, aren't we? What if he doesn't want to be a Chasmite any longer?"

Ragger hoped that his look conveyed all the compassion he was feeling for this troubled girl. She looked truly distressed. Her face was streaked with tears, her nose runny, and, much to her annoyance, a strand of hair kept escaping from behind her ear.

"You love your father. Kynell knows that. And you can trust Kynell to do what's right with him. Kynell is real. Your father knows that now, better than even you or I can know it. And if he loved you, as I'm sure he did, he would tell you to give yourself to the Prysm while you still can."

Teehma stared at the grass. Maybe Ragger was right. Maybe her father would say something like that. She hoped so. The paw on her shoulder tightened.

"But I must also tell you, young miss, that you do not have much time. If, Kynell forbid, the Chasmites win this battle, they will overrun Rhyvelad. If we survive, our lives will be short and difficult—yes, even more difficult than the life you have led. And if we don't survive, we will be rushed to the side of our master. So now is the time to hurry to the god who loves you. Not to Zyreio."

Teehma absorbed the whole speech, but that last phrase stuck in her mind. He had said it before; it seemed like an important point. "Kynell loves me?"

But Ragger had jerked his head up as if he had heard something. He sniffed the air with the most peculiar expression. "Something is about to happen. We must hurry."

Before she could respond to this strange comment, Sirin and Lucio returned from their study of the surrounding timber. Sirin had just opened his mouth to praise Lucio's resourcefulness when Ragger stopped him.

"Sirin, we have to go Lascombe."

"What? Why? Our first priority is to keep these children safe."

"This is more important."

Sirin looked offended at the other munkke-trophe's calm insistence, but in the end, he could do nothing. Ragger did not bother to explain. He only began packing up their things, paying special attention to their rude weapons.

CHAPTER TWENTY-FIVE

The betrayal at the south-east gate had taken everyone by surprise. The defenders had been so intent on the enemy outside that they had not considered potential traitors among them. But the Risen Ones stationed at the gate were putting up a valiant fight. Chiyo's old friend Hunoi, who had been struck down by an arrow in the marshes, seemed to take down three Chasmites with every blow. But the Sentries and fennels pouring in through the open door outnumbered the Risen Ones six to one. By the time reinforcements arrived, Hunoi had fallen under the overwhelming numbers, the invaders had taken possession of the gates, and Chasmites were branching out into the streets. Smoke darkened the sky as the grinning, agitated reptiles and oversized cats began to torch everything in their path.

Tertio had been assigned to the soaking crew for just such a scenario. He and the other members of the crew had been soaking the city for two nights now, ever since Resurrection Night, as everyone was calling it. They had worked tirelessly, drawing up thousands of buckets of water from the city's deep wells, and passing them down lines radiating out into the streets. Tertio had been there in the dark morning hours before the first day of bombardment; not being handy with a sword or siege engine, he had joined in with the rag-tag group of older men, young women, and priests, all of whom were determined to stay above ground. Many had been part of Lascombe's poverty-stricken lower classes, but that seemed like distant history now. To Tertio's great delight, his son Nes had joined him for a time, and Tertio had basked in his company. But then he left, claiming that he had other duties to attend to. His departure had broken Tertio's heart, but there was nothing he could do. Nes was not his son any longer, if indeed he ever had been. He was Kynell's. So he had continued upending buckets, grateful that the splashing water helped cover his watering eyes.

When the rumors of Kynell's appearance reached him, he had shaken his head in wonder. A day ago, he would have disbelieved the messenger, but after seeing Nes, anything seemed possible. His instinct had been to drop his buckets and find him, and he was just preparing to do so, when Kynell came to him—or rather, to his crew of soakers.

As a tall man, Tertio had been assigned to the end of the water line, tossing up the buckets' contents as far as they could reach. The messenger had scarcely departed when he heard an outcry of voices about halfway down the line. It was hard to tell if they were in distress or not, so he and those around him hurried down the road, anxious to prevent any trouble or injury.

What he found was buckets scattered on the ground, dropped from hands that had lost any function. The owners of those hands were solemnly watching the new person that had come among them.

"Is it really?" thought Tertio to himself as he stood at some distance. His insides had frozen and, without knowing it, he had stopped breathing. The man moved with purpose, shaking listless hands, greeting men and women by name, and even cupping the cheeks of a few with his hands. He behaved as a celebrity, a father, and a friend all in one. To those who bowed, he placed his hand on their head.

Then he had come to Tertio, who had dropped his bucket along with the rest.

"Hello, my tall one," he said, for he indeed had to look up at Tertio, a situation Tertio quickly fixed by dropping to his knees.

"My God," Tertio muttered, "do not look at me. I'm not worth looking at."

But Kynell was looking at him, as well as pulling him back up to his feet.

"You are right to kneel, but now I want you to stand. There is much to be done. Please, may I have a bucket?"

Four buckets were instantly pushed in his direction. He selected one then looked back to Tertio. "We shall water these buildings together. It is as necessary a task as all the others."

And so all that morning and the following day, Kynell worked with the soakers, sometimes right next to Tertio, sometimes further up the line. When eager volunteers asked to work next to him, he would always allow it, only sending them back to their duties after they had passed an hour or more in his company. That night he had left without explanation, only to return bleary-eyed but purposeful the next morning.

Whenever Kynell came near him, Tertio had taken the opportunity to protest that surely the god of the Prysm would feel more at ease in the presence of the city's leaders. They could certainly use his help there, he added. In truth, it was making him nervous that Kynell was spending all his time soaking, a task which was only necessary if the worst were to happen. Everyone, Tertio knew, would feel more at ease if Kynell were up on the battlements, deciding how best to annihilate the Chasmites.

"This task is necessary," Kynell had insisted, and his tone allowed for no further questions.

They were seven blocks away from the south-east gate when the fennels and Sentries broke through. Tertio's heart stopped when he heard their roar of triumph. He looked at Kynell, who had calmly dumped another bucket. His expression, difficult to read at times, was solemn, and a nerve in his jaw was twitching.

"Are you scared?" Tertio asked, without knowing why. Of course Kynell could not be scared. But he knew that he himself was terrified; he had no wish to face death, though he hoped he was ready for it.

Kynell seemed cheered by Tertio's question. "You're concerned for me?"

"I would give my life to protect you, if I could."

He smiled, a wonderful sight. "It will not come to that." Then he hefted another bucket and pushed it at Tertio. "Come on. We must work faster than ever."

As civilian mortals, the soakers would only fight with the Chasmites as a last line of defense. Instead, they directed their energy toward dousing the flames as soon as they started. This was not easy, since they had to avoid being cut down by the marauders at the same time. They quickly learned the best evasive maneuvers. Most of the Chasmites were thirsty for a quick kill; they seemed almost incapable of staying in one spot. And their agitated groans and shrieks gave their prey ample warning to hide. So with sloshing buckets at their side, the soakers could run through the open streets until they heard the tortured cries of the enemy. Then they would duck into the nearest door and run the rest of the way through connecting inside doors, if they could. Tertio had never considered a burning building a refuge before, but it was safer than being out in the streets.

Kynell stayed by his side for a time, but then, after offering Tertio and a few others a brief goodbye, he left. Tertio hoped it was to go join the combatants, but there was no way to be sure. If the Prysm god had gone to fight, it did not seem to be making any difference: the wide avenues radiating from the south-eastern gate were soon damp with the blood of mortal victims. But the valor of the Risen Ones was awe-inspiring. They were determined to track down every Chasmite who made it past the initial defense and engage it in face-to-face combat. And Tertio noticed that there were several times when a Chasmite, even if it appeared the stronger, would have preferred to duck aside. But even the weakest of the Risen Ones would face it and die rather than allow it to escape unchallenged.

At one point, Tertio thought that his days would be ended by one of the fiends. It had caught him in the street as he urged his comrades through a smoking door. The last of them had disappeared inside when a snarling fennel knocked him to the ground. He had just time to wince at its pungent breath when the pressure on his chest disappeared. He opened his eyes to see the fennel on his side, writhing pathetically before vanishing. His deliverer was nowhere in sight, nor did Tertio spare the time to look for him. With a prayer of gratitude, he was on his feet again, looking for the nearest source of water.

Vancien and Amarian were determined to fight alongside their father, but Hull would have none of it. He had joined them at Chiyo's headquarters just after word came of the breach. While Chiyo and his officers were already racing toward the gate, he commanded them to stay where they were.

"And do what?" Vancien shouted in agony. "Are we so useless against the Chasmites?"

"Stay here!" Hull roared, exhibiting a temper that they had not seen in a long time. "If I see one of you near a Chasmite, so help me, I'll send you to the Prysm myself!" With those encouraging words, he ran to join the battle, leaving his sons furious at their own impotence.

"Is there nothing we can do?" Vancien said for the third time, pacing up and down the deserted street like a cornered animal. All the other defenders had followed Chiyo's example. In the distance they could hear the taunting sounds of the battle.

Amarian crouched on his haunches, scanning the streets, praying for a task to appear.

"How serious do you think he was about staying here?"

Vancien stopped his pacing. "Like staying physically here? I think maybe he meant just don't fight a Chasmite."

"Then the best thing we can do is take care of that smoke. Those soakers won't be able to do it by themselves."

Vancien agreed. "Yes, yes, you're right. And Thelámos can help."

"No, Vance. Wait!"

But before Amarian could stop him, Vancien was sprinting toward the stables. They found the great Ealatrophe tearing his stall apart in frustration. In the work of a moment, Vancien had him out of the stables and was sitting astride him.

"Vance, this is not a good idea."

"It's the best way to put out the fires. I'll carry some water and Thelámos can simply breathe on them. I've seen him do it."

Without protest, Amarian located a well and filled as many buckets as he could find and carry. He carried them to Vancien, who took one of them himself while Thelámos hooked two in his mighty claws.

"Vance, I'm still not sure this is a good idea."

But Vancien cut him off. "We've got to do something, 'Ian."

"Yes, but perhaps we should think about it."

But Thelámos had propelled into the air. Amarian was left on the ground, helpless, as his brother raced toward the smoke. Bedge arrived just as they disappeared behind the buildings.

"Sir is okay! Bedge saw bad fennels are in the city!"

Amarian reached down a weary hand to rub her head.

"Yes, I'm okay. Thanks, Bedge. But I'm not sure about Vance." He stared at the sky where his brother had just been.

"Sir's brother not careful. Goes very low with the big wings."

"He's trying to help put out the fire."

Bedge shook her head in disapproval but, for once, did not respond.

"Bedge, do all the Risen Ones know of the breach?"

"Oh, yes! As soon as Bedge heard the big door move, Bedge told the light-ones to hurry, hurry to the gate."

"Good girl."

He heard a hoarse shout. There was a solitary man running down the street, covered in soot and looking badly wounded. Amarian was surprised to see that it was General Tengar.

"Tengar! Are you all right?"

The general shook his head and pushed Amarian away. "Amarian, you have to go," he gasped. "Your friends are in trouble. The Risen Ones are trying to protect us, but we fool humans keep charging in. They cannot protect us and fight the Chasmites at the same time." These last words were little more than a whisper. As he slumped to the ground, his hand moved to reveal a nasty wound in his side. To Amarian's surprise, the deep slice was an ashy gray.

"So that is what the blade of a Chasmite does."

Tengar nodded and closed his eyes. Before Amarian could do anything for him, he was gone. Amarian had been around death enough to know that, with a few exceptions, you could not help a corpse. So after mumbling a prayer over the departed general, he jumped to his feet and ran toward the fighting. Bedge ran alongside of him.

By the time he arrived, his armor felt like it weighed twice as much as he knew it did. For a fleeting moment, he wished he had Ovna back with him. A dragon would come in very useful right about now.

From his street-bound perspective, it took him a few moments to find Chiyo. Telenar was with him. They were penned in by a circle of Risen Ones who were grimly keeping the invaders at bay. The little nucleus was surrounded by hundreds of howling Chasmites. This particular group had forgotten about taking over the city in their desire to taste living blood, though Amarian could hear the progress others were making through the streets.

He stood there for a moment, undecided. Bedge, too, though she was keen on battle, seemed out of her depth. They could try to hack their way through to the protective circle, but what would that do? Give the Risen Ones more foolish mortals to protect? As he racked his brain, he noticed one of the Sentries stop its agitation for a moment and look at him. It tilted its head to one side, as if recalling something.

"He recognizes me," Amarian thought. And indeed, Amarian recognized him, too. It was Tsare, the Sentry whom he had first sent to destroy Vancien.

"Darkness?" it gurgled, unsure of itself.

The Sentry's confused attention gave him an idea. With renewed composure, he stood up taller, adjusted his armor, and sent Bedge away. She resisted, but he would hear no objections. When she had finally skittered up a tower, he raised his sword high in the air.

"Chasmites!" he roared, hoping that his voice would carry above the pitch of battle.

It did. Almost as a unit, the Chasmites stopped and looked at him. It was enough of a pause that the Risen Ones could hasten Chiyo and Telenar to safety, cutting down the enemy as they went. But the Chasmites stared only for a moment. Then Tsare shouted "Traitor!", and a surge of Sentries and fennels rushed toward him. There was no way he could resist them; that had not been his plan, anyway.

What happened next was difficult to tell. Out of the corner of his eye, he saw a blur of movement, then Hull was there, slashing around him with the power of twenty Risen Ones. He mowed through the Chasmites as if they were chaff until he stood in front of his son. Amarian raised his sword to help, noting that a shadow covered his blade a split second before he heard Vancien shout something from above. Then he was in the grip of Destrariae cold. He felt himself lifted up, away from his father, who was still fighting furiously. Then he watched, horrified, as the blade of a Sentry struck true. Hull vanished as if he'd never been there.

Both brothers cried out in unison, but there was nothing to be done. Thelámos carried them both, rider and cargo, to the furthest point away from danger. Numbly, Amarian watched Bedge dart through the streets, following them as quickly as her short legs could carry her. Then she was lost to view. Thelámos, guided by an authority higher than Vancien, carried them to the north-west corner of the city. There he deposited them in a tiny square and retreated a few yards, though his stern gaze never left them.

Neither man could speak. They just stared at the buildings around them. Thelámos had brought them to one of the poorer corners of town. Like everyplace else, it was desolate, though the neighborhood had a bleakness that extended long before the war.

Vancien sat down, paying no heed to the grime of the paving stones. "He's gone," he croaked.

Amarian nodded, not trusting himself to speak. A swell of emotion was threatening to choke him. Over and over the vision of that Sentry's blade played through his mind. Over and over he saw his father disappear, just like that. Tears began to stream down his face. He sat next to his brother, knowing that if he opened his mouth to speak the sobs would never stop.

Bedge found them in this position. Not long after, so did Chiyo and Telenar.

Telenar took one look at Vancien and rushed to his side. He knelt, wrapped him in his cloak, and drew him to his chest as if he were a child. Chiyo laid a hand on Amarian.

"It's okay to cry, son. You just lost your father."

Amarian shook his head, drawing in a deep breath. Then the weeping came, rocking his whole body. His father was gone. And this time, he would not be coming back.

By early afternoon, the full force of the Risen Ones had stymied the Obsidian attack. The bulk of Zyreio's forces were beaten back through the gate; only the occasional jittery Chasmite would escape into one of the many side streets. And then its high-pitched hysterics gave away its position before it could do much harm.

After assuring himself that Vancien and Amarian were safe, Chiyo was ready to return to the vicinity of the battle, though he had learned the hard way not to engage in it unless necessary. If it had not been for his hasty antics, Hull and several other Risen Ones would still be with them. And if Amarian's actions had not been quick and selfless, they might all have been killed. But such self-recrimination would have to wait until later. Now was not the time for regret. The city still needed a commander.

Telenar, meanwhile, went to gather the other priests and direct them down into the tunnels. If the worst happened, there must be some priests to preserve the faith, he protested, although no one was questioning him. He had become a changed man since Vancien had seen him last. Vancien wondered if he had had contact with Kynell, or else just figured that staying in his office doubting the Ages was not getting him anywhere. Whatever the case, Vancien was glad of his presence.

Both Vancien and Amarian, with Telenar's blessing, decided to return with Chiyo, so long as they stayed clear of the fighting. It was easy for them to agree. None of them wanted Hull's sacrifice to become meaningless so quickly after it had taken place. As they went their separate ways, Thelámos flew high above the brothers, ready to pluck them out of danger if need be. To their chagrin, they had just reached the East Wall when yet another alarm was sounded, followed by a series of distant crashes. A human sentry stood on the battlements, waving his arms and pointing to the horizon.

"The walls are down! The army's coming—" An arrow felled him before he could complete his thought. He staggered backwards then disappeared over the wall. Chiyo, standing below, watched him disappear before whirling around to see where the shot had come from. It was a Chasmite Sentry who had escaped from the fray, standing about fifteen yards from them. With a cry of rage, Chiyo picked up the stone nearest him and hurled it at its head. The target hit its mark. The Sentry staggered, held a hand up to its brow, which should have caved in, then started running towards them, bow raised to shoot.

"Run, boys!" Chiyo shouted as they all darted for cover. But there was no need. Before the Sentry could fire another shot, a Risen One had cut him down.

"General Chiyo!" she hailed. It was Jana, smeared with blood and soot but nevertheless looking as fresh and healthy as when she had first arrived.

"Is there nothing we can do against them?" Chiyo asked, exasperated.

Jana pointed back toward the north-west corner of the city. "You have all put up a glorious fight. But the time when you could be of assistance is over. We're sending the soaking crew, the priests, and everyone who will go to safety. There are tunnels in that area and there is no enemy yet to track them. Most of the men-at-arms will go with them under the command of Captain An-Sung. Will you go?"

All four, including Bedge, shook their heads.

"An-Sung will take good care of them," Chiyo said. "Besides, if the enemy gets into the tunnels, we're all dead, anyway. I'd rather stay above ground. What about the king?"

Jana did not bother to hide her satisfaction at their decision. "The king and his brother are being taken to safety." Then she pointed to the battlements. "If we can't keep them out of the city, we're going to funnel them along this wall. Our numbers are lessened, but we have enough to do that. We're asking those of you who remain to get to the battlements. When the fight comes beneath you, send a barrage of anything you can find down on their heads. It won't destroy them, but it will distract them long enough for us to strike. Understand?" When they agreed, she allowed herself a smile. "Good. Just make sure not to hit us in the process. Now I've got to find the others."

Without further conversation, she ran off. Chiyo stared after her. "That's one remarkable woman," he observed.

Amarian and Vancien looked at each other; it was odd to see Chiyo affected by anything, let alone a woman. In another situation, they would have chuckled at the sight. For now, they were just grateful to have a sense of purpose. All four of them hurried to the nearest tower, gathering rocks and other missiles as they went. When they reached the top, they found that the battlements were already strewn with remnants of shattered siege engines, stones from the wall itself, and in some cases, bodies of defenders. These last they refused to use as weapons, but they stripped off the armor—a steel helmet would make a useful projectile.

Only after they had gathered everything in their immediate vicinity did they think to look at the approaching army. It was a sight well worth watching. The temporary exterior walls were swaying as it if were being pushed by a mighty wind. In the sections that had fallen, regiment after regiment of Chasmites were marching through, displaying an uncharacteristic and chilling amount of discipline. When anyone fell into a trap or through the ground over the buried jars, his comrades simply trampled him in their determination to keep ranks. The front lines of the force were about four hundred yards from the Sentries and fennels, who were falling back.

Chiyo gave a low whistle. "Looks like there were a lot more followers of Obsidian than of the Prysm."

Vancien shook his head. "Could there be that many more gone to the Chasm than to Kynell? Maybe it's just that we're all bottled up inside this city."

"Yes, but that bottling may save us," Amarian responded. "If we can keep those Chasmites coming through that gate, then the Risen Ones can slice them down as they come."

"And if we can't?"

"We have to" Chiyo said.

There was movement in the tree line.

"Look there!" Vancien said, pointing to the trees to the south.

"And to the north!"

With a roar, hundreds of Risen Ones raced from the trees to meet the army. It was Ruponi's men to the south and Brag the Risen Sentry's men to the north. They were not a large force, even combined, but they charged with such intensity that the leading half of Obsidian's army had to slow to turn and face them. At almost the same moment, the Risen Ones of the city pushed the last of the Sentries and fennels out. The would-be invaders tripped over themselves in their retreat, only to be held down by the Risen Ones who were fast on their tail. Soon the entire Prysm army was in the field, their backs to the wall and their faces toward the Chasmites.

The Obsidian force had its hands full dealing with Ruponi and Brag. When the Sentries and fennels fell back into them, they stopped completely. A few moments passed and then the Risen Ones from the gate smashed into them, causing the whole line to shudder.

"Whoo-hoo!" Bedge shouted, unable to contain herself. "Whoo-hoo for the light-god!"

Vancien shared her joy and cheered right along with her. Amarian and Chiyo watched in tense silence. It looked as if the Prysm forces were gaining ground. The Chasmites were stumbling in upon themselves, hemmed in as they were on three sides. Then a large groan pierced the air: another panel of the wall was falling. It came down with a crash, trapping not a few struggling combatants underneath it. And over it poured yet another column of Chasmites, twice the size of the one that had gone before.

The Prysm had no more reserves. Before they could disentangle themselves and retreat, the column was upon them. As Vancien and the others watched, the bright figures who were their friends, allies, and last hope disappeared under the Obsidian tide.

CHAPTER TWENTY-SIX

Once the first column of Chasmites had begun their march, Gair found it a simple task to blend in. All he had to do was keep step with the others, careful not to get out of line and attract the attention of the officers with the whips. Then, whenever a soldier unable to control himself would get out of line, he would take advantage of the distraction to slip further into the ranks.

Up close, the Chasmites were even more grotesque than he had imagined. Their agitated state was so constant that he had to fight the feeling that he himself was also tormented. The females were the worst. Their eyes would roll back, their heads would jerk to one side, and they would let out a screech of terror and fury that could still the blood of any living thing. Then they would take to scratching their arms with their long, pointed nails until a mortal would have bled. Gair tried his best to avoid eye contact with them; one mistaken look had almost exposed him. The woman (if she could be called such a thing) had met his gaze then ran toward him with blinding speed. She fell at his feet, begging for mercy and cursing him at the same time. He stepped backward through the ranks as fast as he could, but she followed him on hands and knees. Only when he turned his back and refused to make further eye contact did she stop chasing him. When he looked again, she was gone, replaced by just another row of her twitching colleagues.

How he would be able to find Verial in this mess, he did not know. He could see the barrier wall in the distance. One great panel had already fallen. Once he passed through it, he knew there would be no hope of escaping the battle. He had to march against the tide without getting himself noticed.

He had made it through almost the entire width of the column when he noticed that another massive column was forming off to his right. This column, about thirty yards away, was not yet moving. He hazarded a look behind him. If Verial was in this group with him, she was marching along just like the others. He suspected that such was not the case: Zyreio would be keeping a close eye on her. Gair doubted if he would risk her being lost to anyone less than himself.

That meant she was most likely in that other column. He looked again across the expanse of land. The remains of the camp stretched between the two groups. There were not any tents to speak of, since the Chasmites did not sleep, but there were the charred remains of some siege engines along with other, intact machines that were no longer in use. It might just be possible to move from engine to engine without being detected. And perhaps if he were detected, he could pass himself off as one of the troops, though he shuddered at the thought. He was having a difficult enough time scratching, cringing, and gesticulating at the rate of the others; he could not imagine trying to spit out the proper combination of venom and groveling that would be required if he encountered an officer. Still, there was no time like the present. Kynell had been with him so far. He had no doubt that the Prysm god would see him through to the end, whatever the end may be.

He waited until they were a few paces from the burnt remains of a trebuchet. After checking to make sure there was no officer nearby, he gave a great groan as if he could not take it anymore, then marched behind the cover. If the other soldiers noticed him leave, they were too preoccupied with their own gnawing fear to call attention to him. He ducked himself down between the two long timbers that comprised the machine's vertical shaft, crawling on hands and knees until he reached the blackened tip. Then he adopted a quick, agitated jog that took him to the next piece of debris. This strategy carried him almost to the other column. But as he prepared for the final leg, he heard a voice to his right.

"HEEY!! Sss—irrk!"

This call made no sense to him, but he turned, scratching his arm and averting his eyes. He decided not to speak unless commanded.

"Sss—irrk! Waahtt er yoo 'oin 'ere?"

The man's speech, as Gair saw out of the corner of his eye, was affected by his habit of rubbing his sleeve across his face every few seconds. He performed this maneuver with a violent compulsion. And when his mouth was free to speak, he held his lower jaw in such tension that he could barely form words. Yet none of this seemed so important as the whip he clutched in his hand.

Gair did his best to mimic another Chasmite he had seen. He scratched his arm even harder. "I-I-I-I I'm goin' t-t-there." He pointed a cringing finger to the column.

"Sss—irrk! 'errr yoo ss-ssignedddd?"

Gair could not tell what the man was saying, but he gave an educated guess.

"Oh, oh, oh yes, sir. I-I-I-I-I w-w-was sent. I was sent. Ss-sir."

The man pushed his sleeve across his face again, jutted out his lower jaw even further, and raised his whip.

"Sss-irrk! 'en yoo'd BETTER G-GO!!"

Gair took the hint and set off running toward the column, not daring to look behind him. Since he did not feel the whip across his back, he assumed he had been dismissed. With relief, he blended into the ranks, careful not to push anyone out of line yet determined to make it through to Verial, wherever she was. The task was more difficult than before since the column was not moving. Yet the stationary position made the Chasmites even more agitated than normal, so between the cocking heads, jerking knees, and flexing arms he was able to dodge among them. At one point, to his surprise, he heard what sounded like a reasonable conversation. There was a woman and a man standing not too far from him. The first was flicking his pointer finger against his thumb while the second rolled her shoulders over and over until Gair thought she would lose her balance. But she spoke as normally as any woman he had ever heard.

"I believe you're over-thinking this, Martin."

The Chasmite named Martin flicked his finger. "How is that possible? My thinking creates the reality. It's all perception."

"The perception is yours, of course," the woman interjected. "Not mine."

Finger-flick. "Never said it was. Anguish is intensely personal. It can't be shared." "Just like love," she responded, rolling her shoulder and digging her toe into the ground. "Love personifies you. But it needs an Other."

Martin shrugged. "Just like anguish. They are the same. But they're not based on external realities. They're only perception."

Gair shook his head. He had followed the speech of the officer better than he understood the conversation of these two. He left them to their debate in order to push further in. The sea of Chasmites seemed endless. No matter where he went, he seemed to encounter the same combination of specimens: they were either drooling and mutilating themselves, shrieking the foulest of language, or rationally reducing everything meaningful to nothingness. It took repeating the words of the Ages to himself over and over for him to maintain his sanity and his purpose.

After an eternity of searching, he saw one figure taller than the rest. He looked as if he were perched on a beast of some sort, perhaps a voyoté. Since this was the first shape in the Obsidian army to stand out, he headed towards it, feeling his heart sink deeper within him as he went. As he suspected, he was soon a stone's throw away from Zyreio himself. Not that the figure looked at all like the man they had encountered in the woods. This character was sitting on a voyoté. He was tall, robust, the very picture of a genial king. Verial stood beside him.

As Gair watched, Zyreio tried to engage her in conversation.

"Come, lady," he roared, but in a friendly manner. "What do you think of me now? Don't you see that I command this world, even as I command my own self? Nothing escapes my attention or my grasp." He flexed a gloved hand and gave a wide smile. "Don't you see that my hand extends to the ends of Rhyvelad? Come now. Call me your king."

Verial said nothing. Nor did she look at him. *Brave girl,* Gair thought to himself.

Zyreio did not seem troubled by her reticence. He reached down and cuffed her on the ear. Her face turned red, which caused him to laugh some more. "So quiet, my dear? Maybe I have wasted time giving you to my Advocates. I should have kept you to myself. All of these inhabitants of the Chasm are *so* dreary," he sighed. "A little bit of living flesh would be a nice treat."

Verial blushed even harder. Gair had seen enough. It was obvious that Zyreio was not planning on letting her out of his sight. That meant that if Gair were going to rescue her, it would have to be out in the open. Indeed, Gair was not so sure Obsidian could not see him even now.

"You know, my little pet," Zyreio was prattling on, "I've lost many good men in this fight. Oh, yes. My one-time Advocate. Well, you know what's going to happen to that one. And then there's the little turncoat. The turnling, I call him." He chuckled at his own joke. "Once upon a time, the turnling decided to betray his master. But then the turnling got too big for his boots and he thought he *was* the master—of a sort, you understand. Well, this little turnling made quite a fool of himself, so I hear. I haven't had the chance to take care of him yet, of course, but someday I will guide my little waif again."

Gair shuddered at the speech. This new guise of Zyreio's was even more disturbing than the last. He was grateful now more than ever that Corfe was under Kynell's protection. Yet he wondered what Zyreio meant about Corfe thinking he was the master. He twitched extra hard to distract himself. It was Zyreio's tongue that had corrupted all of Rhyvelad, after all. Now was not the time to start believing what it said.

Gair watched as Zyreio continued to talk. He was putting on quite the show, gesturing with his arms, laughing deep belly laughs, and sparkling with manly health. What was he trying to accomplish? Was he trying to win her over? Then, before his eyes, the lord of Obsidian changed form. Whereas once there was a hearty, beefy king, now there was a grizzled young man with a scarred face, long hair, and misshapen legs. Gair found himself looking at his mirror image.

The drastic change elicited Verial's attention. Her quick glance showed a flash of such radiant anticipation that Gair knew there was still hope.

"So this is what you want, my silent consort? I figured as much. Perhaps if I dismount and drag myself over to you." The mock Gair stiffly climbed down from the voyoté and limped over to his prey. "I have given you many forms, Verial. And I have tried to be nice, to show you I am not all bad. But I do not understand your hesitation. You have made your choice, otherwise why would you be here?"

Of all the words he had spoken, these hit their mark. She was shaking all over and from under her breath, Gair thought he heard her say Kynell's name.

Zyreio heard it too. "What did you say?" he purred.

Tears streamed down her face as she trembled harder. She looked just like a child who had gone off with a stranger and now wanted to go home. "I want Kynell now."

In the blink of an eye, Zyreio had slipped back into the short, greasy man they had encountered in the woods. "Kynell, you say?" he sniveled. "Funny, all this time, I could have sworn you wanted him." He waved a hand in Gair's direction. The Chasmites among whom Gair had been hiding shuffled to the side and he stood exposed.

Verial was startled. She blinked, wiped her tears, and blinked again. "Gair? Is that really you?"

Gair nodded, trying to think of something to say that would convince her that he was not one of Zyreio's tricks. "Yes, it's me. And I praise the name of Kynell, god of the Prysm and of all creation."

225

To Gair's regret, Zyreio did not look put out over his declaration. Instead, he seemed pleased. "See? This is the one you want, the one you've been dreaming of. Take her, Gair, with my blessings."

This was an unexpected strategy. Did Kynell have him march through the Chasmite army just so Zyreio could hand her over?

But Verial was shaking her head. "I love you, Gair," she said, as simply as if she was telling the time of day. "You're the only person on earth I've ever loved. But you're not the one I need right now."

Now Zyreio flinched. "Oh?" he said. "And who do you think you need?"

Verial looked him straight in the eye. "Take me to Kynell."

The words hung in the air for a moment. Zyreio winked, smiled, and then reached for her. "Kynell? And what do you think Kynell would want with you? It's not as if you're the freshest flower in the field, if you know what I mean."

Tears were streaking her cheeks, but she held her ground. "I just want to see Kynell."

"You don't know what you're asking, sweetheart. He does not want to see you."

"But I want to see him."

Zyreio's face was getting flush with anger. He moved toward her. "How about I take you to the Chasm where you belong?"

But Gair was too quick. In a flash, he thrust his body between them. Zyreio barely touched him before he recoiled in fury. Then he started whining. "Traitors!" he spat. "I'm surrounded by traitors! To the Chasm with both of you! Get out of here! Go find your—" His tirade stopped in mid-sentence. Something else had caught his attention. Gair looked around to see what it was, but to no success.

Zyreio clamped his jaw shut, clutched his hair and stamped his foot. He looked for all the world like he was about to throw a temper-tantrum. Gair would have laughed at the sight, except that he had learned the hard way not to make light of Obsidian. Second to the Prysm, it was the most powerful force on Rhyvelad. He watched in amusement, though, as Zyreio started marching through the ranks, toward the falling barricade walls.

"Follow him," Verial said.

"Follow him? Why?"

She did not offer an explanation, but since Kynell had been with them so far, he decided to obey her instructions.

"We must hurry!"

Ragger was keeping up a frightful pace. Munkke-trophes were stronger than they looked, plus they had a long, loping stride that could cover a great deal of ground in a short amount of time. The children were too large to be carried by their smaller guardians, so Lucio and Teehma were forced to run through the trees behind them. Low branches scraped across their faces, but they did not have time to assess the damage; every time they stopped for a breath, Ragger outdistanced them by several paces.

"What's the rush?" Lucio gasped.

Ragger did not answer, nor did he slow down. After an eternity of running, they began to hear the Obsidian army. The wails, cackles, and howls filled the air with ominous familiarity.

"They're still here, huh?" Teehma panted.

"Hasn't our side done *anything*?" Lucio asked.

When they could see the glint of the enemy's weapons, Ragger slowed to a jog. Staying in the trees, he turned west. To even Sirin's surprise, he did not bother traveling quietly; in fact, he made as much noise as a jogging munkke-trophe could make. The enemy did not seem to notice. From Teehma and Lucio's perspective, it looked like it was on the move.

They passed through a dense set of trees that, after they climbed over gnarled trunks and branches, deposited them in the woods on the other side of the barricade wall. Teehma noticed with a sinking heart that the army had already pierced that defense. Now it was amassed in what looked like a victory mob on the other side. There was nothing left but a few half-hearted traps between it and the city.

"We are here," Ragger said, stopping when they were about level with the head of the army. "Now we watch."

"Watch what?" Sirin snapped. "The city get overtaken by hooligans?"

Ragger shook his head and caught his breath. "Just wait. You will see."

Lucio and Teehma were only too happy to collapse to the ground. Together, the four of them watched as the Obsidian forces gathered themselves for the final attack.

CHAPTER TWENTY-SEVEN

Ever since they had arrived in the tunnels, N'vonne had had very little contact with the mother of Hull's children. It was not that she avoided her; it just felt awkward to seek her out. Then halfway through the end of the second day of being underground, Chera walked up to Alisha's tent, where both N'vonne and Bertrice were playing with the children.

"Lady N'vonne," Chera said. "May I speak with you a moment?"

Surprised, N'vonne waved her in. "Of course, Chera. Come on in."

But the Risen One shook her head and remained outside the tent. "If it's all right, I'd prefer to speak with you in private. No offense," she added, nodding to Alisha and Bertrice.

N'vonne finished putting the tower on the edifice she and Trint were building. Then she brushed off her hands and rose to her feet. As soon as she stepped out of the tent, Chera led her to a quiet corner, where they stepped beyond the lights marking the edge of the precipice.

"Something's going to happen soon," she said in a low voice. Her voice had become intense and not at all soothing.

"What's going to happen? How do you know?"

"I just do. And I do not think it's going to happen as we have planned it." She held up a hand to forestall another question. "There are some things you need to know. First, there is another group coming down. They should be here very soon. Don't attack them. They are not the enemy. Instead, send a guide to all the main entrance points. Each guide must have to wait at her post for many hours. We do not know which way they're coming from." She took a deep breath, as if checking some inner source for the truth of her next statement. "The second thing is that I do not think we will be with you for much longer. I don't know why, but Kynell is going to call us back before we have a chance to protect you."

N'vonne felt as if she'd been punched in the stomach. "Why would he do such a thing?"

Chera could not hide the tremor in her voice. "I don't know, N'vonne. I really don't. The Prysm knows I do not want to leave." Her voice faded for a moment before returning with fresh vigor. "But we have to trust him. Whatever he is doing is for the good of those who love him. Of that I'm sure."

Trust seemed the furthest thing from N'vonne's mind at the moment. How could she trust in the wisdom of taking away their only protectors? What was the point in providing them in the first place? She did not say these things aloud, of course. But for the first time since she had met Hull, she felt hopeless.

Chera was already leading her back to the tents, telling her to make haste. Despite her alarm and anger, N'vonne followed. When they reached Alisha's tent, Chera took her hand.

"I will talk to the guides. You go to the queen." Her voice dropped to a whisper. "And may Kynell bless you. Do what you can for my boys."

N'vonne nodded, unable to respond further. She would have preferred to return to Alisha's company, but it was impossible to disobey Chera. In truth, she had forgotten about the queen. Lady Quinia had kept to herself since they went underground. Though she refused trepofam duty and would go nowhere near the dining tent, she had condescended to live in a two-room pavilion, keeping only an old male servant who would fetch her meals for her. N'vonne knew she had little interest in the things of Kynell, but Chera was right: she must know of this new development.

As she approached the royal tent, she could see Quinia's servant out front, tending a boiling kettle. His hair was just a shock of white and he was bent over almost double, but he stirred the contents with the vigor of a younger man.

"Hello, Oren. Is the queen in?"

Oren gave a wrinkly smile and gestured toward the door. "She is resting now, Lady N'vonne. Perhaps you could come another time?"

"If it's not too much trouble, I need to see her right away. I have some new developments to report."

Oren nodded, trundling to the door. He gave a low cough then politely batted at the tent flap with a small paddle. N'vonne wondered how long it had taken the queen to establish that little arrangement.

"Yes?"

"Forgive me, my queen," Oren muttered. "Lady N'vonne is here. She says there are new developments which she would like to discuss with you. I believe it is urgent."

A groan issued from within the tent. "I cannot solve one more debate over dirty dishes, Oren. Tell her that the hosts will just have to take care of it."

Oren gave N'vonne an "I told you so" look before turning back to the flap. "I believe the dishes are under control, my queen. This appears to be a more pressing matter."

There was the scrape of a cot from inside. A moment later, the flap was pushed aside, and Quinia appeared, still dressed in her mourning robes. Oren bowed and backed away, leaving the path open for N'vonne.

"Lady N'vonne," Quinia said. "Please come in."

N'vonne curtsied then followed her inside. Quinia bade her sit on a little camp stool across from the cot, then produced some fresh bits of melon from who knew where. Only after N'vonne had been obliged to pick one of the treats off of a silver platter did the queen sit herself. N'vonne allowed her host to nibble on some melon before asking permission to speak.

"Yes, of course," Quinia said sharply. "We cannot play court all day in these canvas prisons, can we? Tell me what has happened."

N'vonne bit back a reply. Did this woman really think that her royal blood would matter when the Chasmites started choking up the tunnels? Did she not understand that all of her posturing was now nothing more than a game of pretend? She decided to take another piece of melon to cool her temper.

"My queen," she began, "I have been told by the Risen Ones that we will soon have additional arrivals here at Haven."

Quinia snorted. "Is that a euphemism for the Chasmites coming to slaughter us?"

"No, my lady. I've been told that the next group is friendly, though I don't know who they are." She desperately hoped that Telenar and Vancien would be among them, even though their evacuation would indicate the fall of Lascombe.

"So we will have to share our tents? So be it. I suppose we could all do with half-rations at the dining tent."

N'vonne swallowed. She had never had much regard for Quinia, but now the queen was attaining a new level of shallowness. A quiet voice within her told her to keep her calm and behave. After all, the woman's world was being turned upside down.

"There is more, my lady. I was given to understand that the protection of the Risen Ones will not always be with us."

Quinia paused mid-bite. "What do you mean?"

"It is possible that Kynell might remove them from us more quickly than we had hoped. I don't know when, but I think it will be very soon."

"And what if the Chasmites find these tunnels?"

N'vonne looked at the dark stone floor, only half-illuminated by Quinia's candle. Shadows flickered across the granite, covering part of her foot in darkness. "I don't know what Kynell has in store for us. We must have faith."

But Quinia cut her off. "Faith! I've had enough of that. I'd rather find my protection behind stone walls and the cool steel of a sword. We've suffered with these 'Risen Ones' as you call them, but they seem ineffective at best. And now they're leaving us? Relgaré could run a better campaign than this."

There was nothing more to say. N'vonne had done her duty. She stood, straightened her dress, and asked permission to leave. Quinia was taken aback by her request for such a hasty departure, but she had no objection.

"Fine, fine. I'm sure you have much to do with this new development. Do keep me posted."

"Yes, my queen."

———————

Telenar had mixed feelings about whether to evacuate along with the other priests. He had allowed the tide to sweep him away toward Lascombe's northwest corner, but he had no peace about doing so. He told himself that the best thing he could do now was to pray, and also that he owed it to N'vonne not to throw his life away. After all, a man could pray in the tunnels just as well as anywhere else. To stay in the city alone would be suicide. And, besides, Kynell could raise his hand at any time and stop all of this nonsense.

Yet the Risen One who had told them to evacuate had looked quite grim. She did not say all was lost, but Telenar could read resignation in her eyes. So what was there to pray for? Victory? That seemed laughable. Deliverance? But what if it was Kynell's will that they all perish?

On top of these misgivings, he could not believe that he was leaving Vancien behind. He would be fine, he told himself. Well, fine in that he was with his brother and Chiyo. But what if Amarian, so recently come to the Prysm, could not withstand the lure of Obsidian? What if Chiyo were to be cut down early, leaving Vancien alone? It was all right to be separated from Vancien if they were in the same city, but to sneak underground while the boy stayed to fight? N'vonne would be furious to hear that he had allowed Vancien to face Zyreio by himself.

The thought was sobering enough to bring him to a stop. Corfe bumped against his back.

"What is it, Telenar?"

Telenar looked at his young face. His shaved head was starting to grow bristles and his eyes were red from lack of sleep. Telenar wondered if he looked just as bad.

"Corfe," he said, scarcely believing what he was saying, "I'm not sure I should leave. Not yet."

Corfe shifted. He was no coward, but he was not prepared to face the Chasmites, let alone Zyreio. "Telenar, if we don't go, I don't think we're going to get another chance. Think of N'vonne."

He looked so scared that Telenar forgot about his own troubles and laid a hand on his shoulder. "I believe I am thinking of her. That is why I need you to go down and tell her that I've decided to stay with Vancien. Tell her I love her." Despite his best efforts, his eyes filled up with tears. "Just tell her I love her and I'll see her soon," he concluded gruffly.

Corfe nodded. "Maybe I should stay with you?" he asked without conviction.

"No. There's no need for that. You had better get going. Remember to find N'vonne the first thing you do."

"Of course." Corfe tried not to show how grateful he was to have a mission that would justify his retreat.

There was an awkward pause, then Corfe nodded again and ran to catch up with the evacuees. Telenar took off at a jog toward the south-east gate, praying that he was not too late.

———————

Three men and a fennel stood on the East Wall and watched the last Risen One fall under a Chasmite blade. The second it happened, it seemed that the entire Obsidian army knew it. They stopped surging forward and began cavorting like fiends, dancing and shouting. Perhaps it was just a reflection of his own grief, but Vancien imagined that he could also hear wails of despair. It was the most horrible cacophony any of them had ever heard.

Bedge curled up beside the battlement wall, quivering.

Amarian knelt down beside her. "Shh, Bedge," he soothed, smoothing her brown and tan swirls until they shone. "Remember the light-god. He won't abandon us."

Bedge continued to shake, so he scooped her up in his arms. Vancien and Chiyo paid him no attention; their eyes were fixed on the grim celebration. But just as Amarian was about to suggest they take refuge somewhere, Vancien pointed.

"Look there."

Chiyo pulled out his range glass. "Where?"

"There, about a hundred yards past the gate. Who is that?"

"It's Kynell. What's he doing?"

"No idea."

By now, both Amarian and Bedge were looking. Bedge perched her furry paws on the stone wall, her eyes round. The Obsidian army continued its celebration, oblivious to the solitary figure in front of them.

"Is that the light-god?"

Chiyo nodded, passing the range glass to Amarian.

"Looks like he's building something."

It was true. Kynell was pulling together pieces of the useless traps, disarming them and arranging them in a line. Then he disappeared into the gate for a moment, only to reappear with a few planks of wood, which he balanced on the traps. They watched this procedure continue until he had produced a rough table. He had dug up his first chair by the time Vancien proposed that they go to him. The others agreed.

On the way, they saw Telenar huffing and puffing down a side street. When he caught sight of them, he looked mightily relieved. "Vancien! Thank Kynell you're safe! N'vonne would never forgive me if anything had happened. It's good to see you all."

Vancien had never been so happy to see him. "Telenar! You came back for us!" Before the priest knew it, he was swallowed in a great hug and receiving multiple pats on the back. Even Bedge purred and rubbed up against his legs.

"All right," he said, attempting to pull himself free. "Now we can all go to glory together. Which I guess is where we're going, because I haven't seen a Risen One since I started back. Where are you all running to?"

They told him about Kynell building the table, which piqued his curiosity just as it had theirs. "And what about the Chasmites?"

"They're just standing there celebrating. They haven't moved toward the city since they defeated—" Chiyo cut himself off. "Anyway, we'd better hurry. They could start at any time."

When they reached the gate, Kynell was still there. He had managed to assemble nine chairs around the table. To their amazement, he had also found some food—not dried meatsticks and bread but a feast of roast, vegetables, savory puddings, and pitchers of a delicate pink juice made near Vancien and Amarian's hometown. All five of them, including Bedge, stopped, at the gate. Kynell was just putting the finishing touches on the table settings when he saw them. He polished a fork on his tunic, which was now quite clean, and set it to next to a plate before gesturing for them to come over.

Cautiously, they stepped outside beyond the wall. The invading army remained at a distance, persisting in its blind celebration. Bedge was the first to act with any eagerness; she trotted out in front of them, purring loudly. Amarian tried to keep up with her while keeping a careful distance. When she reached Kynell, she pressed herself up against his legs. Amarian himself arrived half a second later. Vancien came right after him, with Telenar and Chiyo behind.

"My Lord," Vancien began, waving an arm toward the army. "What are you doing?"

"Hello, hello, hello," was Kynell's only response as they all gathered in an uncertain semicircle. "I'm glad you could come enjoy my feast. Some others should be arriving soon, I expect."

No sooner had the words come out of his mouth than they saw four figures emerge from the trees to their right. As they drew nearer, Vancien recognized Sirin and two of the children he had rescued, plus another munkke-trophe. The newcomers looked just as confused as they were, but Kynell greeted them in the same way, asking them all if they would be willing to stand for a bit until the last two guests arrived.

Vancien stole a look at Telenar. Last two guests? What was he talking about? He had no idea how long Obsidian's army would continue its absurd celebration but it could not be long. In fact, he thought he saw an ominous character pacing in front of the soldiers, vainly trying to bring them back to order. Kynell followed his gaze.

"Oh, yes. He'll be trying that maneuver for a while. Isn't it true how evil fails to control itself, let alone overcome the good?"

Vancien and the others nodded absently as they watched yet two more figures appear from the midst of the Chasmite crowd. They were not too surprised to see Gair, but there was a collective gasp as Verial came into view. She was holding Gair's hand.

Kynell clapped his hands. "Wonderful! We'll just give them a moment to reach us. There!" he proclaimed, as Gair and Verial arrived, looking around for an explanation. None of them had a clue what was going on, except perhaps for Bedge.

"If you please," Kynell was saying, having rolled up his worn sleeves. "Would all the men and women find a seat?" He tilted his head to Sirin, the other munkke-trophe, and Bedge, who had gathered into a knowing little group. "You three have done remarkably. Your reward will come later."

Sirin nodded and to Vancien's surprise, made no move to take a seat. Vancien would have asked about this, except that the munkke-trophe did not appear to take offense and Kynell was already motioning for them to get started.

CHAPTER TWENTY-EIGHT

Kynell went on. "You are probably all wondering why we're gathered here in this, ah, open setting."

They stared at him.

"If you will allow me," he continued, taking up Amarian's plate and beginning to heap it with food. "You must be starving. Here, try some of the beans."

Amarian was so unnerved that he could not object, nor could the others as Kynell went around the table, filling their plates.

In the end, it was Chiyo who found his voice. "My Lord, what are we doing here?"

Chiyo's words had a profound effect on Gair, Verial, Teehma, and Lucio. None of them had known of Kynell's arrival, and certainly none of them expected to see their god in person. Even now, the title "my Lord" could not bring them to the conclusion that they were actually seeing him. It was too far-fetched an idea to occur to them. But they did begin to look on him as if he were a messenger from the realm of the Prysm, which was awe-inspiring enough.

Kynell finished the last plate and sat down, not bothering to fill his own. In the midst of his hosting activities, he had appeared very calm and efficient. Now that he was seated, he exhibited great authority. He was in command of the situation, strange though the situation was.

"You've always been one to get straight to the point, General Chiyo. It is one of your great strengths, though occasionally it blinds you."

Chiyo frowned, but Telenar took a tentative bite of his pudding. "You set a fine table, my Lord. Although I admit that I'm amazed we can eat like this with Obsidian's army breathing down our necks." Then he choked at a sudden thought: Zyreio would not be above deceiving their eyes and ears. "This isn't.—"

Kynell's face darkened. If Telenar had wanted to imply the wrong thing, he had succeeded. "I am disappointed, Telenar. After all these cycles together, and these past few days in the streets of Lascombe, you think I would be part of an Obsidian trick?"

"You are from Kynell," Gair whispered.

Kynell nodded.

"But you can't be one of them Risen Ones!" Lucio interrupted. It was the first he had spoken since they had left the trees. The tantalizing food had shut down his awareness of anything else for a time. Now, he spoke with sudden urgency, gravy dripping down his chin. "We saw all of them get cut down by the Chasmites!"

Kynell nodded again. "I am sorry you had to see that. It will help you to know that the ones you call Risen have returned to me. Their mission has been accomplished, though it may not seem like it."

Gair had started muttering to himself. He had watched the Risen Ones ride out to battle. They had been glorious. But was there some sort of chief Risen One he did not know about? And why would they return to him? As he tried to reason it out, he could feel his heart slowing down beat by beat until it stopped at the only solution. "You're not *from* Kynell, are you?"

Kynell watched him, waiting.

Then, slowly, like an old man, Gair pushed back his chair and dropped painfully to his knees. Lucio, catching on, did the same and before long, they were all kneeling before him. Their questions were momentarily forgotten; now, even in the shadow of Obsidian's celebration, it felt right to give him homage.

Only Teehma had not moved. She sat there, spoon in hand, watching him.

"What are they doing?" she asked, although she was intelligent enough to suspect what was going on.

He turned to her. "Why are you confused, child?"

She flushed a deep red and set down her spoon. "They seem to know you, sir. But I don't think we've met."

"Haven't we?"

"How could I want to meet you if I don't know who you are?"

238

He did not answer her question. Instead, he told the others to get up and resume their seats. "There is much to discuss," he said, picking up the pudding to help them to a second round.

Vancien had turned frightfully pale as the immensity of Kynell's coming pulled again at him. "Lord, what are you doing? We should be serving you!"

"Sit down, Vance," Kynell responded. "I'm going to serve you today. Trust me, you will soon be serving others."

Gair was grinning ear to ear and eating heartily with his left hand. For the first time that he could remember, he felt whole. With his right, he squeezed Verial's hand. She leaned over and whispered to him.

"I should not be here," she said. "We've just come from Zyreio!"

"My dear, none of us should be here! Look at him!" He nodded in Kynell's direction. "He's here. Actually here with us! Do you think any of us deserve that? But I can't think of a better place to be after being so close to Obsidian."

Verial did not respond. Instead, she stewed the food around her plate.

Kynell arrived to deliver more pudding. He raised an eyebrow at her full plate.

"Come with me."

She followed. She was accustomed to obeying divine commands, and though she was beginning to prefer him, she was not convinced that Kynell was much different than Zyreio. He led her several paces away from the table. Only then did she notice that Teehma had followed them.

Kynell asked her and Teehma to sit down on the grass before taking his place next to them. "My girls," he began, "I would love to have you sit at my table with me. But there is something that prevents it."

Verial hung her head. The moment had finally come. She could feel her past overtaking her. The sea of her selfish choices seemed endless and now Kynell was going to call her on it, as he had every right to do. Still, it would be hard to be sent away from him, and from Gair. Where else could she go but back to Zyreio?

"Verial," his voice cut through her thoughts. "Look at me."

She dared not. Of course he already knew all that she had done, yet to look at him seemed like an open confession.

His tone was stern. "Verial, unless you look at me, you will have no part with me."

Reluctantly, she raised her eyes. Might as well get it over with. Yet he was not glaring at her, though, nor did he seem to be appraising her.

"Do you still believe that you can make yourself good enough for me?"

"No, Lord. How could I ever be good enough for you? Those men," she waved a rough hand toward the table. "Those men have given their whole lives to you. They deserve you more than I—"

"I am the Creator of all that is," he cut in. "Of Rhyvelad. Of the Eastern Lands and the West. I put the howl in the voyoté and the humor in the munkke-trophe. I, not Zyreio, made men, women, and children to feel as I can feel, see as I can see, and choose as I can choose, so that one day, we would be together as a family. Do you truly think that any member of my creation can earn my affection more than it has already been given? Can a newborn infant earn its father's love?"

Her reserve faded, to be replaced by anger. With all the injustices she had seen and perpetrated, how could she listen to platitudes? "But we're not infants! We have hated, perverted, and chosen poorly, over and over again! Even your own Advocate Vancien is capable of being selfish and rash! None of us, not even this girl here," she pointed harshly to Teehma, "is a helpless infant."

Teehma did not know how she felt about Kynell yet, but if he was a god, then surely he would put this lady in her place. But he did not look offended. Rather, he had picked up a stick and started toying with it. Then he used it to draw a short line in the dirt.

"Vancien is not innocent," he said. "He knows that he has been forgiven of his faults and his poor choices." He drew another line. "We know Amarian is not innocent. But he sought me out, and I have forgotten his crimes." He drew another line. "Chiyo can be a hard man. But he has never assumed that he could earn my love." He drew another line. "Telenar is proud, but he humbles himself before me." He drew another line. "Lucio is young, proud, and afraid. He needs guidance, as well as the deliverance that only I offer. He knows that." He drew another line. "And my beloved Gair battles against fear and often loses. But still we have made our peace." He started to draw another line, but stopped. "Verial has run from me her entire life. She has chosen against me, denied me, cursed me, and rejected me. Can she believe that I will ever forgive her? Or will she run away yet again, piling crime on top of crime?"

Verial did not answer at first. Instead, she glanced back at the table, where Gair was looking in their direction. Kynell followed her gaze.

"It is impossible to be by his side until you make your peace with me."

As he waited, recent images of Zyreio flashed through her mind. There

240

she was, standing by him, terrified of his every move. Then Gair appeared, but she had known that Gair was not enough. Zyreio had tried to make her think that he was, but she knew better. Gair could take her to the farthest corner of Rhyvelad, but he could not cleanse her past, nor could he guarantee her future. Kynell could. But just look at all the wrong she had done! She was the consort of Obsidian! How could the Prysm forgive her for that?

After another tense moment, Kynell made her look at him. She was surprised to see that he looked sad—very sad, as if he had lost something very precious. "There is a price to be paid for every wrong committed in Rhyvelad. But if you trust me, you will not have to pay that price. I do not want you to pay it."

Her vision started to blur with tears. What a gift it would be not to have to pay for her own crimes! To not feel, every day, her past chasing her like a monster that could never be satisfied? Why would the god of the Prysm offer this to her? Especially if it caused him such pain?

He was speaking again. "Time is short, my dear. Do you trust me or not?"

Through a haze of tears, she nodded then gave a little cry as he hugged her. He was smiling and she began to feel as light as a feather. She almost floated back to Gair.

Kynell remained with Teehma for a few more minutes. Nobody heard what he said to her nor what she said to him. Yet she returned to the table a quiet and changed young lady. When Lucio asked her what they had talked about, she wiped her nose on her sleeve and said she would tell him later.

Kynell followed her back, taking his seat just as they finished dessert. He looked a little more sober than before, and he spoke with a quiet urgency.

"My children, I have a great deal to say to you, and I am sure you have some questions for me. I will not always be with you like this, so let us talk together now. I have chosen you out of all Rhyvelad, not because you are the best," he inclined his head toward Chiyo, "nor because you are the least." He nodded toward Verial. "Take careful note of the words I am about to say. If necessary, I will carve them onto your hearts."

They began to murmur as he continued. "I have chosen you to do my bidding until I come back."

"Are you going somewhere?" Lucio chirped.

"I am. And I am leaving you with a hard road to follow. There will be many who do not understand what has happened, and you must tell them. Most will not listen, even those who seem to have loved me in the past. They will become your enemies, but I require that you love them. You must serve *them*," he pointed to Lascombe, then to the world in general, "as humbly as I have served you today. Tell them what I have told you. Keep telling them until I return."

"And what have you told us?" Telenar blurted out. "Where could you possibly go?"

"I tell you what you already know: all of my creatures have become stained with Zyreio's corruption, and with their own. But I am going to heal Rhyvelad for every man, woman, and child who desires to be healed."

Telenar opened his mouth to say something more, then closed it. Amarian had gone silent and pale, while tears glistened in Vancien's eyes. Teehma and Lucio fidgeted under the Prysm god's weighty pronouncements. Only Gair moved with any sort of purpose. He stood up, limped over to Kynell's side and knelt at his feet. When he spoke, his voice was choked.

"Lord of the Prysm," he began as formally as he could, "please do not leave us, not so soon after having arrived. But if you must leave, I will wait day and night for you to come back. And I will tell anyone who will listen what you have said, though I don't understand it."

Kynell, who was crying now, placed a hand on Gair's head. "My dear Gair. How much you have already gone through for me! Speak to those who will listen, and let your actions confirm what you say. And though I will not be as I am now, I will still be with you." He bent down and touched Gair's shoulder. "Remember me by this."

Gair nodded stiffly, moving to resume his seat. But as he rose, strength and flexibility flooded into his limbs. He looked down in amazement. Not only was his crippled leg whole, but his prosthetic limb had been replaced by flesh and bone. He stepped down experimentally on it, relishing the delightful tingle of his restored nerves. With a cry of joy, he fell back down at Kynell's feet.

"Thank you! Thank you! THANK YOU!"

Kynell laughed. He dragged Gair again to his feet then wrapped him in an enthusiastic embrace. With an arm still draped around Gair's shoulders, he addressed the rest of them. "My children! I will give you strength to live as I desire and love as I love. I will never leave you. But right now I am going to die for you."

As one, they jumped to their feet, shouting their protests. But Kynell was already starting toward the army. Sirin, Ragger, and Bedge followed him, only to be stopped after a few paces by his upraised hand. "Continue to serve my children," he told them. "Be generous with them and remember the Sentries."

They nodded as Kynell resumed his march. Vancien was the first to run after him, followed by a light-footed Gair and the others. But they were all stopped by the three creatures, who had become very hostile.

"Bedge!" Amarian barked. "Get out of the way! We've got to stop him!"

Sirin cracked his knuckles. "Might as well stop the sea from churning, human."

Chiyo muttered under his breath to Telenar. "They are only three. We can easily take them."

But Kynell's wisdom had already started to seep into Telenar's spirit. "No, I don't think that would be smart. He obviously meant for us to stay here. Besides, have you seen Bedge fight?"

"So we're supposed to just stand here and watch him die?" Lucio demanded.

Vancien eyed the short sword Ragger had pulled on them. The three creatures looked ready to kill, or at least neutralize. "Maybe he's just going to fight Zyreio," he suggested hopefully. "He's God. He can't die."

So eager were they for reassurance that they all accepted his theory without question. They forced themselves to watch as Kynell drew closer to the figure pacing in front of the Chasmite hordes. After a few moments, Amarian cajoled Bedge into allowing them to move closer in order to at least see and hear what was happening. The fennel agreed, although the munkketrophes only followed suit after Lucio and Teehma tearfully begged them to do so. So the whole group skirted slowly to the south, gaining an oblique angle from which to view the proceedings.

To Amarian, it was all moving too fast. He had felt the fear of the Prysm from the claws of the Ealatrophe. He knew Kynell to be the stronger. But then why was everything going wrong? The only conclusion he could come to was that his crimes had shaped these events. If Kynell had to die, then surely Amarian had caused it. He was Darkness. He deserved darkness. The light could not tolerate him, and now it was about to die to escape from him.

"Kynell!" he shouted.

Kynell stopped and looked back at him.

"Take me!" Amarian continued, calling out as loudly as he could. "Kill me instead! I deserve it!"

Kynell shook his head, and Amarian felt something inside him break.

"Then forgive me! I cannot live knowing that I caused this!"

243

Kynell did not open his mouth, but Amarian felt a verse from the Ages press down onto his heart: *Kynell overlooks the crimes of those who love him, who are called according to his will. By the blood of the Prysm, the sin and the sinner are separated.* Amarian had never understood that passage before—how could the Prysm bleed?—but now the truth of it was obvious. Neither a chunk of glass nor an idea could bleed. But a person could.

CHAPTER TWENTY-NINE

The orbs were setting as Kynell approached the Obsidian line. The Chasmites had stopped their festive, tormented jubilation and now stood as calmly as their anguished spirits allowed. In front of them paced Zyreio, who was shifting shapes every few seconds. He stopped pacing, however, as Kynell drew near, settling on his jovial king costume.

"Well met, brother!" he called.

Kynell stopped within a few paces of him. A moist early autore breeze was blowing, giving the air a slight chill, not that either of them felt it. The fading orbs cast the whole scene in a rosy light, and their position behind Kynell forced Zyreio to raise a hand to cover his eyes. Kynell watched him, but did not speak.

"Being in the flesh sure does have its weaknesses, doesn't it?" Zyreio persisted, "The glare and all that, I mean." Nerves were giving his voice a waver that he was trying to hide. "Not that we let it affect us, of course! We are stronger than the flesh, you and I. Sure, we have our turn on Rhyvelad now and then, but ultimately our home is elsewhere. Don't you agree?"

For a moment, it looked as if Kynell would continue his silence, leaving Zyreio to watch him hungrily. Then the Prysm god spoke.

"Do what you have come to do."

Zyreio assumed an air of royal innocence. "Do? I'm not really doing anything different than I usually do. Just taking my turn, that's all. My turn at Rhyvelad."

Kynell slowly unwound a cloth that had been wrapped around his wrist. "Rhyvelad is not yours. It never has been. And we are not brothers."

"Co-rulers, then! Mighty monarchs who rule at turns with an iron or a velvet hand. Rhyvelad is blessed to have us!"

Kynell did not answer. Instead, he continued to unwind the cloth until he held a long linen ribbon. This he began to twist in his hand until it became a tightly wound cord.

"So what do you say? Why don't I and my army take a bite out of that city there? When we're through, you can come along in about five hundred cycles and fix it all up again. Is it a deal?"

Kynell shook his head, the cloth hanging limply by his side. "No deals, Zyreio. Do what you have come to do."

Zyreio's kingly facade faltered as he ground his teeth in frustration. "Listen, I don't want to fight you. Just let me pass!"

"I will not let you pass."

"Come on, Kynell! It's my turn!"

Kynell crossed his arms and remained silent.

"You force me to do this!"

"I force you to do nothing."

With a growl, Zyreio stalked up to the Prysm god until they were nose to nose. "You know I cannot beat you," he hissed under his breath.

"That has never stopped you before."

"Fine!" With that, Zyreio swung around and grabbed a blade from the nearest Chasmite. He held it up as if preparing for a duel.

Kynell flicked his wrist, sending the cloth in his hand spiraling around the sword blade. Then he yanked the weapon out of Zyreio's grasp.

"With your own hands. It is for their benefit." He nodded toward Vancien and the others.

Zyreio growled even more. "You want them to see you suffer?"

"I want them to see that I do this willingly. I am their sacrifice." With that, Kynell laid the cloth on the ground and clasped his hands behind his back.

"Fine!" Zyreio said again, not bothering to understand what he meant. He cracked his knuckles, let out a lusty roar, then charged.

Kynell held his ground, neither moving nor bracing himself against the attack. Zyreio hit him with the force of a thousand orbs, concentrated into one seismic shock wave that rocked Kynell back on his heels. Beyond this, his blow had no impact. Kynell regained his position and invited him to try again. This time, Zyreio took up the sword and charged, meaning to impale his victim upon the blade. Kynell stepped aside, allowing Zyreio's momentum to carry him several feet beyond his intended target.

"I said no swords."

The blade dropped to the ground with a thud, leaving Zyreio looking at his hands.

"You were always so arrogant," Zyreio said, his voice low and trembling. "You always had to set the rules and make me play by them. Now you change them on me again. You are no brother. You are a tyrant! You are a calm, deceitful, over-bearing, simpering, petty king. Well, I am done with you!" his voice had reached a high screech now, causing the Chasmites to writhe even more, echoing his sentiment with their own small screeches. "I will be patient no longer! I will be obedient no longer! I will be kind no longer! I will no longer hold my hand, waiting for your go ahead, for your permission, for your condescension. Do you hear me? DO YOU HEAR ME!?"

"Here," Kynell said, stepping toward him and taking him by the wrists. Then he placed Zyreio's hands on either side of his neck and started to squeeze. "Do it this way."

Zyreio, enraged at Kynell's condescension but equally thirsty to triumph over him, squeezed with all his might. At first it seemed like nothing happened. Kynell looked at him but continued to breathe as normal. Then he sighed, looked to the darkening sky, and closed his eyes. A moment later, he started to kick and jerk like any human, and a moment after that, his final breath gurgled out of him. His body slumped to the ground.

———————

If the world took no notice when Vancien died, it went into convulsions when Kynell did. His still form had no sooner touched the soil of Rhyvelad than it groaned and shook its mantle, as if the weight of a dying god was more than it could bear. The three lunos, which were beginning to rise, shimmered as if losing focus. Then one of them began to fade around the circumference, giving the appearance that its outside edges were crumbling. This indeed seemed to be the case, for in the space of a heartbeat, the lunos faded and crumbled so drastically that it disappeared altogether. The heaving world now became a third darker.

The groundswell knocked the entire Obsidian army off its feet. It destroyed the table where Kynell had dined and went on to shake the foundations of the capitol city. Vancien, Amarian, Telenar, and the others were thrown to the ground. They lay there, with tears streaking their faces, listening to the city behind them shudder. Then as suddenly as it had come alive, the ground stilled, with only dust and a fallen army to prove that the quake had taken place.

Chiyo spoke first, his voice raw with dust and emotion. "We have to get out of here before that army gets up."

"Let me die," Vancien whimpered.

But Chiyo was not listening. Neither was Amarian. Together, they were hauling everyone else to their feet and shoving them toward the trees. Bedge led the way, looking behind her to make sure all the humans were following, while the munkke-trophes guarded the rear of the small procession.

"His body!" Vancien gasped as they entered the trees. "We can't just leave it to be butchered!"

As one, they looked back to the spot where Kynell's body lay. Zyreio had not touched it yet. He was just staring at it. Then, finally, he held up a hand and three Chasmites came forward. He was obviously ordering them to move it, but they obviously had no desire to do so. He gestured angrily and they vanished—presumably sent back to the Chasm for their disobedience. He brought forward three more, and these obeyed, if reluctantly. Jerking, twitching, and acting as if Kynell's body was going to set them on fire, they leaned down and hauled him up to their shoulders. Then, with another gesture from Zyreio, they carried it back into the ranks until it disappeared from view.

Vancien and the others watched all of this, helpless. But their grief was interrupted by another great rumble. This time it was not Rhyvelad. Obsidian's army had recovered and was on the move again, marching toward the broken city. And now there was no one to stop it.

N'vonne had known the moment the Risen Ones left. It felt like a collective gasp, followed by shouts of confusion as those left behind realized what had happened. She was in the process of calming those nearest her when she heard another noise from beyond the firelight at the plateau's edge. She panicked for a moment, thinking that the Obsidian army was already upon them. Then she remembered Chera's assurance that these newcomers would be friendly. After that, who knew?

She hurried to the top of the long, narrow staircase with several other women who had heard the sound. There they waited impatiently, watching the distant glow of the host's torch come nearer and nearer. Only when she could see the girl's face, calm but worried, could she breathe easy herself. Thank Kynell she had warned the defenders to hold off their attack.

The girl reached the plateau, quickly handing her torch off to someone else so she could catch her breath. She was followed by the queen's man, An-Sung.

"Lady N'vonne," he bowed. Behind him, the men and women, looking exhausted and confused, spilled out onto the plateau.

N'vonne silenced him with a gesture. "Not yet, Captain." She motioned hurriedly to the women around her, instructing them to conduct all the newcomers to the dining tent, then ordering a chair and a bottle of water for An-Sung. Only when these provisions had been made did she allow him to speak.

He sank down gratefully into the chair but only took a sip of the water. "We cannot rest long, Lady," he began. "The Risen Ones have sent us down here. They fear the city will be taken soon. We must start planning our escape."

N'vonne nodded. The news was horrible but not altogether unexpected. "If what has happened down here has happened above, the Risen Ones are gone already."

An-Sung's face fell. Clearly he had been trying to hold out some hope of success. "Already? Then we are all lost."

"We're not lost yet, Captain. We are safe here, remember?"

He shook his head but did not answer. "Where is the queen? I would like to see her."

She told him where he could find her then asked him to meet her at the dining tent in an hour's time. He quickly consented and with great force of will, she waited until his back was turned before she directed her attention to the continuous stream of people emptying out on the steps. Telenar and Vancien must surely be among their number.

An hour later, N'vonne stood in front of the dining tent, swallowing her grief in great gulps and trying to maintain her composure. She had searched everywhere and asked everybody about Telenar. She had seen Bren, Chiyo's young aide, but he had only seen Vancien, and that had been when he had ridden out on Thelámos for his night attack. Finally, she had found Corfe. With unmasked bitterness, she listened to him tell her that Telenar had chosen to stay with Vancien, that he thought it was better this way, and that he loved her. As she watched Corfe's lips move, a voice inside her head began to scream, *"Why not you, you miserable coward! Why didn't you stay behind and send my husband and son to me? Why did they have to die instead of you?"*

She said none of this and only listened to Corfe inanely repeat his message over and over. He was obviously grieved by what he had to say, but she did not care. All she could feel was a cold, growing ache as the absence of Telenar struck her again and again, like a slap in the face. Finally, she saw him bow low and excuse himself. She watched him go, glad of his absence.

She had wanted to be alone, to walk to the edge of the plateau, past the firelight, and cry out her loss to the distant roof of the cavern. But An-Sung would be waiting, so she collected herself with a trembling breath and went to meet him at the front of the dining tent. On her way, she saw Alisha reunited with Tertio. Ester and Trint were with them, clutching at Tertio's pant legs to assure themselves that he was real. Alisha was weeping loudly on her husband's shoulder. Knowing she could not bear their relief or their questions, she moved quickly past them.

An-Sung was waiting. Quinia was nowhere to be seen.

"She is with her sons," he explained. "The king will come soon to address us. In the meantime, he felt that it would be more suitable for you, as head of the evacuation process, to calm everybody's fears."

The cold hatred she had felt before toward Corfe suddenly boiled over. "Is the house of Anisllyr so cowardly that it cannot lead its own people?"

He stiffened, and she immediately repented of her rash words, though her outrage remained. "Never mind. What do we do now?"

"My lady, I was under the impression that you would already know."

He was right. There was no other option. They had to leave Haven and break open the exit tunnels that led under the Duvarian Range. And they had to do it quickly, before the Chasmites were at their doorstep. So she made the announcement. She gave all the appropriate orders to start the preparations. She pandered to three royal egos, themselves trying to maintain their authority but frightened to death of what was happening. And when, in the midst of this new evacuation, she felt the stone around her rumble and roll, she knew that all was truly over. Whatever they did now was no more than a farce, a game of chase where it was only a matter of time before Obsidian swallowed them. Yet as she saw the frightened faces of Trint, Ester, and the host of other children trapped underground, she knew she had to make the game last as long as she could. If the children could see the light of day just one more time, it might be worth it.

End of Book Two

ABOUT THE AUTHOR

Lindsey is the youngest of the family—the fifth child—and youngest children like to think they have the most sensitive souls. When one of her older brothers introduced her to the fantasy genre, she was hooked and has enjoyed it ever since. It was her love of a full, mysterious, majestic world that led her to get an MA in Medieval Welsh history and then a PhD in Ancient History.

During her academic career she has written and presented several scholarly papers, but her heart has always been with creative writing: C.S. Lewis is her literary hero because he had a gift of helping readers understand and enjoy the most complex ideas.

Her website, www.lindseyscholl.com, is dedicated to exploring truth in a colorful and sometimes humorous way. She is married to Dr. John Scholl, a fellow historian. Together they have twelve nieces and nephews.

You can find more information about *The Advocate Trilogy* at www.theadvocatetrilogy.com.

www.ingramcontent.com/pod-product-compliance
Lightning Source LLC
Chambersburg PA
CBHW071830020726
47502CB00004B/1300